Pleasing and Interesting Anecdotes

An Autobiography of Giacomo Gotifredo Ferrari

D1547736

Title page of the First edition of Ferarri's *Anedotti* printed in London

Pleasing and Interesting Anecdotes

An Autobiography of Giacomo Gotifredo Ferrari

Edited by Deborah Heckert

Translation by Stephen Thompson Moore

LIVES IN MUSIC SERIES No. 12

PENDRAGON PRESS

HILLSDALE, NY

Other Titles in the LIVES IN MUSIC Series

No. 1 *Hugues Cuenod: With an Agile Voice* Albert Fuller

No. 2 *Nicolae Bretan: His Life His Music* Hartmut Gagelman

No. 3 *Entrancing Muse: A Documented Biography of Francis Poulenc* Carl B. Schmidt

No. 4 *Pied Piper: The Many Lives of Noah Greenberg* James Gollin

No. 5 *Peggy GlanvilleHicks: A Transposed Life* James Murdoch

No. 6 *Alessandro and Domenico Scarlatti: Two Lives In One* Frederick Hammond

No. 7 *Chevalier de SaintGeorges: Virtuoso of the Sword and the Bow* Gabriel Banat

No. 8 *Irving Fine: An American Composer in His Time* Philip Ramey

No. 9 *Torn Between Cultures: A Life of Kathi Meyer-Baer* David Josephson

No. 10 *Xavier Montsalvatge: A Musical Life in Eventful Times* Roger Evans

No. 11 *Massenet and His Letters* Anne Massenet & Mary Dibbern

No. 14 *The Experimental Music of Hermeto Pascoal and Group* Luiz CostaLima Neto

Library of Congress Cataloging-in-Publication Data

Names: Ferrari, G. G. (Giacomo Gotifredo), 1763-1842. | Moore, Tom, 1956- translator. | Heckert, Deborah.

Title: Pleasing and interesting anecdotes : an autobiography of Giacomo Gotifredo Ferrari / translated by Stephen Thomson Moore ; edited by Deborah Heckert.

Other titles: Aneddoti piacevoli ed interessanti. English

Description: Hillsdale, NY : Pendragon Press, 2017. | Series: Lives in music series ; No. 12 | Includes index.

Identifiers: LCCN 2017030174 | ISBN 9781576472231 (alk. paper)

Subjects: LCSH: Ferrari, G. G. (Giacomo Gotifredo), 1763-1842. | Musicians--Italy--Biography.

Classification: LCC ML410.F298 A3 2017 | DDC 780.92 [B] --dc23 LC record available at https://lccn.loc.gov/2017030174

Table of Contents

The Anedotti

PART ONE

PART TWO

Table of Illustrations

Acknowledgements

In looking back at my time editing Ferrari's *Aneddoti,* it is clear to me how indebted I am to many people and institutions that supported me along the way. I could not have finished this project without the generosity and enthusiasm of friends and colleagues who have offered knowledge, advice, and often a sympathetic ear when needed. Thanks to all of you who have listened and contributed!

First, I need to thank Ferrari's translator Stephen Thomson Moore, who gave me a wonderful translation to work with, and who was incredibly patient along the way with the setbacks. Of course, thanks also goes to Robert Kessler of Pendragon Press, whose conviction over the merit of the project kept encouraging me to finish. Keith Johnston was a regular source of information and help with the material covering Ferrari's Italian years and beyond, and David Yoon offered consistent editorial advice when I needed it. Sarah Fuller, as always, acted as a wise mentor during the process. Thank you also to Christina Bashford, Jeannice Brooks, Catherine Garry and many other scholars working on the music of Georgian Britain for specific comments and information that were extremely helpful along the way.

For more personal support, I have leaned heavily on friends and family. Thank you so much to Margarethe Adams, Rachel Begley, Daniel Ucko, and Janet Ward. And especially warm thanks to my family, who over the time spent on this project tolerated my actual and virtual absences, and listened when I most needed it.

Introduction
Ferrari's *Aneddoti*

The decades surrounding the turn of the nineteenth century were a period of intense change in the lives of musicians in Western Europe, professional and amateur alike. The rise of public concerts and virtuosi, the shift away from domestic chamber music, and the increased professionalization of musical performance created challenges to older forms of music making that depended on private patronage and the collaboration between professionals and amateurs changed the way of life for many professional musicians. Older research on the period minimizes, or worse ignores, the continued presence of private patronage and domestic chamber music performance in the private home apart from solo piano and vocal genres. Recently, however, there has been a turn towards a more nuanced view of this transitional period. New sources in particular can help us to move beyond misconceptions based upon ways of constructing a musical historiography for the period that prioritizes composition or public virtuosity. It can help us to challenge social attitudes towards music and gender that stigmatize domestic musical performance and led to a public reticence about this activity of music making. Investigations into the real lives of musicians of the period can open up new understandings of how professional musicians combined activities of composition, teaching, and musical collaborations with amateur patrons, and ways in which amateurs and professionals both negotiated the spaces of private as well as public musical performance.

This new English edition of the autobiography of the Italian composer Giacomo Ferrari, published in London in 1830, can serve as one small piece in this puzzle. Prior to the seeming downturn in opportunities for musicians in the 1820s, and touching on issues of gender and patronage, amateur and professional interaction, and the lure of the foreign and cosmopolitan, Ferrari's entertaining autobiography, the *Aneddoti piacevoli e interessanti occorsi nella vita Giacomo Gotifredo Ferrari*, shows how personal reminiscences can be important sources for uncovering the invisible world of domestic music and its patronage, and can offer insight into the transitional period occurring during the years around the turn of the 19th century.

Giacomo Gotifredo Ferrari was born in the year 1763 in the small town of Rovereto, in the region of the Italian Alps north of Trent, to a family involved in the manufacture and sale of silk. Ferrari was destined to continue in the family business, however early on he manifested a strong talent and passion for music, and his father was pleased for him to receive instruction in singing, the flute, and basic music theory, first from local musicians then from more established teachers in Verona. In his teens, to further his education and perhaps to separate him from the musical activities he was pursuing in Rovereto, Ferrari's father sent him to the Abbey of Marienberg near Mals in the Alps on the border between Italy, Switzerland and Austria. The irony is that Ferrari's father was not aware of the amount of music-making pursued at the monastery; all of the monks were musicians, secular and sacred music was performed every day, and students at the monastery could get an extensive education in music theory and instruction in a wide variety of instruments. Ferrari took full advantage of these opportunities while he was a student, and even considered remaining as a monk at the abbey. Upon hearing this, his father removed him quickly.

After his return from the abbey, Ferrari returned to Rovereto and began playing music with local noble and land-owning families in the area. He also began to compose. Upon the death of his father, he became convinced that he did not want to continue working in the family silk business, but instead wished to continue his musical studies, and with the support of Prince Wenceslas Lichtenstein he decided to go to study in Naples where he had letters of introduction to the eminent composer Paisiello.

He arrived in Naples in the autumn of 1784, and immediately went to make the acquaintance of Paisiello. The two instantly struck up a close friendship, but Paisiello was too busy at that point composing his opera *Antigone* and coming to terms with his new position as a composer in the service of King Ferdinand IV of Naples to make the time to directly instruct Ferrari. Instead, he recommended several teachers to Ferrari, and acted as a regular advisor to him, looking over his compositions frequently. Paisiello crucially introduced Ferrari to useful acquaintances among professional musicians (most importantly the singer Celestina Coltellini), composers, and wealthy patrons, and Ferrari made important strides in establishing himself as a composer and performer. Very early in his stay in Naples he was introduced to Thomas Attwood, the young British composer, and the two became very friendly. They eventually shared lodgings and both received counterpoint lessons from Gaetano Latilla, the then-elderly Neopolitan composer of opera buffa and other formerly popular vocal works. The two continued their friendship even after Attwood had gone to Vienna to study with Mozart, and it is through Attwood that Ferrari came to know Mozart's music, which he idolized. It also can be assumed that Attwood's friendship was one encouragement to Ferrari's subsequent move to London.

In the Spring of 1787 Ferrari was invited to accompany Chevalier Campan, a majordomo to Queen Marie Antoinette, to Paris, where he hoped to establish himself among the aristocratic families connected with Campan, whose wife was chief lady-in-waiting to the Queen, and a woman highly-respected within court circles. He was quite successful at creating a viable musical career in Paris, carving a niche for himself as a casual composer-in-residence and voice teacher. During his most successful period in Paris, he was employed by Marie Antoinette as a composer and keyboard instructor, though this was not exclusive employment, since along with his private patrons he was engaged as conductor at the new Théâtre Feydeau and composer at Théâtre de Montansier. The second edition of Sainsbury's Dictionary of Musicians tells us that during the four years he remained in Paris, he "composed and published several Italian notturni, duets, modern canons for three voices, some sets of romances, several sets of sonatas for the piano-forte, and for the piano-forte and violin, or flute, &c. &c."[1]

This was short-lived, however, since the looming threat of political upheaval that eventually erupted into the Revolution made Ferrari anxious and determined to leave Paris, and upon the advice of friends, particularly various diplomats and ambassadors he had come to know, he decided to decamp to England and try his hand at establishing himself in London. This was facilitated in an important way by the fact that he already had connections and introductions to London's musical elite through his network of aristocratic patrons and students.

Ferrari arrived in London in February of 1792. A few days later, he visited Haydn, who told him an extensive version of the story of his life and gave him a sonata in A-flat as a parting gift. Haydn became a regular acquaintance of Ferrari's while he was in London, as did Muzio Clementi. Quickly Ferrari became established as a teacher, making a very good living not only teaching, but also, as he had done in France, by acting as temporary composer-in-residence and chamber musician in the houses of various patrons, both in London and, through extended stays, in their country houses. Some of his most important patrons throughout the 1790's and early years of the 1800's were the fifth Duke of Devonshire and his wife, the (in)famous Georgiana Spencer, the Duke of Queensbury, the Duke and Duchess of Richmond, and the Princess of Wales. Around 1800 he began teaching at exclusive schools for girls, which augmented his income even more, and in 1804 several of his Scottish students in London persuaded him to take a tour of Scotland, with time spent in Edinburgh before embarking on several months where he stayed with several key families such as the Stuart Wortleys, the Dukes of Athol and Argyll, and Lord Douglas. Ferrari seemed to have taken a liking for Edinburgh, and he spent the remainder of his life splitting his time between the environs of London and Edinburgh, though he made several extended trips back to France and Italy, experiencing post-

---

[1] John Sainsbury and Alexandre Choron, *A Dictionary of Musicians* (London: Sainsbury and Co., 1827).

Revolutionary Paris under Bonaparte, the drastic changes to Northern Italy, and witnessing Paisiello's impoverishment and the rise of Rossini's popularity. The last chapters of his memoires describe the effects of the first symphonic concerts offered by the Royal Philharmonic Society and how it came to be organized. He died in 1842.

Many, many people are described from personal knowledge; a range of characters from servants to chevaliers. They include composers such as Paisiello, of course, and Haydn; performers like Michael Kelly, Cramer, Salomon, Clementi, Dussek, Corri, Dragonetti and many others. But he also describes interesting people he encountered in his life, ranging from Emma, Lady Hamilton, with whom he was terribly smitten, to Thomas Broadwood, the son of the piano manufacturer with whom he travelled in Europe. The memoir is packed with the folklore of regions through which he travels, quotes and sayings that were offered to him that struck him as wise or funny, and bits of poetry and other writings.

Because of the intensely immediate, personal and detailed aspect of the memoires, Saint Foix, in a *Musical Quarterly* article from the 1930s, theorizes that the *Aneddoti* are based on journals kept throughout his life, rather than being the distant memories of an old man, and this interpretation does seem to be supported within the memoires.[2] The richness of the autobiography and its sense of the immediacy of his encounters would be difficult to recapture decades later. That being said, Ferrari continually hastens to let the reader know that these are "observations," and rather than representing any objective truth, represent his particular perspective on the events he witnesses and the people he meets. It is equally important to add here – and a point I will return to – that everything about the *Aneddoti* declares the voice of the musical diplomat, a professional musician who has throughout his life been dependent on the patronage of the aristocracy and famous professional musicians, and it is equally enlightening to see how such a diplomat walks the fine line between the tell-all storyteller and the careful servant.

One can easily read the *Aneddoti* for the fun of it. There is Ferrari's name-dropping, with little glimpses into contemporary views of some of the most important people of the day, musical and otherwise. Some of the stories are quite funny, and there is the challenge of puzzling out what is implied from what is said. Poetry, epigrams, morals – all are there not only to entertain but to offer insight into the range of materials a reasonably well-educated, well-traveled, and well-connected professional musician from the decades surrounding 1800 might know.

---

[2] George de Saint-Foix, "A Musical Traveler: Giacomo Gotifredo Ferrari (1759–1842)." *Musical Quarterly* XXV (1939): 455-6.

Beyond being an enjoyable book to read, it is an important account for the scholar of late eighteenth- and early nineteenth-century music for the view it gives us of the life and attitudes of a type of musician who we rarely get to learn much about. It is an invaluable glimpse into a life that was both ordinary and extraordinary. It is extraordinary in the range of people that Ferrari counted as acquaintances and colleagues throughout his life. For instance, we meet Paisiello at several important points in his life during his last decades, from the all-important and newly-appointed court composer in Naples during the 1780s, to a composer virtually destroyed by the vagaries of Napoleon's patronage in the first decade of the 1800s. There is the lovely image of the older Haydn, happy to go on and on about his life to his new acquaintance Ferrari, and with piano sonatas to give away to visitors. As well, we see reflected in Ferrari's anecdotes important early 19th-century attitudes towards the great composers of the day, such as Beethoven and Rossini, but most importantly, Mozart, for whom Ferrari's passage on his genius contained in the *Aneddoti* offers a sense of how a mythologized ideology of Mozart was being constructed at the time, particularly in England. We are also given a snapshot of the range of patrons during the period, and how patrons interacted with musicians publically and privately.

The range of his acquaintances was aided, of course, by the fact that he worked in important centers for musical performance and consumerism, and in each of these areas his contacts and types of professional activities were quite different. During the first part of his life, when he is still marked to become a silk merchant like his father, we are introduced in Rovereto to the type of music making typical of a small, relatively rural milieu in which local merchants and visiting gentry contribute to create a remarkably vibrant musical scene. At this point in his life, Ferrari was a young man, a local son of a well-to-do merchant who could easily have continued the pattern of his life thus far, pursuing music as a hobby. But once he broke with his life in Rovereto and moved on to Naples, Ferrari was jettisoned into the circles of Paisiello and Celeste Coltellini that were at the heart of vocal performance in a city that was one of Europe's most important for opera at the time.[3] There he made the transition from amateur to professional, developing not only his craft as a composer, but the ability to participate in a musical environment that mixed professional virtuosi and aristocratic patrons.

In Paris, he seemed to have divided his time between professional employment in the music theaters of de Monsieur and Montansier, and private

---

[3] For more on Naples at the end of the eighteenth century, see Anthony DelDonna's *Opera, theatrical culture and society in late eighteenth-century Naples* (Farnham: Ashgate, 2012).

instruction within the court circles surrounding Queen Marie Antoinette, for whom he served as singing master in the Italian style. Many of his contacts were with diplomats and government leaders through continuing links with patrons back in Naples.

It is in England, however, where many of these circles overlapped, and since Ferrari spent several decades there, he managed to create for himself a particularly rich and varied network of connections that spanned the professional virtuosi of the capital and the aristocracy and landed gentry. It is the scope of this network which is surprising, as Ferrari seems to be one day dining with Dussek and Dragonetti, and the next with Georgiana, Duchess of Devonshire. It is hard to exactly gauge how respected Ferrari was among this wide network, but he seems to have easily moved between various sets of people in a way that shows a great deal of fluidity in the role of the professional musician possible during the period. By the time he arrived in England in the 1790s, Ferrari had an extensive set of recommendations from his network of patrons in Italy and France, and so was easily absorbed into musical circles in and around London consisting of professional musicians, wealthy amateurs, and combinations of the two. When the season was over in London, he would move to the country, staying with this family and that, for weeks on end. Ferrari's life seemed to consist of teaching singing and keyboard lessons, casually performing and assisting in performances in the domestic context, giving an occasional public concert, and composing pieces suitable for his students and/or suitable for the impromptu concert on demand. Most of these pieces were some form of chamber music – not formal genres like the string quartet, but quite logically, works for small numbers of instrumentalists appropriate for more casual performances. Many of Ferrari's works were accompanied vocal pieces as befits an Italian composer/ teacher trading on the caché of the Italian supposed superiority in music for voice. Sainsbury's Dictionary mentions the following compositions from Ferrari's time in England: "a great deal of music di camera, such as sets of Italian and English canzonets, duets canone for three voices, sets of sonatas for the piano-forte, sometimes with an accompaniment for the violin, violoncello, and flute, &c. A great many duets and divertimentos for the harp and piano- forte, the first of which (Op.13) has been deemed quite a model for a duet for those instruments." [4]

As far as professional accomplishments, Ferrari is not known for his legacy of compositions in the canonic sense. His range of musical publications feature a few operas and works for stage, though often he was writing or adapting additional music for other composer's works. The majority of his published works consist of songs, vocal arrangements, and chamber music of the type that his students or friends might perform at small domestic gatherings. These

---

[4] John Sainsbury, *A Dictionary of Musicians.*

works were obviously very successful of their type, as they frequently appear in bound volumes of miscellaneous pieces found in the collections of various country houses of the period, often collections that were collated from personal favorites by amateur musicians in the household.[5] His works range in the level of difficulty and complexity, from highly virtuosic arrangements for the soprano Angelica Catalani to very easy pianoforte sonatas for his students. Many of Ferrari's works fall into the genre of the accompanied sonata, a genre particular to late Georgian and Regency England, which features a relatively dominant and complex piano part accompanied by less demanding parts for instruments, such as the flute or the violin. As Elizabeth Morgan has described, the point of many of these works was to provide for relatively flexible performance forces which would support the more musically important and virtuosic part of the keyboard player. Morgan also emphasizes that these types of sonatas were largely played by women, for performances within the domestic sphere.[6]

Besides the *Aneddoti*, Ferrari published two popular music treatises. The *Breve trattato di canto italiano* was published in 1818 and appeared both in an Italian version and an English version translated by William Shield, a well-known English composer of vocal and stage music of the time, who must have been a personal friend of Ferrari. This volume seems to have circulated widely, and points again to Ferrari's reputation predominantly as a singing teacher and a composer for the voice in Britain above all. In 1830 he published *Studio di musica teorica pratica*, further capitalizing on his reputation as a teacher.

I have gone on at length about Ferrari's life because it is exactly that life – in the shape given to it by Ferrari in his memoires – rather than his achievements as composer or performer that make the autobiography a valuable resource. It offers us a glimpse into kinds of domestic music making at the beginning of the long nineteenth century and the role of the professional musician in that domestic, private performative arena. What is captured in Ferrari's *Aneddoti* is one record, seen through the prism of personal experience, of shifts in patronage and domestic chamber music as we move into the nineteenth century. The value of the *Aneddoti* does not lie in the autobiographical utterances of a canonic composer, but instead in the view that it gives us of a successful musician who combined composition, performance, and teaching in a way that created a lucrative career within contemporary French and British society at the turn of the nineteenth century. Ferrari's autobiography reminds us that musicians

---

[5] For example of how these bound volumes functioned as extensions of domestic music making and performance, see Jeanice Brooks's "Musical monuments for the country house: Music, collection, and display at Tatton Park," *Music & Letters* 91, no. 4: 513-535.

[6] Elizabeth Morgon, "The Accompanied Sonata and the Domestic Novel in Britain at the Turn of the Nineteenth Century," *19th-Century Music* 36, no. 2 (Fall 2012): 88-100.

served communities of people in a variety of ways, and that connections among communities and patronage were often important reasons for a musician's success. In particular, Ferrari's account of his life shows the often-hidden role of domestic music-making and the kinds of patronage it engendered, particularly the patronage of women, both professional and aristocratic amateurs.

For clearly, Ferrari could never have made a living as a composer or virtuoso performer exclusively, for all of his many professional connections and publications. He is honest within the autobiography's pages of the limitations of his pianistic skills, for instance, particularly once he moved to London and would have needed to compete with the new virtuosity represented there by Clementi, Cramer, and Dussek. He also eschewed composition in the abstract genres of the time – there are no symphonies, string quartets, or concertos within his publications. Instead, Ferrari traded on his "Italian-ness," on the connections in his training to Paisiello and Naples, and on the caché within the French circles around Marie Antoinette and within British aristocratic society as a whole for the Italian singing school in order to create a large network of patrons and students for whom this caché increased his cultural capital.

Throughout the autobiography, Ferrari is concerned to connect his success to a sense of his character and personal attainments rather than his abilities as a performer/composer/teacher. The picture Ferrari paints of himself (and of course self-description is always problematic) is that of someone who was a witty, educated man of the world, who knew how to handle himself in society, and who functioned in a certain way as a kind of musical diplomat. He is the first to say he wasn't the greatest performer in terms of skill, but other personal characteristics made his musical performances seem to be better than they were. Skill anyone could attain; for the kinds of success that Ferrari strove for, something more was required, and the habits of a lifetime promoting himself as a cosmopolitan musician who could fit easily and naturally into wealthy circles of domestic music patronage are reflected in the *Aneddoti*.

The experiences recounted in the autobiography support the view that the opportunities Ferrari had within London musical circles were due to the fact that he was Italian and that he had a wide experience of music on the continent. In London, the cosmopolitanism of a teacher like Ferrari was valued above what was on offer from native-born musicians and composers, and Ferrari shows how extensive those opportunities could be. Those who invited him to their home to perform and who hired him to teach and play with them attained a certain cultural capital from the fact that he was foreign with connections to the rich, powerful and famous of Italy and France, and he in turn traded on the prestige given to him by wealthy English patrons. As Sainsbury's Dictionary describes in his entry, Ferrari was "highly recommended to some of the first noblemen's and gentlemen's families, as well as to several foreign ambassadors, by whom he was constantly well received and employed for musical tuition, particularly in singing."[7] Additionally, as Ferrari discusses professional musicians he numbered among friends and acquaintances, most are foreign, and most of them seem also to be participating in the same range and mixture of public/private, individual/corporate musical performances as is Ferrari.

Ferrari thrived on private patronage; obviously the intelligence, wittiness, humor, diplomacy, and conversational skills that permeate the pages of the *Aneddoti* made him a valued addition for dinners, parties, and other kinds of get-togethers, as an appropriate companion for the music-making of professionals and well-to-do amateurs, and as a suitable teacher for adults and children alike. Whether playing for members of the diplomatic community in Naples, teaching the daughters of the French aristocracy, or forming part of house parties at the palatial country houses in Britain, Ferrari seemed to fit in well and know exactly how to balance his talents and contributions. Ferrari clearly knew that he had been fortunate in the support patrons had given to his career as a musician, and he exhaustively details the names of the many, many people who served as his patrons, both to thank them, but also as a way of proving his own value. The reader of the *Aneddoti* senses that for Ferrari patronage was a mutual exchange; yes, he received a livelihood from his patrons through his teaching and informal performances within the domestic sphere, but the patrons, too, gained from what he had to offer them. Ferrari does not inflate his professional accomplishments, but neither does he underestimate what services he can offer at a relatively high level and what those services are worth.

For the scholar interested in the social context for music at the turn of the nineteenth century, the *Aneddoti* is particularly rich in the view it offers of the roles of women in patronizing musical composition and performance within the domestic spheres that they mainly controlled. Yes, Ferrari had many male patrons; for instance, Ferrari might never have left the area of Rovereto and its environs without the financial support of Prince Lichtenstein (a local branch of the famous family) and the letter of introduction he provided for the young Ferrari to Paisiello and other important people in Naples. Towards the end of Ferrari's stay in Naples, two men encouraged him to leave Naples for more lucrative fields; Count Skavronsky, a relative of Catherine the Great and an obsessive music dilettante, greatly appreciated Ferrari's talents and would have taken him to St. Petersburg, following in Paisiello's footsteps. Instead, Ferrari decided to attach himself to the Chevalier Campan and head for Paris, hoping to use the chevalier's connection to Marie Antoinette and the French nobility.

---

[7] John Sainsbury, *A Dictionary of Musicians.*

Once in England, the Dukes of Devonshire, Richmond and Queensbury often invited Ferrari to dine, to make music with them, and to stay at their country houses.

But it was women who were particularly important patrons for Ferrari. Scholars are coming to a more complete understanding of the importance of women as patrons during this period, and Ferrari's autobiography offers ample material for deepening these understandings. Ferrari was frequently hired by women through connections with other women. He played with women in their home, provided instruction for their children under their supervision, and adapted his compositions for their tastes. The sheer number of women mentioned in his memoires is a testament to the fact that Ferrari understood their power, an understanding reflected in the number of dedications of his compositions he made to women. Furthermore, Ferrari was often honest, albeit diplomatically so, about the musical abilities of many of his patrons, and it is clear that many of the women with whom he was involved were highly-skilled performers, albeit amateurs, and were using the power of their wealth to engage professionals in order to participate in making music on the highest level. Qualities of discernment and taste are also important considerations as Ferrari evaluated his patrons, and considerations of their taste are intertwined with their understanding of what Ferrari can bring to the table (literally!) when he is invited into their domestic circle.

A quick review of three central women, one from each period in Ferrari's career, demonstrates the range of women who were integral to Ferrari's success. The first is Celeste Coltellini, a soprano who was well-established as prima donna in the opera theaters in Naples. She spent most of her career there, apart from two brief sojourns in Vienna, where she knew Mozart and performed several of his works. Her fame was secured by her premiering the role of Nina in the hugely-popular Paisiello opera of that name, and when Ferrari arrived in Naples, she was a well-known figure in the city. Her long residence in the city and her professional standing meant that she knew all of the important musicians in Naples, but she also often sang privately for Neapolitan and visiting dignitaries. She knew everybody, and had a distinct group of friends with whom she socialized and performed. She quickly came to appreciate Ferrari's talents as an accompanist and took him under her wing, having him to dine very often and taking him with her to parties and performances. This was incredibly beneficial to the young Ferrari, creating connections not only with the music connoisseurs of Naples, but also with other important visitors to Naples, such as Emma, Lady Hamilton. By the time Ferrari left Naples, Coltellini had retired from the stage to marry the wealthy Swiss banker Jean-Georges Meuricoffre. The Neapolitan section of the autobiography is full of accounts of meetings between Ferrari and Coltellini, and shows the respect and affection Ferrari had for her, and the kindness she showed him in helping him to develop his career.

While the Chevalier de Campan brought Ferrari with him from Naples to Paris, it is the chevalier's wife Henriette de Campan (or just Campan) who proved to be his most important patron.[8] Campan was an incredibly intelligent and educated woman, the daughter of a high-ranking clerk in the foreign office, which allowed her early access to aristocratic connections. Her learning marked her as distinctive, and as a young woman she became the governess/teacher to the daughters of Louis XV, and eventually she became the chief lady-in-waiting to Marie Antoinette and a greatly-respected figure in court circles. An accomplished musician herself, Campan had an important role in the music performed by and for Marie Antoinette and her household. Campan met Ferrari through her husband (with whom she was virtually estranged at the time), and she instantly decided to introduce him to the Queen, concocting an elaborate ruse in which to bring Ferrari to her attention. Ferrari's Italian connections, and the Queen's passion for Paisiello and Italian opera made it almost a foregone conclusion that the Queen would engage Ferrari; the ruse worked, the meeting happened, and Ferrari entered into the service of Marie-Antoinette, but not in an exclusive arrangement. Campan's influence and introductions brought Ferrari many other students, and the Queen's patronage probably explains his involvement with the Théâtre Montansier and the Théâtre de Monsieur (later the Théâtre Feydeau). Unlike his involvement in operatic musical circles in Naples and that of his later high-born clientele in England, Henriette Campan brought Ferrari into direct contact with the royal court society and the advantages that offered to him as he established himself in Paris. Again, Ferrari remembers the kindness of his women patrons; after the Revolution, when he revisited Paris, Ferrari makes sure to contact Campan, and visits her at her famous and exclusive school for girls, and is incredibly impressed by the quality of the music he heard there.

Finally, while Ferrari played with many aristocratic women during his time in Britain and taught many daughters of the nobility, it was Georgiana, Duchess of Devonshire who perhaps was his first great woman patron in that country and who arguably established Ferrari as the most desirable singing master and pianoforte instructor in London. The two met after the Duchess had returned to England a somewhat chastened figure, and the Duchess was living in a sort of ménage à trois arrangement with the Duke and Lady Elizabeth Foster, who

---

[8] For new research on Campan, see Rebecca Geoffroy-Schwinden, "A Lady-in-Waiting's Account of Marie Antoinette's Musical Politics: Women, Music, and the French Revolution." *Women and Music: A Journal of Gender and Culture*, vol. 21, 2017, pp. 72-100.

Ferrari also mentions, though of course says nothing about her relationship to the Duke.[9] Ferrari had letters of introduction to the Duchess from friends in Paris, and he made his way to her house almost immediately on arriving in London. She instantly engaged him to teach her daughters, introduced him to the Duke, and Ferrari seems to have become a valued member of their circles. The Duchess made sure that Ferrari obtained other students among the British nobility, and frequently invited him to her homes both in London and for more extended stays at Chatsworth House. In a real act of kindness and sense of responsibility, once her daughters were grown and no longer required a music teacher, she sponsored a benefit concert for him, and remained an important patron up until her death. It is not going too far to say that Ferrari's success in Britain was very much dependent on her offices as advocate and her love for music, which she fostered in her domestic circle.

I have briefly discussed three of Ferrari's most important female patrons, but it is important to realize that these were just a few of the many women who significantly impacted Ferrari's life, and that they existed within larger circles of women who supported music and music making around them in large and small ways. Ferrari's *Aneddoti*, and other sources like it, are important sources for looking at how patronage functioned during these transitional decades, and how musicians depended on networks of patronage within communities of women.

Another way in which Ferrari's *Aneddoti* contributes to a more complex view in our understanding of private music making during the early 19th century is the interaction of professionals and amateurs in the circles he describes, and the value professionals had within amateur circles. As Deborah Rohr argues, we often over-emphasize the polarization between private, direct patronage and the market competition of the public concert and the like during this period, with the traditional view being that the late 1700's and early 1800's saw a waning of private patronage. Rohr states that, "musicians' careers reveal a much more subtle and complex range of personal, professional, and financial arrangements than can be subsumed under these two categories."[10] Ferrari's career clearly demonstrates this kind of complexity, as he moves freely in England between public and private spheres, drawing financial support from a mix of the musicians' roles available. Even his teaching – perhaps the activity most connected to private patronage and the domestic sphere –intermingled with less-defined services offered by Ferrari as part of cultivating connections.

---

[9] For more on the infamous Georgiana, see the highly entertaining account in Amanda Foreman's *Georgiana, Duchess of Devonshire*, (London: HarperCollins, 1998).

[10] Deborah Rohr, *The Careers of British Musicians, 1750-1850* (Cambridge: Cambridge University Press, 2001), 40.

And while the *Aneddoti* discuss at length Ferrari's interactions with aristocratic patrons, the memoires also reveal the extent to which the lines between aristocratic, middle-class and professional connections were blurred, and how Ferrari seems to enjoy moving among various circles.

Movement also happened between private and public spheres, for instance, through the dedication. Ferrari shows that the act of dedication of a composition was an important transactional aspect with regards to his dependence/independence from his patrons. Much of Ferrari's instrumental and vocal compositions are dedicated to important patrons, most of them women, and this encourages us to consider the link that existed between public and private, since songs like these would have been initially designed for private performance, probably performed by Ferrari, other professional musicians, and household members in a private or semi-private performance, and then, once published, would have moved into the public sphere and its attendant wider dissemination. His Sainsbury's entry highlights several latter publications dedicated to patrons such as Lady Lewison Gower, Countess Cowper, Lady Stuart Worsley, and the King himself. It is noteworthy, I think, that Sainsbury's Dictionary is careful to mention not only the title of the pieces but also to whom the works are dedicated. These are pieces that came out of circumstances of private patronage and private performance, and the dedications help to locate where as they move into the public realm through publication.

The visits to the country estates, such as the Devonshires' Chatsworth, the Richmonds' Goodwood and Viscount Hampden's Bronham, which are enumerated extensively in the last part of the autobiography, were a particular kind of experience in encounters between Ferrari and some of his wealthiest patrons. This sort of exchange between professional and amateur, tingeing on hospitality, is less tangible than other, more formal arrangements, and it is here that sources such as Ferrari's autobiography can be helpful. Ehrlich and many others have posited that private patronage began to wane during this period, and this is incontrovertible on many levels.[11] But what Ferrari shows us from a personal perspective is that through visits and stays, amateur male and female performers both could interact musically with professionals in many ways, accruing some of the benefits of having a household musical establishment, no longer in a formal, permanent arrangement, but more casual and short-term. An important question is whether Ferrari's experience was part of a transition from the structures of patronage prior to 1800 to what

---

[11] Cyril Ehrlich, *The Music Profession in Britain since the Eighteenth Century* (Oxford: Oxford University Press, 1985).

we seem to see in the later 19th century, or is this a view into the kinds of "invisible," obscured domestic music making of the type described by Christina Bashford.[12] How much record do we have of the kind of country house stay available to Ferrari later in the century?

Ferrari's Aneddoti are charming, light memoires of a successful composer who can look back at a life in which he met interesting and important people, composed music for well-known professionals, adult amateurs, and young students alike, and played in a wide variety of settings with a wide variety of fellow chamber musicians. If accounts such as those by Cyril Ehrlich and Deborah Rohr of the professional life of musicians during the long 19th century are valid, Ferrari's career, particular his achievements and success in Britain are not typical of the broader spectrum of musicians' lives.[13] However, the version of British musical life offered by Ferrari, despite its uniqueness, augments new research into domestic music making and the people involved in private music in valuable and interesting ways. Ferrari's Italian nationality, continental connections and cosmopolitan character gave him a certain caché within certain musical circles in London. These attributes were highly valued, and opened doors to a world of teaching, impromptu music-making, and compositions as payment in gratitude predominantly organized and supported by women. One must ask how common was the experiences had by Ferrari of being invited to spend weeks on end in some of the great country houses, valued and appreciated when the possibility could have been that he was treated as a servant. The Aneddoti offer a tantalizing glimpse into the possibility that other musicians found rewarding careers in similar ways, essentially as professional aids to private music making, via the means of private patronage. The Aneddoti and other sources like it should be explored further in order to grow our understanding of the interactions between professionals and amateurs in the hazy spaces of private music making during this period of transition in patterns of patronage and the spaces of musical performance.

Deborah Heckert

December 2017

---

[12] Christina Bashford, "Historiography and Invisible Musics: Domestic Chamber Music in Nineteenth-Century Britain" *Journal of the American Musicological Society* Vol. 63, No. 2 (Summer 2010), pp. 291-360.

[13] Cyril Ehrlich, *The Music Profession in Britain since the Eighteenth Century* and Deborah Rohr, *The Careers of British Musicians, 1750-1850.*

Chronology of the Life of Giacomo Ferrari

1763	Baptised in the town of Rovereto, in the Alto Adige, or Italian Tyrol, the son of a prosperous silk merchant
c. 1777	Is sent to Verona to continue his education, and Ferrari uses the opportunity to study music beyond the limited possibilites he had in Rovereto.
c. 1779 -1781	Is a student of Marianus Stecher at Marienberg Abbey, where he was sent to study languages. Instead he spends all of his time learning several instruments including flute, violin and viola, improving his keyboard and accompaniment skills, an studying basic composition.
c. 1782	Returns to Rovereto, where he continues to develop his music talents while half-heartedly working for his father. He seizes any opportunity presented to him to make music within the upper class circles of the area, both as an accompanist and player of chamber music. He also begins to regularly compose.
1784	After his father's death, he travels to first Rome than Naples under the patronage of Prince Lichtenstein. There he is befriended by and moves in the circles of the opera composer Paisiello and the singer Celeste Coltellini, and studies with the composer Gaetano Latilla.
1787	Under the protection of Chevalier Campan, whose wife was a favorite lady-in-waiting to Queen Marie Antoinette, Ferrari moves to Paris. Once established in Paris he becomes a court musician at the Tuileries and active as accompanist to the queen, voice teacher to the nobility, and maestro al cembalo at the Theatre de Monsieur.
1792	Leaves Paris for London, fearful of the rumors of coming revolution. Is introduced to Haydn and Clementi within a few weeks of arrival.

1793	Establishes himself as a leading singing teacher and accompanist in London, including acting as teacher to the Princess of Wales. He is patronized by a number of leading women of the nobility, including Georgiana, Duchess of Devonshire and Emma, Lady Hamilton. Friend to many of the leading musical figures in London during the Late Georgian – Regency periods
1799	Travels to Vienna, where he purchases scores of Mozart's operas
1802-3	Travels to Paris and Brussels, where he meets Napoleon and others in the then First Consul's circles
1804	Marries Victoire Henry, a well-known pianist and student of Cramer
1809-1812	An illness leaves, Ferrari almost completely blind for several years, but he luckily regains his sight
1814-16	Extensive trip to Italy with Thomas Broadwood, including a visit to Roveredo
1818	His 2-volume Breve trattato di canto italiano is published both in Italian and in an English translation by William Shield
1820s	Resettles for a few years in Edinburgh, but disappointed by the lack of appreciation for Italian singing in that city, he returns to London
1830	Publishes both his *Aneddoti* and *Studio di musica teorica pratica*
1842	Dies in London

Part One

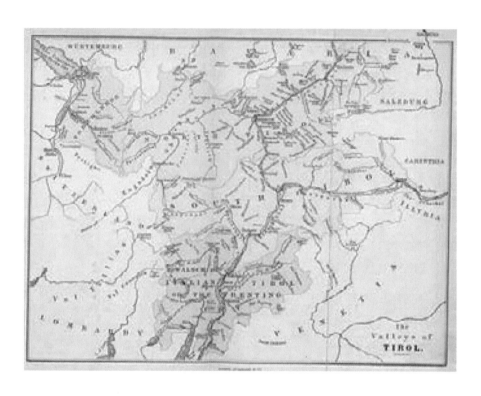

Fig. 2. Map of the Trentino-Sud Tyrol area.

Chapter I.

Description of the most pleasant part of the southern Italian Tyrol to the frontiers of the German Tyrol- Jests, etc. – a Sonnet of Cavalier Vannetti

Roveredo, or Rovereto, is a little city in the Venetian Lombardy, in the Val Lagarina, an area incorporated a long time since into the Italian Tyrol.[1]

The etymology of the name of this city derives from a forest of *roveri*, or oaks, which existed there before its foundation, and whose arms correspond exactly to the emblem of Charles II, King of England, though with a different meaning, which is expressed through a 'c.r' on either side of an oak tree: c.r. *Carolus Rex* - c.r. *Civitas Roboreti*.

Roveredo contains between eight and nine thousand souls. It has Venice to the east, Milan to the west, Verona to the south, and Innsbruck to the north. The River Adige snakes its way not too far off, now humble, now proud: it flows through Saco, a kind of haven for rafts and small boats which is a spot inhabited by many members of the nobility, less than a mile from the end of the town and the monastery of the Capuchins of Roveredo. The little Leno River flows from another end of the area by the town of San Tommaso, and whose bridge links the town to the gate and streets of the city.

The Leno is very useful for the inhabitants' work, but upon the melting of the snows, or after the rains, which are regular there in the autumn, it becomes a rapid and furious torrent, swelling and raising itself sometimes to twelve feet or more above its usual level. Then it brings terror, havoc, and ruin wherever it goes.

In Roveredo there is a castle, a theatre, two hospitals, six monasteries and many churches, plazas, fountains, etc. There is the *Corso*, embellished by various workshops, and especially by the palaces of the Counts Fedrigotti and Alberti and of Baron Piamarta, by the theatre itself, the convent of the Frati Zoccolanti of San Rocco (nearby which is found the Palazzina Bridi), and by a little temple erected to commemorate and honor Palestrina, Handel, Gluck, Jommelli, Sacchini, Haydn, and Mozart. There are a great number of silk and flour mills which run freely using water wheels and other machines set in motion by the diverted waters of the Leno.

---

[1] Known today as Rovereto, the city is located in the Trentino region of Northern Italy, close to the Dolomites. It is within the Vallagarina valley, through which runs the Adige River. Historically it was situated on the border between the independent bishopric of Trento and the Venetian Republic. (Fig. 1, opposite.)

The institution of the grammar school, intended for the study of the Italian, Latin, and German languages and for mathematics, does great honor to the happy memory of Joseph II, who founded it at the end of his reign. There is there also an academy named "*degli Agiati.*" But before these establishments were founded, the local Cavaliers Vannetti, Rosmini, and Fontana distinguished themselves in *belles lettres,* as did the abbots Tartarotti, Scarperi, and Pederzani who, to a larger or smaller degree, brought honor to Italian literature.

The mountains in the vicinity are steep and rugged, but of a moderate height. In the winter they are covered with snow and in the summer, according to their position with respect to the sun, they display on their slopes a quantity of vines, mulberry trees, olives, citrus, fruit-bearing trees, beeches, and an infinity of oaks. Excavations of their bowels have found immense masses of flint, antimony, granite, and superb marbles painted by nature with one or more colors, shining like a mirror.

The vegetables, fruits, and grape vines are excellent in all these little villages; the tobacco—Oh, the tobacco there!—is stupendous, absolutely stupendous! About a mile from Roveredo to the east one crosses the bridge of San Colombano, which is worth seeing, being made from a single arch, and thrown, so to speak, from one mountain to the other. A few miles from there one finds seven little springs a few yards one from the other, which are called the Seven Albi and which contribute the most to maintaining the perennial waters of the little river—the Leno—which runs a half mile directly under the above-mentioned bridge.

From Roveredo to the border to the German Tyrol region is about twenty-five miles; one goes through Acquaviva, a little village of few houses but in a picturesque location. Then comes Trent, a city renowned as much for its ancient bishopric as for the Holy Council that was held there in the year 1545, during which the celibacy of priests was definitively established. The bridge over the Adige offers a not-too-bad view; close by is found the village of Mezzo-Lombardo. The Cathedral of Santa Maria Maggiore is not to be despised. Inside can be seen a good painting which depicts the Council, and an organ, which, though old and possessing a moderate range, always gives pleasure to those who hear it. The *Trentini* praise it to the stars and consider it to be one of the many marvels of Italy, listing these as the Duomo of Milan, the Arena or Coliseum of Verona, the Garesenda Tower of Bologna, the Vatican of Rome, the Forum of Piedigrotta at Naples, the four bronze horses and Rialto Bridge at Venice and the organ of Trent. These fanatics relate that a celebrated professor, having arrived there and desiring to hear and play the instrument which was the subject of such ballyhoo, was introduced to the church in question. At the sight of the painting he was impressed, but so much more when he observed the majesty of the organ. When brought to the organ loft, he essayed some improvisations, and in hearing the emanations of the harmonious pipes and the powerful yet sweet sounds they sent forth, was almost delirious from ecstasy. He exclaimed, "O what a wonderful instrument this is! Just its bellows are worth more than all the cardinals of your Council!"

A few miles beyond Trent the land begins to become sterile and boggy, the air bad, the people enervated; enough about that. Finally one arrives at San Michele, the border between the two Tyrols, but a miserable and unhealthy little spot. Here the language changes; one begins to hear the guttural and corrupt accents of the Tyrolian Germans, who give occasion to foreigners, and especially to the Italians, to make fun continually of a language as rich, beautiful, and sweet as German, if it is properly articulated. Here is what Abate Casti says on the subject:

> The eminent Poet, in one of his very gracious stories, relates that a young woman, harassed and insulted by a Moor, was called to an examination, and when interrogated as to why she had let herself be insulted, answered that she was very afraid. - And who was he who insulted you? He told me that he was the devil? -What did he look like? – He was a robust man. - His face? -Black.- His hair? - Curly. - His nose? -Flat. - His mouth? - Oh, what a mouth! -and what language was he speaking? Here the malicious Casti observes, "If he was the devil then it is natural that he speak German."

Bravo, witty Casti! But it seems to me that he has forgotten that in Italy as well may be heard guttural and risible accents like those of the Tyrolian Germans. In fact, the Florentine tongue does not caress one's ears. The speech of the Bolognese is certainly not worth an *Alleluia* by Padre Martini. And with respect to the execrable dialect of the Genoese, well, here one can say with more truth than Casti - O, what a bedeviled tongue!

Now I would like to offer to the reader a sonnet by the celebrated Cavalier Clemente Vannetti, without doubting for a moment that it will be favorably received, and one in which will be found another criticism of the Tyrolian Germans.

Sonnet:

> (O *Morocchesi*, these valleys were
> Made subject to the government of the
> Tyrol one day by accident; otherwise
> We are Italians, not Tyrolians;
> And so that, in the judgment of the villages,
> You may not go astray with the squint-eyed folk
> Who do not see, and do not know the truth,
> I have here set out a rule for you.

When you are in a place where you find
Speech turned to shouting, and the soil barren,
The sun in Capricorn in every season,
An immense flock of fat men and wagon-drivers,
Pointed houses, and rotund folk,
Then say to yourself: here is the Tyrol.)"

Sonnetto

Del Tirolo al governo, O Marocchesi
Fur queste valli, sol per accidente
Fatte suddite un dì; del rimanente
Italiani noi siam, non Tirolesi.
E perchè ne giudizio dei paesi
Tu non la sbagli, con la losca gente
Che le cose non vede o il ver non sente,
Una regola chiara io qui distesi.
Quando in parte sarai dove il sermone
Trovi in urli cangiato, arido il suolo,
Il Sole in Capricorno ogni stagione:
i manzi e carrettieri immense stuolo,
Le case aguzze, tonde le persone,
      Aller di' francamente: Ecco il Tirolo!

Bravo Vannetti as well! But even if the German Tyrol ends at San Michele and at Mezzo Lombardo, and if we are not originally true Tyrolians, it must be allowed that at Trent, at Roveredo and also at Ala is spoken a very correct Italian, but one also meets often the most awful accents that can only draw forth compassion.

Chapter II.

My Grandfather - The Establishment and Matrimony of my Father - My Childhood - Bird Hunting

My grandfather was born in Roveredo, which, I was told, he never left. I did not have the advantage of knowing him, but I heard so much of him from my father and from others that I am able to say a few things about him. He was trained for business, in which he spent his entire life. He was, moreover, a complete connoisseur of the qualities of silk, for which he had a singular eye and feel, nor did he ever lack for honored and lucrative enterprises through which he could maintain his family properly. He was, as well, a religious man, though far from being a bigot or a pedant. He used to say to his children:

> Let it be a law to you to never lie, nor to use subterfuge; always do your duty; if you are fathers or bosses, command; if you are children or servants, obey. Be faithful to the government that protects you. If you are presented to whatever family, behave with the same affability and decency on the fiftieth time as on the first; and never be proud of your honor and of the talents that you have acquired. Always be ready for appointments well before the time that has been set. Trust in your religion; don't distract yourself in desiring to plumb its mysteries, because everything is a mystery in this world. Have no animosity towards other religions, for they are all good since they all aim toward the same end. Read and reread the divine teachings of Jesus Christ; nourish yourselves with those sublime and natural sentiments and principles; and what is more important, put them into practice yourselves!

Then that brave and valiant man disappeared in a flash, leaving five sons and a daughter. The first-born, Bartolomeo, he had already made a priest, according to the custom in Italy, and he had trained the other four for business. The youngest, Francesco, was the most able, active, and industrious of all of them. Endowed with the sweetest temperament, and always intent on his duty, he easily deserved his father's love and the goodwill of everyone. Assisted by his father's unending concern and inspired by his example, he was able to learn much so that when he experienced the bitter shock of losing him, he was not only able to provide for himself, but also for all his brothers.

He took a little house on the Piazza del Podestà where he ran a small silk business, and by force of effort, economy, and industry, within a few years he saved a fair amount of money. He was then supported by the noble Giuseppe-Maria Pedrigotti of Saco and by his nephew, the noble Angelo Rosmini of Rovereto. These two noblemen had him rent a grand house called the Casa Rossa, which seemed truly made to order for his establishment.

In it were all the comforts of life. As well as an office and storerooms of every sort, there were rooms for raising the silkworms and working the silk, great kettles for spinning and dyeing it, a stable, a shed, a chicken coop, and a garden full of the bounty of God's grace. All this cost the firm of Ferrari and Co. only two hundred florins a year in rent, that is about twenty pounds sterling. Franceso, thus being situated in such a prosperous way, was behooved to marry and take to wife a certain Maddalena Reisevitz of a mercantile family, wise, attractive, but maybe a little too devout. He was already religious enough, so that they got on very well and were always happy together. The husband looked after the affairs of the business and left those of the house entirely to his wife, which she was extremely capable of managing. They had ten children, of which number only the youngest and myself - that incomparable flower of virtue - are still alive.

From the age of three until the age of five years I went to the school of a certain Siora Checca Smitta, where I learned nothing but playing games. At five I went to Don Trener to learn to read, write, recite the catechism, etc. At ten I entered the public school and at eleven I was awarded as a prize for my memory a beautiful, well-bound edition of Virgil, on the frontispiece of which stood the inscription which follows:

Memoria minuitur nisi exerceas, Jacobe dulcissime![2]

(Memory diminishes, unless you practice, sweet Giacomo!)

Such a maxim, which later I found to be so true, was of the greatest utility to me. From that hour on I have never ceased to learn, retain, or repeat by memory, so that I have the consolation of having a memory that is as fresh now as it was when I was twenty years old.

In spite of all this, study was not my dominant passion; I had one that prevailed over it and over every other boyish diversion.

In the autumn I used to get up with the dawn to go hunting for little birds, something that is done in the Italian Tyrol from the beginning of August until the end of December, as much for pleasure as for economy and need. Beef or mutton are too scarce and expensive for the poor of the village, and there is no well-to-do noble or shopkeeper who, during the season, does not have daily on his table a plate of birds or of roast game.

The peasants of those parts make an immense slaughter of chaffinches, blackbirds, thrushes, greenfinches, and others, which they catch in two very cruel ways, which I here describe.

In the clearest paths or passages of the densest thickets they hang a quantity of snares made of horsehair. They tie each row of these to two tree branches of equal height, where they believe that the birds must pass to seek food or drink; and thus it happens again and again. As soon as the bird has stuck its head through the loop, its open wings pull on it violently, and it is caught by the neck.

Another way of catching birds is that of setting up little arches formed by a folding rod beneath the trees and hedges along the paths, in the midst of which, by a certain curious device, the poor birds are caught by their legs. An owl, native to those rocky areas, surrounded by twigs covered with lime; horizontal nets, known in every country in Europe; and vertical bird-catching nets not known

---

[2]From Cicero's De senectute.

in England offer another three ways through which the industrious birders can entertain themselves, or make a living.

The robins are more numerous, and more easily snared, and it is incredible the quantity they catch and eat in the Italian Tyrol, while in the German Tyrol were anyone to touch one of these birds, he would be dishonored and insulted. The German Tyrolians have a religious respect for the robin, or rather a superstition, since they call it the Virgin Mary's bird.

Another very pleasant hunt is that of shooting the large wild birds as they fly past, which they do particularly a mile from Roveredo on a little hill, and in the forest in Valle Longa. By agreement, the proprietors of these lands choose spots intended for the hunters that are a half mile distant from each other, and the first of these hunters who arrives is the master of it; nor is there anyone who would desire to hunt between one post and the next. They sometimes go the evening before to be the first, and sleep under a tree, a hedge, or a rock so as to be ready at sunrise to shoot birds. If the day is calm, there are few birds that go by, but if the weather is cloudy or rainy, they pass by in the thousands, in swarms that look like clouds. The greater part of these birds are made up of starlings, doves, ducks, and geese, as well as swans, crows, and cranes. The first four kinds fly together and in order, but they are so cunning and so skilled that if you shoot at them from the front or from the side, in the blink of an eye the swarm moves as if it were a single bird, and thus avoids death or injury. You need to shoot from the back, once they have passed by, and then one is able to drop twenty or thirty in a single shot. The other kinds fly so high that a shotgun cannot reach them, though they can sometimes be taken with rifles.

It is incredible to see these peasants arrive at market laden with strings of birds, and even if they sell them at a low price, yet given the quantity they catch, they earn enough to buy yellow and black corn flour, which is wonderfully cultivated in the village, and with this they make polenta which serves as sustenance for them every day of the year.

In addition to these peasants there are also owners of the woods who make a living from such hunts and who employ various peasants whose job every day during the season is to set up to a thousand or more snares and as many arches, and who they then have sell the birds they catch in the public market.

At the same time that I used to entertain myself in frequenting all these hunts, I had also a passion for music, which touched my ears and my heart. I never failed to go to sung masses or to other musical functions. If in the summer there was a serenade outside, I used to get up at any hour of the night and go to the window half naked to listen. If there was a virginal, a violin, or a guitar, I diverted myself by plucking it to make it sing. I even had a passion for ringing the noonday bell, which was the largest in the city. My mother, discovering the innate sentiment which I already was showing for music, and the plan I had hatched with a close friend to go to Italy to become musicians, made me learn solmization by myself, secure in her opinion that music could only be an advantage to me in whatever situation I might find myself in the world.

At that point in time, in 1775, a pianoforte had not yet been seen in Roveredo, nor could a harpsichord be rented. There were virginals and clavichords, passable, of three and a half octaves, made by a certain Chiusole, a tobacconist and a natural genius for mechanical things. My mother asked if he would make me a harpsichord of four and a half octaves; he took on the job for the sum of ninety florins and succeeded so well that my instrument was admired by the entire city. (Author's note: A florin of the Tyrol is worth a little less than two shillings, English money).

I had Pulli for a teacher, a solid professor and a master at solmization the like of which I never heard after.

But in addition to giving me a music teacher, she also gave me a confessor. This was a Salesian father of the Zoccolanti, called the Blind Father, because he was. Every Sunday she made me go to confession with her, she on one side of the confessional, and I on the other side. Some evenings he took me out to walk and to be pardoned at the church of the nuns at Saco, where there was a certain Mother Teresa who passed for a saint. She would bring me into the parlor and I would be left alone with her. This Mother Teresa used to tell me my sins. I asked her one evening how she knew them, and she answered that she learned them from her guardian angel. I, innocent - so innocent - and a simpleton like a true Tyrolian in those days, believed positively that the saints here below were in contact with the angels up above. My father, more open-minded than his wife, never ceased to tell me about my grandfather, and he often repeated that which I said above. In fact, he looked for any occasion to inculcate those healthy principles he himself had internalized. Happy to see that I was listening to him, one day he said that if the whole world thought the way my grandfather had, there would be more peace, more morality, and more friendship between men, nor would one see the rise at every moment of so many new sects which corrupted the true religion.

Chapter III.

My Father's Vow - Sanctuary on Montebaldo - My Education at Verona - Pasquinades

My brother Lodovico caught a mild case of smallpox, and one of the two pox he had injured his right eye, which caused him to lose his sight. My unhappy father, due to this misfortune, made a vow to the Madonna della Corona to visit that shrine with his wife and two elder daughters if Lodovico was healed. He spared neither means nor gold, but there was no remedy. In spite of this, he believed that he owed an offering to the Virgin and resolved to still go since my mother had decided to send me to Verona. I thus went with them.

We left Roveredo in the morning and stayed in Ala for a few hours, a prosperous and pleasing town. That night we slept in Peri, a little village, but well-situated; it is about a quarter mile from the Adige, beyond which is the Rivalta gate, where there are two ferries covered with benches for transporting passengers and merchandise back and forth across the river. Facing Peri one sees the very tall Montebaldo, which protects Lago Garda. Halfway up the hill the canonry and the church - or the shrine - of the Madonna della Corona appear.

We stayed at the post house, kept by a certain Signor Ventura, a placid and hospitable man. He gave us an exquisite meal, at a good price, and what is more, some excellent *vin santo*, made in the house. Two silk makers from the area, correspondents of my father, dined with us, and while chatting after the meal they were asked if they could give us any correct information on the history of the Madonna della Corona. One told us that the shrine appeared unexpectedly one day to the unutterable surprise of the vicinity and of the wayfarers and that the great miracles done by the Virgin were innumerable.

The other added without ceremony that the story was false, but that a hermit and his friends, having gone up Montebaldo and having brought up machinery with ropes, built the canonry and the church in secret in the forest. Then, having cut down the trees that were covering it one night, the above-mentioned shrine appeared in full view the next day. He had heard tell of the quantity of miracles done by that Virgin, but that he had not seen a single one. (Author's note: However what is not false is that after the battle of Rivoli, Napoleon miraculously brought his army over Montebaldo, pulling along with them large artillery, counterweights, and with a cannon of an immense bore, whose roar brought panic to the entire valley).

This did not discourage my parents in the least. They left at the next dawn with my sisters and with the postmaster, who courteously accompanied them beyond the Adige to the Riva Alta gate, where they found the asses already in order and ready to slowly ascend that very steep mountain. A mile from the sanctuary they were obliged to leave the asses at a kind of shelter, only being able to ascend from there on foot. Having arrived at the church and made their devotions, they returned to Peri and from there to Roveredo, with the hope of finding Lodovico cured by a miracle, but they found him as unhappy as they had left him.

In the meantime I had kept on in the carriage, passing through Volargne - the end of the Tyrolian Alps - where the rich plain of the Venetian Lombardy majestically presents itself. Having arrived in Verona, I had myself brought immediately to my fated preceptor, the justly venerated Don Antonio Pandolfi. He instructed me a little in Italian and Latin, and gave me an idea of mathematics, of geography, of Muratori's moral philosophy, and of the works of Metastasio, which interested me more than anything. But the enthusiasm and the prevailing taste that I had for music detracted not a little from the instruction of Don Pandolfi.

Cubri was provided as my master for solfège, a dull and knavish priest, good only for bringing a beginner along. Still he gave me lessons in accompaniment, and after a year I knew my solfège and accompanied tolerably at sight, taking lessons every weekday and holiday and paying a Bavarian dollar for every sixteen lessons.

My preceptor and his friends, seeing that Cubri could do no more for me, arranged for me to have Marcolla as a a singing master, an excellent teacher, and Borsaro, much better at the keyboard than Cubri. I paid them the same price for every twelve lessons as I had Cubri, but my father's money was better spent, since in the following year while I remained at Verona I made rapid and visible progress.

During this time something happened which has always weighed on my heart, and confessing it has given me some consolation.

Shortly before I went to Verona my mother wrote there to the archdeacon of Santa Maria Antica to ask him to be my confessor while I was in that city. He agreed to her request with pleasure, and I went often to him immediately after my arrival, but rarely thereafter, as much because he seemed to me a sort of Salesian father as through a circumstance which I am about to tell that proved to me that his principles were not liberal.

He and other fanatics or religious bigots encouraged me to despise, rather to hate, the Jews, calling them the greatest enemies of we Christians. It did not take much to persuade me, and when I went walking through Verona with my companions, if we met a Jew, we would mock him with impunity, with words, with gestures, now caricaturing the songs of his synagogue, now the shouts that those poor folk make in their ghetto or in the streets.

One day, while I was playing ball with some boys in the courtyard of the Palazzo Zenobio, a Jew passed by there with a sack on his shoulders, shouting as usual, "old clothes!" We left our game and began to torment the poor man. He became angered and upset, took his burden from his shoulders to throw at me, who was closest to him, but I, younger and more agile than he, ran out of the palazzo. He followed me, but when I was at a certain distance, I took a stone from the street, and threw it at his head. Stunned by the blow and the wound he stopped, and I escaped to Don Antonio's house, passing through the pharmacy that his two brothers kept.

It was not long until the mistreated merchant of old clothes presented himself in the same shop, complaining justly and bitterly of me. My preceptor came down, and hearing my misdeed obliged me to ask pardon of him, and give him that little money which I had in my wallet. The Israelite was satisfied, and after being placated by Pandolfi, he went back to the ghetto. Don Antonio then brought me into his chamber, and chastised me severely, making me to understand that I ought not to mingle with any but those of my own religion, nor to have scorn for any other, and above all for that of the Jews, since we Christians as well believe in the Old Testament. And further than that, I should note that our Savior himself was born of a Jewish virgin.

That was enough to emancipate me from the prejudices of my archdeacon and his like; when I later got to know some of those persecuted people I considered them always as my friends.

In that spring an *opera seria* was presented at the Teatro Filarmonica. Danzi, in her first youth, a singer of surprising agility, performed, as did David, father of the present David, who was in his prime, as well as Paccherotti, a model for singers of that time. In spite of all that the opera was a failure.

Since I have spoken of the theater, I will relate here two rather biting satires.

When Maestro Mortellari left England, he departed London with his patron Cavalier Pisani, a noble Venetian. Having arrived at Padua, the good Cavalier saw to it that his protégé was engaged to write an opera and a ballet there. The company was certainly poor, but Mortellari was one of those stubborn old men who would not adapt themselves to the good taste of the day, and, what is more, his music was weak and bare of harmony. He produced a fiasco, a grand fiasco, and was served with this compliment:

> Singers without voice,
> Dancers without legs,
> Music by Mortellari!

The last appearance made by the celebrated Mombelli, known as the *tenor dei terzetti*, was as Pergola in Florence. He was over seventy years old, and still wanted to sing; the little voice that he still had was trembling and failing in a disgusting way. Since for twenty years he had been the idol of the Florentines he was respected, but when he went to the theatre the second evening to get in costume he found on the door of his dressing room, written in red pencil:

At seventy, one doesn't sing or dance!

Now, changing the tone, but not the subject, I ask permission to tell another story that I find brilliant.

The Republic of Venice had been on the brink of its decline for more than a century; various senators with good sense and other great politicians had died or retired, and some dandies and ignoramuses with little intellect had taken their place. In consequence, the affairs of the Republic were going to the dogs. One day the initials reproduced below could be seen affixed to a door of the Palace of the Doge:

PPP

III

RRR

G.

These produced great suspicion and fear on the part of the new senators. There were spies at the balls, secret denunciations one after the other, and arrests everywhere.

Finally, they offered a great sum of money and a pardon to whoever might be able to explain the meaning of the above-mentioned letters. Their author had no need of money and neither did he trust the promised pardon. In consequence, some time later, he caused the letters to be filled out as follows:

Patres Patriae Perierunt.

Iuvenes Ignari Imperant.

Respublica Recens Ruit

Gratis.

(The fathers of the fatherland perished/ The ignorant young reign./The recent republic collapses. /Gratuitously.)

Chapter IV.

Promise of Matrimony - Return to Roveredo - Death of my Mother - Scabrous Situation of my Father

A few months before leaving Verona I was invited to the nuptials of two of the brothers of Don Pandolfi, who with him made up a family all living in the same house. Seeing that they were so contented and happy, the notion of taking a wife popped into my head as well. I confided my plan to my friend Gujerotti, and he suggested to me his sister Giuditta, who was boarding in a convent of nuns. I told him that first I wanted to get to know her and let her get to know me. Thus I wrote her, and with a little bribe she seduced the convent doorkeeper to let me, along with her brother, into the parlor. The young virgin was already present; she came to the grate, I bowed to her, she did the same. "Your servant! - your servant!" She pleased me, I pleased her, and with a mutual smile and no further conversation we agreed to be betrothed. She was eleven, I was thirteen and a half. In leaving the parlor we came face to face with the wolf - the prioress was at a window. She saw us, became suspicious, and informed the family of my friend, and from that moment on I never saw my dear betrothed again. It bothered me terribly, because she was truly very beautiful, and as long as I was in Verona I did not cease to yearn for her. What became of her hasty love I do not know, only that mine must have vanished on my trip home, since having arrived at Roveredo I thought of Giuditta no more.

It is easy to imagine the consolation and delight that I felt in seeing my fatherland once more and in embracing my parents and relatives, but the anxiety of providing evidence of my progress in music and further of showing off my silvery and very high voice topped everything. I was hoping to induce my father to allow me to devote myself entirely to music instead of commerce, but it was all for naught.

My mother, as anxious to hear me as I was for being heard, on my arrival put together a little recital, inviting some friends, among whom was my first teacher Pulli.

When I began to sing, I felt hoarse. I tried and tried again but in vain, or rather I could not begin a note. Pulli came up to me, and having as an old master already discovered from my speaking voice that the change of voice was upon me, exhorted me not to force it, since I might lose it. I wept like a baby, and could do nothing further that evening. To console me my dear father permitted me to take flute lessons from Signor Francesco Untersteiner, a miserable player! Yet after only one month I played the pieces from those days passably well with a one-key flute.

My mother then tried to recommence her tricks between the Salesian father and Mother Teresa, without noticing that living for two consecutive years in a large city had opened my eyes and my mind a bit and that my ideas were beginning to develop. I took pity on her, however, once only, and went with her to confess with the Salesian, then in the evening she left me alone in the parlor with Teresa. She, as she had done before, told me my sins. I thanked her ironically, and then looking at her keenly, I winked. She became as red as a lobster and ran off immediately to tell my mother of my words and gestures. I then became suspicious, and returning home declared to my mother that I wanted to change my confessor and that I was too old to be paying attention to the chatter of a Theatine. That was enough that I never heard any further talk of the Salesian or of Teresa.

Up until that point my father's business had had the wind in its sails; he had saved money, bought a nice field, and a *filatojo* or silk mill, where he employed at that time up to twenty-five or more people. He had also set up two of his brothers in Verona, one as a broker, the other as a silk merchant, which had cost him a pretty penny. But his first mistake was to take into his house and as a partner his brother Giambattista, and to change the firm from Francesco and Co. to Ferrari Brothers.

Giambattista had a wife, two daughters and a son, the last of which became the bane of my father and of my brothers and myself. Sometime thereafter my uncle died, and my father made the mistake of taking my uncle's son for a partner, and agreed to give him five hundred florins a year in salary, a share of the profits, free housing and more. He also arranged a marriage with Signora Teresa Fuiten of Trent, an heiress of thirty thousand florins, which sum was given to my cousin under the responsibility of my father.

At that time there were four of us brothers still living, and four sisters, two of whom were twins who then died in infancy. There were two others mouths to feed at the hearth - an uncle who was a priest, and a marriageable aunt, who, both favored by nature with happy appetites and very refined tastes, employed themselves marvelously well choosing the best foods and the best wines, especially since it cost them nothing.

The worst then that could happen to my father was to lose his consort. Her life ended at the premature age of thirty-seven years, leaving her husband in the greatest desolation and all the affairs of his numerous family in turmoil. My mother was grieved not only by her relations but by everyone who knew her, for even if she was overly devout, as I said above, she nevertheless had a generous heart and looked after everything that pertained to her family as the most active and economical housewife possible. My father's situation then became one to cause pity. My uncle the priest occupied himself with nothing but making good wine; he went walking, hunting, to the confessional, and every evening to play trumps or tressette at the house of Vigagnoni, with his penitents. My aunt was always at her rosary, with the office of the Madonna in her hand, or with her fingers in the holy water as soon as she saw a font. My two remaining sisters were sickly and pious to the greatest degree. (Author's note: I will never forget my sister Barbara, when I took her to Saco to hear an opera buffa, which was performed marvelously by the noble musical dilettantes of that little spot. She came along only for my sake, but it was observed by those who were next to her that she never raised her eyes to the stage, nor moved them from the catechism which she had brought along, and which she read and reread until the curtain fell!) My cousin, humbug and hypocrite, was looking forward to when he might undo his uncle and benefactor.

Of four brothers I was the oldest, but still too young to give assistance to my father, and besides, I hated business and adored music. Instead of frequenting the office and the silk rooms I was almost always at the harpsichord or with the flute at my lips. My voice had changed and I exercised it as much as possible. Pulli counseled me wisely not to force it on the high notes, but to seek little by little to unite the chest voice with the head voice, the falsetto, in order to acquire, he said, the violoncello of human voices, the Tenor. But still, other nuisances were disturbing my poor father not a little. Since there was no longer a mistress of the house, the affairs of the family remained in the care of my unhappy sisters and my emaciated aunt, the three of them not making up one between them. I, in addition to music's distraction, had also taken up the custom of going now and then to visit the silk-working women, and their conversation interested me more than the account books and the silk cloth organzas of the business. Among these young women there was a certain Orsolina Vitadèo, daughter of a wig-maker who lived two doors down from my father's house. She was polite and striking, and she struck my eye and pierced my heart a little more than Giuditta of Verona. The sly girl noticed this; it did not bother her, nor was it unwelcome. Not being able to visit such a family openly, I visited with her when she came to work the silk.

One evening as it was getting dark I came out of our granary and clambered like a cat up the neighboring house, then launching and dragging myself with my legs apart up on the roof, I arrived at the window of my beauty's granary. I jumped in, but in jumping bumped into the heads for the wigs and into other obstacles, making a great clatter. Vitadèo heard, and believing that it was thieves he armed himself with a large club to assault them, but tender Orsolina, knowing what was going on, and concerned for my bones, confessed everything to her father. He came up into the granary, and even if he was a little angry, he couldn't keep himself from laughing at seeing me so frightened, agitated and confused by my imprudence. He shouted at me more for having exposed myself to the danger of falling to the street than for having tried to seduce his daughter. She wept with compassion for me. He embraced her, pardoned her, then accompanied me from his house to mine and made me promise that I would no longer get up to such tricks.

Informed of this, and of what I related a little earlier, and seeing that he could not make of me what he desired, my father proposed to me that I should go for two years to the monastery of the Benedictine Fathers at Mariaberg, to learn the German language, but his aim was to remove me from the temptations of music, of Orsolina, and of the fair sex in general. [3] As I was seduced by a great desire to travel, by curiosity about living in a monastery, and for learning the German language, without thinking about anything else I immediately accepted the offer, and my departure was fixed for the fifteenth of September.

Chapter V.
Departure from Roveredo - Brief Description of Bolzano and the Valleys which lead to Mariaberg - Part of my Stay in this Monastery - School and Music

Being always intent on stimulating my interest in business, my father took advantage of the occasion of accompanying me as far as Bolzano to give me a taste for attending the fairs which they used to hold there four times a year. He chose the fair of San Bartolomeo, since it was the most brilliant and pleasing of them all. We left therefore, going by stages from Roveredo to Trent, then San Michele, Egna, Bronzuolo and finally Bolzano. This is quite a considerable and rich city, as much for its fairs as for its geographical position, which allows it to do business without great difficulty with Switzerland, Alsace, Bavaria, Carinthia, Carniola and the northern part of Italy.

---

[3] More often called Marienberg today, the Benedictine abbey is located high in the Tyrolian mountains near Mals, Vinschgau. Rebuilt several time during its 1300-year history, by the time of Ferrari it was a large Baroque edifice close to how it looks today. It was known for the quality of the education it offered, and for the quality and amount of music studied and performed within its walls. St. Foix notes that religious music was performed three times a day in the abbey church, but much music was performed informally as well. As Ferrari recounts below, Fr. Marianus Stecker, a noted keyboardist and contrapuntalist, was the director of music.

The surroundings of Bolzano are picturesque, the soil is fruitful, and even though they are fifty miles north of Roveredo, we must give them the advantage in the production of grain, fruits, vegetables etc., etc.

Their silks and tobaccos are not worth much, but the wines that the Bolzanesi make are exquisite, and they drink them copiously with much enjoyment. They have a proverb that they repeat and put into practice daily:

> *Qui bene bibit bene dormit*
> *Qui bene dormit non peccat;*
> *Et qui non peccat in Paradisum volat.*

> (He who drinks well sleeps well,
> who sleeps well does not sin,
> who does not sin goes to heaven,
> so who drinks well goes to heaven.)

I stayed there about eight days, and as I was not able to be of any use to my father I asked permission to go to my destiny; he granted this, and I left with horse, seat and guide, commended to the Reverend Father the Prior and the Prelate and Most Reverend Father Abbot of the Benedictines of Mariaberg. This monastery is located in the Val Venosta, just a hundred miles from Bolzano. We were three days journeying to get there, which was not excessive, considering that the roads are rocky, badly kept, and almost always climbing upwards. Eighty of those miles offer a perpetual monotony; one passes through the lugubrious and sparsely-populated city of Merano, which would give Pulcinella hypochondria; after which one enters and exits valley after valley, seeing nothing but the same sort of trees, greenery, and boulders. Sometimes one can go ten to fifteen miles without seeing a house or hovel. A kind of little river runs continually alongside, slow and mute, which makes you cold, or rather chills you.

But at Val Venosta, however, there is a complete change of scenery. Slaunders is the first village located on the right, built on a great rock. From there, the little city of Glurentz can be seen not far off, built as a square, girded with a wall and four gates on the sides which are always open and without any sentinels. It was under the orders of a captain who had no other soldiers to command but his wife and children. Beyond Glurentz is seen the entrance to the Valle Enghedina, which leads after a few hours to Choira, the capital of the Grigioni. Straight ahead, and three miles from Slaunders, the Church and Monastery of Mariaberg faces you in an elegant and pompous perspective, situated a vertical mile above the plain of the valley. At the foot of that mountain is seen the village of Purgaitz which contains few houses but a beautiful little Church and a little fort where a judge resides with two invalid soldiers, who have nothing to do but eat, drink and sleep, since it has never happened that these heroes have been called out for a brawl, a theft or a homicide. The good inhabitants of these valleys being so good, religious, and honest, there is no need for force to keep them at peace. They are moreover so devoted to their sovereign as the beggars of Naples are to San Gennaro, and if they find themselves sick or in misfortune they pray God that he may beseech the Emperor to allow them the grace of which they have need. If you offer them alms of a single penny, they load you, almost molest you, with thanks and blessings; and say in their peasant tongue, and from the bottom of their heart: "*Vergelt's God in Himmel ham; vergelt's God, truila, truila, tansend male*" (God give you thanks in heaven, God give you thanks, three times, three times, a thousand times!) To see them on Sundays at Mass, the devotion with which they genuflect, bow at the consecration, elevation and communion, kissing the earth, even, and giving tremendous blows of contrition on their chests, as if they had committed horrible sins, is a thing to edify you and make you laugh at the same time! O blessed mountaineers, how I admire you and envy you! How appropriate seem these two strophes:

> Happy age of gold,
> fair ancient innocence,
> when virtue was no enemy
> to pleasure!
>
> By pomp and decorum
> we find ourselves oppressed
> and make ourselves
> our own servitude.
> Metastasio, *Demetrio.*[4]

> *Felice età dell'oro*
> *bella innocenza antica,*
> *quando al piacer nemica*
> *non era la virtù!*

> *Dal fast e dal decoro*
> *Noi ci troviamo oppressi,*
> *E ci facciam noi stessi*
> *La nostra servitù.*

I left my guide and rig at Purgaitz, and went up by foot to Mariaberg, the road being too steep and stony to go up in a carriage. Having entered the

---

[4] One of Ferrari's few memory slips, it is actually from Metastasio's *Demofoonte*, Act II, sc. 8. Ferrari may have known Paisiello's 1775 setting or Jommelli's slightly earlier setting, both which premiered in Naples.

monastery, I sent my references to the appropriate persons and was received with the greatest affability. The Father Prior presented me to his Reverence the Prelate, before whom, according to custom, I bent my right knee, kissing the gleaming and blessed ring he was wearing. I was then introduced to the schoolmaster, Father Mariano Stecker, a young man of twenty-five years, of peasant origins but with the best manners. He had an aquiline nose, grey eyes, red hair, but altogether a sweet and pleasing physiognomy. He did not know Italian and I did not know German at all; so that at the beginning we communicated using the little Latin that I had learned. But not many weeks passed before I was making myself understood marvelously well in the elegant German-Tyrolian dialect. (Author's Note: Stecker was already at that time a great musician, and by studying Fux and other masters of theory he later became a great composer, especially of organ fugues.) I guessed my father's intention in sending me there was so that I might be safe from the fair sex, since there were no other women in that place but three ugly old peasant women to milk the cows, make cream and butter, to wash the laundry and to do other typically feminine tasks; but he had gravely erred in believing that he would distance me from music. The rule at this establishment was to not admit any brother or cleric if he did not know how to sing or play some instrument extempore; the laymen were admitted there as doormen, cooks or servants, without knowing music, but there were always twenty or more musical fathers and brothers who took as boarders thirty-two scholars, who were provided with everything, except for wine, without tips or gifts, for only ninety florins a year per head, being obliged, beyond their maintenance, to instruct them in the German and Latin tongues, in arithmetic and in whatever branch of music was practiced by the monks.

A day did not pass in which there was not some service with music in the Church of the Madonna. I immediately took lessons on violin and viola, along with a little tuition on the violone and French horn. During free hours from school, Father Stecker was good enough to give me some harpsichord lessons now and then, or permitted me to practice on his instrument. This was a spinet or clavichord of three and a half octaves with hammers of tin. In spite of the poverty of the instrument, I delighted in hearing the sonatas of Schobert, of Metzger, the fugues of Handel, of Bach, among others, and with what precision and spirit that brother played them! He had a precious collection of music that he had nabbed and copied, and he permitted me to copy everything that pleased me as well. It wasn't long before I became a confidant and accomplice in Stecker's musical thefts.

Among the monks in the monastery was a certain Father Bonifazio, the fattest man I had ever seen. His body resembled a barrel, his chin rolled halfway down his chest, his hands looked like two feather pillows, and his fingers like so many Verona sausages. He played the violin and harpsichord like a bagpiper and sang like a barn owl. But he had his own wealth, and spent considerable money to have sent f the newly published music which he desired from Leipzig, Frankfurt, and Mannheim. He even had sent from Augsburg a grand fortepiano of four and a half octaves, a phenomenon that had never yet been seen in the Tyrol.

Father Mariano was an intimate friend of the Father Prior; he, according to the rule of that institution, possessed a skeleton-key with the right to open at will all the bed chambers in the monastery. He lent this key to my maestro from time to time, who, not obliged by the night duties of these monks, used to choose the moment to open Bonifazio's chamber when they were at first matins. He took the music that he desired and carried it into the school; at second matins, he brought it back to the before-mentioned room without its owner noticing. What is more, Father Mariano would sometimes visit Father Bonifazio and play the works he had copied on his pianoforte. The disappointed Bonifazio went into a rage, not knowing how someone else could have the music of which he believed he was the sole possessor.

As soon as I was informed of this scam I offered my assistance, which was accepted with pleasure. Stecker often came to wake me at midnight, and I would get up, ready as a puppy and content and happy to honestly steal the music of someone who was not able to make good use of it.

I had great difficulty in the beginning, but then I accustomed my eye and ear on how to abbreviate, and wrote as fast as my preceptor; and in that way copying three sonatas for harpsichord or pianoforte in one hour was no big deal for us. It is true, of course, that the music was not as long, or so filled with notes and accidentals, as is that of the present day.

I had the pleasure, moreover, of taking breakfast every Sunday with my preceptor. He treated me to fresh eggs, toast and butter; I served him the coffee that I had brought along with me from Roveredo, and I made it not with water but with cream, which produces an exquisite beverage, which I recommend to all gluttons. (Author's note: The cream at Mariaberg was skimmed from pure cow or goats' milk and not from the corrupt and adulterated milk that is sold with impunity in all the streets and dairies of London!)

After breakfast we set ourselves to filling out our abbreviations; then to church to make music; then again to writing, lunching, writing again; back to church again; and thus passed my Sundays, with holy religion, good meals, and divine music. Copying, filling out the sketches, and seeing and hearing the copied music performed was of unutterable advantage to me in reading at sight.

But with such occasions and temptations what else could I become! Goodbye, office! Goodbye, silk-rooms! Goodbye, deluded hopes of my father! Viva la musica!

Fig. 3. Revereto in the 19th Century

Chapter VI.

Continuation of Mariaberg - Meals - Hunting.

The responsibility of Father Mariano was that of instructing his students in German and Latin and in arithmetic. He presided three times a day at our table, and we were served as follows.

Each day, at seven in the morning, we had breakfast; on "fat days" it was a bread soup with gravy broth made with meat of chamois or hart. At midday lunch we had the same sort of soup, boiled with the same sort of meat, ragu of coney, rabbit, and of many types of birds, as well as of marmot and joints of bear, which with a bittersweet sauce makes the eating more delicate and exquisite. We also had roasts of every sort of game hunted there, ranging from partridge to hart. Poultry was only consumed on great feast-days; likewise vegetables and fruits that had to be brought from a distance, and at a high price. At seven in the evening we supped, and supper was, with the exception of the ragu, a repetition of lunch. On "thin days" we were served even better: a soup of pot-herbs; barley or oats with butter and fresh scrambled eggs; *canedlen* or *klösse*, which are kinds of ravioli; *nudlen,* a kind of cooked pasta with butter, eggs and spices; pastries of every kind; and a variety of freshwater fish, among which a kind resembling mackerel called *Engedeiner Fish,* whose flesh is red, salty by nature, and very delicious.

On holidays or feast days they would give us one, two, or even three extra dishes, which were devoured one after the other, as if they were nothing, but the serene air, the crystalline water of that are, and the scrambling and leaping we did on those rocks would have given an appetite to the listless, and made one able to digest steel.

It will perhaps seem strange that they were able to maintain such a school so well, and at such a low price, but the venerable monks were not thinking about money, but only of spending the admission fees and teaching the young people. They were also charitable in the highest degree; they used to travel miles to help someone whom they had learned was in need. They visited the sick, sought to console them, and administered the sacraments to them when it was necessary. At the monastery they never failed to attend to their daily and nightly prayers. Having done their duties they were always friendly and jocular. They would entertain themselves now by making music, now by going walking or hunting, now by playing billiards or keels, and always ending with a healthy lunch or supper that providence had sent them and that they shared with their friends. In short they were truly religious, neither Trappists nor "Holier-than-thou." They had four expert and robust hunters who hunted primarily the chamois and harts that were abundant there, and they hunted in the village in the following way.

The hunters would go out two by two, alternately, each with a pennant in his pocket and armed with a double-barreled shotgun, with bread, cheese, brandy, and a canteen full of fresh water; and with such provisions they sometimes would stay out in those woods, rocks, and mountains, sometimes in the middle of the snow, up to three and four days, nor did they ever return without their prey. As soon as they saw a group of harts or chamois from afar, they unfurled their pennant in order to know from which direction the wind was blowing, for if it was blowing towards the animals, they, smelling the men's odor, would immediately flee to a great distance, and as a consequence the hunters would have to make great circuits to surprise them.

The mountain men would sleep beneath a tree, or by a rock, or in a cave, and when one pair returned the other two would go out, and so on. In the winter they also went hunting for the black bears that were to be found in the higher and more frigid mountains. (Author's Note - It is generally believed that this breed of bear is not carnivorous nor sanguinary, and that they are (except for the females) sustained for three or four months of the winter by their fat, neither moving nor breathing. The hunters, however, used to say that they had seen them killing other animals several times, sucking their blood, and that their dens and caverns were full of wild fruit, greens, roots, etc, but so well kept and safe from the bad weather that they seemed to have been put there by the hand of man.) They then go out all four together each supplied with a pair of heavy boots, with iron on the soles for the ice, with the usual shotgun, but in addition with a bayonet and with a pocket knife whose point is sharply curved and as keen as a razor. They know already pretty much where the bears are staying, and go there. As soon as they have discovered a den, three of them hide, the fourth gives his shotgun to his companions, and goes forward with his knife, which he carries in a sheath, in the side-pocket of his trousers. The bear smells the man, and comes out very quietly from the den, advancing with a friendly appearance. But when he is close, the bear rises up on its feet and embraces the hunter, not to rend him but only to drink his blood. The hunter lets himself be embraced, but before the bear has bared his claws, or opened his mouth, he is already wounded mortally by the fatal knife with which the hunter opens and furtively lacerates his belly; the poor beasts faints and falls backwards, and the hidden companions immediately come forth and finish him off before he can notice it or suffer any spasm. Sometimes the timid, or inquiet female bear comes out of cavern, and seeing the father of her children slain, and fearing for her children, she launches a furious assault but is always the victim of bayonet-strokes or shotgun blasts. Then the hunters go into the den, tie the little bears with ropes, and lead or drag them to the monastery. Once they arrive, they start shouting and jumping like maniacs, throwing their green caps in the air, and act as happy and content as if they had found a treasure. The steward receives them with rejoicing, and treats them to a meal *alla* Mariaberg, with excellent wines that they much prefer to brandy.

Chapter VII.

Second Matrimony of my Father - Fanaticism for sacred music for the organ and for religion

A year after my arrival at Mariaberg, my father informed me that he had taken as his second wife Signora Francesca Gottardi, widow of a close friend of his, and mother of a rich heiress named Catterinetta; he had concluded this matrimony as much for the necessity of having a woman in the house, as for facilitating at a later date my nuptials with the daughter, whose fortune would enable us to checkmate his nephew, who was perpetually annoying him. This did not surprise me, since, a little while after my return from Verona, he had already given indications of such a project. But Catarinetta did not please me, nor had she ever pleased me, so nothing came of it.

I answered my father that at that moment I had not the least desire to take a wife, and if I had shown some inclination for the ladies, that only had been a passing fancy. In fact my passion for music was growing daily, and I was encouraged by the progress I was making on my new instruments and by the approval which I received because of it, so that I thought no longer about anything else. Moreover I had taken a liking for church music, and the masses, antiphons and other music that I heard there by Seifert, Seidelmann, Abt Vogler, and, above all, those of Father Arauss, which moved me greatly. There was a superb organ in the monastery, and a certain Father Giuseppe played it divinely. He would take a subject from the beginning, the middle or the end of a piece of music that had been performed a moment earlier, and, as if he were preluding extempore, he would draw from it a delightful fughetta so well modulated and fashioned that it was ravishing.

But another passion no less violent than that for music developed in me and took charge of my mind and my heart: Religion! Every day, whether for duty, or for entertainment, I would serve one, two, or even three masses, and I was present at all the ecclesiastical functions. I had for confessor a venerable and liberal old man, who after hearing my sins would give me a little slap, while saying, "*Ego te absolvo*". Sacred music no longer gave me a feeling of pleasure, but of religion: Father Giuseppe with his organ made me burn and freeze at the same time.

The church at Mariaberg was spacious and elegantly decorated. On the high altar were placed four skeletons of martyrs covered with a painted canvas on which they were depicted. On great feast days they were uncovered, and then they appeared in a large case with glass on the front, but so well preserved that they seemed to be sculpted in marble. In the middle of these was the tabernacle, with a large cross of gold upon it. The church had three naves, and in each of the two lateral naves there were three altars, all consecrated to six different Virgins; the first altar on the right was dedicated to the Madonna of the Snow, represented as a wax figure, dressed graciously in white satin, with earrings and a cross of diamonds, and with a necklace and bracelets of pearls. I took her for my tutelary saint, and went every evening to seek pardon before her altar; almost every night I dreamed of Paradise, and seemed to see angels, archangels, seraphim, cherubim, with my dear Madonna among them.

My fanaticism for religion had grown to such an extent that, having discovered where the monks kept their disciplines, I got up secretly one night and, half-dressed, went very quietly to take them. I beat my naked shoulders until I drew blood, and then I bound my back and legs with a mortifying belt of sharp steel and went to bed. The next morning when the servant came to make the beds, finding my bolster and sheets soaked with blood, he told the master of the school.

Stecker called me to his cell and asked me how this had happened. I would have liked to conceal my little game, but I turned red and had to confess what I had done. Mariano smiled and told me seriously not to do such things anymore, adding that the disciplines and mortifications were nothing but charlatanry used by hypocrites or the superstitious, that they had nothing to do with the true religion, and that if I had not had his counsel in time, I would have lost my head like so many had done, and would have no longer been useful to society, to those in need, and to myself. Such sentiments said and expressed by a man whom I loved and venerated struck me to such an extent that from that time on I thought no more about disciplines or mortifications, nor about other foolishness of the superstitious. As long as I stayed in that monastery I was always content and happy, as I have never been since, nor will be again.

Chapter VIII.

A Religious Theatrical Feast for the Father Abbot and the Monks of Mariaberg

Being aware of and grateful for the favors, generosity, and alms that the philanthropic Benedictines continually scattered about the area, the inhabitants of the surrounding region decided to give them a *festa teatrale*.

The judge at Purgaitz, the captain of Glurentz, the host of Slaunders, and the barber (*der Herr Barbier*) of the convent headed up this enterprise and in a few weeks they collected more than five hundred florins. Some signori of Choira and Merano, supporters of the monks, contributed the most for such an occasion and came there in a crowd. The barber, bearding the muses, took it upon himself to write the poetic script, or better expressed, the one-act program, to which he gave the title *Noah's Ark*.

As there was not a room large enough in any of the villages to serve as a temporary theatre, the host of Slaunders offered his courtyard, together with the granary; the granary was converted into a stage and the courtyard into the seating area. It was surrounded by tables, covered with tents, and adorned with tree branches, stags' horns, and bearskins, ornaments much used in all the taverns of these villages.

In front of the orchestra there was a large chair intended for the Father Abbot, with seats on either side for twelve of his monk, a number of rows of benches for foreigners and the wealthy of the town, then a large platform for the common folk whom the directors had favored by admitting. The stage represented the open interior of the Ark, and the author, realizing that he would not be able to bring in all the animals of creation, planned to paint a large number of them on the scenery. Beyond the end of the Ark the sea could be seen, the sun to the right, the moon to the left, and various sparkling stars scattered here and there. At the front of the stage there was on one side the gate of heaven painted in blue, and on the other side the gate of hell painted in red. Six persons of both sexes were the actors, who, by changing their costumes many, many times, portrayed more than sixty characters; nor was there, so to speak, a class, profession, or degree of society which did not appear in the scenario.

An hour before the beginning of the production the seating gallery was already full of spectators. At the arrival of the Prelate and his monks, all rose and applauded them with the most lively acclamations. Upon the curtain's rising, six mountaineers dressed as hunters appeared on the scene, and six peasant women, dressed as ladies. After bowing before the Father Abbot, they began to sing some of their national melodies, but very well and with natural taste and exactness; then to waltz, with the most gracious attitudes and movements. Then half of these players exited the stage to change their costumes, and in the meantime the others ate, drank, and talked among themselves as if they had been in their huts. Not a single one looked at the public, nor addressed to it a sentence, a phrase, or a single word. The ones who had changed costume having reentered the scene, others went out to do the same, and so it went, for almost the entire presentation.

I now will speak of the denouement. The favored playwright - the barber - having been offered the use of anything that might belong to the monastery or to its friends that would contribute to the success of his sublime poem, had one of these mountaineers appear in the most splendid cope of the Prelate, with his miter on his head, his pastoral crook in his hand, and the cross of diamonds pressing on his chest. To the right of the feigned Prelate he had another mountaineer appear, dressed in a three-cornered hat, decorated with feathers of every color from the wild birds of those mountains, in the uniform of an invalid, with the embroidered vest of the Judge of Purgaitz, with britches of black fur, boots, spurs, a dagger and sword at his side, intending for him to represent St. Michael the Archangel. On his left he had appear yet another mountaineer decorated with two bearskins sewn together, with two chamois horns attached to the head of one skin, and with three large fox-tails attached one after the other, and sewn to the tail of the other skin, believing thus to represent the devil. The three mountaineers were followed by the judge, the captain, the host, and the barber in gala dress, along with their families; then the other mountaineers appeared dressed in caricature, enough to make you split your sides with laughter.

Then the rustic prelate advanced toward the audience, and the others with him. Lifting his hand he blessed the true Prelate and the spectators; at the sign of the cross, the devil made an infernal shout, shaking furiously both his horns and his tail. The archangel drew his sword to kill him, but Lucifer, knowing the power of that blade and quicker than the saint, leapt toward the gate of Hell, and with two or three butts of his horns he forced the door and threw himself in. Flames were immediately seen, and one heard for a few seconds the howls and moans of the damned souls, which caused shuddering and terror. The gate of Hell having then closed, that of Paradise opened spontaneously, and St. Michael, putting his sword in its sheath, respectfully showed his companion inside. After the gate closed, two musicians appeared, each with a trumpet ten feet long made of the bark of a tree, which produces a sound similar to the so-called *corno inglese* or *vox humana*; they skillfully played a pathetic melody and a lively waltz to express that since the devil was already in hell, there would be peace and happiness on this earth, and to announce at the same time the return of the celestial travelers. At the sweet sound of this trumpet all knelt; the sun and moon, animated by various invisible devices, moved together and touched each other as if to kiss, and the stars, moved in the same way, made a circle around them. The entrance to Hell was swiftly transformed into a second gate of Paradise. The trumpets having finished playing, three thunder-strokes were heard to express the Trinity, and at that point the two gates opened wide, beyond which could be seen a myriad of torches with mirrors behind, with transparent glasses in front of a thousand shapes and colors, and which, with the contrast and splendor of the stars in the background, offered the most imposing *coup d'oeil* one could ever see.

Finally, the mitered and armed mountaineers appeared from the second door to show that they had made the tour of all of heaven. They advanced to the middle of the stage next to the orchestra, the first with a superb garland of artificial flowers, the second with a great olive branch, also artificial, in hand. The garland was presented to the Father Prior and the olive branch to the Superior; these, through prior agreement with the poet, put the garland on the head and the olive branch into the right hand of the true Prelate. He rose, and turning all about, gave four blessings to the spectators with the celestial branch. The curtain fell, and then the applause, the *strilli*, the tears of joy and contentment made the walls of the granary and the courtyard echo. The author was called onto the stage, and the applause doubled and tripled to make all the valleys resound. Finally, after there was moment of calm, a voice cried out, "*Es lebe der Herr Barbier!* Long live the barber!" Then everyone in chorus repeated with the greatest passion and furor, "Long live the barber!" (Author's Note: This fortunate poet was not only the barber of the monastery, but also the surgeon, according to the German custom.

He had developed a plan that succeeded marvelously well. Every year on the first of January he made all the monks and scholars take medicine, and he prepared the ingredients according to the age of the ill or the well. On the first of April he bled everyone. On the first of July he gave an emetic to all, and on the first of October he bled them as before. During the two years that I passed at Mariaberg I never once heard of a cold or of any other disease.)

Chapter IX.

A Plan to Make me a Brother - Return to Bolzano and Roveredo

How grateful I was to my friend the barber for my admission to this spectacle, and I will not be able to describe the extent to which I enjoyed it. The happiness that I saw among these monks contributed not a little to accelerate the plan that I had already formed of becoming a Benedictine, and I wrote to my father asking his permission. He answered that he did not at all mind that I might nourish religious feelings, but that the idea of becoming a brother seemed to him "a passing fancy like those of my first loves." The jibe was well made and struck me to quick. Moreover, my father said that he had great need of my assistance, as much to help him in his approaching old age as to look after my younger brothers. He added that if I insisted on my plan I would certainly regret it; but that he was expecting to see me return to the next fair of San Bartolomeo entirely cured of my monkish inclinations. I, docile and always a slave to persuasion, abandoned the idea of the monastery and set myself to studying German and arithmetic a little more to please my father, however without leaving my dear music.

Before the time fixed for my sojourn in the monastery could run out, I received the order to be in Bolzano on September 15. Anxious to see my father again, I was very happy about it, but I regretted even more having to leave that sacred and happy place. How many tears I shed at the moment of departing! But the sadness of a young man is like that of an old man: it passes quickly, and is easily dissipated.

I left Mariaberg on the appointed day, at five in the morning, calculating that if it had taken three days from Bolzano to get there on the way up, I would not spend more than a day to get back going down, without thinking that I would have only a single horse for the entire journey. Nevertheless, I succeeded. At Purgaitz I found a little carriage ready, with iron chains for springs and a sack full of leaves for a cushion. The horse was robust, and I had been given a hunter from the monastery for escort, who I supposed was more to defend me from the eagles or falcons than from assassins, unknown thereabout.

As soon as I had mounted my noble carriage, I took the reins and the whip and it was farewell to Mariaberg, to Father Abbot and the Madonna of the Snow; I thought of nothing but seeing my father again. I stopped several times at various small hostelries to refresh the horse, now with beans, leaves, and water, now with grey bread dipped in wine. Halfway along I stopped for two hours, where I found good fodder for the horse. The hunter, strong as a lion, but only used to traveling on his own two feet, was beginning to complain that his legs and back hurt; I had him given a good supper and some good wine, and we got back in the carriage. I continued to be concerned for my horse, but having arrived at Merano he could go no further, and I was obliged to stop for another two hours. The hunter was banged up from head to foot, and for the last forty miles did nothing but take tobacco, smoke, yawn and curse at every step the stones and holes on the road that were giving him unbearable jolts. Accustomed from infancy to travel in every sort of wagon, with iron springs and without, I didn't suffer at all, but rather enjoyed myself greatly at the expense of the unfortunate hunter. Finally, at ten in the evening, we arrived at Bolzano. I found my father at dinner and had the pleasure of dining with him.

The following day he examined me to assure himself that I had studied what he had wanted at Mariaberg, and he was very edified to see that I knew how to add, subtract, multiply and divide with assurance, and that writing a business letter in Italian or German was only a little game for me. He had had a simple education and was very impressed by what his son could do. He set me immediately to correspondence, showing me the way to keep the books and the transactions of the fairs. He made me learn the various coins used and sent me here and there to collect some money or to pay. The custom in Bolzano for making payments was to send out someone from the shop with sacks full of silver and gold coins, but in order not to have to carry such a weight about the city they used to place some of the money some on the counter of a central coffeehouse where the mistress served coffee, and say to her "*Geben sie acht!*" (Pay attention!) and she answered "*Ja, ja!*" (Yes, yes!). One took the rest of the money where it was supposed to go and returned to pick up that which had been left on the counter. Sometimes one could see thirty or more sacks belonging to one or another businessman, nor did one ever hear tell of a mistake or something missing. Happy times! Happy places! The order and exactness in business affairs and in everything was remarkable in Bolzano. If someone came to an appointment five minutes later than the prescribed hour he was received with scorn and bad grace. If he was late in a payment, he lost credit immediately. If a dinner guest arrived late he would have to be content with the leftovers, and without ceremony the others would laugh in his face, declaiming the Italian proverb:

He who arrives late is badly lodged.

When post horses were ordered, the postillion was ready at the designated hour, but if after two or three minutes he did not see baggage or travelers he loosed the horses, returned to the post, and one had to pay for a half trip.

Sometimes I would go with my father to the last mass at eleven-thirty; at the striking of the half-hour and before the bell had ceased its vibration the priest had already made the sign of the cross and said, "*Introibo ad altare Dei.*" Oh, what punctuality, and what pleasure! Towards the end of the fair, there were three days of *giro*, or money exchange, and the noise that was made there in exchanging several dozens of thousands of florins was certainly louder than that made at the money exchange in London in three years, where they negotiate thousands and millions of pounds sterling.

We left Bolzano on the twenty-ninth, going as far as San Michele by post, where, because of the great number of travelers there were no more post-horses to be had. My father not wanting to sleep in such a run-down place, he hired a pair of oxen and a driver to take us to Trent. I hopped on the seat with the peasant, and by poking and tormenting those poor animals we arrived at Trent in two hours. The next day I could scarcely believe I was again in my always-beloved Roveredo.

Chapter X.

A mix of commerce, music and loves

We got down from the carriage at the Casa Rossa about midday and found the family under the portico, which had, as usual, come to meet my father, so hungry and so curious to know his news as if he had returned from the Antipodes. My stepmother welcomed me cordially and was even more anxious than my father to have me marry her daughter, who had already shown some inclination toward me. They immediately sent someone to look for her so that she could dine with us; but poor Catterinetta was so unattractive to me, that I treated her with a chilliness verging on incivility. At about one o'clock my cousin came to his post in the office, and hearing that we had arrived, came and presented himself with his ugly visage upon which one could see engraved sanctimoniousness and hypocrisy, but he forced himself to welcome us as best he could.

After dinner, my father took me to all the rooms in the shop and introduced me to the agents and workers, and then he had me sit next to him in the office. And thus I continued, sometimes often, sometimes rarely, for about two years, also frequenting the silk rooms, etc., but more from obedience and respect than out of love for business.

Around that time a rather singular circumstance took place regarding his business. He had at the same time material commissioned for Berlin and for Amsterdam, orders to send two chests of dyed silk, each weighing two hundred pounds, but of different kinds.

The man whose job it was to mark them erred, and addressed the silk intended for Berlin to Amsterdam, and that for Amsterdam to Berlin. The Prussian dealer had the wit to sell the silk, on my father's account; the Dutch dealer, irritated by the mistake, sent the chest back; but in doing so, he erred himself. Instead of the silk he sent to Roveredo a great chest, which indeed weighed two hundred pounds, but full of tea.[5]

A little after my return I was introduced to the Academy of the Dilettanti, and as no one knew what I had done at Mariaberg, they were all astonished that I knew how to play rather well a flute quartet and flute concerto, and how to play second violin or viola in a quartet, reading at sight. Fama volat. I was immediately invited to Saco and to Foianeghe, the country estate of the noble G.M. Fedrigotti, whose consort was a true lady, a woman of spirit and liberality. Signor Giuseppe Maria played the viola, his brother Domenico the flute, and their nephew Gianpietro (now Count) played the violoncello and sang with a small voice, but very gracefully.

Upon returning to Roveredo I was introduced on the organ of the Cathedral of San Marco, where almost every Sunday and for other feast days, they had some musical performance. There I caused a furor, and was considered as a prodigy or a portent, nor could they understand how I could sing or play anything on the spot. But the furor that I caused was not very flattering for me, since my admirers, who made up the orchestra possessed no great abilities. Since my criticism cannot harm them, I will describe them freely and with all possible truth and severity. The maestro di capella was Don Pasqui, a fantastic and churlish man, a terrible organist and a worse composer. Don Zandonatti, his assistant, was more expert in love than in harmony. The singers were the

---

[5] (Author's note) The manner of making and drinking tea in those countries is this: one takes a pinch with fingers, and places it into a little pot full of cold water; one lets it boil for a half-hour, then one passes it through a sieve, and drinks it warm with some red sugar, as a purgative: sometimes one lets is cool, and then instead of sugar you squeeze in some lemon juice, and take it as a cordial.

worst part, for they screeched like friars. First violin was G. Untersteiner, lawyer, and the final student of Tartini, who bored us to death with the concerti and insipid sonatas of that great theorist and player. First of the second violins was F. Feyer, ex-priest, maker of harmonic strings, which he scraped like a comb in order to be heard. The octogenarian Mascotti played the viola, and played so quietly that you couldn't hear a note. Both the violoncello - the lawyer Bettine – and the violone or contrabass, F. Ranzi, called Franzele (little Franz) delle Madri sawed away at double strength. First flute was played by F. Untersteiner, whom I baptized first flute of mercy, and whose second was a certain tailor Agnoletti, worthy of his first flute. Oboe solo was the emaciated Laurenzi, who played like a bagpiper. The horn players were Don Grase, who was quite young and Tambossi, a tanner and robust man. Checco Corsi, ex-coachman, and now a merchant dealing in rope, played the trumpet. The timpani was played by Madernini, sacristan at San Giuseppe, who made the whole orchestra go sideways, always playing out of tempo. In other words, the purest and most perfect musician among them was the one who pumped the bellows for the organ.

Oh Mariaberg, I would say, why am I here playing in San Marco! I am not saying that the music of the friars was executed with proper expression and delicacy, but one did hear the notes clearly and correctly, the accents, the colors, and the beat like a clock. The scrapers at San Marco seemed like so many blind men playing billiards.

It is true that music had always opened great possibilities for me, but, now, in my circumstances, it was more than a little injurious to me. Where was my true office? - At the house of the dilettantes in Saco. Where the rooms with silk? - At the Academy and at the organ of Roveredo. Where was my desire for celibacy and to become a friar? - In the laps of the most beautiful, eligible young women of the country. I visited almost every family; in the town. The young ladies were all affable towards me, and I fell in love with each one: another temptation to matrimony that manifested itself, but in such a way! I liked one because she had blond or chestnut hair, another because of her dark or blue eyes. This one enchanted me because of her slim waist, this one caught my attention because of her back. One touched me with her voice, another with her spirit, another with her affability or grace. To sum up, the last one seen was always the one that I expected would be my spouse. In the midst of all this, my father enjoyed seeing me welcomed everywhere, but was sorry that I seemed so distracted: my cousin had never wanted to see me at the business, but was croaking with jealousy and rage to know how nobly I was welcomed *chez* Fedrigotti. My stepmother wept and sighed because I was courting this one and that one without ever glancing at her adored Catterinetta. I myself could see that my career was in a terrible mess: I gathered my determination and decided to abandon music and love, and to get down to business. I shared my project with my father, he embraced me, and encouraged me, and knowing that I wanted to learn French, offered me a teacher, which I accepted with such jubilation as if he had offered me a wife the day before.

Chapter XI.

Study of French - Selections of Poetry - Facetiae

The only one who could teach French in Roverado those days was the charming Signor Don Marco Tazzòli, a man of over sixty, from an illustrious family, honest, liberal, and full of anecdotes and facetiae. In his youth he had been private secretary to the ambassador of France at the Court of Turin, and he knew French perhaps better than Italian. He gave me lessons, not so much out of self-interest as for the friendship which he bore for my father and for the esteem and recognition which I showed him, this being the best way to acquire the affection and inestimable care of a master. Beyond elementary instruction he had me read the letters of Madame Sevigny, Telemachus, Seneca's morals, and a little of the ancient story of Roland.

Not content with teaching me the French language, he sought to introduce me to other things which were useful or pleasing to society. I read with him, or copied out extracts of Italian poetry, he told me little stories of every sort, and thus instructed me by entertaining. Here is one story that he said he had heard from his ambassador. A lady of the court of Louis XV went out one day from the Tuileries to walk in the garden. She was over seventy, ugly, her face made-up, and with a nose that would give you a scare, but she was covered by a very rich, embroidered vest, which was out of style, in fact rather ancient. Two servants were following her dressed in gala livery. Having gone into the garden a little way, she met a cavalier who knelt before her, grasped the border of her vest and kissed it. The servants wanted to chase him away, but she did not wish it, and asked immediately of the gentleman what he intended to do. "Forgive me," he said, still kneeling and with his eyes downcast, "Forgive me, *madame*, if I have offended you, but you should know that I am the greatest admirer of and fanatic for antiquities; in seeing your truly superb vest I could do no less than kiss it." "Oh!" answered the gallant Parisian, "if it's only a question of antiquity, then kiss my nose, which is twenty years older than my vest!" The antiquarian arose, and in seeing that great nose, made a deep bow, and went his way.

Conversing one day on the wealth and avarice of certain individuals of the town he unburdened himself against them most severely, and recommended to me to be always generous, never stingy.

See what the celebrated Anacreon says:

> Not to love is hard!
> Loving is hard as well!
> Harder still to me it
> seems to not rejoice in love.
>
> Blood, knowledge, manners,
> Are indifferent or despised,
> Only the gleam of gold seems
> Fair in love,
> May he forever die
> Who first loves gold;
> Father and brother
> He neglects for gold.
> Every grievous woe today
> Is a gift of gold,
> And what is more, for this reason
> Lovers now are no more to be found.[6]

> *È duro il no amare!*
> *Duro è l'amare ancor!*
> *Più duro poi mi pare*
> *Il no goder d'amor.*
>
> *Sangue, saper, costume*
> *È indifferente o vil:*
> *Solo dell'oro il lume*
> *Sembra, in amor, gentil.*
>
> *Pera per sempre quello*
> *Che prima l'oro amò:*
> *I'l padre ed il fratello*
> *Per l'oro ei no curò.*
>
> *Oggi ogni mal funesto*
> *Solo dell'oror è don:*
> *E, quell ch'è più, per questo*
> *Gli amanti più non son!*

---

[6] From Anacreon's Ode 46. The version of this Italian translation is probably by Francesco Saverio de' Rogati, for which there were several editions in the late eighteenth and early nineteenth centuries, including an 1818 edition.

The sentiments of this ode, united with the dispositions which I had already imbibed from the liberality of my father, struck me, but later they were fatal to me, since from that time on I had no concern for money, but to spend it.

On another day I asked my master what the reason was that I heard nothing but laments and complaints all around me. One would say, "What a world of miseries! What a vale of tears!" Another, "I no longer care for life! I want to die!" And this from people who seemed to me to gaily eat, drink, and enjoy themselves. Don Marco answered that I was not yet of an age to know the world, nor to see what was going on inside the families and the hearts of those who I believed to be enjoying themselves. "Read this extract from our admirable Metastasio, the most natural poet and philosopher who has ever lived, and you will have a little idea of the miseries of human life:"

> Why wish to live? What pleasure
> Is found in it? Every fortune is suffering,
> Every age is misery. Boys tremble
> At a threatening glance; as adults we are the plaything
> Of fortune and love; those with snowy locks
> Groan under the weight of their years; first we are
>   tormented
>
> By our yearning to acquire; and then transfixed by
> Fear of loss. The evil war eternally
> One with another; the just battle
> Envy and fraud. Delirious shades,
> Dreams, follies are our cares; and when
> We begin to see the shameful error
> Then we die.[7]
>
>   Demofoonte

> Perchè bramar la vita? E quale in lei
> Piacer si trova? Ogni fortuna è pena,
> È miseria ogni età. Tremian fnaciul

---

[7] More from Metastasio's Demafoonte, here correctly attributed. From Act III, sc. 2.

D'un guardo al minacciar: siam gioco adulti

Di fortuna e d'amor: gemiam canuti

Sotto il peso degli anni: or ne tormenta

La brama d'ottonere: or ne trafigge

Di perdere il timor. Eterna Guerra

Hanno I rei con se stessi: I giusti l'hanno

Con l'invidia e la frode. Ombre, deliri,

Sogni, follie son nostre cure. E quando

Il viergognoso errore

A scoprir s'incomincia, allor si muore.

The old fellow, seeing that I was changing color, that I was agitated, that my eyes were filling with tears, pretended that he did not see me, and he immediately wrote the following jest, which made me laugh greatly:

> *Epitaph:*
> In this dark hole lies buried
> A goat who died following the flock;
> To the shepherd he left his skin and bones
> And his horns for the forehead of the one who reads this.

He also wrote for me, immediately afterwards, a satire, which later became a proverb, directed at a famous preacher, whose eloquence attracted everyone, and converted even the greatest scoundrels, but whose private life was neither prudent nor exemplary, in that he would rather have said, I love you, I adore you, than *Dominus vobiscum.*

The satire is in the Milanese dialect, and says:

> He who does what the priests says
> Will certainly go to heaven:
> He who does what the priests do
> Will go to the devil's abode.

> *Giace spolto in questa oscura fossa*
> *Un capron che morì seguendo il gregge:*
> *Al pastore lasciò la pelle e l'ossa,*
> *E le corna nel fronte a quei che legge.)*

38

Seeing that I was entertained, he was good enough to tell me a little story no less amusing than the epitaph and the satire. A poor bookseller had a stall in the street, and spent his breath constantly crying, "Compendium of the ancient story of Roland…Compendium of the history of France by Millot…Compendium of the history of England by Goldsmith, etc." No one would buy a book. A jokester went by, in whom the bookseller inspired pity, and said to him that he would never succeed with his compendia, which were known to everyone, but instead he ought to have a completely new history, and, if he wished, he would write the title for him. The seller agreed, and the unknown man wrote it for him, then he advised him to have it printed, and to have it glued on to every volume that he had. Thus the poor man did, and a few days later he appeared at his stall with his library, crying, "Complete history of our father Adam, the first man on earth, written by his teacher." Hearing such an outlandish title, everyone ran up, and without thinking that Adam could not have had a teacher, they bought it, and in a very short time, there was not a single copy left: they were all made fools of, and the bookseller was surprised and consoled.

Dear Don Marco, how charming he was, and how well he knew and took delight in teaching and satisfying young people!

In the matter of religion he was an intrepid moral philosopher, and used to say, "I affirm that religion is the most wonderful thing invented by man, or rather revealed by God. Everything is good in the true religion, nothing is wicked. I am so convinced of this, that I would even protect the religious humbugs, if I had not observed during the course of my life that they are generally conniving and egotistical; they give their charity to the poor for show, and their gifts to the church for ostentation. They read the New Testament as hypocrites, but don't put into practice a single one of the many virtues it contains."

Fig.4. Marienberg Abbey

Chapter XII.

Inclination of Commerce - Opening of the Theatre of Roveredo - New Study of the Italian Language- Fragments of Poetry.

The principal aim of my father in making me learn French was so that I might take care of the correspondence in that language. As I had been under the instruction of Don Tazzòli for four months, I knew more than enough for that purpose, but various circumstances obliged me to leave him, though not without great regret. I then applied myself even more to the business, to double-entry bookkeeping, to keeping the file for the fairs, etc., but always cultivating my beloved music, the more so as the business was worsening and I could see that music would be my bread one day. My father was subject to a common malady of the town, the illness of chest pain, and in the last years of his life he had two or three attacks each winter, and each time he was in danger or infirm for six or seven weeks.

In the meantime, his nephew lamented bitterly that all the onus of the business was falling on him. He acted like the owner, and when his convalescent uncle returned to the business he received him with a haughty and disrespectful air. My father suffered like a martyr and I was dying of anger without being permitted to crucify that ingrate! At the approach of a fair in Bolzano, known as the Corpus Domini, both of them fell ill. Thus I was sent to the fair as agent of the Ferrari brothers, which flattered my ambition and amour propre not a little. To make deals in the leading squares of Europe, to accept agreements, to make payments, to receive money! What a stimulus it was to make me love commerce!

Hardly! Returning from the fair I found that in Roveredo they were rehearsing an opera buffa for the opening of the theatre. Cimarosa's Giannina e Bernardone was being presented, which was rather a pasticcio than an opera. But never mind, it was new to the town and novelties please everywhere. The company could be called Italy's leftovers, except for Fucigna, basso caricato, who was not a bad actor, and Casalis, prima donna, who did not sing badly. She claimed to be twenty-nine, but we know the privilege of prima donnas. Still, she had a complexion and voice that were fresh enough. She was a student of the blind Bertoni in the Conservatorio dei Mendicanti in Venice, and knew her business; she visited a number of theatres to applause in Italy, and then went and stayed ten years in Dresden, especially acting in the delicious operas of Naumann, Schuster and Myslivecek. She needed a master to teach her the parts, and since there was none such in Roveredo, she arranged to inquire whether I would do her the courtesy of assisting her.

I answered that I was only a dilettante, but that if she thought I was capable I would serve her for free, as much to do her a kindness as to be useful in the opening of the theatre. She accepted my offer, thus exciting my ambition and my love for music. Anything but being the agent of the Ferrari brothers! Hearing myself called Signor Maestro I felt exalted, filled with joy and contentment.

I was thus introduced to Signora Casalis and she received me with the greatest politeness.

I taught her the part without complication, since her repertory was nothing but old stuff, not classic, and by consequence, easy to decipher. After the opera opened I continued to visit the prima donna, and I am greatly obliged to her. Because of her, I made the acquaintance of, sang, and accompanied a quantity of the music of the masters mentioned a little earlier, the chamber duets of Padre Martini, the cantatas of Cavalier Alessandro Scarlatti arranged as duets by Durante, etc. etc. Seeing the transport that music induced in me she encouraged me to compose, and I, without knowing any rules, began to write serenatas with great success for the good citizens of Roveredo and Saco. I then wrote melodies for flute, violin, viola and violoncello, in the style of Davaux, Saint-George etc., which I called, as they did, Quartetti.

I also entertained myself by giving lessons for free to this one or that one. Prince Venceslao Lichtenstein, canon of Cologne, was then in Roveredo in the house and under the care of his tutor, the brilliant Abbot Tachi. His Highness was my favorite student there, since he had talent, studied, and treated me with the greatest affability.

Feeling appreciated for my musical inclinations, I decided to direct myself to music and to go to study it professionally at Naples as soon as I had reached my majority. The only difficulty that I foresaw in going to Italy was that I did not know the language well, speaking it as I did like a corrupt Venetian, but a happy circumstance favored me in this matter. I became friends with a cousin of mine, Annetta Parisi, a young woman with good manners, and fanatic for the Italian language and its literature. We got along very well, and had it not been for a match offered to her and which she accepted, I believe that from cousins we would have become consorts, but our nascent love was not to be, and we remained always true friends. Although I had the occasion to see her almost every day, yet she wrote me the most polite letters, and so well, that I was ashamed to answer. I said as much to her, and she counseled me to take lessons from her teacher. I asked my father's permission, and he, who was unable to refuse me anything, granted it.

Signor Don Giuseppe Pederzani was my new Italian language teacher: he came to give me lessons at the house of my Parisi cousins. He was a young man, a little peevish, but also serious, sardonic, critical, gallant with the ladies, satirical with those with whom he did not get along, but also a linguist and literary man of great merit. He was later recognized as such in Verona, Florence, and throughout Italy. I was only under his instruction for three months: had I only been able to continue! Nevertheless, he corrected those errors, great or trivial, with which I was infected, and set me up so that I could help myself. If thereafter I was, and am, able to make myself understood, I certainly owe my principal obligation to the brilliant and severe Pederzani. He instructed me with Corticelli's grammar, and by making me read, copy out, and learn by heart fragments of prose and poetry by authors who write in the literary style. If there was some doubt or difficulty, he would immediately resolve it by running through the pages of the Italian classics, which he kept on the table where he studied, but with such quickness and assurance, that it seemed as if he knew them all by heart. If there ever appeared a word which was old, or out of use, he would then take the Decameron, and with that excuse would let me run through some rich passage, but always written with the purity of language of Boccaccio. Here are some excerpts of poetry that he had collected, and which I hope will not be unpleasing to the reader.

AVARICE
Among these marbles lies
The stingy soul of a cruel miser
Who bemoaned, when death came near,
The cost of his tomb, and not his life.[1]

Giovan Francesco Loredano

*(Avarizia
Sen giace qui fra questi marmi unita
D'un avaro crudel l'alma mexchina,
Che pianse, quando morte ebbe vicina
La spesa del sepolcro e non la vita.)*

Giovan Francesco Loredano

[1] This and the following poem are frequently to be found in collections of Italian verse from the late eighteenth and early-nineteenth centuries. Both, for instance, can be found in Angelo Vergani's 1802 Poesie italiane: tratte da' migliori autori.

INGRATITUDE

I saw a woman wandering in the naked sand,
Languishing, and burnt by the summer heat,
A plant arises, full of apples and leaves
And a brook appears, limpid and lively:
She, seated in the sweet serene shade
Now feeds on apples, now drinks at the shore;
Refreshed in spirit, and restored.

Silvio Stampglia

(*Ingratitudine.*

Donna vidi raminga in nuda arena
Languida, ed arso dal calore estive,
Pianta sorger di pomi e fronde piena
E un ruscello apparir limpido e vivo.
Ella assisa all dolce ombra servena
Or di pomi si pasce or beve al rivo:
Spirto ripiglia, e ristorata appena
E quelli prende e prende questo a schivo.
Alfin superba in piè si leva e poi
Con atti otraggia sconoscenti e rei
Il ruscello, la piñata e I fruit suoi.
Seccansi e l'acqua e I rami in faccia a lei.
Pastorelle, scacciatela da voi!
L'iniqua ingratitudine è costei.

SLEEP

In Arabia there lies a pleasing valley,
Far from cities and villages,
Which in the shadow of two mountains is all full
Of ancient firs and beeches;
The sun roundabout brings the bright day,
Which may never penetrate there with its rays,
Since its path is blocked by the dense branches,
And there one enters, underground, a cavern.
Beneath the dark forest a broad and
Spacious grotto enters the rock,
Whose front the avid ivy
All twines about with twisted step.
In this abode heavy slumber lies.

Leisure, on one side, corpulent and fat,
On the other, Laziness sits on the earth;
Who cannot walk, and can barely stand.
Forgotten Oblivion is at the door:
He lets no one enter, nor recognizes anyone;
He hears no entreaty, nor report,
And chases each away equally.
Silence goes about as escort:
His shoes are of felt, and his mantle is brown:
And whoever he many see in the distance,
He signals that they should not approach.[2]
Lodovico Ariosto.

(Sonno
Giace in Arabia una Valletta amena
Lontana da cittadine da villaggi,
Che all'ombra di due monti è tutta piena
D'antichi abeti e di robusti faggi.
Il sole indarno il chiaro di vi mena
Che non vi puòmai penetrar coi raggi
Si gli è la via dai folti rami tronca:
E quivi entra sotterra una spelonca.

Sotto la negra selva una capace
E spaziosa grotta entra nel sasso,
Di cui la fronte l'edera seguace
Tutta aggirando va con torto passo
In questo albergo il grave sonno giace,
L'Ozio, da un cnato, corpulento e grasso,
Dall'altro, la Pigizia in terra siede
Che non può andare e mal si regge in piede.

Lo smemorato Oblio sta sulla porta,
Non lascia entrar ne riconosce alcuno:
Non ascolta imbasciata, nè riporta,
E parimente tien cacciato ognuno.
Il silenzio va intorno e fa la scorta,
Ha le scarpe di feltro e il mantel bruno:
Ed a quanti ne incontra di lontano
Che non debban venir cenna con mano.

---

[2] From Ariosto's Orlando furioso, Canto XIV.

Chapter XIII.

Death and Funeral of My Father -Horrible Conduct of My Cousin - My Ruin and Departure for Rome with Prince W. Lichtenstein

With the opening of the theatre finished and my study of the Italian language interrupted, I gave myself seriously to music. I got up at dawn and went to bed as late as I was able, and in such a way I was not absent during the rest of the day from the shop, where my father looked at me so anxiously.

In the winter that followed he was once again attacked by his pain, and for fifteen days was in great danger. On the twentieth day he was much better, and I went to have fun on a sleigh ride until night. On my return I found the serving-girl of the house coming out of my father's bedroom, very agitated; I asked her how he was, and she answered that he was getting worse. I entered then with haste, and hardly had time to kiss his hand, which was almost cold, and with sorrow at the same time, had the consolation to gather his last sigh with my lips.

The impression that such a blow made on me is not difficult to imagine, thus I will only speak of his funeral. He had not only the honors of a businessman but such that no noble had had before. The citizenry, the body of merchants, the clergy, the monks, the confraternities and a multitude of people followed his bier; there were counted more than eight hundred torches lit. That may seem a fabrication, but it is actually true and not surprising. That good man had not only assisted his brothers, his nephew in Roveredo, his nephews in Verona, and provided dowries for their sisters, but did good deeds for whomever he could: charity to the poor, alms and gifts to the friars and to the churches. I will say even more; he took deposits at a rate of five and six percent interest, and then lent to the poor spinners at three and a half or four percent, so they might buy leaf, raise silk worms, and spin a little silk. A few weeks before he died he told me that he had noticed that he had been a little too liberal, but that he did not regret it, that he encountered many ingrates, but that he had still found some grateful people who had made it worth it, and made him happy. But the poor man did not know the degree of ingratitude, nor could he imagine in what ruin his family was about to find itself.

No sooner had he been buried than the sale of the business was negotiated. Signor Rosmini agreed to be my guardian and that of my brothers, but not being able to act either in favor or against himself, nor for his uncle Fedrigotti, he gave ample power to my cousin. My cousin accommodated the affair to benefit himself, dividing what was left of the silks and the good credit between the bankers and himself, and leaving cruelly to us all the bad debts. Not content with that he had the audacity and the infamy to offer me eighty florins a year to remain in the office - as if I should sweep the warehouses - after my father had given him five hundred florins a year, and an interest in the profits upon the death of his father! I refused with scorn and pride the ignoble and scandalous offer of that hypocrite, and prepared to litigate with him as soon as I had come of age.

Everyone in the shop and everyone in the village was outraged by such corrupt behavior. The Fedrigotti and the Rosmini themselves offered me eighty thousand florins of capital to take it from him, on the condition, however, that I marry Catterinetta; but in spite of my great desire for matrimony and to be useful to my brothers, yet I could not resolve to marry that girl for her money alone, and render her and myself unhappy.

Another reason dissuaded me from such a marriage, and it was that I found myself already committed to a certain Livietta Fedrigotti, of the age of sixteen, who had promised me not to marry before reaching twenty-one if I kept my word and had become successful by then.

I told my good Prince Lichtenstein what had happened to me, and about my plan to go to Naples, and he encouraged me to leave everything and devote myself to music, certain that I would succeed. He politely offered to take me as far as Rome, whence he intended to travel several months thereafter.

The celebrated Paisiello, whose dramatic music had touched me more than any other master, was in Vienna at that time and was then composing his famous *Re Teodoro in Venezia*. I wrote immediately to my close friend Bridi, a banker there, so that he might arrange for Paisiello to be my teacher of counterpoint upon his return to Naples. Bridi, always ready to help me, made an effort and succeeded with the help of Marchese Circello, ambassador from Naples, and of his private secretary, Abate Leprini. Paisiello promised not only to instruct me but would not hear of any kind of recompense. During that time I was almost always at my music, nor did I enter the shop, except when I was sure that my cousin was not there, since his person had become unbearable and disgusting to me.

Having arrived at the age of majority, I became guardian of my brothers, and wanted to attack my cousin in court, but a certain Tommaso Hortis, the head clerk of the shop, counseled me not to do so, saying that I could not act without his assistance, and that he could not act against my cousin while I was in Roveredo, but that if I was determined to leave for Naples and wanted him to testify against my cousin, he would do it. I trusted Hortis, who had been such a friend to me, but who, like a new Judas, betrayed me, and ended by ruining the sons of his patron and benefactor.

On the first of November 1784, I left for Rome with Prince Lichtenstein and Abate Tacchi, preceded by the courier Ignazio Sattini of Trent, leaving to my brothers and nephews a little money beyond what was necessary to furnish themselves, and the usufruct for thirty consecutive years of my little rents on the vineyard down on the bottom by the Sega, on the spinning-house up above by the Sega, and on the field by the Sabioni.

Talis pater, talis filius.[3]

Chapter XIV.

My Arrival at Rome and at Napoli - Conversation with Don Giovanni Paisiello

We arrived at Rome on the sixth, where I only stayed for eight days to fleetingly see the tiniest part of the infinite beauties of art which that magnificent and now sad city contains, and which I will not speak of, as they are too well-known to those who travel or those who read.

Having taken a sad farewell from Tacchi and from my Maecenas, I left on the fifteenth in the morning with the courier's carriage, and I arrived at Naples on the evening of the twentieth of November 1784. Oh, what a bother to go one hundred and fifty miles!

The following morning I presented my letter of introduction to the celebrated maestro Don Giovanni Paisiello. (Author's Note: Paisiello was then at the aged fifty-two, charming, tall in stature, and with a physiognomy as sweet as his music; liberal, rather ostentatious, a good friend and a good husband. He always lived in perfect concord with his wife, but never had the happiness of having a single son. He was also elegant in his dress, wore a *frontino* - a wig worn on the front of the head - and spent at least two hours a day at his toilette being shaved and having his hair done.)[4] He welcomed me with the simple and sincere good nature that is characteristic of the Neapolitans. He was about to go out in his carriage and take his usual walk in the Villa Reale before getting down to work. He

---

[3] (Like father, like son)

[4] When Ferrari arrived in Naples, Paisiello himself had just recently returned to the city from his sojourn in St. Petersburg to take up a prestigious court appointment which required him to regularly write operas for S. Carlo. This perhaps explains why Paisiello was too busy to personally instruct Ferrari. During Ferrari's five-year stay in Naples, Paisiello fulfilled his duties as opera composer at S. Carlo and as the court composer in charge of secular music at court, with the increasing duties leading up to what seems to be a breakdown of some kind in 1790, about the time of his composition of *Nina, o sia La pazza per amore.*

Fig. 5.   Portrait of Giovanni Paisiello at the clavichord by Élisabeth Vigée-Lebrun

suggested that I go with him; I almost fainted with surprise and delight. What, I, a poor ignorant young man, in a carriage and going for a walk with such a man! I could not believe it, it almost made me embarrassed: yet I went.

Crossing the Largo del Castello he said to me, "There is the Castello dell' Uovo. And that is Vesuvius. That there up above is the Castello de Sant' Ermo." And a little farther on. "This is the Teatro Reale de San Carlo." And at the turn by S. Ferdinando, "This here is the king's palace." Having passed the Gigante, "There is Puortece. Down there is Pompei, and close by is Castellamare, and then Surriento, the island of Capri...And see Pusilleco, Piedegrotta, etc, etc."

I wasn't seeing anything. My eyes were full of tears of joy and contentment in hearing the dialect and accent of that good man; there next to Paisiello I thought I was in the seventh heaven.

Having arrived at the Villa Reale, and gone in to walk in the garden, the conversation that follows took place, more or less.

"Well then, my dear Tyrolian..."

"Signor, I am Italian".

"That's right, excuse me, be patient. Then, my dear, you are decided to become a composer?"

"If heaven wishes."

"Good, good, I'll take care of it."

"I am well aware of the trouble that you are taking for me, and I will never forget your goodness."

"What the devil are you saying?"

"Signore..."

"Ella, Lei (polite terms of address)...But son, these elaborate and ridiculous expressions are not used in Naples. You never say Signore to anyone! You say voi to a few, and tu to everybody. So don't use these formalities any more with me!"

"As you wish it!"

"Huh? malora! You have read the works of Metastasio?"

"And with what delight!"

"Bravo! He is the poet and the teacher of the dramatic maestri di cappella. Mo, mo - when you begin to write ariette, Metastasio will be more useful to you than the ignorant Paisiello."

"The ignorant Paisiello! You are joking! I have always considered you to be the leading dramatic composer in the world!"

"Mannaggia mammeta! If only it were true! Embé, you should know that in music io songo nu ciuccio!"

"Songo nu ciuccio? I don't understand you."

"I'll say it in Italian as well as I can. I mean to say that I am an ass."

"But, dear maestro, you are discouraging me! What? You, from what I have seen, heard myself, and heard tell from others have delighted all Europe for a quarter of a century, and now you call yourself a nothing? After so many beautiful operas written here and there with success and wild applause, after so many novelties produced by your genius, you call yourself a nothing?"

"My dear, you shouldn't think that I am without amour propre. If you are talking about expressing the worlds of harmonious combinations, of making a shepherd, a buffoon, a warrior, a heroine sing in their proper character, if you are talking about theatrical effects, I will tell you that I'm not afraid of anyone. But in the matter of true music I call myself a zero, because this is an art and a science so deep and inexhaustible that I regard it as hardly begun. As far as novelty, after the creation there's been nothing new on this earth."

"Then I will discover the arcanae and minutiae of music, and after all of that I will not even have the satisfaction of producing something new! My dear Paisiello, you make me despair, you will make me become a beggar, a corsair, or a renegade!"

"Relax, my dear! You are too fiery! You should not think about novelties, nor of delving into the miscellenae of musical science, but let it be enough to seek the truth. Study your counterpoint without interruption, examine the music of good authors, ancient and modern, do not tire of reading Metastasio and other dramatic poets, and when you have scribbled upon some parchment and a few quinterns of music paper, you will write correctly and truly, and that will make your music appear scientific and new."

"I have caught my breath again. And I beg pardon for my inconsiderate and ridiculous passion."

"Be good, my son, and don't be so formal."

"Allow me, dear master, to ask you two more questions."

"We'll see."

"I want to know how it happens that two composers set the same words and their music is different, and how one composer can write so many things, as you have done, without repeating himself at every moment, and always producing something that resembles the truth."

"Mo te capaceto. Seek two men who resemble each other as much as possible; examine their features, and you will certainly find that those of one will not be exactly like those of the other. Thus if the lines of the face differ one from another, the ideas of the mind ought also to vary. And this corresponds to the differences between two composers who set the same words. Let us now come to the one composer. Imagine that you possess a tree which is nourished, rests, and then produces for you at its time a certain amount of fruit, but, however, not all of the same fragrance and beauty, as happens. The novelty of the composers is exactly this, but instead of producing fruit, like the tree, he writes a quantity of notes, more or less sensitive or elegant, but always generated by the same musical tree. As far as repetition is concerned you are wrong, my dear, since there is no composer or author, nor can there be, who does not repeat himself more or less; in fact, everything repeats itself in art, as in nature."

"Dear master of mine, I thank you greatly for what you have told me; I have learned more from you in an hour than I have during the ten years since I began superficially to learn music. But if I am not too indiscreet, I will have another question to ask you, and then I won't annoy you further."

"Say as much as you like: here I am!"

"I would like to know what differences you find between the music of an Italian composer and that of a German."

"I will tell you. If the two professors had studied in the same way, there would be no difference. Do you understand?"

"Hum!..."

"But the Italians begin generally without finishing, and the Germans finish before beginning. I don't know if I am clear."

"Excuse me, master, but I don't understand you."

"Mo' te persuado. In Italy we only pay attention to the melody, whether because of our nature, or by the harmonious effects that the voices, or the manner of singing, produce here. We only use modulations to reinforce the effect of the text. In Germany, however, whether for other reasons or because the Germans see themselves as inferior to us in singing, they don't care about the melody, and only emphasize it but a little, for which reason they are obligated to use an involved harmony in order to make up for the lack of the magic beauty of the voice."

"But is there no one who has studied as he ought, and has distinguished himself?"

"Indeed there are many, both Italian and German."

"And who are these?"

"I will cite you a few. For example, there is no Italian composer who can surpass the very pure melody of Hasse, the ingenious and vigorous choruses of Handel, nor the tragic operas of Gluck. But neither is there a single German composer who can surpass the science of Padre Maestro Martini, the counterpoint of Durante, or the grandiose and robust harmony of Padre Maestro Vallotti. But it's already time for me to write. Let's go."

"If you will permit me, I would like to stay and walk some more."

"Fine. Come to my house at two. You will find a nice plate of maccheroni c' 'o zuchillo, a stufato alla genovese, and after the meal I will give you some work to do."

"I don't know how to thank you, dear master, for such kindness, nor will I ever be happy until I can show you my gratitude."

"Be good, be good....Goodbye."

"Goodbye."

N.B. (Author's Note): Hasse had the fortune to find himself in Vienna when Metastasio was in the service of the Emperor Charles VI, and over the course of twenty years he wrote the music for various operas and cantatas of that divine poet. Such was the fame that he acquired with his elegant compositions that for many years he was called the "God of Song" in Germany and Italy, a title that after his death was transferred to the renowned Antonio Sacchini. Durante was one of the twelve candidates who presented themselves in Naples to become maestri di cappella at the Conservatorio of the Pietà dei Turchini. They were given a madrigal to set to music, in five real parts with double and strict counterpoint. Durante's composition prevailed over the talents of Vinci, Leo, Feo, Porpora and all the others. The great contrapuntist was immediately employed in Vienna by order of Emperor Francis I, but only stayed there for a few weeks, for the following reason. Being taken by his friends to a military review, with its firing of guns, he was so frightened and taken aback by the noise of the artillery that he began to tremble, to laugh, to cry, and to show so many symptoms of madness that it was believed necessary to send him back to Naples, where he resumed his post at the above-mentioned conservatory, at which he trained a great number of eminent students.

Chapter XV.
Soliloquy - Magnificent Eruption of Vesuvius - Scene alla Siciliana.

In spite of the lively desire and ambition I had to go back with Paisiello, still, he had gotten me so confused, demoralized, and agitated that I felt that I needed to be by myself. I walked several times up and down by the Villa Reale, thinking about what I would do and what would become of me. To begin counterpoint at twenty-one! At what age would I begin harmony? And when would I be able to write an opera? Ah, if only I had become a friar! If only I had spent more time attending to the shop and had married Catterinetta! Why not return to Roveredo and bring my cousin to justice?

While my mind was preoccupied and my emotions beaten down by lugubrious and oppressive thoughts, a circumstance came to pass that, even though unexpected and disturbing, nevertheless gave me new spirit and courage. The atmosphere began to darken; from afar one could feel a kind of earthquake and everyone ran as a throng toward the high ground at Chiaja. I asked what it was, and was told that snow had fallen on Vesuvius, that it was vomiting forth a prodigious quantity of smoke, and that an eruption was expected imminently. "Bravo!" I said to myself "Bravo, this is just the moment to come to study counterpoint!" Yet I took heart and followed the crowd. At the sight of the mountain I was astonished and amazed, having seen it tranquil just two hours before. The column of smoke was as large as its basin - the crater - and it seemed to go up as far as the clouds. It was so dense and of so black a color that I was expecting that at any moment it would spread its shadow over the whole horizon.[1]

The Neapolitan people were quiet, and said: "*Madonna mia*, I thank you! The *scirocco* has come, and Naples need not fear! My Jesus Christ, pray to St. Gennaro that there is no change in the direction of the wind before the eruption is over!" This gave me courage, and I went to my lodging, the Albergo di Venezia, across from Paisiello's house. At two I went to Paisiello's to dine, and he introduced me to his wife, Donna Cecilia, and to his uncle Don Ciccio (or Francesco). From that moment on I have always been a friend of the house.

---

[1] Mt Vesuvius, the volcano near Naples most famous for burying the town of Pompei in ash and lava in AD79, erupted several times in the period 1600-1900, including eruptions in 1767, 1779, and 1794. Ferrari was not in Naples during a major eruption, but the volcano was very active during this period, and lava would flow regularly. The lava flow and ash fields were popular tourist sites, as Ferrari describes.

Fig. 6. Joseph Wright of Derby's painting of Vesuvius erupting in 1774-76

liberty of asking her if she wasn't afraid of the eruption that was threatening to explode at any moment.

"What are you saying? What eruption? What eruption? That's a little smoke coming out of the crater. And even if there was an eruption, the wind is the *scirocco*, so there's no worry for Naples."

"But don't you feel the earthquake?"

"What earthquake? It's the fire of the volcano that is boiling a little and makes this noise. It's not an earthquake. But did it scare you?"

"Me? No. I'm not scared, no, no, really."

"Poor little boy!" she said, smiling. "You're used to seeing the mountains of the Tyrol covered with ice, and now you are alarmed seeing ours which smoke! It's better if you don't come to the theatre.

"Me? But to hear an opera by Paisiello I would come even if I were sure to find fiery lava at the entrance to the theatre!"

"Bravo! Wonderful! Be a good boy! Then come back here at seven and we'll all go there together."

"Thank you very much."

After dining my teacher took me into his study, and, having asked me various questions on what I had learned, he set me to work, encouraging me by saying that my course of instruction would be much shorter than usual. He invited me to come to his house morning and evening, if I wished, and that he would give me a lesson whenever possible. I thanked him.

At seven, I went back to the house, and with Donna Cecilia and her friends I went to the theatre where I enjoyed myself greatly, hearing an old but very graceful opera staged by the composer himself.

Returning from the theatre to the Paisiello house, the noise from Vesuvius was much more audible, and from time to time one heard bangs that seemed like little claps of thunder. I trembled like a leaf, but tried to act brave. Donna Cecilia, mischievous as all women are, noticed and made me stay for supper. Various guests then arrived and gave us the news that the eruption had exploded and that it was the most beautiful thing in the world to see. I turned red and pale at the same time, and the others laughed at me. Seeing how cheerful everyone was, I took new courage and climbed up with them onto the roof terrace of the house. Oh, what a spectacle! What a marvel! What a beautiful horror! The night was dark, the air hazy, the sea was slumbering, the earth was immobile, the stars invisible; it seemed in truth that the volcano had absorbed all the elements and the firmament itself. The peak of Vesuvius was covered with snow; three rivers of fire, a little apart from each other, made their way through the snow, rushing furiously and spreading lava at the base of the mountain near Portici by Torre del Greco, and then down to the sea. Beyond the lava, one could see here and there openings that seemed like torches. The mouth of the volcano vomited a column of smoke, now black, now mixed with combustible materials and with fiery stones of immense size, which, bursting in the air, presented to the eye a sort of fireworks. This reminded me of the *festa teatrale* presented to the Benedictines at Mariaberg, but that was nothing but a heavenly fiction, and this seemed like an infernal reality.

A quarter of an hour after us Donna Cecilia came out to call us to supper. As soon as she appeared on the roof, she immediately shouted, "Mamma mia! Saint Gennaro, what a scare this is! Come to supper, come to supper!"

That brave woman, who not long before had been making fun of me, ran away like a lightning bolt. We finally went down, and found a supper prepared *alla siciliana*, with a single large oval platter in the middle of the table heaped with salad seasoned with oil, vinegar, pepper, salt, garlic, with hard-boiled eggs, anchovies, locusts, breasts of chicken, of pheasant and other more substantial things, enough for twenty people. After the salad, refreshments of every sort: pastries, almond cake, *mostacciuoli* biscuits, exquisite fruits, and ices in quantity. And what glasses of Lacryma, Malaga wine, and English punch were drunk to Saint Gennaro and the health of Paisiello! Towards midnight we left the married couple and the old man Don Ciccio, half gone with liquor. The friends of the house accompanied me to my inn, and I went to bed. I will let the reader guess how I passed the night.

The following day I got up early. The eruption was still frightening, and it continued that way for about another month. One could hear the bells of the principal churches of the metropolis constantly, with processions here, and prayers there. Incense, myrrh, and branches of laurel were burned, exhaling a sweet and delicious fragrance; all the lamps were lit before the images set out in the plazas. And, in every street, in the middle of all this, mandolins, guitars, tambourines, songs, dances, and *maccheroni* were everywhere.

Towards noon I went to the Paisiello house to make a visit of convenience and duty, but the maestro was composing *Antigone*, to be presented at the Teatro San Carlo for the birthday of the King, and so I could not see him nor have a lesson with him. From Paisiello's I went to the Coltellini house to present a letter of introduction to Signora Celestina, prima donna at the Teatro dei Fiorentini, of whom I will speak in the following chapter.

Chapter XVI.
Casa Coltellini - Lady Hamilton

Celeste Coltellini was certainly the most natural, witty and perfect actress that could be desired. [1]In addition to being a most able actress, she sang with purity of style and of expression. She was a student of the celebrated Mancini, and even if her voice was not agile nor had much range, yet her knowledge and judgment made up for the qualities that nature had not given her. In the Pastorella Nobile, in the Schiavi per Amore, in the Molinarella, and in others, she was a jewel. In Nina, I was told that she was sublime, that she drew forth tears and almost took

---

[1] Celeste Coltellini (1760-1828) was a well-known Italian soprano during the 1780's and early 1790's, most known for her performances in opera buffa by the popular composers of the day. She began her career in Naples, singing several roles in Paisiello operas, most notably Nina, o sia La pazza per amore. The Austrian Emperor Joseph II heard her sing while in Naples and invited her to Vienna, where she lived for over a year, singing several roles often paired with Nancy Storace and, according to several accounts, moving in the same circles as Mozart. After her time in Vienna, she spent the rest of her life in Naples. She retired at the age of 32, marrying the Swiss banker Jean-George Meuricoffre.

the breath away from those who heard and saw her. She had, moreover, a pretty face, the proper stature, a relaxed bearing, and was without affectation. For many years, she was the pearl of Naples, then married M. Meuricoffre, a Swiss banker who had established himself in Naples, and she retired from the theatre, bitterly wept for by the virtuosi, the composers and even more by the public who so admired her. She welcomed me with her innate amiability

that she never lost, presenting me to her mother, her aunt, to her brothers, and to her sisters Constantina, Annetta and Rosina, one more polite and charming than the next. They were all born in Florence, and, having traveled, they had lost the Florentine burr, and consequentially they spoke so purely, and pronounced and articulated so sweetly that it was a delight to hear them. Those dear Coltellini! Were I a Muslim I would have married all four of them at first sight! Casa Coltellini was a home and port-of-call for artists, literati, and noble travelers, all of whom competed to enjoy the amiable company of those interesting young ladies. They frequently held numerous little annoying Italian conversazione, which are perhaps worse than certain English routs, where one only goes to see or be seen, to criticize or yawn, and from which one leaves insipid and perplexed like the conversation itself. But there it was a matter of enjoying the talents of the visitors.

Someone would sit at the harpsichord to play something, then another to accompany duets or concerted pieces performed by Celestina, Annetta and the others. Celebrated painters would show their portraits and drawings to Costantina and Rosina, then a sculptor or a painter would show his work. An improviser might entertain you all evening, a man of letters might read or perorate on the branch of literature with which he was concerned, or the travelers would tell their stories, the accidents, or of their amours, whether true or ben trovati. All of them kept the company awake and merry. One day Celestina invited me to dinner and asked me to be there early so that she could introduce me to, and have me hear sing, an English young lady whose voice touched everyone's heart, and whose beauty outshone the Venus of the Medici. I smiled, intently fixing my eyes on hers, and she added, "You will see! You will see that I haven't said enough!" I accepted the invitation, and went, nor was I at all disappointed. It was Lady Hamilton, the most beautiful creature I had yet seen. (Author's note: I speak of Lady Hamilton before she had had the honor of bearing such an illustrious name. Her conduct in Naples having been for years and years correct and moral, she won not only the heart and hand of the gentleman Sir William Hamilton, but also the esteem and affection of all those who knew her, so I have thought it well to omit any other name.)[2]

[2] Ferrari claims acquaintance with the infamous Lady Hamilton at two points in his life. When he meets her in Naples, Lady Hamilton had recently arrived in the city as the new mistress of Sir William Hamilton and had not yet married him. She quickly became a court favorite, and was well-established as the hostess of his salon. When Ferrari encounters Lady Hamilton again in

Fig. 7, Portrait of Emma, Lady Hamilton by Johann Heinrich Schmidt

London, as recounted in Part Two, of the autobiography, she is married to Hamilton and is firmly ensconced in a ménage-à- trois with Lord Horatio Nelson. As were so many of the period, Ferrari was instantly smitten with the beautiful and charming Emma.

When a Neapolitan lady married off her daughter, I recommended to her with fervor to follow the example of Lady H. if she ever wished to be respected and happy. When the English beauty went to the theater, or for an outing in her carriage or on horseback, she was always admired, and the people said, "Look! Look! What a divine countenance! She is a Virgin! (Author's note: This title is given often in Italy to any good woman, even if she is married and has children.)

Then Sir Hamilton gave her a musical education. She had Diopioli for a singing master, then Aprile and Millico. She studied accompaniment with Fenaroli, and sang now and then in the new productions of Cimarosa, Paisiello, and Guglielmi. As far as her appearance is concerned, I have never found a beauty to compare to Lady Hamilton.

Ah, if only for a single hour I could be an improviser or a poet. How many beautiful things I would say on such a subject! But, I would like to paint, and I do not draw; I would like to speak and I do not know how; I would like to sing and I do not have the inspiration! Sir Walter Scott, give me your plume and your colors, with which I might describe the merits, the charms and the graces of this beautiful creature!

In order not to leave the reader anxious to hear that which I am unable to express, I will have recourse to my faithful Metastasio, taking as a model the portrait of the beautiful Europa, in order to compare her to this elegant and true Venus of Albion.

On the Rape of Europa
by Pietro Metastasio

It was of Hamilton...

It was of Europe that most flowering time,
When she had scarcely completed fifteen years,
Graceful in her actions and pleasing in her speech,
On her spacious brow in the bright gems
Of her golden tresses some were braided
And others fell unbound and free,
Like waves which in falling ripple,
And rise once more, and slowly tremble
At the sweet assault of the lascivious zephyr.
Two black lights, above which arch
Two brows, black and as fine as may be,
In her slow moving and in her glances are gathered
All the force and the pleasure of Venus,
Full are her cheeks, where the rose and the lily
Alternate their pleasing colors,
Divided by her noble nose.

Her lips strewn with native purple,
More precious than that of the shells of Tyre,
Reveal tiny and compact teeth,
Which seem to be made of polished ivory,
But so well-disposed and so well-ordered,
That there is not one too many nor too few.
The neck, round, subtle and of lucid alabaster
Which ends in the white chest, elevated and mobile,
Of the same color which the snows
Give to the high Appenines,
When, the sun falling into the Ocean,
Its uncertain rays tinge them with a color,
Which moderates and enlivens their exceeding brightness.
Narrow is her waist, and broad her shoulders,
Small her feet, her hands long and tender,
And in her gentle glance united
Sweetly together live majesty and grace.[1]

Era d'Europa quell'età più florida
Che scorre di tre lustri appena il termine,
Grata negli atti e nel parlar piacevole.
Su la spaziosa fronte in gemme lucide
De' suoi dorati crini altri s'annodano,

Altri cadendo poi disciolti e liberi
A guisa d'onda nel cader s'increspano
S'innalzan spesso e lentamente tremano
Al dolce assalto di lascivo zefiro.
Due nere luci, sovra cui s'inarcano
Nere le ciglia ancora e sottilissime,
Nel lento moto e negli sguardi accolgono
Tutta la forza ed il piacer di Venere.
Piene ha le guance, ove a vicenda sparsero
La rosa e 'l giglio il lor colore amabile;
E dal naso gentil poi si dividono.
Le labbra sparse di nativa porpora,
Che torrebbero il pregio al tirio murice,
Talor minuti e spessi denti scoprono
Che sembran fatti di pulito avorio;
Ma così ben disposti e con tal ordine,
Che non mancan fra loro e non eccedono.
Tondo, sottile e di alabastro lucido

---

[1] One of Metastasio's lyric works, published as part of his six-volume opera omnia in 1735, and repeatedly after that.

Rassembra il collo, che davanti termina
Nel bianco petto rilevato e mobile,
Il qual si mostra del color medesimo
Che dall'alto Appennin le nevi rendono,
Quando cadendo il sol dentro l'Oceano
Gl'incerti raggi d'un rossor le tingono
Che il soverchio candore avviva e modera.
Angusta è la cintura e larghi gli omeri,
Picciolo il piè, la man lunghetta e tenera;
E nel gentile aspetto unite albergano
In dolce nodo maestade e grazia.

Chapter XVII.
Continuation of Vesuvius and of Paisiello - A New Counterpoint Teacher - The King, The Queen of Naples and the Cavalier Acton of England - The Miracle of St. Gennaro

Towards the end of December the eruption had diminished quite a bit. The smoke was less copious and dense, the explosions neither so frequent nor so strong, and the molten lava ran invisibly under the cooled lava and the burning cinders, just as one might believe the tide runs under the surface of the Mediterranean without lifting or lowering its waters.

This offered the English travelers the opportunity to visit the crater, though accompanied by the usual guides and by the Hermit who lives at a certain height on Vesuvius inaccessible to the lava. But how many pairs of shoes were burnt on those cinders, and how many feet were cooked by the lava unsuspected below! This, however, is nothing for them - the English traveler is more curious, more enthusiastic, and perhaps more imprudent than that of any other nation. There is not a cavern, a precipice nor an abyss which frightens him, and which he does not wish to confront.

My study with Paisiello was going slowly, in fact, miserably; in spite of his good will he did not have the time to instruct me, and in five weeks I did not have four hours of lessons. I waited patiently until the performance of his *Antigone*, hoping that I would be able to profit by his lessons afterwards. This opera caused a furor, and in fact revealed the talents of three celebrated singers - Pozzi, Rubinelli, and David - sacrificed the year before in productions of operas by Sterkel, Martini (the Spagnuolo) and Pleyel, three composers of merit, but

Pozzi, Rubinelli, and David - sacrificed the year before in productions of operas by Sterkel, Martini (the Spagnuolo) and Pleyel, three composers of merit, but not of Italian opere serie. The great maestro was at the harpsichord for three consecutive nights, according to Italian custom, and on the fourth day he left to write an opera for Rome, leaving me under the instruction of his old friend Nasci, but that was worth nothing to me. I was patient until his return, since he was engaged to the Florentines to write La Grotta di Trofonio. There I was, still without a teacher, and half despairing.

Donna Cecilia and Don Ciccio gave me great hopes that he would assist me more extensively in the summer, but my friends the Coltellini and others encouraged me to take a teacher who was less busy, and to pay him. It happened that at their house I made the acquaintance of a certain Thomas Attwood, an Englishman, who was there to study counterpoint.[1]

We immediately struck up a friendship; I told him of my situation, and he told me that he had a good teacher, Latilla, an older man, and that if I also wanted to study with him he was sure that he would accept me with pleasure. I went immediately to Paisiello to inform him of my circumstances and of my plan; he liberally encouraged me to put it into operation, offering me his assistance when I would begin to write things for the chamber or the theatre, and furthermore, permission to look over and study all his scores. This last item was useful to me, but at the same time damaging, since having imbibed from his excellent models, I was taken, when starting out, for a poor copy of him. I went then to my English friend, and since he was on the verge of changing his lodging, we took an apartment together in the house of a certain Seidler, a German clockmaker, and we had for some time the same teacher.

Latilla had a deep knowledge of counterpoint. He was a little lazy, but good, as are all those lazybones, as long as they have the means of finding a plate of maccheroni.[2] Latilla took a carlino for each lesson (four and a half English shillings) from Neapolitan musicians, two carlini from foreigners in general, and three carlini from the English. I offered him two carlini as a regular

---

[1] Thomas Attwood is best known as Mozart's favorite pupil. He was in Naples at the same time as Ferrari to study composition, supported by the then Prince of Wales. After a couple of years in Naples, he moved to Vienna, where he studied with Mozart. He returned home to London, where he spent the rest of his life as organist at St Paul's and as one of the first professors at the new Royal Academy of Music.

[2] Ferrari never supplies his teacher Latilla with a first name, but it seems clear Ferrari was studying with Gaetano Latilla (1711-1788), who was living in Naples during this period, and who taught Thomas Attwood as well. Latilla had been trained at the Conservatorio di S Maria di Loreto, and his first comic operas were performed in Naples. In the 1740s and 50s he was at the height of his fame as an opera composer, composing both in Rome and then Venice, where he had several important posts, before running into trouble with Venetian officials. He returned to Naples to live out his last years, subsisting mostly through his teaching.

foreigner, but he said to me, "No - you are Tirolese, it rhymes with Inglese, ergo you have to pay me what your friend pays me."

I got into an argument as heated as it was ridiculous, and then found myself happy to have an educated teacher who came to me four times a week and stayed with me for entire hours. He instructed me in how to dispose the voices in two, three, and four, first in stepwise motion, then with leaps of a third to an octave, with ties and simple modulations, then with canons, fugues, and church music. I continued thus for a year, after which I took no more than two lessons a week, having then occasional lessons from Paisiello, who from time to time corrected arias, duets and concerted pieces that I had written. Moreover, I went to the rehearsals of all Paisiello's new operas, and after the third evening I took the place of the maestro at the harpsichord for practice, and he was very happy to let me have me do it so that he could go home to bed.

La Grotta di Trofonio pleased infinitely. By that point, Coltellini had gone to sing at Vienna with the permission of the King of Naples, as a gift to Emperor Joseph. Cioffi and Moreschi alternated as prime donne, and performed together in the opera. Cioffi sang well, but did not please, because she was neither an actress nor beautiful. Moreschi scarcely sang, but pleased because she was a good actress and was charming. The celebrated Casacciello (father of the present singer), Gennaro Luzio, both Neapolitan buffos, and Morelli, a Tuscan buffo, contributed much to the success of that opera. The King and the Queen were present the first evening with their faithful companion Sir William Hamilton, and it was the first time that I had the honor of seeing Their Majesties.

Having seen Emperor Joseph II pass through Roveredo the previous year, and Pope Pius VI in his return from Vienna, I was moved not a little in seeing for the first time a king and a queen. I immediately inquired about her as sister of my sovereign, and was told that she was a most excellent princess, but a little too partial to the Germans. Her consort was a respectable man, a good husband, a good father, and a liberal prince, but that as king he did not take part in the affairs of state or of the family. Instead, he entertained himself by making music, playing billiards, going hunting for wild boar or fishing, but the queen commanded in the Palace, and Sir Acton, an Englishman, minister of the Navy, was the factotum of the Kingdom.

Some time later I saw appear the pasquinade that follows, which doesn't seem too bad:

Hic Regina,
Haec

Hic haec hoc Acton.[3]
(The king is queen, the queen is king, and Acton is both)

Ferdinando IV played the hurdy-gurdy, and was truly transported by any sort of music.

If a distinguished professional arrived in his metropolis he wanted to hear him and encouraged him liberally. A certain Antonio Mariotti, a Bolognese, had arrived there before me, a celebrated trombonist and perhaps the only one at the time who played such an instrument in Italy. Passing through Rome, he saw the Easter services and the benediction the Pope habitually gives on that day from the Vatican. It made such an impression on him that for a number of weeks he could not get His Holiness out of his mind. The King of Naples, hearing that a new virtuoso had arrived there with a new, unusual instrument, called him immediately to his palace at Caserta to hear him play. Mariotti played the bass timidly in a quartet, yet it pleased his Majesty; he then played the bass in a noisy overture with courage and force, and put in certain trombonisms that caused the King to get up from his seat and approach the player. The overture being finished, he put a hand on his shoulder and said to him, "You are the trombone of my Chapel and of the Theater of San Carlo!" The poor Mariotti, happy, confused, and with his Pope on his mind, answered him,"Blessed Holy Father, I thank you for your good will!" His Majesty, bursting with laughter, turned to the Queen, and called her: "Wife, come here, come here! Did you hear? This peculiar Bolognese called me Holy Father as if I were the Pope!"

The Mariotti of whom I speak is the same who, for many years, has been first trombone at the Italian Opera in London.

At the end of April of the following year (1785) the eruption was almost over; there had been processions and prayers to Saint Gennaro, but they said he was hard of hearing. Finally, when the ministers saw that the lava was for the most part petrified, that the smoke vanished, the explosions had ceased, and the other symptoms they knew had terminated, they had the bells of the chapel of the saint rung to announce the miracle that was awaited with such impatience.

I asked a Neapolitan friend of mine to take me to see the spectacle, and he made me understand that, as I was a foreigner and living with an Englishman, if I was ever recognized in the chapel I would be taken for a heretic and abused. This didn't frighten me, and I again asked him to take me with him, promising him that I would pretend not to know him until the miracle had been done. And so we went. The chapel was almost full of beggars and fish-sellers, some foreigners, but few decent Neapolitans. The priest stood already turned to

---

[3] A witticism, pointing to Acton as the one that does everything, i.e. the factotum.

Fig. 7. Map of Naples and its musicasl establishments during the late 18th century

the altar, and half genuflected before the ampoule of crystal with four faces containing what was believed to be the Blood of Saint Gennaro. His bust in gilded silver was on the left. After some prayer *sotto voce*, the priest turned back to the public with the flask in his hand, to show that the blood was coagulated. Then everyone kneeled; the priest came down from the altar, and had the sacred ampoule kissed by everyone who came forward. And after having gone around the chapel, he went back up, showing that the blood was still coagulated. Then the people, who had been peaceful and praying before, began to murmur against the bust of Saint Gennaro, calling him beggar, boor, etc. etc.

The priest made a second circuit, which didn't work any better than the first. Then the beggars and fish-sellers began to yell out blasphemies and imprecations with gestures and words it would not be proper for me to repeat; at that point I was more frightened than I had been the first night of the eruption, but the shrewd priest, seeing that they were threatening to destroy the bust and the ampoule, hurriedly made a third circuit, and then came triumphantly to the altar, and having turned around, he lifted his hand with the ampoule into the air, letting it be seen that the crystals were half transparent, the blood liquified, and that the miracle had been obtained, without those poor beggars having noticed that the eruption had already ceased. Now they changed their blaspheming into benedictions for San Gennaro, for the Virgin, and for all the saints; there was embracing between men and women, and merriment as if they had been in a tavern.

I asked my friend as we were leaving the church what such buffoonery and scandal meant. He answered me that in certain countries one keeps the people in check with laws, in others with force, and in still others with superstition. "We agree," I answered, "but I will never again believe in the miracle of San Gennaro."

Now I believe even less in the charlatanry of that dear Prince Hohenlohe, *requiescat in pace.*

Chapter XVIII.
Latilla- Paisiello-Clementi-Haydn- Praise of Mozart- Haendel.

Latilla never failed me, and entertained me now and then with his conversation. I asked him one day how it could be that Jommelli, Piccini, Sacchini, Guglielmi, Paisiello, Cimarosa - all students of Durante - could have been so well instructed by that master alone, and yet each acquired a different style. He answered that a teacher of counterpoint could not form the style of a student writing dramatic music; those that I cited already had a natural taste, and that, by force of study and effort, had acquired a true genius and a different style. Even Durante, though the leading teacher of the Neapolitan School, could not boast of having shaped them, but only of having instructed them and set them on the road.

Another day I showed him the so-called "Octaves" Sonata, op. 2, by the celebrated Muzio Clementi, that my friend Attwood had lent me. He examined only the first Allegro, and then exclaimed, "This, yes, this is a nice piece! But if Clementi is able to play this with ease, then Clementi is not a man, but a devil! And I tell you that he will be the Durante of future pianists!" (Author's note: What would he have said if he had known that Clementi knew as much of literature and science as of music! And what would he say now, if he were living, to hear that sonata played with facility by dozens of noble young ladies?)

Attwood then left for Vienna to finish his studies under W.A. Mozart.

My friend arrived in the metropolis at the moment when that groundbreaking composer had just published his six quartets dedicated to Haydn, and he sent to me in Naples a copy as a gift, with a letter in which he advised me not to judge them without having heard them several times. I tried them with professionals and dilettantes alike, but we were only able to play the slow movements, and those poorly; I scored some passages, including the G major fugue from the first quartet. I showed it to Latilla, and he, after having examined the first part, told me that it was a very nice thing. Scrutinizing then the modulations and ingenious combinations in the second part, and having arrived at the reprise of the subject he put my copy back on the table, exclaiming, stupefied, "This is the most beautiful and astonishing piece of music I've seen in my whole life!"

"Don't you think that it's too ingenuous for a real fugue?"

"What are you saying? This is the best! *E nu zuccaro*! This is a real fugue, it's not scholastic! It's new! It's new!"

"Then can there be novelty in music? Paisiello told me that there was no such thing."

And he answered me that there is and is not; that there are three sorts of music that may be distinguished one from another, the elementary, the expressive and the original. The first is that which we make as boys, imitating the composers which we hear or whom we study; the second is when our own ideas are heard and propagated; the third is when, endowed by a natural genius, by force of study and tireless work, we arrive at creating, so to speak, novelty.

"But Mozart is still young, nor can he have studied much."

"I'm not saying that he is old," he added, "but his pen is well-seasoned. And I predict that this man will soon be not only Attila, the Scourge of God, but Attila, the Scourge of composers!"

Some time after Paisiello's return from Rome, a certain Gasparino arrived at Naples from the capital, a broker and a dilettante of the theatre. He took himself to Paisiello to ask him if he could find for him a *maestro di cappella* who was out of the ordinary, since, as he could have neither him, nor Guglielmi, nor Cimarosa, who were always under contract at Naples, there were no other masters in Italy who were worth two *bajocchi*. Paisiello suggested Mozart to him, as a youth of a transcendent and extraordinary talent; he added that it was not certain that his music would please, being a little complicated, but that if Mozart ever did please, he would surpass many masters in Europe.

In order not to abandon a man and a subject that capture my interest so much, I must make a little jump in my account in order to mention another case.

When the maestro Cimador reduced the six superb symphonies of Mozart into septets, they were rehearsed in the house of a certain Mr. Horring, a Viennese then living in London. He invited me to hear them and invited Clementi also. Cimador gave them his manuscript, and I had the double pleasure of reading along while they were performing the symphonies. When they arrived at the end of the last movement of the Symphony in G minor, Clementi said to me, "Mozart has arrived at music's gate, and has jumped over it, leaving behind ancients, moderns, and posterity itself!"

Now having presented the favorable opinions of Latilla, Paisiello, and Clementi, and with the support of these three renowned composers, each in a different branch of music, will I be blamed if I desire to attempt an appreciation of the numerous works of that singular and sublime genius? In the course of my youth I read, reread and examined a quantity of classic music of ancient and modern composers, and I found in this music beautiful, superb and sublime things. But from the year 1799, while I was in Vienna and there procured for myself all the works of Mozart that could be had, I have always considered him the most eminent composer who has ever lived, appearing like a phenomenon, like a comet which passes and returns several centuries later, or which perhaps is never seen again. His music is natural, original, elegant and varied, full of simple melodies, with clear modulations, reasoned and not superfluous, without the extravagances or the din which dumbfounds the mind and the ear, as often occurs today.

Really, by now I expect to see a piece of music begin on an augmented sixth chord, continuing chromatically and harmonically up and down the scale, and resolving at the conclusion on a diminished seventh chord, with the accompaniment of a ship of the line's hundred and twenty cannons, along with two frigates of sixty, which fire in unison five shots a minute. After this there will be nothing more for reinforcing music but the thunder of Jove and the forge of Vulcan, with the hammers and tongs of all the devils of hell. And who will be able to cite me a composer who has written in so many genres of music, who has distinguished himself and has surpassed everyone, as has Mozart, except for Haydn in his symphonies and Handel in his choruses, music for which Mozart himself had always a profound veneration? And the proof of this is that he was never ashamed to follow in the footsteps of Haydn, and to call him figuratively the legitimate father of his children, in his dedication to Haydn of his first six quartets. And he did himself the honor of adding certain wind instruments to the choruses of Handel, which brought forth once again the potent music of that great man, and which, without a doubt, he would have done himself, if such instruments had been in use at the time and in the place where he wrote his music. [4]

[4] In the following passage Ferrari reflects emerging attitudes towards Mozart in England during the 1820s that focused on the uniquely "characteristic" aspects of Mozart's music, in tandem with an aesthetic emphasizing the beautiful and classical nature of his output. It would be fascinating to know which works Ferrari acquired for his collection while he was in Vienna in 1799. For more on the reception of Mozart during the early 19th century when Ferrari was writing his *Aneddoti*, see John Daverio's "Mozart in the nineteenth century" in *The Cambridge Companion to Mozart*, ed.

Who has written like Mozart, and so well, for the piano: variations, caprices, fantasias, sonatas both solo and with violin, duets for four hands and for two pianos, trios and quartets and a real and magnificent fugue for cylinder organ? Who has written true quartets and quintets for the violin and other string instruments in real parts? Overtures, symphonies, ariettas in various languages, cantatas, canons, *opere buffe* that are not vulgar, and noble *opere serie?* Church music, sublime rather than academic? But what a fool I am! I almost forgot his piano concertos, which ought rather to be called dramatic operas, speaking to the ear, the mind and the heart of the musician. In them are enchanting combinations, combinations to transport one, and to raise the dead! And add to all this the fact that Mozart passed on at the premature age of thirty-five. Now I invite you, young composers, to take Mozart for your model. Entertain yourself by putting his concertos and other pieces into full score; examine his vocal scores, observing and admiring in them the disposition of the parts, the counterpoint, the concatenation of the subjects, the expression of the words, the theatrical coups, and the portentous effects arrived at by that demigod!

Hoping that the jump that I made in my account has not broken the thread, I will take the liberty of continuing on a little, not to criticize modern music, nor the two composers - Beethoven and Rossini - whose works have caused such a stir for *diversi lustri* throughout all of Europe, but only to sustain, and rightly so, the fame and superiority of the immortal name of Mozart.

Among the composers of instrumental music who made a name after Haydn and Mozart, the celebrated Beethoven took the prize, and every connoisseur can do no less than agree that he possessed a very great talent. But at the same time, he must confess that in his music are found episodes, prolixities, and extravagances that are not found in that of Haydn or Mozart, his models. It seems that he wished to surpass them, but he was deceived: one does not surpass a creator, a complete genius like Haydn, and even less a formidable colossus like Mozart, in every branch of music. But Beethoven is no more. And I will say no more of him, respecting forever his memory and all the beauty and good that he left during his happy passage over this earth.

Simon P. Keefe (Cambridge: Cambridge University Press, 2003).

Chapter XIX.

Continuation of the preceding chapter – Beethoven - Rossini - Singers-Orchestra -Inscription of the Celebrated Diderot.

In the case of dramatic music, the renowned Rossini created a general revolution, though who would wish to compare his operas with the originality, the solidity and the variety of those of Mozart, written, as I have said earlier, before arriving at the age of thirty-six? However, let those ignorant critics who are jealous and envious of the merit and of the extraordinary success of the citizen of Pesaro, talk. Let them chatter; there is no one who can deny that Rossini's operas are full of taste, imagination, and energy; that his scenic eye is most perspicacious; and that his effects and his musical cabalettas go much further than those of so many other masters.

If then they say that he makes the singers burst, the violins exhausted, the wind instruments run out of breath, and that he deafens the audience with his unique, calamitous din by means of those cursed little flutes, piccolos, whistles, triangles, trombones, drums and all of that Turkish music with which he overloads his scores... then perhaps they are correct. If they say that he rumbles here and there, that the parody is repeated at every moment...then again perhaps they are correct. But what difference does that make to Rossini? He will continue ever onward, as long as his star continues to shine, and if it should ever go out, he will laugh at his critics and say to them, "Behold my invincible and unsheathed sword; behold my banner, triumphant, and swirling in the breeze. Take arms and enter combat, if you have the spirit. I am abandoning the joust and peacefully retire with a reputation spread over both hemispheres and with my wallets full of coins."

Now perhaps it will be thought that I am against Beethoven, Rossini and the music of today, but this is not the case; in fact I approve and admire all of it, though up to a certain point. When I was studying counterpoint in Naples, instrumental music did not signify much in Italy, and vocal music found itself in a deplorable decadence.

Outside of Sarti, Paisiello and Cimarosa, who wrote with commitment and love, one heard nothing pleasing in the works of many other composers, but for a rondo imitated from one to the next, a trio likewise, and a stretto of a finale likewise, with repetitive harmony lacking in interest. For the rest of the music, there was nothing but a muddle, melodies which were old hat, paltry accompaniments, perfect chords and dominant sevenths one after the next; modulations from the tonic to the relative, and back again immediately, which produced a tedious and unbearable monotony.

Today we have arrived at another excess; everywhere instrumental music has made giant steps, as much through the development and propagation of harmony as by the brilliant publications of eminent masters, and by the perfection of wind instruments. But vocal music, which does not have mechanical techniques, has remained behind. Now it is a matter of bizarre melodies with variations or ornaments on every note; of *concertante*, noisy accompaniments; chromatic chords of every kind; modulations on every phrase, if not on every word; and most of the time without expressing the sentiment.

If Paisiello modulated in the romance from his inimitable *Nina,* passing from the tonic in the major to the submediant in the minor, he did the right thing, and here is the reason: the text of the romance says, "When will my dearest come to see his sad friend?" And this is where he places the transition to the minor mode, which is ravishing since in such a way he expresses the sentiment of the words on the words themselves. Then he continues modulating sweetly on, "The sunny shore will be covered in flowers." At this point one is back on the tonic in the major, likewise expressing the sentiment of the words. Today such a transition has become a cliché of most composers and is used practically without any other purpose or reason than for changing the mode.

Here is another example. A troop of soldiers advances into the theater preceded or followed by a military band. One hears a majestic march, beginning in the major mode, and the first part ending in the minor, as if these warriors had become fearful, tired, or wounded; the music modulates, and finishes in the major mode, so as to make you think that in the meantime twenty or thirty surgeons had arrived, who had healed the soldiers in a moment, and put them back on their feet, so that they could courageously continue their march to the field of battle.

At one time the instrumentalists sought to sing on their instruments; now the singers seek to play, using their voices. And the composers try to please them and spoil them, and the public applauds them, and makes them lose their sense.

At one time the orchestra accompanied and sustained the voices; now the voices have become the go-betweens and servants of the orchestra! And to whom does the applause go? To the noise of the orchestra, and to the unnatural forcing of the crucified singers! The inscription that follows seems to be applicable to my argument:

Hic Marsyas Apollinem.

(Thus Marsyas did to Apollo.)

This was written by the celebrated Diderot, and was intended to be placed on a new curtain for the Grand Opéra in Paris, where the singers were

Chapter XX

Excursion on the Lava at Vesuvius - Anecdotes – Operas, Etc.

Celestina pleased in Vienna, as she had in Naples, and as she would any-where she might show off her talents. I, in the meantime, often cultivated the society of her sisters, and to recompense them for their courtesies, I would first have Annetta sing, and then Rosina play, since, as there were not many players there ready to hand, I could serve for anything. I made many pleasing acquaintances in their house, among others that of one called Monsieur Pierre. He was French, and by consequence full of vivacity and spirit. Towards the middle of May, he proposed to the above-mentioned to make an excursion on the lava, already cut in many places, beaten down and leveled. The proposition was joy-fully accepted, and a company of about twenty people in various vehicles was formed: I was in a carriage for two with Monsieur Pierre. We went to Portici, and between that city and Torre del Greco we drove on an immense avenue of lava that projected up to a half mile into the sea, where you could have sailed until a few months before. We then made a turn around the foot of Mount Vesuvius, always on the lava, and, having brought cold provisions with us, we had a sumptuous meal al fresco, in the middle of and upon the flakes of that already extinguished volcanic river. What most surprised and entertained me on that excursion was to see the appearan-e of flowering branches of almond and germinating suckers of vines, of figs and other things in the places where the lava was most spongy and soft. This led me to believe that the lava running pre-cipitously down from the crater coagulates and cools without immersing itself in the earth and without doing much damage to the vegetation.

In returning to Naples Monsieur Pierre told me some stories, two of which seem like they may divert my reader.

Three friends - a friar, a priest, and a military man - found themselves on a trip in a public carriage with a poet for the theatre whom they did not know. Anxious to know who he might be, they asked him many questions, but he only responded with monosyllables. Having arrived at an inn where one could dine, they invited the unknown man to drink a bottle of Malaga wine with them after supper. He accepted such a compliment. Then the friends, having become more courageous, asked him, now one, now the next, if he was traveling for entertainment. - No. - On business? - No. - For political reasons? - No. - Then, you are an artist? - Precisely. And in what genre, if we may ask? - I am a poet for the theater. - A poet for the theater! We had taken you for a signore! You are so well dressed and polished! You spend your money! Where does the false and ridiculous proverb come from which says, "He is poor and miserable like a poet for the theater?" "I will tell you, gentlemen (looking at each of them in turn), you know that there is no rule without an exception, but the proverb is just and sensible. If you see me well-dressed, it is an accident, for the poet for the theater, generally speaking, is as lazy as a friar, gluttonous as a priest, and drinks like a soldier. How could you think that he could get rich?" The friar, the priest and the soldier looked at each other, not knowing what to say.

A gentleman of high rank, very rich, and yet even more miserly, had an eighteen-year-old son, as handsome as Adonis and generally good, but puffed up with nobility and haughtiness. His father kept him on a very strict budget, and only rarely would allow him a couple of scudi to entertain himself. A woman of low degree, but extremely rich, became enamored of the young man, and, knowing his circumstances, wrote him a letter and included in it a money order for a thousand zecchini, beseeching him to accept her little present. Upon seeing the money order he felt consoled, but learning from whom it had come he became offended, put the order in with the letter in order to send the whole thing back. At that point his father appeared, who, having heard from his son what he intended to do, took up the money order, called his major-domo, and sent him immediately to the bank to deposit it in an interest-bearing account. Then he said to his son, "You are a fool and an idiot. Write this lady a letter of thanks immediately, and for the future make it your law to always take everything that is offered to you, and to never refuse anything, even if it may come from an enemy's hands." Not long thereafter the miser fell gravely ill, and three days before dying he made his last will and testament. To save on ink he left out all the periods and commas. The next day, feeling worse, and fearing death, he did not order his dinner, so that it might not be served in vain. Finally, on the night of the third day, in his death throes, he put out the little lantern that he kept on his bedside table so that it would not burn after his death, and on so doing he expired with the greatest sweetness.

I also had the pleasure of meeting Cavalier Campan chez Coltellini, the major-domo for the queen of France and husband of the renowned Madame Campan, first lady-in-waiting for the unfortunate Marie Antoinette, and who later raised the Napoleonic dynasty at St. Germain en Laye.[1]

---

[1] Mostly known as the husband of Henriette Campan, who we will meet in Part Two of the *Anedotti*, his full name was Pierre-Dominque-Francois Berthollet Campan, and he was the son of the secretary of the royal cabinet. Campan had at this point obviously been some time in Italy, pursuing his twin passions of music and the opposite sex. Ferrari calls him a major domo to the Queen, and it seems that he had some official capacity, probably because of the prestige of his wife within Marie-Antoinette's household. The couple were unhappy and separated in 1790.

The cavalier was a charming man, mad for the fine arts, but yet more mad for the fair sex; he knew music well, and played the violin passably. I composed for him some sonatinas for pianoforte with obbligato violin, which, though neither good nor bad, nevertheless made an effect wherever we played them. I cultivated his acquaintance because he treated me so well, and we made great plans, which later were put into effect, as I will say in a moment.

In the autumn Guglielmi wrote Enea e Lavinia for the Teatro San Carlo. He had Morichelli for the prima donna, Roncaglia for the leading man, and the celebrated tenor Mombelli, a magnificent trio, who supported the whole opera. For the following carnival season, Paisiello wrote L'Olimpiade for the same theater and for the same singers. Piqued with honor and jealousy, natural to every artist, he did not want to listen to the friends who advised him to finish the second act with a quartet, he wanted to write a trio to surpass that by Guglielmi, but although it was beautiful it did not please. Yet L'Olimpiade held the stage with other pieces, and above all with the famous duet "Ne giorni tuoi felici, etc."

That same autumn an old opera of Cimarosa's, Le astuzie teatrali, o femminili, was presented at the Teatro reale del Fondo. La Galli and Moreschi, dueling prima donnas, sang there together. It also included as well Mengozzi, mezzo carattere, Casacciello, Trabalza, and Ferraro, a Tuscan buffo. That opera pleased to the extreme. It included a duet, "Lasciate che passa la bella Damina," in which the two donnas were supposed to mock each other.

Galli sang her first solo elegantly and to much applause. Moreschi sang the second solo with dexterity and had her applause. Then came the duet, and between the merit of the music and that of the singers, it pleased, and was repeated after loud applause. Galli sang the first solo with delicious variations and ornaments; while Moreschi was insulting her sotto voce. Then Moreschi came forward with the second solo with graces and seductive looks, and Galli insulted her as well. When they came to sing together, they lost their heads, forgot they were in the presence of the public, and came to blows.

Moreschi ripped Galli's handkerchief and clothes, and Galli, knowing that her rival was using a wig, pulled off her cap and artificial tresses. Casacciello, always looking for a laugh, came from backstage with a huge shotgun on his shoulder and stood in a military posture between the two to separate them. He succeeded, but the poor Moreschi was the victim in the battle, since she remained on the stage with her head bald and nude, more so than nature had created, after which she never again returned to the stage.

Chapter XXI.

Anecdotes - Facetiae - Pasquinades - Little Trip to Rome with Cavalier Campan - The Duchess of Albania - The English Pretender - Sonnet to Cardinal York.

After the Christmas holidays (1786) Guglielmi wrote an opera buffa, Adalinda, for the Teatro Nuovo, performed by Bennini, prima donna, her husband Mengozzi, mezzo carattere, and Gennaro Luzio, buffo caricato. Guglielmi was knowledgeable of dramatic music but was lazy, avaricious, and without self-respect. He wrote two or three complete pieces in each opera, and then had the rest of the vocal lines of the arias and of the concertato pieces orchestrated by his students and by his Neapolitan copyists as well. At the first performance, the composer of the opera was booed, as was deserved, so that by the middle of the second act the discontentment became so general that they were obliged to drop the curtain and everyone was happy to leave and go home. Guglielmi left the theatre and invited some friends to dinner, in order to make a cabal the second evening with a trio that had already been written and prepared for this reason.

In the morning he went to the Caffè del Veneziano, rendezvous of the virtuosi. There he found the impresario of the Teatro Nuovo. He went up to him, greeted him, took a folder of music out of his bag, and presented it to him, saying, "This is the piece that will resuscitate our Adalinda. Give me sixty ducats and I'll be satisfied."

The impresario looked at the title of the manuscript and read, "Vaga mano sospirato, posthumous trio from Adalinda." Knowing the theatrical cunning of the maestro, he took the trio, asked the cafe owner to pay Guglielmi, hurried to the copyist, arranged a rehearsal, and it was produced the same night.

The news spread through Naples in the blink of an eye. That night, an hour before the curtain, already one could only get into the theatre with difficulty and patience. Finally, the opera began. The public, in expectation of the new piece, passed over and applauded the material preceding it. The trio came, and it was encored three times. That made the finale of the first act stand out, and the pieces in the second act that had been booed the first night, were almost all encored, especially a little duet with wretched music and horrendous words.

"To hell with the theatre," Paisiello often said to me, "And to hell with the caprices of the public!"

In Lent of 1786, an oratorio entitled Gefte was given at the Teatro del Fondo, under the direction and production of Count Don Peppino Lucchesi, son of the Prince of Campofranco, and a fanatic for music. He made a miscellany or pasticcio, but one that was so well arranged it seemed like an original work. Singing in the piece were Marchetti, prima donna assoluta (Oh, what a beautiful creature, and what a lunatic!), Mengozzi, tenore, and Carlo Rovedino, basso cantante. Maestro Cipolla and the able Millico wrote various pieces for the occasion, but what carried the palm were the two arias that Cipolla wrote for Carlo Rovedino. He had a deep and high voice both, sonorous and mellow, vibrant and sweet; he could unite the chest voice to the head voice like two pieces of silk, and sang the cantabile like an angel.

Don Peppino triumphed with his success, but he did not have enough money to sustain such a magnificent and costly spectacle. He thus asked permission of Ferdinand IV to give four extra performances on the first Sundays of Lent, but during the day, and for the friars, priests, and laity, without women, neither in the boxes nor in the orchestra. Permission was granted, and there were four very full houses. There was a throng, as much to see such a quantity of friars in a theatre as to hear and see the crazy Marchetti spin out her voice, ornament her lines, and make the most curious gestures and attitudes to entertain the sighing reverends. The rich among them paid, but the poor Franciscans and Capuchins were let in free. One evening a capuchin, finding himself in a box near the orchestra and anxious to see and hear, leaned out over the railing and his beard caught fire from a candle of one of the contrabass players. The contrabassist put down his violone, grabbed the Capuchin by the jaw, pulled out his beard, put out the fire, saving him from being burned or at least disfigured.

Towards the end of Lent, Cavalier Campan kindly offered to take me with him to Rome, in order to be present for the services of Holy Week and for the feasts of Easter. Nothing more pleasing at that moment could have happened to me. To travel with a gracious gentleman; to meet my little Prince Lichtenstein, who had already sent me an invitation; to see the pomp and the splendor of the services; and to hear the music of those classics (Palestrina, Vinci, Leo, Hasse, Haendel, Durante, Marcello, Padre Vallotti, Pergolesi, P. Martini, Jommelli), was for me a gift not to be forgotten as long as I live.

We left Naples on Thursday of the week of the Passion, and arrived in Rome on Palm Sunday, with our sonatinas, with the favorite pieces from the Grotta di Trofonio, which I had transcribed for piano and violin, and with twenty-four variations that I had composed in imitation of those whom I admired in my early youth.

I will not speak of the liturgies and services, for the same reason that I did not speak of the innumerable monuments of that city. I went immediately to see my good Prince, who welcomed me with his customary affability. Holy Thursday I was introduced with my first violin at the Academy, which the noble Signora Flaviani held every week. My sonatinas made a great effect, and the variations caused a furor, even if there were two pianists in Rome at the time who were much more able than myself, the Masis, father and son, who then settled in London for many years. What pleased and touched me the most at the Academy was the Stabat Mater by Pergolesi, performed with orchestra, and sung by two old musicians of the Sistine Chapel, with weak and problematic voices, but who shaped and modulated them so well that they brought tears in my eyes from the first note to the last.

On the eve of Easter I went with my cavalier to make a little music at the house of the Duchess of Albany, where there was a small and pleasing society of dilettantes, and where we also had great success and enjoyed ourselves quite a bit. The Duchess had a noble appearance, a superb figure, and, had her face been unmarked by the pox, I would be able to compare her to Lady Hamilton, who I have already praised. As far as her affability, spirit, and sweet and seductive manners, I have never found a lady more charming. The music being over, she invited us to follow her to the salon of her father, Charles Edward Stuart, the pretender to the throne of England. He was seated on a little throne, where he welcomed each person with the greatest courtesy, and you could note in his face his joy and contentment in seeing everyone bend the knee before him, and in hearing himself called Majesty.

The next day we dined with Signor Campan at the house of his doctor and friend, Dr. Martelli, a man of spirit, and knowledgeable, encyclopedic, and sharp - all in all, a sort of Muzio Clementi.

He had a little wife who was more charming than any Roman woman I had ever seen. He served us a sumptuous banquet, with wine from Orvieto, Cyprus, etc., after which there was a little music. To end the day, the entertaining Martelli read us some most charming anecdotes, a few of which I have the honor to offer to the reader.

It is known that Pius VI began to drain the Pontine bogs, for which reason he came by the name of Seccatore [translator's note: literally, dryer, but figuratively, a nuisance] by the wits of Rome. When the good Pius traveled to Vienna in order to calm the wrath of Joseph II against the friars, Marforio asked Pasquino where the Seccatore had gone. Pasquino answered, "that he had gone to dry [annoy] the Emperor". A few days later, Marforio asked again, "but, dear Pasquino, you are always joking! Now, tell me seriously, what did our good Pontifex go to do in Vienna?" Pasquino added – "Oh, if you are talking to me seriously, I will answer you seriously, and tell you the truth. He went to Vienna to sing two masses: one without a Gloria, for himself; the other without a Credo, for the Emperor."

During the papacy of Benedict XIV, Lambertini, the leader of the Bolognese Senate of Forty, sent two ambassadors to His Holiness to ask for a favor. They chose the two leading nobles of that city, both from the Forty: His Excellence Orsi, and His Excellence Bovi. Benedict's secretary, who was apparently an idiot, instead of announcing them in the way that I have said, turned things around and announced them as follows: "His Excellence with the forty Orsi [bears], His Excellence with the forty Bovi [oxen]," to which the charming prince answered, "Send the eighty beasts in at once."

His Eminence Cardinal York lived for many years in Rome, as is well known, and his remains were left there in holy peace. During his life he was loved and respected by everyone, and assisted liberally, like his brother Charles, by the Papal court, but even more by the generosity of George III, King of England. Cardinal York was an excellent man, liberal, a fanatic for Italian literature, and most of all for improvisers. He had as secretary and major domo a certain Abate Cantini, faithful, pleasant, and devoted to His Eminence. Another celebrated improviser, Abate Gavazza, appeared in Rome. Cantini introduced him to the Cardinal, and not knowing that he was the greatest libertine and spendthrift in the world, offered him an apartment in his palace, his table, carriage, and an honorable salary. Gavazza, without a penny in his pocket, would have accepted the job for two farthings.

At the end of each year, Cardinal York used to balance his books with Cantini. Gavazza would buy on credit and send the creditors to be paid at the palace: his impudence went unchecked for a year or two, but at the end of the third year his debt was more than a thousand scudi. This offended the Cardinal, who ordered Cantini to only pay half, and to let the improviser know that if he did not show better judgment in the future, he would chase him out of his palace. Some days later the major domo went very sadly to the apartment of his friend. "What is it, Cantini, are you sick?" – No, but I have bad news for you." - "And what is it?" - "His Eminence is angry with you, and only wants to pay half of your debt, and if you continue to behave like a madman, he wants to dismiss you." "Oh, if that's all it is, sit down, and you shall see how you make peace with a man of spirit." In a few minutes he wrote the sonnet found here, gave it to Cantini to present to the cardinal, from whom Gavazza obtained that which he desired.

To his Eminence Cardinal York

Sonnet

Your Royal Highness, by your goodness,
I know that you spoke to Cantini the other day
And moved by your good will
Paid half of that debt.
I thank you for your charity
And am as grateful as may be;
But to say "I absolve you" by half
Is not done in God's Church.
And will your Highness do so with me?
You, who are always a mirror of virtue,
Prince, Cardinal, Son of a King?
Oh, no; lift you hand a little more,
and say: I absolve you entirely,
For this year, I will bother you no more.

The wretched improviser Abate Gavazza. On Dec. 31.

(Vostra Altezza Real per sua bontà
So che al Cantini l'altro di parlò,
E mossa dalla sua benignità
Mezzo di quell tal debito pagò.

Io La ringrazio di Sua carità,
E le son grato quanto mai si può,
Ma il dir Ego te absolvo per metà
Nella Chiesa di Dio mai non si usò.

E vostra Altezza l'userà con me?
Ella che è sempre specchio di virtù,
Principe, Cardinal, figliuol di re?!

Eh, via: alzi la mano un po/ più in su,
E dica: Ego to absolvo *come va:*
Che per quest'anno non la secco più.)

Chapter XXII.
Continuation at Rome - Return to Naples with Mr. Albert, Englishman

I was also presented to the daughters of Mr. Lagrené, a celebrated painter and director of the Royal Academy of France in Rome. His daughters were fanatics for music, despite the fact they had no talent for it! Though they were far from being beautiful, their amiability and their good-hearted natures made them pleasing without the passing charms of youth, and the delightful ornament of musical ability. They had a salon that was the most brilliant that I ever attended; a great number of artists were its basis along with many literati, and every respectable rank of person was represented, up to the leading nobility of Europe. Monsieur Lagrené was a nice old man, and seeing that I gave pleasure to his get-togethers with my little sonatas and with some canzonettas that I had composed after my arrival in Rome, he took a liking to me, and when I was not busy with my princeling, or with the cavalier, he would always have me to dinner at his house. I thus made some acquaintances that were shortly to be of great use, among them a certain Mr. Albert, an Englishman, young, independent, and a lover of music. I found myself often in his company at Mr. Lagrené's, and knowing that I was about to return to Naples, he offered to take me in his carriage if I promised to give him piano lessons during the few months when he was planning to stay in that metropolis. I accepted the proposal, and we left the fourth Monday after Easter.

I left Rome with the greatest unhappiness, having been so well received, encouraged, and celebrated there by the personages that I have mentioned. Yet the idea of making progress in the career I had decided upon consoled me a little.

Mr. Albert was a pleasant young man who was received in the best society; he spoke French well, and Italian passably, but I did not know anything more about him. I could not have possibly imagined that he might be one of those English tourists of which I had spoken above. He made an agreement with the ordinary courier for Naples to travel with him, offering moreover an escort of four dragoons for the two carriages. However, wishing to see the tombs of the Orazi and Curiazi, which were to be found a few steps outside the city of Albano, and informed by the courier that he would pass by there about midnight, he promised him that he would be ready at that hour with his carriage, and with the escort mentioned. We left at ten in the morning and, after having seen the tombs, we had an excellent meal with some exquisite white wine, which is so renowned in that city. At nine, Mr. Albert made his servant go out and ordered him to bring him his weapons. He gave two pistols and a saber to the servant, two pistols to me, and kept two more pistols and another saber for himself: I wondered at his precautions and apparent prudence, but I learned some time afterward that he had taken such an escort and so many weapons in the hope of going into battle with the assassins which are always found in these places. About ten we lay down fully-dressed in bed, awaiting the courier, and slept like logs.

At three in the morning, the servants came to wake us up. We were surprised that it was so late, but the courier had just arrived, and they told us that he had been caught in a tremendous storm, which had frightened the postillion and the horses, and they had thrown him in a ditch, which he could only get out of with great patience and effort. While he was drying his clothes and taking a little food and drink, they hitched up the horses and sent once more for the escort, even if there was no need for it; for after such a storm, there was no likelihood of finding assassins on the road, since they have a sort of instinct or superstition that makes them more frightened of thunder or lightning than of the devil himself, whom they have never seen.

At three-thirty we left armed like bandits: our pistols all had two barrels, our sabers were strong, pointed and sharp, but unfortunately for my companion and luckily for me there were no skirmishes. At three in the afternoon we were surprised by another storm. The rain poured down violently, the hailstones were like grapeshot; flashes and thunderclaps came one after another, with some perpendicular strips of pallid fire, which seemed to come from the heavens, stretching out precipitously, first disappearing into the air, then falling to the earth, and which redoubled the horror of the tempest. Mr. Albert's carriage was half-open, but with curtains on the sides, and with a leather cover in the front, but to no avail: we were soaked to the bones. At four a bolt fell with an enormous din only a few yards from the heads of our horses, who, being frightened, stopped as if they had been struck by an apoplectic fit, nor was there any way to make them continue. The courier, who saw the critical situation which we were in, had his two dragoons gallop to Messa, to ask for help; they immediately sent us a postilion and two colts, and a half-hour later we took refuge in that inn, or post-house for horses.

The courier for Naples was supposed to continue his journey, but seeing us half-drowned, languishing and dismayed, he thought that we would not follow him, and advised us to stay in that in for the shortest time possible, since the assassins in the region came to get all their provisions there. Mr. Albert began to laugh, gave a tip to the courier, and immediately ordered dinner and three bedrooms; I didn't say a single word. After having changed from head to toe, and having dried and warmed ourselves, we went down to dinner, but before we sat down, the host came out with a great key in his hand, and said to us the following, "Here, gentlemen, is the key to the shed for your carriage. If you have valuable things in your trunks, I advise you to bring them into your bedrooms, since I won't guarantee anything. My house is like an island in the middle of the sea, with no other islands nearby, and no other defenses but a little rock. My rock is that barracks that you see there, where there are twelve dragoons to escort the travelers who pass by. In the caverns of these mountains there is a band of thieves who come to get their provisions from me, and if I were to refuse them they would put to fire and sword everything that I possess, and myself first of all; but they are honest and pay liberally when they have money. They are all known; their families wander here and there, nor do they have any other way of supporting them but by assaulting and robbing the passersby; and if a postilion were not to stop when they present themselves, he would certainly be killed upon his return."

"Do they ever come to rob in your house?" asked Mr. Albert.

"Yes, sir," answered the host, "when they know that there are foreigners at my inn; but I think that there is no reason for fear tonight, since the immense rain that has fallen has made the water rise in the marshes, nor would it be possible to cross them."

"What a shame!"

"What a blessing!" said I.

Finally, dinner was served, a veritable dinner for assassins! Three-day-old fish from fresh or boggy water, fresh meats, vegetables full of sand, spiced wine - nothing that you could enjoy. I proposed a frittata, and they made it with duck eggs, fried in oil, which we could not touch. We made do with bread and cheese, but my little Englishman was careful (according to the custom in his country) to get some butter.

After dinner, visiting his bed, he found that the mattresses were stuffed with corn leaves. "Goddamn it," he exclaimed, "I will never sleep on such a bed," and at that moment he ordered one of the escorts to hitch the horses, and thanks be to God, we left that dangerous and unhealthy hostelry. We ate, with great appetite, and late at night, at Molo di Gaeta, and we arrived at Naples at sunrise, with no assassins or other obstacles, much to Mr. Albert's regret, but much to the consolation of the writer.

Chapter XXIII.
Adventure of Mr. Albert- Padre Giordano.

The same morning I went to see my dear Paisiello. He was busy; he was writing his most gracious *Schiavi per amore*, nor could I see him. Donna Cecilia and Don Ciccio had gone out. I spent the day with Latilla, in order to ask him to come so that I could recommence my studies with him, then I went to the Coltellini's where I gave a report on my journey to Rome, and my success there, and also of my return with my English student. They advised me to ask of him ten carlini per lesson; I remarked to them that I only paid three carlini to the leading teacher of counterpoint in Naples and that I didn't feel like asking so much. They replied that I was a professional, Mr. Albert an English dilettant, and therefore rich.

That same evening I went to see Donna Cecilia, where I repeated the story of my trip, and I asked her if the Coltellini's had advised me well concerning my student. She told me yes, and that I ought to know that the English were particular on this point, and that if I were not to make my student pay an honorable price, that he would not consider me at all. I took her advice, and came out well by it, since he had no problems with my request, and at his last payment gave me a few ducats more than he owed me.

In the course of the conversation I let her hear the ariettas that I had composed at Rome, as well as the variations which I had not yet played in Naples; naturally, in the house of my teacher, and before his friends, I could not fail to be applauded. There was in that company a certain Padre Giordano of the Dominican order, who encouraged me greatly, and of whom I will speak after having said something of my little Englishman.

Mr. Albert was a most affable young man. He did not have a great inclination towards music, but spent a fair amount of time at it, and did me many favors. One day he proposed that I make a trip up Vesuvius with him to go into the crater. Knowing that the eruption was entirely over, nor seeing any smoke emerging from the mouth of the crater, I accepted, but the evening before we were to go I was told that that morning two Englishmen had been suffocated and lost there. The next day, when my student came to meet me, I told him what I had heard, and declared that I certainly did not want to go up the mountain, but that, as he had planned to dine at Portici, I would accompany him as far as that town, would look after ordering the meal, and would await him there until he returned. And so it happened. He went up with two English friends, with his servant, with the guide, and with the hermit whom he found along the way. As soon as they had entered the crater they heard a shaking. The guide immediately ran off, shouting, "Every man for himself! Every man for himself!" They all escaped with the exception of my friend, who was surprised by an explosion of searing smoke, which burnt his face and hands, and lightly charred his hair and clothes. Then he escaped as well, but in rushing down the mountain he fell on the ice, broke his watch, wounded his face and hands; in short he arrived at the inn at Portici, where I was waiting for him, like an *Ecce homo*. They immediately washed him from head to foot with sweet almond oil, and in a few minutes he felt better, as merry and joyous as a butterfly. I couldn't resist telling him that having the luck to avoid the assassins he should not have exposed himself to an even more threatening danger. "What!" he replied with force and enthusiasm, "What an honor to die in battle against the assassins! What glory to lose one's life in a volcano!" "Bravo, Signor Albert", I added, "bravissimo! But as far as I am concerned I will prefer to die tranquilly in my bed, and of old age if possible." He burst out laughing, and we were always good friends.

Padre Giordano was one of those men who seem to have been sent into the world for the delight of those who meet them, and was one of those priests who uphold their religion with honor and decorum, without puerility or cant. He was the model Neapolitan: good, indulgent, charitable, and known and esteemed by all of Naples. He knew music well, both in theory and practice, since he was sensitive to every chord, and sang everything easily extempore. Having finished his ecclesiastical duties, he spent his life (as much as he could) at the pianoforte with Paisiello or Cimarosa, singing their music with them, and hearing a buffo duet of one of these masters with Padre Giordano, with the expression and emphasis which they put into it, everyone forgot the leading *buffi caricati* of Europe!

Such was the enthusiasm of the good friar for music that he used to call it the greatest gift given to man by God. And he would say, "God did not create the musical art, but gave to nature the means of producing it. He gave a singing voice to certain male birds and to mortals of both sexes, and which produces melody; he has given sound and resonances or harmonic vibrations to various metals and crystals, which produce a general harmony. He determined a diatonic scale of only seven notes, nor is there art nor science which is able to extend it without repeating the tonic at the octave and so forth; and through augmenting or diminishing the tones or semitones of the said scale and of its repetitions all the imaginable combinations of artificial harmony may be found. Music has one sole consonant and perfect chord, and the inverted and dissonant chords all derive from the natural and perfect chord; and they are excellent, superb, if used with moderation and judgment, indeed they are the embellishment of the harmony and of the melody after all, attracted by the power of the tonic or of the fundamental bass, they gradually fade away and are lost in the natural and perfect chord.

Music sweetens the passions of the violent man, and inflames those of a weak man. Is there anything in the world than more inspires true religion than the sound of an organ in a church, or hearing sacred music performed? No.

Therefore music is the greatest gift given to man by God.

Chapter XXIV.

Coltellini's return. Opere buffe. Baroness Talleyrand. Excursions to the Island of Ischia. Pirro.

The charming Celestina arrived from Vienna, laden with garlands, to collect added laurels in the country in which she began and was to end her theatrical career, and she was welcomed with the applause she justly deserved. She appeared in the opera *Le Gare Generose, o gli Schiavi per Amore* with her sister Annetta, who was then making her debut, alongside Viganoni, Casacciello, Trabalza, *secondo buffo*, and Ferraro, a Tuscan buffo. Even if this opera was considered one of Paisiello's weaker ones, yet it pleased extremely, having being written with such naturalness and truth, and sustained moreover by the rare and natural talents of Coltellini, Casacciello and Viganoni.

For the second opera of the spring, Guglielmi wrote the *Pastorella nobile*, and for this work that cunning and lazy old man wrote a superb quintet for the first act and then a *duettino da piazza* for the third act, both of which were enough to sustain the entire opera.

At the beginning of that year a new ambassador from France, Baron Talleyrand, whose wife played the piano very well, arrived in Naples with his family. Already seduced by Paisiello's music, Baroness Talleyrand fell even more under its spell hearing it performed by Paisiello himself, or under his direction. She showered him with favors and courtesies, hoping to induce him to give her voice lessons, which the composer detested doing. It did not take long for him to become the idol of the family, nor could he be found anywhere but at the French embassy: he went in the morning to give lessons to the Baroness, who had had an apartment prepared where he could study and write his music; he dined with her and her family, and only returned home to sup with Donna

Cecilia. Madame Talleyrand had a chambermaid, Mademoiselle Julie, who, though neither young nor beautiful, was nevertheless so merry and playful that she was Paisiello's pet. It was her duty, when he was studying, to bring a cup of chocolate or some fruit, with French wine, etc., and the good maestro, following the example of Molière with his serving-girl, had her hear the pieces which he had composed, and she, impudently, though always jokingly, would praise them or criticize them according to her opinion. "And sometimes," Paisiello said to me, "she hit the nail on the head."

After dinner every day, the ambassadress was accustomed to taking a spin around the city in her carriage. Paisiello would follow her in his little carriage alone with Mademoiselle Julie. That platonic affair used to make everyone who knew them laugh. But what was an even greater source of mirth was to see Guglielmi, who, jealous that his musical rival was following the coach of an ambassadress of France, set himself to following Paisiello in his open carriage driving the horses himself, and sitting next to his beauty, a half-century younger than the sickly maestro.

The following autumn Baroness Talleyrand rented a large country house on the Island of Ischia, about sixteen miles from Naples. She invited her singing teacher there and had an apartment prepared for him. By then I already had written, with Paisiello's corrections, much chamber music and music for the theater, and was writing an opera buffa based on Goldoni's *Le Pescatrici*, which my master had suggested to me. He left for Ischia, and a few days later Lieutenant Gamerra of Mantova arrived from Vienna, bringing with him his famous poem, *Il Pirro*. I made his acquaintance in conversation with Donna Cecilia, and he invited me to hear him read his libretto: I went and was very impressed. He told me that he was leaving soon for Ischia, with the hope of seducing the great master to set his poem to music, and that if I wanted to give him a letter, he would be happy to take it with him. I seized the occasion to kill two birds with one stone, as they say, as I recommended the poet and his libretto and I asked permission to visit him at Ischia to show him the pieces I had already written for *Pescatrici*. The poet was welcomed with the same warmth as his *Pirro*, and I had a verbal answer from the lieutenant that I would be welcome in Ischia anytime I wished to go. As I was known by the majordomo at the French embassy, I easily obtained permission to embark with the sailing boat that brought fresh provisions to the ambassadress each day.

It was the beginning of October when we left, an evening about midnight, with the most splendid moonlight and on a sea that was

Fig. 8. Portrait of Celeste Coltellini by Antoine-Jean Gros

placid and gleaming like a mirror. Shortly after passing the Island of Procida a strong wind started to blow, which carried my hat, and almost myself, into the sea. The boat was heading toward Ischia, and my hat towards Procida, so I asked the sailors to retrieve it if they could, but they answered that it had fallen into a current, and that if they were to go after it they would risk shipwreck on that little island, or at least to be stuck there until the current shifted. This made me suspect that the current must have been a sort of Mediterranean tide. However, as it was I was more than happy to arrive at Ischia using my nightcap for a hat, since, as soon as we disembarked, there was a frightening agitation and tempest on the sea. I found refuge in a fisherman's hut, where I rented a room for a week, and I struck an agreement that they would give me breakfast, dinner, and supper for a total of two carlini a day, i.e. eight English shillings. *Mirabile dictu*! And what fish of various kinds I ate there! And what exquisite Ischian wine I drank there whenever I pleased! I went the same morning to my dear master, who showed the greatest pleasure in seeing me, and who gave me a lesson worth ten. He then presented me to Mademoiselle Julie, and she conducted me to his chamber, giving me refreshments in profusion, along with the ambassador's French wine; she then accompanied me on a walk in the garden and the woods. Thus I continued every day I remained on that delicious island.

The seventh day I went to have a lesson and take leave of my master, and he encouraged me to stay another week in order to finish the first act of my *Pescatrici* with his help. I thanked him and decided to stay. After the lesson, he told me that the ambassadress was expecting some musical dilettantes to dinner, that her piano was quite out of tune, and that if I could and would tune it, I would do him the greatest favor. In order to make that good man happy I agreed, though I had never done such a thing before. I then presented myself to the Baroness, and she asked me what my method was; I turned red, but I told her that I had thought to tune all the fifths, then the octaves, the thirds etc. As she didn't know anything more about the matter than I did, she found my method sublime, thanked me for the trouble that she had put me to, and left me alone with the instrument. I began to tune all the fifths quite perfectly, and trying two or three chords I heard a discord that was enough to skin your ears. I then tried tuning all the major and minor thirds, and the confusion was still worse. Then I lost my head: anxious to succeed, and fearing failure, my hand shook, I broke ten or twelve strings, and left the instrument in such a state that it could not be listened to. Confused and humbled by my defeat, I figured a way out: I went immediately to Mademoiselle Julie's room and begged her to let me write a note to Paisiello, in which I informed him of my disgrace, but promised him that Her Excellency's piano would be put in order in time to divert her company that evening. I then asked the chambermaid to take the letter to the addressee, and while she was carrying this out, I ran off like a racehorse, and I went to my fisherman, and gave him reason to believe that I had dispatches for the embassy. He immediately called his son, put their skiff in the water, and the three of us, rowing like galley slaves, arrived in Naples in four hours. I had the boatmen stay at the pier, and went immediately to my tuner, Mosca, and he left in just a few minutes for Ischia in the same boat.

The next evening I went to Mosca's house to get the news, and was very happy to hear that Paisiello and the ambassadress were appreciative of my attention and industriousness, inviting me to return to the island whenever I pleased. I returned ten or twelve days later with the first act of my little opera finished. The Baroness welcomed me with the greatest good will: she wanted to hear my music and was very happy with it. She did me a thousand favors, and later became my student in accompanying, three years after, in Paris. I also stayed there a week on that occasion, and it was very useful to examine Gamerra's poem and compare it with the music to which the composer set it.

In the middle of November Paisiello returned to Naples, with the vocal parts of his *Pirro* completed, and the principal roles written for Danzi le Brun, Roncaglia (*primo uomo*), Manzoletto (*secondo uomo*), and David (tenor), then at the height of his powers. The rehearsals began, and the master wanted me to be present for all of them at the harpsichord - what glory for me! The singers, not being aware that I already knew the music, took me for a prodigy. Danzi called upon me to take on the musical education of her little daughter, and David and Manzoletto were later of great help to me. *Pirro* was finally presented and had the success that it deserved.

The feature of introducing finales into opera seria was very well received, as were Danzi's bravura aria, Roncaglia's rondo, the arietta (written as a gesture of friendship for the weak Manzoletto), and the duo, and the trio. But in the final estimation, David's magnificent *scena* carried the day and crowned the efforts of both the singer and the composer.

Chapter XXV.

Count Skavronsky - Illness - Departure from Naples.

At that time there was in Naples a Russian ambassador, Count Skavronsky, a man of middle age, charming, liberal but rather extravagant and fanatical for music.[1] He had four regular professional musicians in his service - two violinists, a violist, the other a violoncellist - whose duties were none other than playing duets, trios or quartets while His Excellency took his meals. Having been taken to see Paisiello, who he had met in Russia, he was so touched by his *Pirro* that, from the moment in which he heard it presented, he no longer wanted to hear any other vocal music but that of Paisiello. For this reason, he held little recitals, and his favorite singers were Annetta Coltellini, David, Carlo Rovedino and the buffo Manzoletto, who entertained him more with his little stories than with his febrile singing. As these were all friends of mine, they quickly introduced me to the Count as an accompanist. Happy with the way in which I performed the music, he took a great liking to me, and wanted me to make music with him almost every day and every evening. He took me in his carriage, and to his boxes at the theatres. He played billiards with me, and when he lost he paid me, but when he was the victor, he would say to me, "You'll pay me in Paradise." Moreover, I had the advantage of meeting various distinguished persons at his house, such as the Abate di Bourbon, the interesting Lady E. Forster, and His Royal Highness the Duke of Cumberland, who was traveling with his teacher and violinist F. Giardini.

All these honors certainly flattered my *amour propre*, but eating so many foods and drinking so many liquors to which I was not accustomed was greatly injurious to my health. Staying up until one or two in the morning was killing me because I needed to get up early in order not to interrupt my study. In fact, a few

---

[1] Count Pavel Skavronsky was the son of a relative of Catherine I of Russia, who created him a count. Pavel's widowed mother settled in Italy and took her son with her, where he became a devoted music enthusiast, and in the 1770s and 80s surrounded himself with musicians and constantly attended music performances. His cousin the historian V. Mikhnevich wrote of him: "Skavronksy's love for music is that of a nobleman's frivolous willfulness and caprice...Always surrounded...by artists, singers, and musicians, always concerning himself with music...he ordered his attendant to speak to him in recitative, according to exact pitch. His footman, trained according to a score written by his master, would announce the carriage's readiness in a pleasant alto. The head waiter would call out in a festive tune. The coachman would communicate with the Count in basso profundo. During festive lunches and receptions, all the servants were organized in duets, quartets and choirs, imparting the atmosphere of an opera house. His Highness himself gave instructions to his servants in musical form, singing his orders. (recounted in Marina Ritzarev's *Eighteenth-Century Russian Music*, Routledge, 2017).

Fig. 9. Portrait of Count Pavel Skavronsky

months after having met this gentleman, I began to become weak, and found myself so ill that I was obliged to call a doctor, who, finding that my tongue was white, gave me, according to the custom of the time in Naples, a potent emetic, and continued thus for eight straight days. He made me observe, moreover, the most strict diet, and after a week he had reduced me to a skeleton, unable to stand up. I told the good Count Skavronsky of my situation, and he was kind enough to come see me with his doctor, the renowned Doctor Cotugno. He forbade me the emetics, ordered me to chew rhubarb root and swallow the juice, prescribed me a bearable diet, and in a few weeks I was back to life.

But before I finish talking about this Count, I must tell an anecdote told throughout the theatres of Europe, but whose origin is hardly known.

One day I found myself alone with the ambassador, he at the pianoforte, I next to him. He was improvising, modulating, or rather arpeggiating, and he asked me from time to time if it was correct. I could only tell him yes, since he was only modulating from the tonic to the dominant or the subdominant. A footman arrived and presented a servant who had been recommended to His Excellence by the Princess Gragaring at the time of her return to Russia. The servant came forward, and the Count, still practicing modulations, asked him his name.

"Bartolomeo, slave of Your Excellence."

"Do you know music?"

"No, Excellence."

"Do you sing?"

"No, Excellence."

"Do you play a little violin?"

"Not at all."

"The contrabass?"

"No."

"The *colascione*?"

"No."

Then, impatient, the noble musician, without leaving his arpeggiating, declaimed, to a popular tune, the following words:

"Bartolomeo, you're not for me! Bartolomeo, you're not for me! "

The servant, astute and impudent, answered him in the same tone of voice, and using the same tune:

"I really don't care a fig! I really don't care a fig!"

The charming ambassador, enchanted by the very fine ear of the clever rogue, rose from the piano, called the footman, and ordered him to fit him out in livery, and he took him into his service."

This anecdote is the basis for a scene between Biscroma and Don Febèo, in the opera *The Fanatic for Music*, in which the celebrated Naldi distinguished himself both in Lisbon and in London.

After my return from Rome to Naples, I continued to stay in constant communication with Cavalier Campan about musical matters, his plans, and about the gracious offer that he had made of taking me with him to Paris.

At that time there was no other topic of conversation in Europe apart from the famous diamond necklace that had so compromised Madame de la Motte, the Cardinal Rohan, and the queen of France herself. It was said that Louis XVI was about to convene the Estates General, that there were great disturbances in Paris, and that there would certainly be a revolution. Such a word was always unwelcome to my ear — I was scared by it - and I wavered on whether or not I should go.

During my illness I received a letter from Monsieur Campan, in which he told me that his father, secretary to the Queen of France, had ordered him to be in Paris the following July, and that, as he wanted to tour Italy, he had arranged to leave Rome at the beginning of May, and was inviting me to join him there towards the end of April so that we could let our friends hear what I had written for him. I showed the letter to the good count who said frankly that he very much regretted it, but he would advise me to take advantage of the occasion. I showed the same letter to Paisiello and Latilla, and they honestly declared that it was a stroke of luck for me, since I no longer needed a teacher, but that I should study and work by myself if I ever expected to become something in the world.

That convinced me I should leave, but woe is me! What a parting! What farewells! My heart was full of friendship and gratitude for the Coltellinis, for Paisiello, and for Skavronsky, who, after having been so good to me, gave me on my departure a golden box full of twenty louis d'or for having dedicated my *Twenty-Four Variations* to him. Moreover I was very attached to the good and affable residents of that city, to its picturesque location, and to the healthy climate tempered by the winds. The strolls on the quay, at Chiaia and in the Villa Reale, the delightful views of the countryside and the sea which were presented to your eyes at every moment; Vesuvius, Capo di Monte, Zolfatara, Pozzuoli, all were so many hooks in my heart which I had no idea how to release. The moonlight, the serene and starry sky, the sea gleaming like crystal, with the stars and the planets reflected in it, all inspired in me sublimed sentiments of respect and adoration for the divinity.

What I regretted not a little in having to leave that metropolis was not being able to be present at the rehearsals and the first performances of the opera *La Nina*, which was nearly completed, the more so since Paisiello had shown me the French libretto and had said that if he set the libretto well, which he guessed to be the case, he would die happy. In fact, he had written very beautiful music before that opera, and wrote as many beautiful things after, but he was never able to surpass *Nina*. It was written for the two Coltellini sisters, for Lazzarini, Tasca, Trabalza, di Giovanni and Bollini, and presented for the first time at the Teatro Reale in Caserta to such an outcry as has never been matched since. It was very well liked throughout Europe, but what a difference to hear an opera staged by the master who composed it, and performed by the company for which it was written, rather than to hear it sacrificed to the whims of those directing or performing it after!

Finally, on the twentieth of April I left Naples, and in taking leave of my friends there it seemed to me as if I were leaving my heart itself in that promised land, in the terrestrial paradise. There is no doubt that the Neapolitans are right in being proud of their city, continually saying, "See Naples, and then you may die."

Chapter XXVI.

Arrival at Rome - Trip to Frascati - Anecdote of Pope Lambertini - Meeting with Count Skavronsky - Departure for Florence.

I arrived at Rome on the 25th, sad, tired and isolated like a pilgrim, annoyed to excess by the slowness of traveling with that tedious and unbearable courier. I went immediately to Cavalier Campan's residence, where I found a letter inviting me to join him in Frascati, where he was staying in the countryside with his dear Doctor Martelli and with the charming Martellina. He asked me to bring my viola, the trio and quartet that he already knew I had composed for him in Naples, and to bring with me a violinist and a violoncellist to try them out. I spent the evening half at my prince's, half at the Mademoiselles Lagrenès, and in the morning I took care of that which Signor Campan desired. As soon as we had arrived at Frascati we tried out my pieces; the cavalier and the two musicians were very happy with them, but the little doctor criticized me, claiming that I had imitated Pleyel and hence the German style. I answered him that, having heard Pleyel's Op 2 quartets on my arrival in Naples performed by Pleyel himself, and then having heard them again and again for two and a half years straight after that, it was no surprise if I had fallen into his style, but that it seemed to me that the melody of that composer was more Italian than otherwise, and that I would be happy if my instrumental compositions could resemble his.

He added, "Everything you say may be true, but Pleyel is a German, and you ought to have nothing to do with German music."

Monsieur Campan and the amiable Rosinella laughed; I spoke no further, but realized at that moment and for the first time that even men of judgment have their prejudices and weaknesses.

My trip to Frascati consoled me a little for the regret that I felt in leaving Naples. I would make long excursions, morning and evening - now on foot, now by donkey - through spacious fields and on the flowering hills that surrounded them. During the day I would make music, or read, or play; sometimes I would compose, sometimes the amiable Martelli would entertain us with his stories. All in all, we passed the time without tedium. One day I asked the doctor to write words for me for an *arietta buffa* to divert our company, and he did so. He declaimed his verses for me, and I wrote the arietta in a few minutes in his presence and then let him hear it. He was happy with the music and amazed by my quickness, but I was more amazed by my speed than he, since up until then I had sometimes needed hours to find a pleasing melody not already used. But I noticed immediately, and much more thereafter, that it was the fact that I heard the declamation of the poet that helped me find the subject and write the whole of the arietta so quickly. It was applauded at Frascati, as one could imagine, and it was later one of my little triumphs in Rome, as throughout all Italy, at Lyons, and for some months thereafter, in Paris also.

Among the stories that the amiable little doctor told us, I recall one that seems not too uninteresting to me.

It is known that Pope Lambertini was a man of talent and of great spirit. During his reign, he held a jubilee. He came forward in front of the people, as is the custom, followed by cardinals, prelates, bishops, archbishops, etc. In facing out the window of the Vatican and seeing the immense plaza of San Pietro thronging with people, and that the crowd went all the way to the bridge by the Castel Sant'Angelo, he was stupefied and asked his secretary the cardinal:

"What does all this mean, my dear cardinal?"

"Holiness, it is a jubilee!"

"Yes, yes; but don't you see how many signori and how many horses adorned with fancy feathers and rare gems there are? How many carriages festooned with velvet, satin, damask?"

"Holy Father, from the poor to the rich, from the peasant to the ruler, we are all sinners on this earth, excepting your Holiness."

"Very well, but I cannot understand how all those people can support themselves and dress so well."

"Holy Father, it seems quite clear."

"How is that?"

"They are all swindling each other."

"Well, if that is the case, then they all need to be absolved," and upon saying so he gave the blessing.

On the third of May, M. Campan brought us all back to Rome, and I stayed there with him until the twelfth, going out almost every day with him to have my music heard here and there. I had even more success than the year before, but that did not puff up my pride at all, since I knew that I wasn't a great player, and, as far as composition was concerned, I had already been smitten by the sonatas and quartets of Haydn and Mozart, whence I could see my lowliness and their superiority; in fact I was nervous of having to be heard in Florence, Venice or Milan, where instrumental music was more commonly cultivated than it was in Rome and Naples. I could never have believed that my cavalier would think of presenting us in Paris, but he was not afraid of anything. He believed himself to be the most perfect violinist in Europe, and before leaving Rome he made me promise that I would not have my sonatinas played in Paris with just anybody, but with him alone. This displeased me extremely, yet I was obliged to submit to his wishes.

On the tenth, crossing the Piazza di Spagna, I unexpectedly met Count Skavronsky, who asked me urgently if I was no longer going to Paris. I told him that I was leaving in two days. "That is really a shame," he added, "that is really too bad. I advised you to go there myself, but then affairs in France were not the mess that they are now, and everywhere an imminent revolution is feared. It would be better if you came with me to Crimea; I leave tomorrow morning, and in fifteen days we will be in Kerson, where you will see the coronation of my sovereign Catherine, Empress of all the Russias. You know that for eight years Paisiello was her favorite composer at St. Petersburg, and that he gave singing lessons to the Grand Duchess. I will present you to both of them; I am certain that you will be very welcome, and you will make a quick fortune in Russia."

What a temptation! To travel like the wind, to see a coronation, to avoid a revolution and the annoyance of always having to accompany my sonatinas!

I was almost at the point of accepting the offer, and of making my excuses to Cavalier Campan, to whom I had already expressed my fear of going to Paris several times, but Skavronsky, thinking to tempt me even more, had me enter the house he was leaving in order to have me see his traveling carriage. It was a sort of vis-à-vis carriage, very low, half closed, and with some chains of wrought iron for springs. It would have been enough to break the bones of a bear. Having examined the carriage, I turned back to the count, thanked him for his offer, and made it clear to him that, having just recovered from an illness, I would not have been able to bear a quarter of the journey without perishing. He smiled, said that I was right, and that he wished me peace and happiness in Paris.

I took my leave of the friends that I have mentioned, and on the twelfth we left for Florence, preceded by a certain Pippo, courier and servant of Monsieur Campan.

Chapter XXVII.

Eminent persons at Florence. Bologna and Venice. Conversation with the younger son of the Banker Luisello.

We arrived on May 17 in the capital of beautiful, rich, and well-cultivated Tuscany, and from the 18th to the 26th, we dined every day with the French ambassador, Count Durfort. After dining, we sometimes played music among ourselves, sometimes we played billiards, sometimes we went to the theater and then we returned for supper, and always with the lovely and elegant Parisian, Countess Venture. She was an extremely accomplished woman, around fifty, and yet through her hairstyle, lipstick, ribbons, jewels, etc., she looked like a young woman of fifteen. She claimed to be mad about music but knew nothing about it and could not hear anything. When she began to sing, she was a true caricature of the old French school, so as to make one feel pity on the one hand, and to get your nerves on the other.

I introduced Monsieur Campan to Cavalier Fontana, who welcomed us with the greatest grace. He let us see at our leisure all the chambers of his natural history collection, renowned throughout Europe, but as this was put together by one of my countrymen, I can do no less than praise it myself, and recommend to all travelers to see such a singular and superb establishment.

On the 27th we left for Bologna, where we had been before; we slept at Covigliaio, near Montefuoco, called Monte Fuoho by the Florentines, a phenomenon which seems more extraordinary to me than Vesuvius in Naples and Mont Blanc in Switzerland, since it is always on fire, and yet burns nothing. If it rains, it blazes more, and is more beautiful.

We stayed in Bologna at the palace of Count Odoardo Peppoli, friend of the Cavaliere, and remained there two days only in order to see once more the famous Observatory, of which one can never see enough, and to meet the celebrated Maestro Padre Mattei, a charming man and learned composer, full of taste, and to whom Liverati and Rossini, his students, owe much. Count Peppoli was one of those fine Bolognese, affable, not standing on ceremony, and of the sort that Goldoni presents so well in his clear and witty comedies in the character of Doctor Balanzon. He played the violin very well, and was so impassioned of his instrument that he offered to bet anything whatsoever that he could play twenty-four hours straight, without ever rising from his seat. He gave us two lunches and two sumptuous dinners, nor have I ever forgotten his exquisite Bolognese mortadellas. We stayed two days at Ferrara, two at Padua, and on June 5 we arrived in the always marvelous Venice, where we stayed until the 29th to see the regatta, the wedding with the sea, the cockaigne, and the other amusements that one could see at Ascensiontide.

From Rome to the lagoons of the Adriatic, we had always had great success with my music, but once in Venice, we experienced a rather hard setback. The day after our arrival we dined with the French ambassador, the charming Count Challon. Among the others present were Madame Las Casas, the ambassadress from Spain to Parma, who was traveling throughout Italy, and Madama Lamberti, from Milan, who was returning from Naples to her homeland. They were two rare beauties, traveling with their husbands, who, in contrast, looked like two children. Everyone hurried to court the ladies; no one bothered to pay any attention to the cavaliers. The latter were, however, happy - very happy - to see their spouses admired.

There was there a certain Marquis d'Hautfort from Paris, the best amateur violinist I had heard up until then. He was traveling with three professionals who he kept at his table and paid a salary, and, everywhere they stopped, they enjoyed performing, and letting their friends hear, the quartets of Vanhall, Stamitz, Daveau, Pleyel, and also some by Haydn, which the Marquis played very well. Having agreed with the ambassador to make a little music after dining, he began to play a quartet by Pleyel with his professional musicians; it surprised everyone, and was applauded by some. Mr. Campan, however, not convinced of the marquis' superiority, had the courage to ask his players to accompany him in my quartet, which M. D'Hautfort permitted most politely. But! My cavalier began to tremble, could not attack a note, played terribly out of tune, and was sweating blood out of anxiety and shame, so that in the middle of the first allegro he was obliged to put down his bow. He apologized, asserting, which was true, that he had had an asthma attack the night before that had weakened him so that he was unable to go on. He was excused, and the triumphant marquis continued to delight the company.

When I saw that M. Campan was tranquil once more, I approached him, and said, "But dear Signor Cavaliere, if playing here is a problem, what will we do in Paris, when we will perform before Bruni, Giornovichi, Mestrino, Viotti, etc.?" "Leave me alone," he answered, "I received quite a slap in the face. I am quite fascinated by those two beauties. Don't speak of music tonight."

By luck, the great violinist left, which made space for the beaten Cavalier to reappear with my sonatinas.

We passed many pleasant days in the company of Monsieur Challon, but I had an even better time at the house of an old correspondent of my father, Signor Pietro Luisello, a banker whose younger son was a charming hunchback, sardonic, full of natural wit, like all Venetians. Several times he took me in his father's box to the Teatro La Fenice, where they were presenting *L'Orfano della China*, a rather weak opera by Bianchi, sustained however by the sweet voice and charming manner of Babbini, and even more by the singular and transcendent merit of Pachierotti, whose expressive and elegant ways of singing were transformed into flights, flowers, and miracles.

He also introduced me to various very nice families, and wherever we went, and at whatever hour of the day or night, as soon as we entered the salon a servant or serving girl arrived with two cups of coffee. One day I happened to ask a question, which led to the following conversation: "Do tell me, dear Signor Luisello, how many cups of coffee do Venetian gentlemen drink in the course of twenty-four hours?"

"My dear friend, I couldn't say precisely, but I am sure that sometimes we drink as many as the twenty-four hours in the day."[2]

"Marvelous – but don't you get overheated, doesn't it prevent you from sleeping, doesn't it burn your intestines?"

"Whatever are you talking about?....You know that what we drink in Venice is all coffee from Alexandria of the most perfect quality. You roast it, cool it, grind it, boil it, and clarify it. Then one drinks it, cool or hot, and you sit and sip it, passing the time with some beautiful young thing. Good things, well made, that you enjoy with taste and love, don't do anyone any harm."

"Wonderful!"

[2] Translator's note: all of Luisello's speeches are in Venetian dialect.

"Have you ever heard the Venetian proverb in Latin, on the number of cups of coffee that we drink?"

"No."

"Now I will tell you."

> Prima juvat
> Secunda nocet
> Tertia necat,
> Et quarta placet.

> (The first helps,
> The second harms,
> The third kills,
> And the fourth pleases.)

The fifth, then, the sixth, the seventh, etc. are always pleasing, and you drink one after another, without burning your intestines."

"Viva!"

"Tell me, Signor Maestro... how do you like Venice?"

"Very, very much!"

"I tell you – this is a real city, eh?"

"Superb."

"What do you think of Bologna, Florence, and Rome?"

"Famous cities, one more beautiful than the next."

"But all three together are not worth a single Venice?"

"I wouldn't say that."

"Did you ever see a Rialto Bridge in those three cities?"

"No."

"A Piazza San Marco?"

"No."

"The Procutoria, the Ducal Palace, the Riva dei Schiavoni, the Bronze Horses, the Lazaretto, San Zarzi, etc."

"No."

"Then Venice alone is worth more than all those three."

"What a fanatic!"

"And what do you say of Naples?"

"Here you cut me to the quick. That region was, is, and will always be, in my heart."

"But what do they have in Naples that is so extraordinary?"

"My dear Luisello! The landscape, the climate, the phenomena!"

"The phenomena! And you don't call Venice the greatest phenomenon in the universe? A great city built 1300 years ago, in the midst of the sea, so that one would say the Omnipotent himself had created it there? A place where not a plant, a tree, or a beast is born that doesn't give a mouthful of water, nor a drop of wine; which does not produce grain, nor rice, nor barley, nor gold, nor silver: and in which you can find anything you could imagine in the blink of an eye, in profusion and at a good price? This is the greatest phenomenon in the world if you will be just."

"You are right to praise your fatherland, but you know well that all travelers agree that Naples surpasses all, and that all agree with the ancient proverb about Naples which you must know."

"Chatter, chatter, from children. All are just travelers, monkeys, and gigolos, and they go from one place to the next for fashion, as the sheep move from place to place for a little grass. If Neapolitans say to me, "See Naples, and then you may die," I answer them, pure and simple, like the true Venetian as I was born: "See Venice, and then go hang yourself."

Chapter XXVIII.

Departure from Venice - A Pleasing Parting with the Owner of the Locanda - Arrival at Verona, Milan, and Genoa - Embarkation for Nice and Gale on the way there - Arrival at Marseilles, Lyons and Paris.

A half hour before leaving Venice, Monsieur Campan settled his accounts with the owner of the inn, and, happy with his moderate bill, asked him amicably if all Venetians were as honest as he. The host smiled and answered him, "Your Excellence asks me a delicate and complicated question, and I tell you in truth that I don't know how to answer you, on my word as a gentleman."

"I will tell you; since I have been at Venice I have observed every day, morning and evening, a great number of persons of every class walking up and down through the Piazza San Marco and under the Procuratie. I then go into the cafes to eat and drink, into the theatres, the casinos, and always the same faces.

I would like to know how these people of leisure, these merry folk, can always be entertaining themselves and still earn their bread."

"Oh, Blessed Excellency! If you are talking about those vagabonds who walk up and down by San Marco, who go here and there to any place where there is diversion or entertainment straightaway, I will give you the satisfaction of a solid jest, and I will tell you a proverb that does not err:

> With art and deception
> One lives half the year,
> And with deception and art
> One lives the other part.

> *(Con arte e con inganno,*
> *si vive mezzo l'anno:*
> *e con inganno ed arte*
> si vive l'altra parte.)

"Bravo, signor padrone!," exclaimed Monsieur Campan. "Here are two silver ducats, and favor me with a copy."

Our host took the money, and as we were embarking he secretly gave me the proverb written down, and a bottle in straw of maraschino to drink on the voyage, not daring to give it himself to the cavalier.

Having disembarked at Fusina we went by post as far as Vicenza and stayed there a half-day to visit Monte Calvario, or the Madonna del Monte, a most celebrated sanctuary, and erected in a truly holy location. From the summit of the mountain, a view is revealed to the naked eye that I do not know how to describe. The horizon seems to extend to the sky; with a telescope one may see a large part of the plains of Lombardy, the Veneto, and Romagnola, a great number of cities, towns, and villages, various rivers, bridges, towers, castles, palaces, monasteries, and more. What a beautiful sight!

On the thirty-first, we arrived at the Inn of the Two Towers in Verona. Here I left my companion for two days, and, as soon as I had arrived, took a horse and carriage to make a trip to Roveredo, as much for the pleasure of seeing my brothers again as to look after the affairs of my family with my cousin and with Hortis, if this were indeed possible. But these two bandits, informed of my sudden and short stay, were not to be seen. I left on the third day from Saco, on a boat of merchandise, and arrived at Verona, after having traveled fifty miles in seven hours on the Adige.

Having arrived at the inn, they told me that Monsieur Campan was out and that he was expecting me at four. I immediately seized the opportunity to make a visit to the good Don Pandolfi, and I can say that we were both happy to see each other. I then went to see my friend Guierotti solely for the curiosity of learning news of my old Giuditta, and was happy to hear that she was already married. I dined with the cavalier, and then went to the Arena to see the hunting of the bulls, and the day after, the race of the *barberi* or thoroughbred horses; two spectacles, one crueler than the other, but which are viewed, with a certain anxiety and with a certain pleasure, by everyone. The following day we visited Marchese Carlotto, a famous dilettante player of the contrabass. In the evening there was a little music; we were edified by the Marchese, and he was very happy with us.

How I regret not being able to devote more space to talking more and more of this joyous and elegant city! But so much has been said about it that I would be importuning the reader were I to say any more. What consoles me is knowing that its sovereign adores it, knows the merit of its inner beauties, the good nature of its inhabitants, and the precious value of the soil which surrounds it.

On the sixth of June, we left for Milan without stopping at Mantua or anywhere else except to changing horses, since Monsieur Campan had already visited these cities during his trip from Paris to Rome. Arriving at Milan, and not finding certain persons that Monsieur Campan had expected to find there, it was decided to leave for Genoa soon. The evening before our departure, we went to the Teatro della Scala, where a miserable opera by Tarchi was being presented. The company was neither hot nor cold, except for Marchesi, who was not, however, the perfect singer that he later became, though his voice and execution pleased his compatriots, the more so as he had offered to sing gratis on this occasion. But we were already infatuated with Pacchierotti and so left the theater after the first act.

The day after we left for Genoa, where we stayed until the eighteenth, in order to be present at the procession of *Corpus Domini* that is so famous in that city, and which is certainly worth seeing. The streets are covered with fresh roses strewn in abundance everywhere. A quantity of young green beeches, cut on purpose for the occasion, and planted or tied by the sides of the streets offer a most gracious scene. From the windows of the first floors of the houses can be seen, displayed with great pomp, the most elegant fabrics of every color, and from the houses of the rich one sees many in damask, velvet, and satin. What disgusted us greatly in the procession was to see a number of noble Genoese competing to carry in turn the large cross, which is of immense size, and of a weight to crush an elephant. Four strong porters lifted it with great effort from the leather holder which hung from the shoulders of the superstitious one who was carrying the cross, in order to put it on another's shoulders. This ceremony seemed to us to be the most ridiculous, tormenting and ludicrous thing one could find. Nevertheless, we entertained ourselves infinitely at Genoa, having been recommended with great zeal by the Counts Durfort and Challon to the French Consul, Monsieur Raulin, a man of middle age, amiable, hospitable and generous, but without extravagances or needless superfluities. He had a very beautiful house situated facing the gulf, elegantly furnished. He kept the most perfect table, and offered everything in abundance, with a good heart, and without the least ceremony.

As long as we were there, he invited us, or rather forced us, to lunch and dine with him, and between the two meals we went to the comedy, or its annex, now for a walk, now to row or to sail on the sea in his boat. The position of Genoa reminded us of Naples; the factories and the palaces erected outside the town, the mountains, the pleasant hills, and the most varied rustic views charmed us at every step. The inhabitants are good, as are almost all the Italians, and would be happier if they were reunited and governed by one single sovereign. But....poor Italy! You have too many masters and too many internal and external factions to overcome to ever be happy.

He who knows you admires you, and at the same time is sorry for you, and everyone says something close to that which one of your illustrious poets expresses:

> "Italy, Italy, o thou who fate made
> a woman unhappy in her beauty...
> Oh, were you less beautiful and more strong!"[3]

> *(Italia, Italia, o tu cui feo la sorte*
> *Donna infelice di bellezza...*
> *Deh, fossi tu man bella e almen più forte!)*

On the nineteenth, after having said a sad farewell to the Consul, to Genoa, and to all of proud Italy, we embarked on a small sailboat with eight oars to go down the coast to Nice, but having gotten halfway there, there came a storm and terrible gale that forced us to seek land as quickly as possible. We disembarked in an arid and uninhabited place, but the sailors told us that behind a certain hedge there was a hut where a hermit stayed, and that they were sure that he would give us asylum if we were to go there. Indeed, having gone towards it an old man with a long white beard came out, with a hood on his head and a rope at his waist, inviting us to enter.

His habitation was nothing but a large room and a little workshop, where he spent his time working as a woodworker, and a garden whose produce was only a little lettuce and some radishes. He offered us some hard biscuits, some salted eels, and some oil, but then some excellent wine that had been given to him by the good people of the neighboring area. Having been informed of the nearby town, my companion immediately sent Pippo to look for provisions. We were half

---

[3] The opening of Vincenzo da Filicaia's famous Sonnetto LXXXVII

dead of hunger, not having been able to take any nourishment on the boat, being disgusted by the odor of the onions that the sailors were chewing continuously, and by the tobacco that they were smoking. The servant returned in less than an hour with prosciutto, salami, fresh bread, eggs, and more, and between these, the lettuce, the hermit's wine, and the devouring hunger that was gnawing at us, we had one of the most appetizing dinners you could imagine. We slept in our clothes on a large straw mattress, the cavalier on one side, I on the other, and the hermit in the middle; Pippo laid himself down on the ground wrapped up in his cloak.

We were obliged to spend another night in the hut, but on the third day, at five in the morning, the sailors came to wake us and we embarked under a serene sky on a tranquil sea, favored by a light breeze that carried us happily to Nice. As soon as we had unloaded the cavalier's cabriolet, we attached the horses, and crossing Provence, arrived at Marseilles and from there, Lyons, where we received another musical setback that does not bear speaking of.

Finally, on the thirteenth of July, 1787, our journey ended in the proud, majestic and ever-happy city of Paris.

END OF THE FIRST PART.

PART TWO

Fig. 10. Portrait of Jeanne-Louise Henriette de Campan by Joseph
Boze

Chapter I.

Paris- Choisy- Versailles- Royal Mass- Unexpected meeting with Monsieur- Music with the Queen.

The grand metropolis of the continent was then, as it had been for many a year before, in its highest degree of wealth, honour, and influence. Foreign powers admired it, feared it, and envied it. Frederick the Great, King of Prussia used to say to his friends, "When I dream, I wish I were the King of France; and if my dreams were to be realized, I would not allow a single cannon shot in Europe without my permission." In Paris, amicability, pleasure, and concord reigned. Every nation exerted itself to learn French and to imitate the manners, dress, and the spirit of the Parisians. It was the earthly paradise of the arts and of artists, but above all of music and musicians. The most distinguished talents were venerated, adored, and admitted into whatever society, sitting at the same table with the highest nobility of France, and sometimes with the princes of the royal family themselves. Less-distinguished talents and masters were respected, well-paid, and welcomed in the best families, and young people making their debuts were encouraged with money, gifts, or other pleasing things.

Oh, Paris, Paris! You were the illusion of youth; the luxury of middle age; but, of old age, the rest and happy tomb.

In the space of eight days I discovered and saw almost all that there was of note;

I also made the acquaintance of various relatives and friends of the cavalier, in whose houses we produced an incredible effect with our music. I couldn't believe it, but my first violin being desirous to be heard in a numerous company, in the presence of professionals and able dilettantes, it was not long before he received certain comments *sotto voce*, which are not worth repeating here, which caused him to think better of this. I said to him plainly that he was compromising himself, and that I was the victim of his *amour propre*. Luckily he was persuaded, and from that moment on resolved that he would only be heard in his own house or among his relatives.

Several days later he brought me to Choisy, between Paris and Versailles, where his father lived in a most beautiful country house, and where I spent two delicious weeks.

His father was a man close to seventy, but whose spirit and vivacity seemed to be that of a man of less than forty. He entertained the most pleasing guests, and was always happy and in good humor. The Sunday after our arrival, my friend brought me to Versailles, to attend the so-called *Messe du Roi* and to present me to his wife, the renowned Madama Campan, a lady of singular merit, but too well-known to have need of my tributes.[1] Having arrived at the palace, and gone up to the apartment of the Queen, and after a little conversation with Madame C., we went to mass, going through an immense salon called *l'Oeil de Boeuf*, and entered into the galleries of the Royal Chapel. From there I was able to see at my ease Louis XVI, kneeling next to his illustrious consort, facing the altar, by the orchestra, and surrounded by his royal family, the high nobility of the court, and by a few grenadiers.

The mass being finished, and I, being anxious to see where the sovereigns, the nobility, and all those people were going, lost sight of my companion. I looked for him in the grand salon, and not finding him, I returned to the galleries, and thus went back and forth until I found myself all alone in *l'Oeil de Boeuf*. Having approached the door by which I had entered earlier, I was about to open it, but it opened wide by itself, and I bumped into a corpulent man, whom I had never seen, and who asked me with disdain, *"Que voulez-vous?" "Je cherche le Chevalier Campan." "Passez."* ("What do you want?" "I am looking for Chevalier Campan." "Pass through.") Observing a throng of cavaliers following him, I thought that he was the king himself; but having finally found my companion, and recounting what had happened to me, he told me that I had bumped into His Royal Highness, Monsieur the King's brother. "My God," I added, "if that had happened in Turkey, they would certainly have cut off my head!" "And perhaps impaled you," answered the Cavalier, joking. (This reminds me of the case of a Capuchin, imprisoned by the Turks, and condemned in Constantinople to either become a Mahometan or be impaled. "I, a Mahometan? Never, and again, never!" "Then you will be impaled." "And why?" "Because you do not wish to become a Turk." "But this is not possible". "Then you will be impaled." Why impaled?" And finally, the wretched Frate added, "Do with me as you wish, as long as you speak no more of impaling.")

Having taken a turn through the palace, and seen what was possible to see in the time during which the court remained there, we returned to Choisy and found we had the company of the secretary of the Queen, who had just sat down to dine. Among others was Madame Campan, who had preceded us in a hurry from Versailles, and was anxious to know from me personally what had happened to me in *l'Oeil de Boeuf*. I related my adventure with the vivacity of youth, and in the Italianized French that I was speaking then, which made the

---

[1] Jeanne Louise Henriette Campan (née Genet, 1752-1822) was a remarkable woman from the period before and after the French Revolution. The daughter of a civil servant, she was very well-educated by her family, and gained distinction early in life because of her learning, rising to the position of reader to the daughters of Louis XV, and an established and respected figure at the court. When Ferrari first met her, she was the chief lady-in-waiting to Marie-Antoinette. As a result of her experiences at court, she wrote her valuable Memoirs of the Private Life of Marie Antoinette, published in 1823.

whole company laugh tremendously. As it is well known that the French take advantage of any minutiae to entertain themselves, nothing else was discussed at that meal other than colliding, impaling, and *l'Oeil de Boeuf.*

In the evening there was music, and Madame Campan wished to hear my compositions; she then gave me some pieces by Piccini, Sacchini, and Gluck to accompany at sight, without preparation at the pianoforte, as was the custom at that time. She was very happy with my music and with my sight-reading, and promised to speak of it to the Queen, and introduce me to her at whatever cost. I was never able to learn why Madame C. didn't bring me directly to her Majesty, nor for what reason the Queen did not order me, directly, to present myself to her, but the affair took place as follows. The charming lady of the chamber invited me to dine on the following Thursday along with her husband. It was arranged that M. Campan would begin tuning his violin to my pianoforte in the apartment of the Queen's first Lady of the Chamber at the same time during which the Queen was accustomed to cross a corridor leading to one of her rooms which was next to this one. The Queen, hearing music, was supposed to stop at the door of Madame C.'s salon to listen, and at the same time Madame C. was supposed to open the door, as if by accident, and seeing her Majesty, invite her to enter. Marie Antoinette would enter, ordering all to follow her; and so it happened.

Cavalier C., who had had the honor of teaching the theory of music to that excellent princess, was expecting that she would want to hear him play, and I was trembling, but she happily paid no attention to his violin, nor to my sonatinas. She made me take out the score of *Re Teodoro in Venezia* by Paisiello, which was her favorite. I played the overture, then she seated herself at my right, and I accompanied her and we sang together, and along with the cavaliers and ladies of her court, we performed the concerted pieces, and the two superb finales of the opera, which they all knew already by heart. As I knew them even better than they did, it is not surprising that they all found that I accompanied marvelously. The Queen, however, said to Madame Campan, *"Votre protégé est un excellent musicien, mais il a le défaut de prendre le mouvement trop vite, comme font tous les jeunes gens."* ("Your protégé is an excellent musician, but he has the fault of taking movements too quickly, as is the habit of all young people.") This observation of Her Majesty was natural enough, since she had the habit of always taking the movements too slowly, and she could not imagine that I, although young, was so fanatical for Paisiello that I would rather have been whipped rather than sacrifice the music of my master to satisfy her.

During this period the affairs of France began to get into a dreadful mess. Their Majesties were living almost continuously at Versailles, they were no longer frequenting the theatres, etc., and I heard no more said of the Queen until the year 1792, of which I will speak at its proper time.

Chapter II.

Anecdotes - Return to Paris - The Marquis Circello - Abate Leprini - The Countesses of Tessé, of Tott, and other distinguished personages.

During the last days we spent at Choisy, Monsieur Campan the senior entertained us a great deal with his anecdotes, which he told with such naturalness and character that they gave the greatest pleasure to those who heard them, two of which I have the honor to offer to the reader.

A certain Adami, a young guitar maker, took a wife, who, a year after the wedding, gave him a child. Content and happy to have become a father, he ran immediately to his close friend Rigoni, and said to him, "I have come, friend, to give you some nice news, the greatest, most extraordinary, most marvelous news, that you could imagine."

"By Bacchus! Tell me then what it is about."
"Guess what it is."
"Did you win the lottery?"
"No."
"At cards?"
"No."
"Were you made pope?"
"Don't be ridiculous."
"Did you receive an inheritance?"
"Anything but an inheritance."
"Well then, tell me what it is, since I will never be able to guess."
"My wife has given birth."
"And this is the extraordinary news?"
"And what do you think?"
"It is just great."
"Now guess what she produced."
"A boy."
"No."
"A girl then."
"Who told you?"
"O what an idiot! Were you expecting maybe that she would make you a guitar?"

When Joseph II succeeded to the throne of his mother, the illustrious Empress Maria Teresa, his first aim was to prepare for a war against the Turks, his sworn enemies, but needing money, soldiers, and supplies, it was necessary to suppress the monasteries, to take their immense holdings for the public good, and to form from the laymen an army of well-fed and robust soldiers. He suppressed the convents of the nuns as well, in order to acquire their wealth, permitting them (with the agreement of the head of the Church) to give up the veil and to take husbands. This produced a whispering throughout Vienna and a scandal in all the convents of nuns. The nuns said to each other, "What? We who have taken the veil, and made a vow of chastity, to have a husband! What indecency! And it is the Emperor's idea? And the pope agrees? It is not possible."

The abbess of the Convent of the Sisters of St. Elizabeth, tormented perhaps more than any other by her reverend mothers and sisters about this business and wanting to know the truth of the matter, wrote a courteous letter to the confessor of the court, the archbishop of that metropolis, begging him to find out from the Emperor himself if what was being said was true, since her nuns were all afflicted and made desolate by the idea of being able to have husbands.

The confessor, liberal and flippant, no less than his imperial penitent, brought the letter immediately to His Majesty. Joseph read it and laughed heartily. "What a disgrace!" he said with sarcasm. "Go immediately to the convent to console them, and tell them that the edict will be put in force, that the pope has consented to it, and add, moreover, that I permit them even to have two husbands if they desire them." Monsignor flew with his carriage to the convent, and as he went, he made up a little story. Having entered the parlor, he called for the abbess and all the nuns. They crowded toward him with the greatest anxiety in order to learn the Emperor's answer. The archbishop asked them to be seated and to keep calm. Then he told them that he had been authorized by the sovereign to assure them that all that which they desired to know was true, but that His Majesty, having been informed of the aversion they had for matrimony, would only allow those nuns with soft voices to have a husband. Hearing this, they all began to purse their lips, and murmuring *sotta voce*, and with their lips only half open, "O Mother Abbess! Mother

Vittoria! Sister Soffia! Oh what a horror! What a shame! What cruelty!" The Monsignor continued by saying that His Majesty, ever just in his decrees, would permit two husbands to the nuns who had big mouths. Then, opening their mouths from one ear to the other, they all shouted at the top of their voices, "O Highness! O Monsignor Archbishop! O Father Confessor!"

On my return to Paris, I immediately sought to obtain free admission to the Grand Opéra, in order to see the classic operas of Gluck, Piccini, and of Sacchini. Viotti, the Queen's first violinist, and Sapio, her *maestro di canto,* procured me this favor, nor will I be able to describe how delighted I was to attend there, nor how many tears I shed hearing the music of these three celebrated composers. I hurried then to present the letter of recommendation Paisiello had given me for the ambassador of Naples to the court of France, his old friend the Marquis Circello, which began thus: "Your Excellence has recommended a scholar to me; now I have the pleasure of recommending to you a young master, who does himself honor and whom I am sure that You will be happy to protect and encourage!" The good marquis welcomed me in the Neapolitan manner and invited me to dinner for the same day. He had me sit next to his private secretary, Abate Leprini, saying, "Here is your spot; come when you like, and if I or the Marquesa are out of the house, you will always find the Abate, with whom you will be able to eat a bowl of good soup or a nice plate of macaroni."

The Marquis Circello was an excellent gentleman, grand and at the same time economical. He lived in the elegant Hôtel de Poyane, Rue de Fauxbourg St. Honoré, and had the finest table in Paris. Monsieur had generously granted him the famous M. Grillon to be his chef, the same man who for many years has maintained a hotel in Albemarle Street, and who, in the year 1814, had the honor of lodging his first patron, Louis XVIII, when he passed in triumph through London, having been reestablished as King of France.

He also had the finest pastry chef that could be found in Naples, a certain Romualdo, who died years ago in Duke Street, Manchester Square. Abate Leprini was a respectable and religious man, but certainly not a fanatic; he spoke to me often about morality, calling it the handmaid, or rather the sister, of religion. He used to say to me, "There are sins of malice and of weakness; let us avoid the first, and hope that God will pardon us the second." He recommended that I not read the works of J.J. Rousseau, as they were too philosophical and hypocritical, and even less those of Voltaire, they being too shameless and waggish.

Having little by little gotten to know this gentleman, and both finding him and leaving him in his room with the works of Voltaire in hand, I asked him why he counseled me not to read that which he was reading continually. "It is true," he answered, "Voltaire is a great rogue, but one who I find myself unable to give up. But I am old, nor can I be corrupted; you are still young, and could be easily seduced by the elegance, the genius, and, I am sorry to say, by certain truths of this great writer. "

I was then introduced to the Countess of Tessé and she gave me as a student Mademoiselle - that is, Madame - the Countess of Tott, a most beautiful creature and a protegée of the Queen.

It became known in Paris that I had made music with His Majesty and that I was giving lessons to Madame de Tott, and so singing and accompaniment employment sought me out from all over. Among those whom I cannot forget, nor omit naming certain families from which I received the greatest courtesies, include the Duchess of Castries; the Countess Joigny (her sister); the Duke of Guines (their father); the Marchesa Beauharnais (Josephine); the Duchess of Richelieu; the Baroness of Stael; the Marquesa of Belsunce; the Baroness Talleyrand; the Duchess of Polignac; the Countess of Noailles; the Princess de Bergnes; the Count Charles de Noailles, now Prince of Pois and Duke of Mouchy; the Countess du Saillant; the Marqusa d'Aragon and the Princess of Craon; M. Louis, the architect who erected the superb theater of Bordeaux and the Royal Palace at Paris; M. De Boulogne; M. and Madame Dupin, etc. Of some of these I will speak in a moment.

In spite of the extraordinary encouragement that I received daily in that metropolis, I was exceedingly bored and always had Naples before my eyes and in my heart. Little by little, however, I got used to it, and I eventually enjoyed myself a great deal.

Chapter III.

Mestrino - Dussek - Steibelt - J.B. Cramer - Shmerczka - Plantade - Portraits - Romances -Theatre de Monsieur.

Through various circumstances and reasons which are not worth mentioning, I was obliged to leave Signor Campan's house at the beginning of November, remaining always on good terms with him. I took lodging in a hotel with the celebrated violinist Mestrino, one of the greatest talents possible; an amiable young man and a trickster. At that point, for many years there had been in Paris three celebrated masters of the pianoforte: Hullmanndel, Küffner, and Adam. Then arrived successively several other renowned pianists. First came Dussek, called Handsome Dussek, who was the most amiable wit in the world, always merry and gay, and never bothered by matters of any sort. He was a great player and had a natural and insinuating genius for composition. Steibelt was a scatterbrained and dissipated man, clear in his writing and full of taste, but incorrect and confused in his playing. How many notes and how many beautiful phrases disappeared under the hands of this player! But being aware himself of his own errors he introduced the use, or rather the abuse, of the pedals, which certainly can make a delicious effect in slow and diatonic movements, but in rapid and chromatic movements one is unable to distinguish melody, or harmony, or phrases. But in such a way the sloppy player saves himself.

Cursed be those pedals! If twelve Dragonetti were surrounding me, playing their contrabasses at full volume, I would hear at least a sound, an accent! But if a damsel of only twelve years plays on a little pianoforte à la Steibelt, I hear no more than a whispering, a buzzing, which pierces my eardrums.

After him came J.B. Cramer, who with his manner of playing surpassed all, and except for Adam, they left, one after the other, for England - Steibelt, Küffner, Hullmandel, and Dussek. Cramer was a handsome young man, a surprising player, a great reader, and a great musician. He was considered to be Clementi's greatest student, and he executed the difficult music of that composer with the greatest facility. I learned later that he had taken lessons with Schroeter as well, and played the works of that sensible and sweet master with grace, elegance, and with perfect taste. In the field of composition, he had not yet produced the beautiful, classic pieces he wrote later, and which are always admired.

Charmed by his talent, and though older than he, I asked him for lessons out of friendship, which he gave me, and I owe him for having opened my eyes to the manner of fingering and playing on the pianoforte.

A short time before, another pianist (or rather fortist) had arrived in Paris, a "croque note" not to be compared to those named above, but nevertheless recommended warmly to the Queen by some German prince.

He was greeted with that princess's usual affability, and after having played in her presence, she said to him (more to honor the recommen-dation than the recommended) that she desired to take lessons from him, to which that dolt answered, *"Madame, je tacherai de m'arranger avec mes élèves de Paris, pour venir doner leçon à vostre Mayésté à Versailles.* ("Ma-dame, I will try to arrange with my pupils in Paris, to come and teach Your Majesty at Versailles.")

I, in the meantime, encouraged from every side, inflamed by amour propre and emulation, and free from the formalities and considerations which were binding me while I was in my Cavalier's house, began to work in earnest; and even though I had many students, yet I found the time to study, to practice at the pianoforte, and to compose, not without diverting myself from time to time at the theatre or in conversation. I wrote three sonatas for pianoforte and violin, my Opus 2, which were much superior to what I had written up until then, and which were well received in Paris, Naples and also in Vienna. But seeing that the school of Clementi was spreading itself throughout all of Europe, and that young pianists were popping up everywhere and putting me to shame, I only studied that instrument further for entertainment and interest. I applied myself seriously to vocal music. I composed twelve Italian *notturni*, and then another twelve which had a good reception, then three books each with six French romances, a few of which developed a truly fanatical following. Here are the texts of two that should certainly not displease the reader.

LA NAISSANCE DE L'AMOUR

Par Monsieur l'Abbé Garron

Quand l'amour naguit à Cythère
On s'intrigua dans le pays:
Venus dit, je suis bonne mère,
C'est moi qui norrirai mon fils.
Mais l'Amour malgré son jeune âge,
Trop attentif à tant d'appas,
Préférrait le vase au breuvage
Et l'enfant ne profitait pas.
Ne faut pas pourtant qu'il patisse;
Dit Vénus, palrant à sa cour;
Que la plus sage le nourrisse,
Songez toutes que c'est l'Amour.
Soudain la Candeur, la Tendresse,
L'Egalité vinrent s'offrir;
Et même la Délicatesse,
Nulle n'avait de quoi nourrir.
On penchait pour la Complaisance,
Mais l'enfant eût été gâté:
On avait trop d'expérience
Pour penser à la Volupté.
Enfin sur ce choix d'importance
Cette cour ne décidant rien,
Quelqu'un proposa l'Espérance,
Et l'enfant s'en trouva fort bien.
On prétend que la Jouissance
Qui croyait devoir le nourrir,
Jalouse de la préférence,
Guettait l'enfant pour s'en saisir:
Prenant les traits de l'Innocence
Pour berceuse elle vint s'offrir,
Et la trop crédule Espérance,
Eut le malheur d'y consentir.
Un jour advint que l'Espérance
Voulant se livrer au sommeil,
Remit à la fausse Innocence
L'enfant, jusques à fon reveil:
Alors la trompeuse déesse
Donne bons-bons à pleine main;

L'amour fut d'abord dans l'ivresse,
Mais mourut bientôt sur son sein.[2]

(THE BIRTH OF LOVE.
By Monsieur L'Abbé Garron.
When Love was born in Cythera,
There was intrigue in the land:
Venus said: I am a good mother,
It is I who will nurse my son.
But Love, too attentive to such attractions
Despite his young age,
Preferred the glass to the beverage,
And the child had no profit from it.

He must not suffer, however,
Said Venus, speaking to her court;
Let the wisest nurse him
You all know that this is Love.
Immediately Candor, Tenderness
Equality came to offer their services,
And even Delicacy.
None of them had anything with which to nourish him.

One inclined to Complaisance,
But the infant had been spoiled:
One had too much experience
To think of Pleasure.
Finally, this court making no decision
On this important choice,
Someone suggested Hope,
And the infant thought this very good.

It is said that Enjoyment
Who thought that she should nurse him,
Jealous about the choice
Kept an eye on him to snatch him;
Taking on the traits of Innocence
She came to offer to sing lullabies
And too-credulous hope
Unhappily consented.

---

[2] This was one of Ferrari's most popular and long-enduring works. It is mentioned several times in articles and accounts of Ferrari during his lifetime and throughout the 19th century.

One day it happened that Hope,
Wanting to slumber
Gave the child to the
False Innocence, until she should wake up:
Then the deceitful goddess
Gives bon-bons, with both hands:
Love was inebriated at first,
But soon died on her breast.)

L'AMOUR ET LES GRACES
(par le même)

A l'ombre d'un myrte fleuri,
Echappé des bras de sa mère,
L'Amour reposait endormi,
Quoique l'Amour ne dorme guère.
Les Grâces jouaient près de là,
Sans le soupçonner au boccage.
Par malheur l'Amour soupira,
Il n'en fallut pas d'avantage.
A l'aspect de ce jeune enfant,
C'est l'Amour s'ecrièrent elles.
Fuir est leur premier mouvement:
C'est celui de toutes les belles.
Cependant l'Amour est si beau,
Mais les Grâces sont si craintives;
N'importe; un sentiment nouveau
Rassure les trois fugitives.
Le perfide est donc endormi,
(Dirent les Grâces en alarmes.
Peut on réunir comme lui
Tant de malice à tant de charmes?
Gardons-nous de lui pardonner,
S'iassissons ses flêches cruelles;
Mais il faut d'abord l'enchaîner,
Car vous voyez qu'il a des aîles.
Elles approchent tour à tour,
Mais tout doucement et pour cause;
Hélas! Pour éveiller l'Amour

Il faut souvent si peu de chose.
L'Amour ne dormait déjà plus;
Bientôt l'effet suit les menaces:
Il résiste: efforts superflus!
On ne résiste points aux Grâces.
Ah, leur dit il, point de courroux;
Brisez mes traits, séchez vos larmes,
Puisque l'amour est avec vous
Il n'a pllus besoin de ses armes.
Partout, depuis cet heureux jour,
Des trois soeurs de Dieu suit les traces:
Elles embellissent l'Amour,
Et l'Amour embellit les Grâces.[3]

(LOVE AND THE GRACES.
By the same.
IN the shade of a flowering myrtle,
Having escaped his mother's arms,
Love, sleeping, rested,
Although Love does not give repose.
The Graces were playing nearby
Without suspecting he was in the grove.
Unfortunately, Love sighed –
Nothing more was needed.

At the sight of this young child,
They cried "It is Love!"
Their first impulse was to flee:
This is the impulse of all beauties.
However, Love is so beautiful,
But the Graces are so fearful;
No matter; a new sentiment
Reassures the three fugitives.

The perfidious one is asleep, then
(The Graces said, in alarm.)
How can someone like him combine
Such malice and such charm?

---

[3] Other sources from the period identify this poem as coming from the pen of Racquit-Lieutaud, a dramatist and librettist active in the last years of the 18th century. See, for instance, *L'Esprit des Journaux Francois et Étranger*, published by the Société de Gens de Letters (Valade, 1787).

Let us avoid pardoning him,
Let us seize his cruel arrows;
But first of all he must be enchained,
For you see that he has wings.

They approach one by one,
But very softly, and for a good reason;
Alas! It often takes so little
To waken Love.
Love was already sleeping no longer;
Soon the effect follows the menaces:
He resists: superfluous efforts!
One does not resist the Graces.
Ah, he tells them; don't be angry;
Break my arrows, dry your tears,
Since Love is with you
He no longer needs his weapons.
Everywhere, since this happy day,
This God follows the footsteps of the three sisters:
They embellish Love,
And Love embellishes the Graces.)

These two romances were very well liked, as much for the elegance and delicacy of the words as for the simplicity of the music, and still more for the care that I took in changing the accompaniment for every strophe, in order to express in such a way the sentiment of the words.

This was a novelty, and removed the monotony of a narrative cantilena.

I then wrote six duets, and six Italian canons for three voices, which also were successful.

In the year 1788, I was engaged at the *Théâtre de Monsieur* to be at the pianoforte, and to be responsible for the scores, now using my music, now using another's.[4] The first opera executed under my direction was the *Villanella Rapita by Bianchi,* produced as a pasticcio.

---

[4] The Théâtre de Monsieur was a theatre begun under the patronage of the king's brother the Comte de Provence in 1789, under the direction of Viotti and other of the Queen's musicians, and its original repertoire reflected her tastes. It originally performed in the Tuileries Palace, but in 1791 moved to a purpose-build building located on Rue Feydeau. During the Revolution, the theater changed its name to Théâtre Feydeau. During the time Ferrari was employed there, the theater was noteworthy for presenting Italian operas by composers such as Pergolesi and Paisiello, with Cherubini acting as house composer. Unusually for theaters of the time, it produced a range of spoken and musico-dramatic genres.

I composed for it an overture, a cavatina, an arietta for the second part, and the mirror scene. Everything went well, particularly the mirror scene, which really established my reputation in Paris. After this came the *Geloso in Cimento by Anfossi,* also done as a pasticcio, for which I wrote a terzet which was encored with furor, and a successful chorus. The principal actors who performed in these two operas were the famous Stefano Mandini, his wife, Carlo Rovedino, the charming Viganoni, and the surprising actor Rafanelli. (Author's note: Rafanelli and Mandini were rivals in the theatre, even though their talents were of different sorts. Having met at the rehearsal of Sarti's *Gelosie Villan*e they began to squabble and had words with each other.

R. sent to M. a card reading as follows:

> "*Signor Cantante* Mandini! You have offended me unjustly, and I demand from you immediate satisfaction. I challenge you therefore to a duel, and will await you tomorrow at seven, at the gate of the Bois de Boulogne.
>
> I leave to your lordship the choice of arms, since I am ready to fight with sword, saber, pistol, or cannon!
>
> The Actor Rafanelli."

Mandini and his wife were dying of fear, but Cherubini and other of their friends took care of the affair with a plate of macaroni and a roast turkey, which Mandini gave to Rafanelli, and to the leading actors of the *Théâtre de Monsieur,* among whom the master was not lacking.

They also had me write many separate pieces for this one or that one with more or less success. The orchestra of the theatre was large and was formed in the blink of an eye, to the surprise of all the Parisians, considering the quantity of theatres that were in the capital.

But with a first violin like Mestrino, with a first violoncello like Shcumerczka (a Czech), with a contrabass like Plantade, and with a maestro who got on with the first violin, the orchestra ought to have gone well, and so it did. Mestrino, as I said before, was a young man of natural genius; he wrote the melodies of his concertos with the purity and judgment of a composer, and then he gave the accompaniments and the harmonic realizations to his friends, who filled out the score for him, and everything was correct even though he could not write it all by himself. He died a few months thereafter, lamented by his friends, by professionals, and by amateurs alike.

Plandate was an excellent professional, and a good young man; his talent distinguished him to the extent that, from the contrabass and modest composer that he was, became one of the *maestri di cappella* of the King of France.

Shcumerczka was the most singular man that I had ever met in my life. He was about thirty, of middling stature, with a dark and unpleasing face and little brown eyes, but lively and expressive. He was insipid and annoying in his conversation except for certain moments that I am about to relate.

During the time in which I was living with Mestrino, Shcumerczka came now and then to dine with us and with other friends, and after a few glasses of bordeaux or of burgundy, he entertained us greatly with his fantastic and fabulous little stories, some which I am unable to omit, even at the price of not being believed.

Shcumerczka used to claim that he had been seven times around the world and that he was connected with all the crowned heads of Europe, along with the Great Mogol, the Emperor of China, and Scipio Africanus. He had seen the Temple of Solomon begun and completed. and had played violoncello and harp duets with David, Solomon's father. He had toured America, before it was discovered by Columbus, had hunted there, and killed an infinity of elephants and other ferocious beasts. Indeed, if you listened to him you might have believed that he was born before the Creation. This made us say that he was a man with two distinct brains; one full of folly, the other full of music. In fact, I don't believe that there ever was a professional more intrepid than he.

He played the violin passably, but on the violoncello he could execute anything. He didn't care to throw dust in one's eyes with a flood of rapid notes, harmonics, or squeaking, nor with the *capotasto sul ponticello*, as so many do. He had a grandiose bow-stroke and he produced a just and round tone. He modulated his sounds as one modulates the voice, and he sang on his instrument like a marquee tenor, for he wanted to sing, and not astound. He died later at Little Chelsea, near London, in the year 1794.

On July 14, 1789, the revolution that had been expected for so many years broke out and interrupted the course of my happy career. Marquis Circello and my principal students and patrons emigrated one after the other. To begin with, I was not put out, and got on very well with those who remained, with the salary from the theatre, and the profit from my published works, which was not indifferent. The loss of Mestrino saddened me for a long time, nor could I stay further in the hotel.

I had an elegant little apartment furnished in one of the houses of M. Louis and paid the rent with the singing and accompaniment lessons that I was giving to his daughter. M. Louis was always distracted with his architecture, but he was still a good man, without airs, liberal and splendid. His wife was worthy of such a husband, and their only daughter shared in the merit of her parents. How much I enjoyed that charming family and how many courtesies I received there, I cannot tell!

Chapter IV.

Madame Louis - Madame Du Saillant- Journey to Spa and to Brussels - Return to Paris - Broken-Off Wedding - New Love.

Among the obligations that contracted with M. Louis' family, I cannot forget or omit from my story those that that I bear his consort particularly. She was a charming person, and full of advice; she knew music deeply, and knew harmony much better than I did at the time. She advised me in an amiable way, and with the greatest delicacy, to study the *Dictionnaire de Musique* by Rousseau, which I did, and from which I derived great benefit, that work being the development, light, and guide of harmony. But as I am speaking of that dictionary, I can do no less than offer to the reader an extract on the entry *"Génie"*, which made such an impression on me.

Ne cherche point, jeune Artiste, ce que c'est que le Génie. En as-tu : tu le sens en toi-même. N'en as-tu pas : tu ne le connoîtras jamais. Le Génie du Musicien soumet l'Univers entier à son Art. Il peint tous les tableaux par des Sons ; il fait parler le silence même ; il rend les idées par des sentimens, les sentimens par des accens ; & les passions qu' il exprime, il les excite au fond des cœurs. La volupté, par lui, prend de nouveaux charmes ; la douleur qu'il fait gémir arrache des cris ; il brûle sans cessé & ne se consume jamais. Il exprime avec chaleur les frimats & les glaces ; même en peignant les horreurs de la mort, il porte dans l'ame ce sentiment de vie qui ne l'abandonne point, & qu'il communique aux cœurs faits pour le sentir. Mais hélas ! il ne fait rien dire à ceux où son germe n'est pas, & ses prodiges sont peu sensibles à qui ne les peut imiter. Veux-tu donc savoir si quelque étincelle de ce feu dévorant t'anime ? Cours, vole à Naples écouter les chef-d'œuvres de Leo, de Durante, de Jommelli, de Pergolèse. Si tes yeux s'emplissent de larmes, si tu sens ton cœur, palpiter, si des tressaillemens t'agitent, si l'oppression te suffoque dans les transports, prends le Métastase & travaille ; son Génie échauffera le tien ; tu créeras à son exemple : c' est-là ce que fait le Génie, & d'autres yeux te rendront bientôt les pleurs que les Maîtres t' ont sait verser. Mais si les charmes de ce grand Art te laissent tranquille, si tu n'as ni délire ni ravissement, si tu ne trouvé que beau ce qui transporte, oses-tu demander ce qu'est le Génie ? Homme vulgaire, ne profane point ce nom sublime. Que t'importeroit de le connoître ? tu ne saurois le sentir : fais de la Musique Françoise.[5]

---

[5] The following excerpt is taken from Jean-Jacque Rousseau's *Le dictionnaire de musique.*

GENIUS. Do not seek, young artist, to know what genius is. If you have it, you sense it within yourself. If you do not have it, you will never know it. The musician's genius subjects the whole universe to his art; he paints every picture with sounds; he makes silence itself speak; he renders

Madame Louis also advised me to read *L'Emile*, the *Nouvelle Héloise,* and the *Confessions* of the same author, which, even if incongruous, are nevertheless written elegantly, nor do I regret having read them. She then suggested to me the works of Voltaire, Racine, Molière, Florian, etc., in such a way that in a short time she gave me a taste for French literature, and I continued to read it until my sight became weak and my eyes defective. The Countess de Saillant also deserves a distinguished place in my memoire. She was a sister of the Count and the Viscount Mirabeau; she lived with her husband, who was really a good-hearted grump, with the Marquis and Marquise of Aragon, her daughter, with five other daughters who were all canonesses of Maubeuge, and with her only son. The Countess was an angel of goodness, and had transfused her soul into her family, especially the Contessina Miny, my student, who was really full of talents except for her musical knowledge, who everyone agreed, and she as well, that she played the piano without fingers, and sang without a voice, nor would ever bother to practice.

At the beginning of 1790 the affairs of the National Assembly got even worse, emigration was more frequent, there was talk of a counter-revolution, and everyone thought of nothing but putting aside some gold and silver.

In the summer of that year I received various letters from some of my students and friends who had emigrated to Brussels and to Spa, who, knowing my anti-revolutionary opinions, and fearing for my security in Paris, were encouraging me to join them, sure that they would find for me enough work to pay for my trip. Things were going from bad to worse, so in the month of August I was forced to give into their suggestions. I obtained a leave of three months from the theatre, which I then renewed, and between the lessons and recitals I gave in those two places, I got on marvelously well.

Having been informed that at neither Brussels nor at Spa was there a pianist of note, I composed two sonatas that were not at all bad and that had a great impact,

---

ideas through sentiments, sentiments through accents; and the passions that he expresses – he excites them deep within hearts: pleasure, through him, takes on new charms; the sorrow that he causes to moan draws forth cries; he burns without ceasing, and is never consumed: he expresses frost and ice with heat; even in depicting the horrors of death, he brings to the soul this sentiment of life which he never abandons, and which he communicates to hearts made to feel it: but, alas, his genius is able to say nothing to those where its seed does not exist, and his marvels can scarcely be sensed by those who cannot imitate them. Do you wish, then, whether some spark of this devouring fire animates you; run, fly to Naples to hear the masterworks of Leo, Durante, Jomelli, Pergolesi. If your eyes fill with tears, if you feel your heart palpitate, if you are agitated by trembling, if you are suffocated by oppression in your transports, take Metastasio, and get to work; his genius will heat up yours, you will create after his example; this is what genius does, and other eyes will soon render you the tears that the masters have caused to be shed. But if the charms of this great art leave you unmoved, if you are neither delirious nor swept away, if you only find beautiful that which transports, do you dare to ask what genius is? Vulgar man, do not profane this sublime name. What matters it to you to know it? You will never feel it: make French music.

then two concerti, one rather weaker than otherwise and the other passable, but which were well received and particularly patronized by the indulgence of Lord Malden, now Count of Essex, and by Prince Louis of Prussia, two personages one more charming than the next, and true dilettantes of music.

Having already tasted the pleasure and the luxury of being applauded in the theatre, and finding myself in Brussels without means to carry on my career, I left that city with the greatest displeasure in the month of February 1791 and returned to Paris.

Just after arriving back, I wrote an aria, *"Belle Enée abandonate,"* for my friend C. Rovedino, who sang it for the first time at the Concert Olympique, and which was encored with the greatest applause.

This brought me the pleasure and benefit of being requested immediately to write an opera for the Théâtre de Monsieur, but knowing that two well-known composers were in negotiation to be commissioned for the same purpose, I thought it well to refuse, not desiring to compete with Zingarelli, much less with Cherubini.

I then abandoned the Teatro Italiano, leaving the imbroglio to my replacement and friend Tomeoni, determined to stay in Paris at any cost and hoping at the same time that the beginning of the revolutionary tempest would calm down in the end.

From the moment that I left Roveredo to go to Naples, I had not thought seriously about any other woman but my dear Livietta. Believing myself well-situated and able to maintain her in the way in which she was accustomed in her noble family, I wrote to her and offered again my hand, apologizing for not having been able to do it earlier. She answered that she had waited a year and more beyond what had been agreed upon, and believing that I was thinking of her no more, she regretted to have to inform me that she had already been betrothed to my cousin and friend Signor Clemente Cobelli. Since I could in no way condemn her, I took her decision in holy peace, but regretted it extremely, and it excited in me a new desire for matrimony, more violent than ever. It was not long before I took a liking for the daughter of an artist friend, whose appearance would have made you say that she was the most magnificent and modest young lady in the universe. I began to court her, and having her sing and play the pianoforte for me, and she seemed sensible to my attentions. Finally, I explained myself and asked her for a lock of her hair. She, without saying a word, took the scissors, cut a lock, and gave it to me, saying, *"Monsieur, je vous donne ceci, non point comme un gage d'amour, mais comme un gage d'Hyménée."* I took it, answering, *"Mademoiselle, je vous rends mille grâces, et je l'accepte de quelque manière que ce soit."*[6]

---

[6] "Sir, I give you this, not as a pledge of love, but as a pledge of Hymen." I take it, answering, "Mademoiselle, I thank you, and I accept it in any way it is offered.".

I immediately had the hair put in a ring, an elegant one, with her initial under the glass. I continued then to visit her every day, but my visits were no longer so well received. I complained of it to her, and she answered me that she was suffering migraine, she wasn't well, she was unhappy, etc.

I then discovered clearly that she was attracted to another, and was entirely playing with me. I immediately left her house, not without great regret, however. Some time later I went to visit certain intimate friends of mine and hers, one of whom, a woman, seeing me with the ring on my finger, said, "What! You were tricked, and left your flame, but are still wearing her hair?"

"It's true", I answered, "but she is still ever in my heart".

"And do you really believe that those are her hairs?"

"I saw her cut them myself."

"Well then, you should know that she wears a wig, and has her father spend a great deal of money to hunt for the finest hair that can be found in Paris. You should also know that she rubs her cheeks and lips with aromatic vinegar, which is full of cosmetics, and that she has three false teeth."

In hearing this I turned completely red, and more scornful than ever I took the ring from my finger and threw it to the ground. Then I crushed it into a thousand pieces with the heels of my boots, shouting, "Oh, accursed witch! To offer me as a pledge of matrimony the hair of a corpse! O you monkey, awful monkey, I detest you, I abhor you!"

\

Chapter V.

My first Opera in Paris - Second Journey to Brussels, and Return to Paris - Madame de Craon, Mamoiselle Bonne D'Alpy - Disgust at Paris - Departure from that City with Simoni -Arrival at London.

Liberated from two matrimonies, which would have caused me a great deal of trouble and perhaps entirely ruined me, considering the course of that horrible revolution, I went to see Mr. Neuville, friend, partner, and factotum of Mlle. Montansier, to get the libretto which had been offered me. He gave e three to choose from by a certain D'Hale, an Englishman; *Les Evénements imprévus, L'Amant jaloux,* and *Le Jugement de Mydas,* which had already been set to music many years before by a favorite composer in France in those days, Monsieur Grétry. I, being ignorant of the matter but informed that the three poems were equally excellent, selected the first, and wrote it with no greater difficulty than I would have set an Italian libretto, since the poetry was so sweet and musical. Having learned after the first rehearsal what was being prepared at the Thèâatre Montansier, the newspapers began to fulminate against me, calling me impudent and prideful in wanting to put to music a libretto that had already been set by Grétry. Informed of this, I went to Mr. Neuville and proposed to him that I should abandon my enterprise, not wishing to set myself up as a rival to that maestro and to bring myself into disgrace with the public. Mr. Neuville and other friends assured me that, if I did not carry on, I would lose my reputation at the finest point of my theatrical career, and that it was not the journalists nor the public who were against me, but only certain partisans of Grétry, who had put the articles in the press, which they would not have done if they had not feared a confrontation.

After having seen six performances of my opera, and even though I felt fortunate, encouraged, and flattered in that capital, nevertheless what I noted there caused me to seek a position in Brussels once more, always with the hope there would be a counter-revolution to follow.

I presented another academy there, and composed a new sonata and a new concerto, which did me great honor, but knowing that the Prussian troops were not advancing and that the army of Coblenz was not being organized, I resolved to return to France to look after my affairs and then continue to England. Towards the end of January 1792, I arrived in Paris, the city once considered the most brilliant in Europe, which then had become the least charming, and the most perplexed and insupportable.

Not many days after my arrival I had the honor and the felicity of becoming acquainted with the excellent and well-known Princess De Craon, from whom I received an infinite number of kindnesses. She had no other defect than that of not being rich; one day, talking with her of fortune and degree, she said jokingly to me, *"Mon bon petit ami, je suis princesse de l'Empire, il est vrai; mais en meme temps je suis bien a court d'argent, et sans principauté"*.[7] She was living with a protegée of hers, Mademoiselle Bonne d'Alpy, a creature with truly suave manners. She was rather small in stature: she had a fine head of hair, a lively eye, a nice little nose, pearly teeth, arms and hands of a model, and she was a little lame, which made her even more interesting. She knew Italian and English as well as she did French; she drew and painted like an angel; she played the piano so well as to make her teacher Dussek say that she was his only student. In sum, she was full of charms and graces, and so loveable and modest, as to make me forget Giuditta, Livietta, and the fake tresses.

At about that time the queen let me know through Madame Campan that I should send her everything that I had published during the last three years, and to have copies made of everything which I had in manuscript. This was the most flattering of commands for me, and which I carried out immediately. She also let me know that, as soon as the affairs of state were taken care of, she would take me as her singing master. But with affairs moving at breakneck speed, I was disappointed, a victim, as were so many others, of a revolution which put all Europe to sword, blood, and fire, and the consequences of which are still not finished.

How I regretted not being able to be in the service of such a good, liberal, charitable and obliging ruler, whose memory was dear to me after her undeserved fate. In her salon she could be seen with the majesty of an empress, the manners of a lady, and the graces of a shepherdess.

I will not speak further about her beauty, but will only say that the arms and hands of Marie Antoinette were made to put in shadow all the most beautiful ancient sculptures of the Greeks.

My situation then was truly enviable, and the more so as I did not merit it. On the point of having the Queen for my student, wealthy from the sale of my compositions, and with a liberal salary from the Montansier, what more could I desire? *J'étais dans l'embarras des richesses.* Welcomed in the households of Madame de Craon, of Madame Louis, of Madame de Saillant, and of others, *comme l'enfant de la maison,* I was happy, most happy. But then! To see those unhappy sovereigns held in prison, and treated disrespectfully by the rabble

---

[7] My good friend, I am a princess of the Empire, it is true; But at the same time I am short of money, and without estates.

in their own palace of the Tuileries, so many innocents strung up from the lampposts or with their heads on pikes, so much looting, and so many horrors already being committed in Paris irritated me so, and caused me so much anger as to cause me to expose myself to being slain myself at any moment.

Finally I decided to leave and, having taken my leave of various friends, I went to see Mr. Louis, to ask from him the favor of keeping my apartment until my return, which he courteously granted me. With a friend, Mr. Chabert, I left the care of my furniture, with a part of my linens, with many engraved plates of music, and of two hundred pounds of tobacco *della Ferma*, which I had procured at the point when the National Assembly had lifted the tariff on it, so that instead of paying six francs for it, as was usual, it cost only two francs a pound.

I then went to Madame Campan, asking her to write to me in London as soon as the Queen might honor me with her commands. *"Allez, allez, mon fils,"* she said to me, "and stay in England as long as you can."

Knowing that a certain Simoni, from Dresden, a serious tenor, was going to travel to London, having been hired to sing at Salomon's academies, I offered to be his companion, and he accepted me with pleasure, on the condition, however, that we should not travel in public coaches. I gave in to his wishes, the more so as I believed that by renting a limonière carriage, taking post-horses, and giving good tips to the postillions, we would arrive more quickly at Calais; but I was mistaken. It took four days and three nights to get there from Paris. Simoni was a young man of thirty to thirty-five, with large, sad eyes, a sorrowful face, and a misty voice. He was a good singer and a professional, but an actor who could freeze a volcano and the sun itself, and a traveling companion to make a hermit lose his patience. He carried along with him a little pharmacy; he had his pockets full of flasks of scented water, chocolate pastilles, sweets, and who knows what all. He did not want to start traveling before ten in the morning and stopped at every second or third post to take his medicine. After dining he needed to take a little nap, and as it got dark, he didn't want to continue onwards, for fear of the damp, or of having the carriage overturned. Oh God! What a trial!

Finally, on the evening of the eighth of April, 1792, we arrived at Calais. The following day, at four in the afternoon, we embarked on an English ship and at about eleven we disembarked happily at Dover, where we had a good dinner, and I had a good bed. Simoni, finding himself late, had the spirit to depart at night, in spite of every danger, with two other travelers on the seat of a post.

I wanted to go the following morning, but the public carriages were all full; I thus took a place for the evening, and in the meantime I set about behaving like an Englishman. I went into a bathing machine, a thing that I had not seen before, where, having undressed, I dove into the sea, as my bathing attendant instructed me, splashing about like a seal. I then bought a fine pair of boots, two spurs, a whip, and a hat; then I rented a horse, and having mounted it, and riding in the English style, I thought myself a Marquess of Stafford, a Duke of Portland, and almost a Prince of Wales.

I left Dover the same evening, supplied with various letters of recommendation, and with a letter of credit from my cousin Cobell with the respectable firm of Pattison, and on the eleventh, at six in the morning, I entered, happy and contented, the vast, rich, and pompous metropolis of London.

Chapter VI.
Visit to Haydn - Anecdotes of Haydn, and the Princes Esterhazy and Lobkowitz - The Duke of Queensbury Lord and Lady Hampden - Salomon's Academies - Trip to Brussels- The Archduke Carlo - The Duchess of Devonshire - Lady E. Chruchton, Miss Harvey.

Having arrived at an inn in the city, and having unloaded my baggage, I had a carriage come to take me to the house of Maestro Pozzi, to whom I had been recommended, at No. 2, Great Pultney Street. Although the street was depressing, the soot dense, and the sun showed itself like a candle at night, still I found that I was happy and full of joy, considering the dangers I had survived, avoiding the revolutionary horrors which were threatening Paris and which took place in the months of August and September of that year.

Knowing already that Haydn was in London, and that he dwelt near my lodging, I dressed quickly to pay him a visit.[1] I spoke to him in my Tyrolian German, but, having heard my name, he began to laugh, and answered me in Italian, which he spoke fluently, and in that language we continued our conversation.

---

[1] In April of 1792, Haydn had been in London about a year and a half. He had participated in two series of public concerts promoted by Salomon which featured his music, had been feted by Court and City, had given a few lessons, and had been bestowed with an honorary doctorate of music from Oxford. It had been a busy time, and Haydn had withdrawn a bit from society during the previous summer, but had pushed during the fall and winter to meet all his obligations in London. He returned to Vienna just a few months after Ferrari's visit to him.

I made him sincere compliments, such as those due to such a man, and one that I so venerated. He assured me that up until the age of thirty he had been a nothing, but that then he had had the fortune to study under Porpora; that which he knew he owed to that great master, and in part to his own effort.

I asked him what he thought of Pleyel, of Kozeluch, and of Mozart. "The first two," he said, "are most gracious composers; but the other...Ah!" he replied with an obbligato sigh, "Mozart is an eminent writer!" I asked him then to let me hear a new composition of his own, and he had the good will to favor me with his Sonata in A-flat, which pleased me extremely.

Haydn was a tranquil man, simple but witty, and not without spirit. It is quite well-known that he was protected and encouraged in his youth by the last reigning Prince Esterhazy, (grandfather of the present Austrian ambassador to England) who lived with the greatest pomp and splendor at his immense estates at Eisenstadt, Esterhazy, Tokay, and others, and where he kept at his expense an Italian opera, a chapel, and an orchestra, all most perfect. Haydn had the direction of the orchestra, and in such a way was able to make frequent and precious experiments, and to brighten the obscurity of ancient music, producing new and marvelous effects that opened the eyes of Mozart, of Beethoven, and so many other composers who followed in his footsteps. At a certain point, the prince became disgusted with the players in his orchestra and ordered Haydn to dismiss them all, with the exception of the first violin and the organist. Haydn was compelled to obey, but he regretted seeing so many people ruined, and for himself, the loss of his experiments. He then thought to compose an instrumental fugue and asked the prince to come to hear it performed on a certain Sunday after mass, and the Prince granted his request. After the connected work necessary in a real fuga, the clever maestro introduced a kind of coda with successive rests calculated to make the instruments stop playing one after the other, and ended the fugue with a unison between the first violin and the organ, tasto solo. Prince Esterhazy noted the composer's jest, and it pleased him so well that he ordered that all his performers be retained. After Haydn had written his celebrated and sublime symphonies in London, after he had been applauded as he deserved, he also had the honor of being made doctor of music at Oxford. He then left for Vienna, and a few days after his arrival there, met Prince Lobkowitz, a great patron, musical dilettante and practical expert in music. He asked Haydn why he had never written an instrumental quintet; his answer was that he had never thought doing so before getting to know the celebrated quintets of Mozart, which he had found so perfect and sublime that he had no desire to enter into competition by writing one himself. "It doesn't matter," added the Prince, "write three for me, and I will remunerate you as much as possible." The brilliant master set to work, and sometime thereafter he brought his manuscript to the prince. The prince looked at the first page and found a score with five lines, four filled in and one empty. He believed for a moment that Haydn had begun the quintet in four parts, with the fifth part to come in later, as is sometimes done; but no - paging through the whole manuscript, he continued to find the empty line. Then he turned to the composer and said to him, "But, dear Haydn, have you forgotten the fifth part?" Haydn answered," No, *Signor Principe*, I have left it for Your Serene Highness to fill in, because I couldn't find it."

From Haydn I went to visit Mrs. Hyde Clarke, who I had met in Paris, and who welcomed me with open arms. She was living with her two sons, George and Edward, and with her niece Miss Georgina de Meyer, later Mrs. O'Moran. After a few words, she wrote a little letter to her friend the Duke of Queensbury, fervently recommending me to him and advising me to go there immediately, which I did. He had just dismounted from his horse, completely soaked, as he had been surprised by the rain. He read the letter and signaled to me to follow him into a room where there was a piano, but rather than wanting to hear my music, he asked me to sit down at the instrument to accompany his, which he sang while a servant took off his soaked boots, assisted by another to help put on a pair of dry ones. I saw immediately that he was a fanatic for music, and with what kind of original person I was dealing, nor did I pay any attention to his extraordinary manners.

He sang me various of his ariettas, which all ended with the cadence of "God Save the King," and offered to give me lessons, asserting that Sapio and many others had thus made their reputations and that, without doing so, I would never have the least success in the country. I thanked him properly and told him without ceremony that I had come to London to teach and compose, not to learn. "Do what you like," he added, ringing the bell, "and greet Mrs. Clarke for me."

From there I took two recommendations with which the Marques Circello had favored me, one for His Excellence the Count Woronzow, minister plenipotentiary of Russia, the other for His Excellence the Prince of Castelcicala, ambassador from Naples. They both welcomed me with the greatest cordiality, nor do I have words enough to count the infinity of courtesies and honors I was to receive from these two illustrious personages.

I dined that same day with Mrs. Clarke, and in the evening she took me with her niece to make music for His Excellency the Marques del Campo, Ambassador from Spain, where Miss Georgina distinguished herself with her beautiful voice, doing honor to my music that she sang there. Such a circumstance made me known immediately, and it did not take me long to find students.

In the course of a few days I had the pleasure of finding my friends T. Attwood, J.B. Cramer, Dussek, Sapio, etc.. Having been introduced at D. Corri's house, I became friends with the most eminent professionals of the metropolis. P. Salomon was one of these, and he courteously offered me free admission to his academies, during some of which a scena ed aria I had written for Simoni was performed, which he sang with great success and which brought me much honor. In the middle of June, a period during which the crowd in London used to leave the city to go to the country, I was invited to go to Bromham, one of the estates of the last Viscount Hampden. My duty was to sit at the piano every day after lunch and after dinner to accompany Lord Hampden, who played the flute and who was so transported by the music of Handel that he was happy to hear it played simply by himself and myself, that is, by flute and piano alone. That annoyed me a little, but our playing did not last long, because the viscount got tired quickly and fell asleep. The flute fell to his knees without him noticing, and I then went out with a shotgun to shoot birds.

There I wrote three concertante trios for piano, violin and violoncello, op. XI, six canons for three voices, *La Partenza* by Metastasio for four voices, and twelve Italian arias that more or less pleased. I gave some lessons to Lady Hampden, a most accomplished woman, who treated me with the greatest liberality and courtesy.

I stayed two entire months at Bromham, and I enjoyed myself a great deal, now hunting, now fishing, now composing.

On returning to London I made the acquaintance of His Excellency Cavalier Pisani, ambassador from Venice to the court of France, who had fled to England with his son and daughter, to whom I had the honor of teaching music.

I was then introduced to Her Highness the Margrave of Anspach, both to give lessons and to be present at her little academies and the operettas she gave in the theater at Brandenburg House. I spent the winter, the following spring, and the summer in London, but in September 1793 I made a trip to Brussels to see my Parisian students and friends once more, and to follow the victorious (at that time) armies of the English and Austrians, who it was thought would take Paris, but we were all cruelly disappointed.

And yet a counter-revolution by the French was expected, and for this reason I stayed six weeks in that most gracious city. I gave lessons to my Parisian students, as well as to some from Brussels, among them the daughter of the Duchess d'Ursel, the daughter of the Countess Delapenois, Madame Basen, and the Countess Paolina Metternich, sister of the present prince, from whose family I received the greatest honors.

I also gave an academy, for which I wrote a new piano concerto and a sonata in C, which caused a sensation. The protection of H.R.H. Archduke Carlo drew a crowd of nobility and respectable persons to the concert, and in the morning he sent me twenty-five *louis d'or* for his ticket. I went immediately to his palace to thank him; having been introduced into his apartments, I found him in a small chamber, playing the piano. He immediately got up and welcomed me in the most charming way. I asked him to continue, and he said to me that he was not anxious to be heard in my presence. I sought to encourage him, but it was fruitless. I left him then, offering him the sonata that he had applauded so the evening before, and which he accepted with courtesy and pleasure. (If that brave prince was afraid to play the piano in my presence, he nevertheless had the courage to strike against the armies of Napoleon, and who knows what marvels he might have achieved in that career, had his health not prevented him.)

During my stay in Brussels at that time, I frequently entertained myself by playing billiards with Carlo Rovedino, Amantini (a musician of the Royal Chapel of Louis XVI), and with Noverre, the late renowned composer of ballet, for all three were waiting, as was I, the moment to return to Paris.

One day there was a fight between Amantini and myself; he lied to me, and I said some words to him that offended him. The next morning he sent me a little letter, challenging me to a duel with pistols at the *Allée verte*, a small distance from the city. I, having never shot a pistol in my life, and having been informed of my enemy's skill, was so frightened that it still makes me shake when I think about it. But in order not to seem a coward, I answered him that, as he had been the first to cause offense, I should have the choice of arms, and that if he wished to duel with swords, I would be ready to meet him at the *Allée verte* at whatever hour was convenient for him. But while I was writing, Rovedino, who was with me at home, having learned about the affair, went to Noverre, and with him to Amantini, to make peace. Whether the valiant musician was scared of my blade, or whether our mutual friends had persuaded him that we were both wrong, the affair was resolved *alla* Rafanelli and Mandini by means of a dinner which we were to give to the mediators; but the expense fell entirely on me, as Amantini did not have a penny in his wallet at that point.

Tired of waiting for the counter-revolution, and informed by my friends that my students had returned from the countryside, I decided to return to England. But a few days before my departure, I was invited to a small academy in the house of the Viscountess of Vaudreuil, where I had the honor and the advantage of meeting the Countess of Kermanguy, the Prince of Ligne, the Prince Victor of Rohan, along with the charming Count, now Prince, Diedrichstein, Lady E. Foster, and the Duchess of Devonshire.[2] This last lady

---

[2] Here Ferrari is of course referring to influential and infamous Georgiana Cavendish, Duchess of Devonshire (née Spencer, 1757 – 1806) who became an important patron for Ferrari, employing him as a teacher for her daughters, including him in house parties, and introducing him to other patrons. Her life is a fascinating one, both private and public. By the time Ferrari met her, she had returned from exile in France where she had given birth to an illegitimate child from her

asked me to let her hear some composition of mine, and I sang for her a French romance and an Italian arietta, the texts of which I have the honor of presenting to the reader, in the hope that it will please.

ROMANCE
Pour aimer j'ai reçu la vie,
Et je n'y tiens pour que aimer:
Mon bien est le coeur de Zélie,
Tout autre bien m'est étranger.
De la tendresse,
De son ivresse,
Par toi j'ai goûté les douceurs;
Et de la vie,
Par toi j'oublie
Et les chagrins et les malheurs.
2nd Couplet.
Si quelquefois de ma paupière
L'amour a fait couler des pleurs,
Souvent aussi dans ma carrière
L'amour a répandu des fleurs.
C'est la tendresse,
C'est son ivresse,
Qui toujours consola mon coeur:
Sans ma Zélie
Toute ma vie
J'aurais ignoré le bonheur.
                              Par Monsieur Rivière de St. Charles

(Romance
To love I received life,
And I do not want to love:
My good is the heart of Zélie,
All other good is foreign to me.
Of the tenderness
Of its inebriation
Through you I have tasted the sweets;
And through you

---

relationship with Charles Grey. Many pointed to a change in the Duchess, and she seemed to be quieter and more settled until her death in 1806. Ferrari does mention Elizabeth Foster without alluding to the famous ménage-à-trois between the two women and the Duke, in which the three shared a house, the duke marrying Foster after Georgiana's death. For more, see Amanda Foreman's Georgiana: Duchess of Devonshire (New York: Random House, 1999).

I forget
The distresses and woes.

If sometimes love has
Made tears fall from my eyes.
Also, in my career,
Love has often strewn flowers.
It is tenderness,
It is its inebriation
Which always consoled my heart.:
Without my Zélie
For my whole life
I would not have known happiness.)

Arietta
In making a bouquet
Of beautiful rose,
Among them I include
Hidden Love.
I take him by the wings
Which he has on his back,
And immerse that betrayer
In wine.
2da Strofa.
In vain the tyrant
Shakes his feathers,
For I drown him
In good liquor.
And thus it happens
That at every moment I feel
A pleasing and new
Trembling in my heart.[3]
        Anacreon. Translation by De Rogati..

(Arietta
Nel fare un serto
Di, rose belle,
Colgo fra quelle
Nascosto Amor.
Per l'ali il prendo,

---

[3] This text seems to imply that Ferrari had to hand a volume of Francesco Saverio de Rogati's *Le odi di Anacreonte e di Saffo recate in versi italiani.*

Ch'ei porta al tergo,
Nel vino immergo
Quel traditor.
In an le poiume
Scuote il tiranno;
Poi lo tracanno
Nel buon liquor.
Per questo avviene
Ch'ognora io provo
Un grato, un nuovo
Palpito al cor.)

After my music had been performed, I saw with pleasure that the whole company was impressed by me, and the Duchess of Devonshire did me the honor of offering her daughters to me as students as soon as I might return to London, and everyone may think that I did not delay a moment in accepting such a courteous offer. I left my friends in Brussels towards the end of October. I stayed a day in Ghent to walk about that most spacious and depopulated city. (Under the rule of Maria Teresa, it happened that Prince Kaunitz, her minister of state, presented her with the map of Paris, asking her to note the immense extent of that capital. The empress did not lose her composure at all and had the map of her city of Ghent brought, much larger in extent than Paris at the time. She showed it to Kaunitz, saying: *"Mon cher prince! Vous êtes si étonné par l'etendue de la grande metropole de la France! Mais ne voyez vous pas que je peux mettre Paris dans mon Gan..d."* (My dear prince! You are so astonished by the extent of the great metropolis of France! But do not you see that I can put Paris in my Ghent?)

I then went on to Bruges, embarked at Ostend, and on the first of November found myself once more safe and sound in London. And although I was still not accustomed to the climate, the way of life, and to the English customs, yet all in all, I was satisfied with my situation.

Not long after my arrival, I was called to Devonshire House to give lessons to Miss St. Jules, the present Mrs. G. Lamb, who had a graceful little voice, and who later became a pleasing singer. Then I did the same with Lady G. Cavendish, now Countess Carlisle, and with her sister Lady H. Cavendish, now Viscountess Granville. These two did not have much in the way of voices, yet their taste for singing and the care that they took in their studies meant that they came to be able to sing pleasingly anything at sight.

As soon as I was introduced to that splendid family, Lady E. Foster, intimate friend of the Duchess with whom she lived, arranged for me to have two of her nieces as students, Lady Carolina Chrighton (the present Lady

Wharnecliff) and Miss Harvey, who married Mr. C. Ellis (the present Lord Seaford), who brought me great honor and advantage. At that time I saw a great deal of Domenico Corri and Dussek, through whom I made the important acquaintance of Muzio Clementi. He took an immediate liking for me, and I for him. He often favored me by taking lunch with me, and on this pretext he had me perform his sonatas, and severely criticized my compositions, but always justly and in a friendly way. When I was going well, he said bravo; when I did poorly, he gave me the nice title of "idiot!" His conversation was instructive and interesting to the greatest degree, nor will I ever forget the infinite debt of gratitude I owe to that great man.

Fig. 11. Portrait of Muzio Clementi by Thomas Hardy

Chapter VII.

My first opera in London. - Journey to Roveredo, Vienna, etc. - The Bishop of Derry. - The Princess of Wales. - My second opera. - Travel to Chatsworth, and brief description of the residence of the Duke of Devonshire there.

I continued to give lessons for a number of years, and to write chamber music, both vocal and instrumental, as well as some arias for the Italian theater: Deh se pietà ritrova for Morichelli, Io son capricciosetto for Viganoni, etc. In 1799 I wrote an intermezzo for four voices in one act - I Duè Svizzeri - that was so successful that it was performed for many years running, and its terzetto, "Vieni o sonno" is still not forgotten. Banti, Viganoni, Carlo Rovedino, and Morelli performed the intermezzo perfectly.

Happy with the number of my students and the success of my publications, I treated myself that summer to a trip to Roveredo.

I embarked at Yarmouth for Hamburg. From there, having crossed the Elbe, I went by coach via Frankfurt, August, Innsbruck, Bressanone, Bolzano, and finally to Roveredo.

I remained there only ten days, which seemed as if they were but ten seconds. All my friends were astounded that I could enjoy such a humble spot after having resided for so many years in Naples, Paris, and London! I made them laugh by saying that I would exchange those three capitals together for the San Colombano Bridge, for the seven Albi, and for the rugged mountains of the area, of which I have already spoken in my first chapter.

Further, I was asked if I might know Lord Bristol, Bishop of Derry, and father of the present marquess. I was informed that some years before he had spent a lot of time in Roveredo, where he was an intimate of the families of the noble Fedrigotti and Rosmini. He had lived splendidly during his stay there, and I was told also that he was admired and respected by the inhabitants. He was a great connoisseur of the fine arts, and he had spent a lot of money on making a collection of the most beautiful specimens of marble to be found in the mountains around the city, for which reason he had had some blasting done, and had selected a sufficient quantity of the most exquisite kinds to make a hundred and twenty colossal columns, which he had sculpted with their respective capitals and pedestals. He collected other works of art to the tune of a hundred thousand pounds sterling. Although I had not had the honor of knowing him personally, yet having taught in his family and knowing many of his relatives, I was able to inform my friends that six of the above-mentioned columns that had been sent by him to England, fearing the first incursion of the French in Italy in 1796, had been stopped by customs officials and sold at auction at the customs-house in London, and that the Duke of Richmond had acquired them. All the rest had been taken by the French, who permitted the noble Lord to ransom them with the other works for the sum of ten thousand pounds sterling. A week later they were taken back by the French, and they put His Excellency in prison in Milan, from whence he was able to escape and return to England a few days later.

I found two of my brothers still living, as well as my step-mother, who was happy to have found a good match for her Catterinetta. I spent many pleasant hours with my cousin Cobelli and his Livietta, with whom he was living very happily.

Before leaving Roveredo, I gave my brother the priest the task of buying me a small estate, called the Castle of Lizzana, at a small distance from the city, which he did in a hurry, to my misfortune.

I left my native land and my old friends with the greatest regret and went to Verona, where I saw the victorious army of General Clairfait and the French garrison, which had come as prisoners from Mantua.

From Verona, I continued on to Venice, and from there to Vienna, in order to see my close friend Bridi once more and to see a production of my Due Svizzeri, which was well-received there as well.

From Vienna, I traversed Bohemia, Saxony, etc. and embarked at Hamburg, and after a stormy voyage of twelve days, I was happy to set foot on dry land at Yarmouth on the first of October, and to establish myself for the third time in the great metropolis. I presented myself immediately to the Marquess Circello, who had succeeded the Prince of Castelcicala; he welcomed me as usual, and introduced me to Baron Jacobi, the Prussian minister, and to Count Staremberg (now Prince), Austrian Ambassador Extraordinare, by which, and especially by the last, I was honored and favored in a thousand ways. I then became acquainted with Monsieur Gautherot, a piano teacher. He was a singular man, honest, obliging, and flippant. He had a whole book of anecdotes in his head, and would tell them in a way so succinct as to please anyone. Here are a few of them.

René Onvell, a Flemish wig-maker in London, upon being informed that a customer (Mr. Dizi, a celebrated composer and performer on the harp) was to leave for Brussels, asked him to take with him a letter for his sister and to bring him back the answer. The favor was granted, and the correspondence follows.

Fig. 12. Portrait of Georgiana Cavendish, Duchess of Devonshire by Thomas Gainsborough

"A ma seur[1]

Ma seur de Liège

Très connue sur la place publique de Bruesell.

Ma très cher seur de Liège!

Il y a deux seecle que je n'et entendu de toi. Si tu ai morte, laiss moi savoir comen tu te porte. Quant à moi, je suis toujour avec mes pauvre yeux en compote, et avec mes miserable jambe en fricassè, avec lesquels je suis.

Ton affectionè fraire de Londre"

The answer:

"A mon fraire.

Mon fraire de Londre, Coifeur eminant à

Londres.

Mon très cher fraire de Londre! En Angleterre,

J'avons reçu ta laitre qui ma fai gran plèsir, apprenant la fortitude et la duré de tes jambe et de tes yeux; et je me hate avec lenteur à repondre, pour te dire que notre maire se porte à merveill, et notre pair travail comme un chien. Seure d'Anvers vienn c'accoucher de deux garçons male, et se porte là là. Je t'embrass mon cher fraire de Londre, et je me cigne,

Ta affectioné seur de Liège.

P.S. Ta maire t'envoat deux pair de vieux draps, pour te faire six chemises neuve; et tu trouvera dans le mem paget deux louidor, que ton paire t'envoat à mon insue."

("To my sister.

My sister from Liège

Very well known in the public square in

Brussels.

My very dear sister from Liège!

It has been two centuries since I heard from you. If you are dead, let me know how you are doing. With respect to me, I am always with my poor eyes in compote, and my miserable legs in fricassé, with which I am

Your affectionate brother from London.")

---

[1] All of the misspellings in this section are original! [Translator's note: all the above is written in execrable French]

"To my brother.

My brother from London, eminent coiffeur in London.

My very dear brother from London, in England,

I received your letter which gives me great pleasure, hearing about the strength and hardness of your legs and eyes; and I hasten with slowness to respond, to tell you that our mother is marvelously well, and our father works like a dog. Sister from Antwerp has just been delivered of two boys, and is doing so so. I embrace my dear brother from London, and sign myself,

Your affectionate sister from Liège.

P.S. Your mother sends two pairs of old curtains to make you six new chemises; and you will find in the same packet two louis d'or, which your rather is sending you without my knowledge.)

Another:

One year on the 24th of December, that is, Christmas Eve, an inhabitant of a village was at the window of his house. It was numbingly cold, and he had not gotten dressed and had neither a collar nor a cap on his head. A friend of his, passing by, saw him and called out, "Pietro, what are you doing there?"

"I am catching a cold."

"What for?"

"So that I can sing bass tonight at the midnight mass".

And another:

There was a wealthy man in a country house, and not being able to attend to all his properties, he rented some to an agent. The agent began to build a house opposite to that of the landowner. The landowner was opposed to it and went immediately to a friend of his who was a lawyer and lived in the nearby village to prevent it. The lawyer read the plaintiff's documents, and then wrote a letter, which he gave to him, saying, "Give what is written here to your tenant, and you can be certain that he will stop building." The wealthy man thanked him and asked him what he owed him. "Oh", said the lawyer, "for my trouble, send me some peaches from your garden, and I will be content."

Early the next morning, the owner himself picked a dozen of the nicest peaches, put them in a basket, and sent them and a letter of thanks with his own gardener. The messenger, having entered the lawyer's house, was confronted by a woman who was as ugly as sin, and whose face looked more like that of a monkey than that of a woman. Having been told what the gardener was bearing, she made him go into the parlor, asked him to put the basket on a little table, and went with the little letter to her husband, ordering the serving-girl to give the man something to eat. In the meantime, two monkeys, who were the woman's pets, came from the courtyard into the parlor, as they had smelled the fruit. They were dressed in jackets and scarlet pantaloons, as well as green caps with feathers. They jumped up on the little table, and in a few moments they made the peaches disappear and ran off. The master of the house came down in haste, thanked the gardener for his employer's courteous letter, and asked where the peaches were. The gardener, who had never seen a monkey before, answered, "Oh, dear sir! Your sons have eaten them! What dear creatures! How they enjoyed them!"

At the beginning of the year 1800, I was hired to teach at one of the most respectable and largest schools in London. I immediately had fourteen young ladies to instruct, twice a week, and at an extraordinary price for the time. At the end of the first semester, the mistress of the establishment asked me if I thought I would be able to train some good singers from among my students. I answered that if I were able to make all those voices emanate from a single pipe, all of them put together would not produce a voice that would satisfy me. That was enough to make her seek out and hire another teacher, who made her believe that each of the students had a voice more than strong enough for the needs of a little woman.

If I had been less sincere, or more politic, I would have earned a lot of money at that school, as I did in so many others!

In the month of September of the same year I was selected as singing teacher for Her Royal Highness the Princess of Wales, and for five and a half years running, with few interruptions, I had the honor of giving her lessons twice a week at her residence, Montague House, in Blackheath.

Not long after, I was invited to teach at the respectable school of Mrs. Durand, now Mrs. Chalklen, at Bromley, in Kent. It was very convenient for me to accept this, since from Blackheath I would go to Bromley, and would have the opportunity of sleeping once or twice a week outside of sooty London. That little spot soon became the rival of my native city in my affections, but one needs to live there for some time and to walk around the vicinity, in order to take in the quantity and variety of views and pleasing ambles that can be found there. The institution of the College of Bromley, intended for forty widows of the clergy, is admirable; each of them is afforded a pension of about thirty-five pounds sterling per year, with a little separate house free of taxes, and which contains two good rooms, a little extra room, a kitchen, and a pantry.

Although the college may not have been constructed with pomp, yet it was embellished with a spacious entrance, with fields surrounding it, and with three rows of superb trees of enormous circumference and height, which served as refuge and nesting place for hundreds of crows.

In the spring of 1801 I wrote an opera in two acts, *Rinaldo d'Asti*, which Banti had asked from me so that it could be premiered for his benefit. He seemed to be enamored of my music, but, in spite of that, having had been invited by Billington to sing Nasolini's *Mitridate* with her, he accepted the invitation, hoping to earn more, treating my work as if it were nothing. Offended by such disgusting and cruel behavior, I had my opera sung by Vinci, without taking account that a suit made for a giant would not look well on a dwarf. *Rinaldo* was only performed three times, and I remained a victim of Banti's avarice and thoughtlessness.

The following autumn I received a courteous invitation from the Duchess of Devonshire to spend some weeks at Chatsworth, where she was staying in the countryside with her consort and family.

The residence of the Duke of Devonshire at Chatsworth is on a grand scale.[2] The palace is magnificent. At the entrance there is an extensive square courtyard with gates surrounding it, containing great chambers here, a riding school there. On the first floor there are various richly-furnished salons, a billiard room, a library, a dining room that can accommodate more than three hundred persons at table, bedrooms for the masters, etc.

On the second floor there are sixty bedrooms for visitors. Outside the palace, there are workshops, stables, and sheds in quantity.

Crossing the vast land holdings of the noble Duke, one finds at every stopping place fields with wildflowers, dense thickets, hills, little streams and limpid brooks, ponds, and other rural beauties to fill those who see them with joy and wonderment. The orchards and gardens around the palace, the artificial waterfalls, and the fountains are kept in the best order, without thought for expense.

The Duke's table was served in the most splendid manner and in the greatest profusion. There were always many visitors, and when he was in residence at Chatsworth, he gave a public banquet every week for the wealthy of the area and his principal agents and tenants, and even if he was shy and a

---

[2] Obviously the long stays at Chatsworth House were one of the high points of Ferrari's life in Britain. Chatsworth had belonged to the Cavendish family since the 1500s, and by the late 1700s, the house, which is in Derbyshire on the River Derwent, had reached epoch proportions under the rebuilding program of the fifth duke's father. It was set in an extended landscape designed by "Capability" Brown, and contained important collections of art, books, and other artefacts acquired by the Dukes of Devonshire. The setting would have been augmented by the people Ferrari would have encountered in the house, surrounding the Duke and especially the Duchess, in their roles as important society leaders and patrons of the arts.

Fig. 13. Chatsworth House around 1800

man of few words, yet he approached them with affability and candor, as if they had been his brothers.

In the pantries and wine-cellars one would often see a number of peasants merrily eating and drinking to the health of the master of the house, and the good that he did, and which the illustrious family continues to do, even after the death of that lord, in that county, is something too well-known to need my praise.

I stayed for six weeks in that most delicious locale and was treated with the greatest courtesy by everyone. There I wrote three English ariettas, six Italian duettini, and ten canons for three voices, etc.

A few minutes before I was to leave Chatsworth, the charming duchess showered me with gifts and ordered that a pannier of game should be put in my two-wheeled cart, along with three pineapples, each of which was nearly as big as my head!

The charm of the Duchess of Devonshire was known in every part of Europe. In spite of this, I cannot omit a little anecdote, which proves her tact and nimbleness of spirit.

I had a brown poodle named Lambo, who was quite dear to me and who I took with me everywhere; thus he was also my companion at Chatsworth.

One day while I was walking with him in the gardens I met the Duchess, who, in seeing my dog, exclaimed, "Oh, what a monster! Whose is it?"

"Excellence, this is my faithful poodle."

"Your poodle! What a beauty!"

Chapter VIII.

Return to London - Trip to Goodwood, from the Duke of Richmond - Incidents that happened to me there - Fox Hunt- Poetry of Petrarch.

After having passed a joyful autumn in a pleasant countryside, in a residence fit for a king and in the lap of the most charming and distinguished society, it will not be thought extraordinary if I say that in leaving my heart was oppressed by melancholy.

Leaving, moreover, the picturesque views of Matlock, the opulent plains of Leicester, and crossing the superb estates of the Duke of Bedford at Woburn, to then spend the winter in the dark and smoky city of London perturbed my mind and caused me disgust.

But by fortune, not many days after my arrival, the Duke of Richmond proposed that I spend some time at his elegant and admirable abode at Goodwood, giving lessons to various young ladies and his friends, and to make a little music in the evening, etc.[1]

I promised to go, and I kept my word. But several times I was on the point of ruing having made such a commitment, by reason of the extraordinary incidents that happened to me there.

I left London with my faithful Lambo, in the Chichester stagecoach, on the morning of the fourth of January, 1802, and arrived at Chichester at six in the evening, where I found one of the Duke of Richmond's carriages ready to take me to Goodwood, and before seven I was already at the house.

---

[1] This would have been Field Marshal Charles Lennox, the 3rd Duke of Richmond (1735 – 1806). After an extraordinary life in the military and as a Whig politician, the duke retired to his estate at Goodwood. Despite his active political life, he was throughout his life a keen patron of the arts and music, particularly of painters such as George Stubbs, Joshua Reynolds, and George Romney. The Duke died soon after Ferrari's visit, and, the title passed to a nephew. Goodwood House is in Westhampnett, West Sussex.

His Excellency had already finished dining, and he ordered a little supper for me in his library.

As soon as I had finished a bit of the first course, the servant who had the care of me asked me what sort of beer I would like to have. I, not knowing the flavor of the small beer, nor the potency of the strong beer that the great English lords are accustomed to having in their country houses, asked him for strong beer. He, lacking sense and sensitivity, poured me two great big beakers full in the course of the meal, which I drank, and which, together with a few little glasses of wine which I took during and after the meal, produced the effect that everyone can imagine, though fortunately, only a few hours later.

About eight, I was invited to take tea and coffee with the duke, and with his most noble and most charming company. Then various pieces of music followed, and when I saw that there was no longer need of me, and believing myself tired from the trip, I asked permission to retire. The bell was immediately rung and a servant summoned who might convey me to my assigned sleeping quarters, and I left the hall as tranquil and sober as I am now.

From the change of scene, and in climbing the stairs, I felt that my legs were heavy, and my head in confusion.

Having arrived, and remaining alone in my bedchamber, I got undressed quickly and put on a small table the candlestick, my watch, my box of tobacco and my handkerchief. I then lay down according to my custom with a book in hand, but how much I read that night, I could not say with any certainty.

Waking in the morning, and seeing myself in such a large bed and in such a large chamber, I did not know what had become of me, nor remembered anything at all.

Little by little it came back to me; I looked at the clock, which showed ten o'clock. This was something very unusual for me, as I never stay in bed later than six or seven o'clock. I saw then that the candle was consumed, my tobacco-box burned on one corner, and when I went to pick up my handkerchief, my hand was full of ashes, and beneath another pile of ashes a rather deep hole, made perhaps by the wick of the candle or by the handkerchief having consumed itself slowly. I got dressed hurriedly and arranged to have a maid come up to my room. She came, I told her my problem, asking her to speak neither to the Duke nor to anyone else about it, and she promised.

The week was not out when there was another imbroglio.

One morning there was a knock at the door of my room, and the Duke of Richmond came in. He approached me with a rather sad face and told me that he regretted having to give me bad news. I immediately thought that he had learned what had happened to me on the evening of my arrival at Goodwood, but, no. "You know," he said, "of my passion for dogs, and it gives me great sadness to inform you that your Lambo has come down with a contagious illness, and fearing that he might give it to my hunting dogs as well, I came to propose to you that he should be put in a little stable where he will get on well, and my head hunter will look after him, and certainly cure him." I thanked him for his extreme solicitude and let him know, as much as it was possible, how much I regretted having brought him there. "Oh," added the good Duke, "I know the sagacity of poodles, nor am I surprised that you always bring him with you." He affably shook my hand and went on his way joking.

When I was along I began to think to myself, saying, "Poor duke! If you knew that in addition to the danger of contagion in your kennel, you had also, through my fault, the danger of seeing your house in flames, I don't think you would treat me so kindly."

The setting and the park of Goodwood are two quite singular things, and worthy of being seen and admired by anyone. The hills have plentiful thickets full of evergreen trees, so well-arranged and cultivated that they seem like miniatures. There are an infinite number of little fields, cultivated and leveled with such care that they enchant you, and in crossing them you would think that you were walking on moss. From various heights in the park, you can see one end of the Isle of Wight, which is not far off, and the great arm of the sea that divides it from the county of Hampshire, offering most enchanting and varied prospects.

Fox hunting is conducted with great pomp in the region.

The land and the plantings seem to be designed for such an entertainment, and there is a great abundance of foxes there. The duke keeps various packs of selected hounds in his vast kennel, raised with the greatest care and trained by his expert huntsmen. He also has a great number of robust and superb thoroughbred horses.

One day I asked of my charming host the favor of seeing such a spectacle, and he, without any hesitation, offered me the use of one of his steeds. I thanked him, yet turned down his offer at the same time, making the excuse that even if I were apt at riding, I would not have the nerve to make my horse leap over ditches, embankments, and hedges, for fear of breaking my neck, but if he would arrange a donkey for me, I would be happy with that, so that I could see what I wanted.

And so it happened.

The huntsman pointed out to me a spot where he thought the hunters would have to pass by. I got there in time and experienced a pleasure I would never have expected.

I put myself, with my patient companion, at the corner of a grove, and a half hour after my arrival I heard from far off the baying of the dogs, and the hoofbeats of the horses, which produced in me a new and pleasing sensation, and which made the ears of my little beast perk up.

It did not take long before the crafty fox passed, its mouth open and foaming, chased by the impetuous hounds, the swift steeds, and the horsemen who were anxious and determined to catch up with it and strike it.

At that moment I was beside myself: one after the other I felt courage, fear, shivers, and I could barely catch my breath!

My little donkey, who until that point had been docile, began to bray, buck, and kick so hard that he finally threw me from my saddle and, seeing me on the ground, he seemed to enjoy my overthrow. He kicked a few more times, and went off at a gallop to his stable, leaving me there like an idiot.

Luckily the greenery where I fell was so thick and soft that I was not hurt.

I went back to the house on my own two legs, and coming upon the duke, he asked me how I had liked the hunt. I answered him that I thought it was the most beautiful and most seductive spectacle that I had ever seen in my life, but was too ashamed to tell him of my catastrophe with the donkey.

Goodwood *tout ensemble* pleased me greatly, and so inflamed my fancy that I composed a quantity of music there, including six Italian ariettas, twelve canons for three voices, and three pieces on poems by Petrarch, brought together in a single cantata, the words of which are found at the end of this chapter.

On the eve of my return, the Duke of Richmond graciously offered to have me taken by one of his carriages to the gate of the park, which faces on the highway to London, in order to put me on one of the stagecoaches which pass by at six in the morning, rather than put me to the trouble of going from the part of the estate opposite Chichester and thus travel five or six miles for naught.

I profited by his courtesy without being able to foresee what would happen to me. I got into the carriage on the ninth of February at five in the morning, conducted by the lord's coachman, and accompanied by a boy on horseback, with a lighted lantern in his hand.

It was still dark; a stormy wind, and snow, and hoar-frost was falling in flakes.

Upon crossing the first barrier the light went out, and one could not see a thing. The young man was no good for anything except for opening the other gates. Nevertheless, with the help and instinct of the horses, we arrived a short distance from the final gate. There the coachman lost his way; he wanted the horses to go to the left, and they wanted to go to the right. From the continuous bumps, I felt I realized that we had gone off the road, and had gone into a copse full of thorns, close to a very steep drop. I quickly put down the windows of the carriage and grabbed the side straps to hang on were we to turn over.

In fact, it was less than a minute before we crashed, but fortunately we fell onto some tree trunks that prevented us from sliding to the bottom. Knowing that nearby there was a barrack with soldiers from the Duke's regiment, we called for help, and in a few minutes a number of them arrived with torches and brought us every possible assistance. The coachman had various contusions, one horse was slightly injured, and the carriage quite dented. My Lambo and I did not suffer any injuries and were precisely on time to jump into the stagecoach.

> Cantata
> Selection from the verses and words of the Canzoniere of Petrarch.
>
> Through the inhospitable woods
> That the sun scarcely penetrates,
> I am accustomed to break the silence
> With the sound of my lyre,
> Expressing my bitter sorrow.
> Laura already seems to gaze at me,
> And nymphs with her:
> Then I awake from sleep,
> And only bushes and flowers
> See my eyes.
> Her angelic words
> I seem to hear then,
> But it is the slowly murmuring river
> Or the turtle dove which laments
> The dying day!
> Yet, if vain images
> Are so close to the truth,
> May love grant that I end
> My life's entire course
> By dreaming ever thus.
> Valley, which still is full
> Of my sorrowful lays;
> River, which goes swollen
> With my weeping to the sea:
> Air, still worm and serene
> With my sights;
> Here where love leads
> I come to be restored.
> Alas! I still know
> Your usual shape

But how God has changed
My felicity!
She, through which
This hermit shore pleased me,
Has past the stream of Lethe,
And will not return.
I do not find peace,
I do not how to make war,
Ardor melts me,
The ice which imprisons me
Holds me tight;
It does not want me to be vanquished
And does not giv e me
My liberty.
Without eyes I see,
I am weak, and shout
I ask for help,
I want to die.
Adored deity,
See now
In what state
I am for you! ²

CANTATA

Scelta da versi e voci del canzoniere del Petrarca

Per mezzo I boschi inospiti
Che apena il sol penetra,
Soglio il silenzio rompere
Co suon della mia cetra,
Sfogando il rio dolor.
Laura mirar già sembrami,
E Ninfe insiem con lei:
Poscia del sonno scuotomi
E veggon gli occhi miei
Solo arboscelli e fior,
Le sue parole angeliche
Parmi sentir talora,
Ma è il rio che lento mormora,
O il tortore che plora
Il moribondo dì!
Eppur se van immagini

---

² Beginning with the opening lines from Sonnet 143, this text is a collage of lines from several Petrarch sonnets, such as Sonnets 19 and 260, as well as newly-written poetry to link them together.

Son così presso al vero:
Concedi amor ch'io termini
....
Sognando ognor così,
Valle, che ancor sei piena
De' miei dolente lai:
Fiume, che gonfio vai
Con il mio pianto al mar
Aria, dei miei sospiri
Ancor calda e serena:
Qui dove amor ne mena
Mi vengo a ristorar.
Lasso! Conosco ancora
Invoi la forma usata,
Ma com'è oh Dio cangiata
La mia felicità!
Quella per cui mi piacque
Questa romita sponda,
Di Lete passò l'onda
E più non tornerà.
Non trovo pace,
No so far Guerra,
L'ardor mi sface,
Mi serra il gel.
Chi m'imprigiona
Non mi vuol vinto,
E non mi dona
La libertà.
Senz'occhi vedo,
Son fioco e grido,
Aita Chiedo,
Vorrei morir.
Nume adorato,
Comprendi adesso
In quale stat
Son io per te!

Chapter IX.

Journey to Paris. - Paisiello,[3] Viganoni, and M. Kelly. - Anecdote about Bonaparte and Cherubini. - Complete transformation in Paris.

In the month of July, I made a little trip to Paris, as much to recover what I had left there as for the consolation of seeing my good Paisiello once again, who was there writing his most beautiful, but ill-fated, *Proserpine*. As soon as I had arrived in the city, I went to Mr. Louis and had the displeasure of hearing that he was dead. Madame Louis was living in the country with her daughter, who had already been married for some years to a Monsieur de Corny. I went immediately to my old lodging, and the porter informed me that Mr. Chabert had sold all my property. "What", I said, "even the tobacco!" "Mr. Chabert," she replied, "told me that it had become moldy and that he was obliged to throw it out." The loss of the furniture, linens, and copper plates for music was no great blow, but to lose two hundred pounds of excellent tobacco, aged for ten years, was a dagger to my heart.

I then went to see Paisiello, who displayed the greatest pleasure on seeing me once more, as did Donna Cecilia, who was with him at that time.

Paisiello was Bonaparte's idol, and he in turn was Paisiello's idol. The composer dined almost every day with the First Consul, something that flattered him greatly, but also displeased him at the same time, since it took him away from his work.

Although I knew that Paisiello did not enjoy receiving visitors, yet, being certain of pleasing him, I took the liberty of presenting to him, without advance notice, my two friends Viganoni and Michael Kelly, who he had already met before, and for whom he had written his celebrated *Re Teodoro* in Vienna, giving to the first the part of Sandrino, and to the second the part of the secretary. As soon as we had gone into the antechamber, the mischievous Kelly, seeing that the master's room was open, began to intone the aria written for him from the opera, "*Queste son lettere scritte in inglese.*" Paisiello recognized the voice and the music, and hurried out to embrace the singer with his usual affability, exclaiming, "My dear Kelly, I am happy to see you again! What? You haven't yet forgotten that aria that you refused to sing at first because the

---

[3] The events of Paisiello's biography after 1790 are too complex to fully outline here, but the ups and downs of his career that we see reflected in the *Aneddoti* were a result of his convoluted attempts to balance the patronage of the Neopolitan king and Napoleon, with his fortunes very much tied to shifts in political power at the time. He spent several years in Paris, and by this point had moved away from the composition of operas to concentrate on civic and religious works. For more, see Michael F. Robinson. "Paisiello, Giovanni." Grove Music Online. Oxford Music Online. Oxford University Press.

scoring was too heavy?" Then having turned to Viganoni, he also embraced him, saying, "My dear Sandrino, I was unable to serve you well in that opera, but it was not my fault. I hope however that the aria "*Mi perdo sì mi perdo,*" which I wrote for you for *Modista Raggiratrice*, made up for it." Viganoni smiled and thanked him: one could see joy and delight shining in their faces, and I enjoyed seeing them so happy.

I traveled throughout all of Paris seeking other old friends, but I found very few. Some were already dead, among them Cavalier Campan, others had emigrated, and others were living in the country. Nevertheless, I found Cherubini, who for many years had been oppressed and humbled by the rancor felt for him by the First Consul, due to the circumstances that follow.

During the time Bonaparte was simply a general, he went to the Théâtre Feydeau in Paris to hear one of the best operas by that master, and found himself by chance in a box where Cherubini was sitting. As he had met him before, he complimented him at various times during the course of the performance, but when the opera was over, he took him aside and said, "Dear Cherubini, you have a great talent, but your music is so complicated and noisy that it deafens me." Cherubini answered, "Dear General, you are a great warrior, but as far as harmony is concerned (excuse me), it's none of your business, because you would like me to write music that is only fitting for your ears."

Napoleon never forgave him, and during the twelve years of his reign, he kept him in oblivion as much as was possible!

I also found my old flame with the false teeth, or rather she came to see me with her mother, hoping that I was rich. During the time of anarchy she had had seven husbands in only six months and was divorced from the last at the point when I saw her, and she was hoping perhaps that I would become the eighth. She had lost her complexion and was made up from her chin to her eyes.

She had the impudence of asking me what had become of that ring. I, without ceremony, laughed in her face, telling her to ask our mutual friends about it. Seeing that I was well aware of her insolence, she made a most beautiful curtsey, and went off with her mother, looking more scornful than ashamed.

Although the peace of Amiens had brought a little tranquility to France, nevertheless Paris was no longer Paris.

Most of the nobility that had previously been the source of the wealth and the splendor of that metropolis were still outside the country, or had been the victims of the infernal steel of Robespierre, or of the other monsters who preceded or succeeded him. Those of the middle class one no longer met with the ease, the sincerity, nor the social order that is so pleasant to everyone, and instead there was nothing but suspicion and distrust, even between father and son and between brother and brother.

The plebs were impertinent and brutal.

To sum up, living in Paris during that period was no longer living, but rather dying over a slow fire.

Chapter X
Visit to Madame Campan at St. German en Laye - Great Banquet and Great Party given by her for the leading personages of the time - Exhibition of her students - English Poetry - Return to Paris.

Two weeks later, I received an invitation from my friend Noverre to pass several days with him near St. German en Laye, where he had retired.

I went there, so much the more since I wanted to visit Madame Campan, who (as I have already said) was residing there in her renowned educational establishment for young ladies.[1]

My friend Noverre had a most gracious house, situated on a hill that presented the most beautiful vista of the environs. He kept an exquisite table and a pleasing society, and even if he had passed the age of eighty-five, yet he was always in good humor, excepting when he spoke of Madame Campan, whom he could not forgive for not having chosen him as dancing-master for her school.

One morning I presented myself to the old lady-in-waiting of the unfortunate Marie Antoinette, and after the usual formalities, and with the reminiscences concluded, she brought me up to date on her enterprise.

She was living in a very beautiful palace, with two great houses nearby, which contained in all more than one hundred and fifty persons, between

---

[1] Madame Campan survived the Revolution, but became penniless. She decided to attempt to support herself by starting a school for girls outside of Paris at St. German en Laye. The school became very well-known and quite prosperous, and it is here that Ferrari visits her. Just a few years later, Napoleon appointed her as superintendent of a new school he founded for the orphan daughters of his Legion d'honneur soldiers until the Bourbon restoration. As an educator, she was ahead of its time in advocating for a comprehensive education for women, and her schools were noteworthy for the balance of instruction in academic learning, the arts, domestic sciences.

students and the servants. She had (in addition to the French) a great number of damsels of every nation, religion, and sect from the continent. There were also Indians, Americans, and English students there who all paid a very high price and in exchange they received the most complete education.

The leading teachers of Paris were employed to give lessons to Madame Campan's students. She had in the house various governesses capable of not only having the students repeat their lessons but even of instructing them. The apartments were kept with splendor and cleanliness, and the edifice dominated a vast picturesque and varied horizon.

After having taken me about a great part of that habitation, she conducted me to her boudoir, where I was astonished to see a quantity of busts and portraits, some representing the Bourbon family, others that of Napoleon. There was even one of Napoleon's favorite mameluk painted by Madame Beauharnais!

I asked her if the First Consul had ever been in her apartment, and how he liked seeing the images of the Bourbon dynasty intermingled with those of his own family. She answered me that he had been there several times, but that he was above such minutiae.

I asked her then in confidence what she thought of him. "Oh," she said, "he is an active man, full of genius, and very fortunate. He was on the verge of being killed in the National Assembly, and of losing his army and himself at Marengo, but if his luck doesn't abandon him I expect to see him crowned soon. Come," she continued, "come to dinner with me next Thursday, probably you will meet him in this boudoir, and perhaps you will dine with him. I say perhaps, because from the moment he bore the title of Consul and for the next ten years, he always honored me with his person at dinner every Thursday. Then last Thursday, a few days after he was made Consul for Life, he did not come, and who knows if he will ever come again. At any rate, I will certainly introduce you to some of his relatives, and a few of my little students, who I had the luck to marry to the leading personages of our time; that is, to the adjutants and officials of the great captain."

I thanked her for her courtesy and went there on Thursday, but the First Consul did not come, and I believe that he never went there again.

As far as the dinner goes, it seemed like it was being given by a princess rather than by a schoolteacher, nor was there anything rare or delicate that was lacking. In fact, when I reflect on the events that occurred shortly thereafter, it seems to me that she already had some presentiment of what was to happen to a few of the invitees who came, to offer such a costly and luxurious meal.

She was seated at the middle of the table on one side. She had her chaplain on her right and General Savery on her left. Others there were Marshall Ney with his wife, who was a niece of Madame Campan; a sister of hers; General

Du Roc, prefect of the palace; General Beauharnais, then viceroy of Italy; his sister Madame Louis Bonaparte, thereafter Queen of Holland; Napoleon's sister, Madame Murat, then Queen of Naples; Monsieur Isabé, a celebrated painter; myself; and various others whom I did not know.

Having finished dining, Madame Campan asked me if I had ever set English poetry to music. I answered yes.

"Will you let us hear a few ariettas?"

"Of course!"

"All my students know that language, and there are among them two young Englishwoman, who, I am sure, would be happy with such a gift."

"You are too kind; and if they will forgive my little voice, and strange pronunciation, I am ready."

And having seated myself at the pianoforte I sang the following strophes:

CONTENTMENT.

1.
Contentment! smiling, lovely fair,
    Thou brightest daughter of the sky,
Why dost thou to the hut repair
And from the gilded palace fly?

2.
I've traced thee on the peasant's cheek,
I've marked thee in the milkmaid's smile,
I've heard thee loudly laugh and speak
Amidst the sons of want and toil.

3.
Yet in the circles of the great
Where Fortune's gifts are all combin'd;
I've sought thee early, sought thee late,
And ne'er thy lovely form could find.[2]

THE BUTTERFLY.

Still free from thought and free from sorrow,
Waive lovely fly thy wings in play,
Though time may clip thy wings to-morrow,
An age of bliss in time to-day.\

---

[2] The text is from a poem by Catherine Grey, Lady Manners and later Baroness Hightower (1766 – 1852), an Anglo-Irish poet.

Would that they life's short happy measure
Were mine -but oh! that wish in vain,

Still must thou sport through days of pleasure,
And I still sigh through years of pain.
[3]

Whether because of the circumstance, or for some other reason, these two ariettas had the greatest success, nor do I ever remember them being so much applauded.

Madame Campan wanted to employ me as singing teacher for her students, and Marshall Ney offered to speak on my behalf to the First Consul so that he would take me on as his composer. I thanked both of them, assuring them that I was determined to return to my fatherland after having taken care of my affairs in London.

Then our charming hostess entertained her society with an exhibition, which she was accustomed to having her most expert students perform from time to time in a hall of the palace on a little stage made especially for such occasions.

Two of the young ladies presented themselves on the stage and played a kind of overture for harp and pianoforte. Others came forward who sang a concerted piece, then an aria, a duet, etc.

Soon there appeared still others, declaiming by memory passages of prose and poetry in French, Italian, or Spanish; then the examination began.

Every spectator had the right to question the girls on sacred and secular history, on mythology, on geography, etc. and the girls answered correctly. They were given an unknown piece of vocal music, and although it might have been accommodated to the voices of those who were to sing it, they executed it at sight, and without accompaniment. Three of the youngest then presented themselves, one with a piece of white satin in hand, and each of the others with a half-folio of paper, showing us that there was nothing on them. They then sat at their tables, and in a few minutes one showed us her writings, the other her sketches, and the third her embroidery.

They began once more to make a little vocal and instrumental music, and finished it all, *alla francese*, with a little dance.

The following day I made a visit to thank Madame Campan, nor could I sufficiently express to her how much I enjoyed the day before, above all in

---

[3] This is from a poem by the novelist and poet Matthew Gregory Lewis (1775-1818), the [3]author of the popular and scandalous gothic novel *The Monk*.

seeing her students so well-educated, and able to do her and themselves honor in the presence of their relatives and friends, without subterfuges or charlatanry. I dined afterward with my friend Noverre and returned in the evening to Paris.

Chapter XI.
Abate Casti - Paisiello- Marshall Ney - Review by Napoleon - Academy at Devonshire House.

Unhappy with Paris, my thoughts turned to the happy isle of Britain, but as my friend Bridi was in the area after his trip to England, and Paisiello, Viganoni, Kelly and other friends as well, I let myself be persuaded to remain there a few weeks more.

This caused me to have the pleasure of being introduced to Abate Casti, a great friend of Paisiello, and the author of the libretto of his *Re Teodoro*. He had been in Paris since 1800, where he published his witty poem *Gli Animali Parlanti* (The Talking Animals), in which he introduced a Corsican dog, in order to call to mind politically the destruction that General Bonaparte had caused in Italy.

Casti was already somewhat old and frail in health, but full of spirit and fire. As far as jibes or riposts were concerned, he was extremely quick and comparable to a Chevalier de Bouffler or a Sheridan. He was full of infinite regret at having published his poem, which had drawn to him the ire of the First Consul.

One day while I was examining with Paisiello some piece of music from his Proserpine, reviewing French prosody, which he did not know at all, Casti appeared.

"Addio, Maestro, how are you?"

"Oh, my dear Abate! I am well - and how are you?"

"I am doing quite poorly."

"I am sorry - and what is the problem?"

"I am sick in body, mind and spirit."

"And why?"

"Because the First Consul does not wish to see me, because he detests me, and that makes me unhappy."

"But he has a great regard for your talent."

"Who told you that?"

"He himself."

"When?"

"Yesterday, at dinner."

"Ah, if I could dine with him! Listen, Paisiello, you are both my friend and his: try to make peace between us. Tell him that I have the greatest consideration for him, and that I feel the greatest tenderness for him. Tell him that I will change my poem from beginning to end if he desires it, and that instead of introducing a Corsican dog, I will make appear a timid and innocent little lamb." The maestro smiled, and I went on my way, admiring his poetic sincerity.

Paisiello and others worked for such a reconciliation, but it did not succeed. Bonaparte did not wish to pardon Casti, just as he had not pardoned Cherubini.

The prolongation of my stay in Paris also gave me the opportunity of being present at a review of the First Consul. Marshall Ney, who had taken a certain liking for me, kindly offered to take me with him to the palace of the Tuileries Palace in order to see the display, and I accepted.

Ney was a very handsome young man: tall, blond, with blue eyes, a fresh complexion, and a noble bearing. On his brow one saw a military air, but at the same time a very sweet physiognomy, accompanied by the most affable manners.

On the day fixed for the above-mentioned review he came to pick me up with his own carriage, and as we were on the way, and seeing that I was treated in such a friendly way, I took the liberty of asking him if it was true that which I had heard from here and there in Paris, that General Moreau had been honorably exiled to America because of Bonaparte's jealousy.

"*Ah, mon Dieu Seigneur! Que dites vous, mon cher ami?*"[1] he exclaimed impetuously. "For the love of God, let such a blasphemy not issue from your mouth, or you will have great woes! Know that the First Consul has the greatest esteem and veneration for the general, and that in fact, he calls him the savior of France. If Moreau goes to America, it is only on his own initiative, as much to leave the military life as to attend to the considerable estates that he possesses in that country, and I assure you that Bonaparte has nothing to do with it. "

I asked him to pardon me for my curiosity, and having arrived at the Tuileries he took me to the apartments of the great warrior, from whence I saw the review, which did not make a great impression on me, having seen so many others before.

The review being finished, the First Consul went out with haughty and ferocious air, which I did not like at all.

The charming marshall took me back to my lodging and did not cease to admonish me not to speak further of General Moreau. Before dismounting from the carriage I thanked him for his extreme courtesy. However, from the

[1]Oh my God! What are you saying, my dear friend?

effort he had put into trying to persuade me about the said affair, I had no doubt about his attachment for Napoleon, just I had no doubt that what I had heard in Paris about Moreau was only too true.

By the end of the month of August I decided to return to England. I took leave of my friends. Paisiello was almost in a rage with me for not wishing to be present at the premiere of his Proserpine. I told him that he had still not finished the first act, and that as I had neglected so many affairs in London during the preceding season, not to return immediately would too much injure me. I asked him to tell me of the success of his opera, which he did, in a letter to be found at the end of this chapter. He was persuaded and we parted good friends.

Having arrived at Dover, I read in a newspaper that the Duchess of Devonshire was going to take the waters at Ramsgate. I immediately changed my travel plans and went that instant to present my homage to her, and to tell her what had happened to me in Paris. She welcomed me with her customary good will, and after several days I left for London, where for seven months running I was busy from morning till night.

As soon as she had arrived in the metropolis, the charming duchess called me to Devonshire House, and announced to me with the greatest delicacy that her daughters had finished their education, and in consequence they could no longer employ me, but that, desiring to be useful to me, she was offering, with the consent of the Duke, her house for a benefit evening the following spring.

Who would have refused such an offer!

On the 30th of May, 1803, I gave a most splendid academy there, assisted by the rare and well-known talents of Mrs. Billington, Braham, Viganoni, Carlo Rovedino, Morelli, Weichsell, Lindley, Dragonetti, etc.

Various princes of the blood appeared, as well as almost all the foreign ambassadors, the leading British nobility, and the continental nobility that were in London. My profit matched the heights of the society that attended, and my honor no less.

Letter from Paisiello

Paris, 2 June 1803.

My dear friend Ferrari,

It is already a month and more since Cavaliere La Cainea left here for London. I gave him an envelope for you containing the arias, duets, and the overture of my opera Proserpine that are already printed, though the score is not yet finished being printed. The same Cavaliere took it upon himself to deliver to you the envelope, saying that he knows you, but from that time to this, I have not yet been able to learn, either from him or from you, if you have received it. Thus, I have decided to write you to learn from you the outcome of the said affair. I hope that you will answer, because I am still waiting an answer from you on other things I have written, letting me know to whom I should send what I owe you for the expenses made on my account, both for the twenty-four handkerchiefs, as well as two wigs,

and thus I hope that you will answer me, and quickly. I had hoped to return home, but I am obliged to remain here, the First Consul having desired that I compose another opera, and at the same time making me a gift of a superb gold box containing 250 louis d'or inside it, to bear witness to the satisfaction and pleasure that he had with the music for Proserpine. Be well, give me your commands, and with affectionate regards, together with my wife, I am ever,

Chapter XII.

Trip to Scotland - A Turn around the Mountains - Return to London by way of Manchester.

At the end of that season, I received invitations from several of my Scottish students to make a tour in their country during the following summer, which was soon approaching. Moved by the description they made of it for me, and by the desire to gratify them, I went; nor have I ever regretted the trip.

I found my friends Natalie Corri and Stabilini in Edinburgh. The pleasure of seeing each other again was mutual, and I spent many pleasant days with them.

The capital of Scotland pleased me exceedingly. The situation of the old city is beautiful, and noteworthy for its antiquity, nor have I ever seen a modern city as elegant as the new city of Edinburgh. I liked it so well that, if I had not arranged to repatriate myself the following year to the Tyrol, I would have settled there. Corri and Stabilini encouraged me to stay, assuring me that I would do my work as well as in London and that I would create a vogue for Italian music in Scotland.

I visited the family of my student Miss Gordon, who lived at Braid, a gracious spot, nearby the city. I then spent two weeks at Seaton House, Aberdeen, visiting Mr. and Mrs. Forbes, whose daughter, a student of mine, is the present Lady Hames Hay. From there I went through Perth and stopped in Belmont at the house of the Honorable Mr. Stuart Wortley. There Miss Wortley, the present Honorable Mrs. W. Dundas, and Miss L. Wortley, now Countess Lovaine, arranged for me some letters of recommendation, as well as a horse, a little carriage, and a guide to continue my trip in the mountains of the west. Having mounted the carriage I thought I was with the hunter of Mariaberg, since my Caledonian did nothing but smoke and take tobacco from morning till night.

I passed through Taymouth and Killing without stopping, and then stopped for a half day and a night at Dunkeld, which is a little paradise of nature and a jewel of art.

The family of the Duke of Athol was at his famous estate of Blair, where I went as quickly as possible, and there is no need to say how I was received there by the inhabitants of that region in general, since everyone knows Scottish hospitality. Blair is a renowned site, as much for its greatness and beauty as for the hunting of deer, which are found there in quantity. For my taste, however, I would trade three Blairs for one Dunkeld.

From Blair I went to Inverary to the Duke of Argyll. In that spot it seems that nature has been prodigal with her beauties. The greenery of the meadows delights and ravishes you; the cascades and the basins of water are as limpid as crystal, and the mountains thereabouts are wild, and covered with superb trees of every sort.

Loch Fyne forms a sort of gulf that rises and falls every six hours with the tides. When the ebb and flow of the sea enters that little inlet, then goes out of it - now peaceful, now tempestuous - it presents you, everything together, with new, pleasing and magnificent scenes. The loch is celebrated for the herring, who breed there by the millions, and for its shifting, sandy shoals.

While I was there, something most lamentable took place. Four poor fishermen, crossing those waters in search of fish, were carried instantly, without noticing it, onto those banks, and as the tide was going out rapidly, they found themselves very shortly, so to speak, aground. Without having any assistance, as if they had been on a soft sandbank, they were immersed little by little in that limpid mire, where they unhappily perished.

At Inverary, I had the honor of meeting Marquis Lorn, now the Duke of Argyll, along with his sister Lady Carlotta Campbell, who was then in the flower of her splendid beauty.

After having crossed a good piece of the county of Argyll, I traveled along the shore of Loch Lomond for many miles, which is worth seeing. From there I arrived and stayed a day at Glasgow, a considerable city, it is true, but too melancholy, and smokier than London.

I left my guide in that fog, and took a seat in a chaise to make a visit to Lord Douglas and his pleasant estate of Bothkeld Castle, which I always called a miniature of Dunkeld. Being rather late, I was barely able to view the surroundings and to enjoy the society. Two days later I caught a carriage which was returning South, and traveled in it for a distance along the famous lakes of Westmoreland, down to Manchester.

The factories within this city are renowned and very numerous. The cotton mills are amazing, surpassing greatly the silk mills of Italy. How entertained I was seeing the wool beaten by four artificial iron arms moved by a water-powered machine, having in each hand a striking rod, and striking so equally as to make it appear like a well-woven fabric in just a few minutes. The machines for working the cotton are most ingenious, and the wheels, the distaffs, and so many other tools for spinning and refining it are made to perfection. The factories of pins, needles, and paper *mâché* are no less worth seeing. But what gave me even more pleasure in Manchester was the acquaintance of a certain Mr. Cheese, a fine organist and master of the pianoforte. He was entirely blind, but had a memory so happy and extraordinary that he could retain in his mind any piece of music after having heard it only two or three times. But what surprised me, even more, was to hear a student of his - born blind, and only twelve years old -playing the music of Clementi, Cramer, Dussek and others, almost without missing a note!

Up until then I had never traveled with the postal carriage, called the "mail coach," and I wanted to give myself that satisfaction.

Thus on the fifteenth of September I left that city at four in the afternoon and arrived at London at six on the sixteenth. To make 185 miles in twenty-four hours is a much quicker journey than being the four or five days on the road to travel only 150 miles with the eternal courier from Rome to Naples!

Chapter XIII.

My Wedding.

At the beginning of the year 1804, my future prospects being particularly favorable since I had been awaiting since the end of the season for a large stipend, I planned to repatriate myself in the autumn and settle in Roveredo, having always desired to live in a small city or even in a village rather than in a great metropolis. I thought that, between what I owned in Roverado combined with the little that I would bring from England, I would have put together a sufficient income to be able to maintain myself properly, and even in comfort, saving the profit of my subsequent compositions as a surplus, whether for saving or for entertainment.

But man proposes, and God disposes.

For a number of years, I had greatly admired the musical talent and the style of pianoforte playing of a certain Miss Victoire Henry, daughter of a

French father and an English mother, and herself born in London.[1] I had the pleasure several times of meeting her at the Italian opera and at various recitals, and even if I had not visited her parents, yet I knew them well enough through conversing with them. Little by little I became captivated by her manner and struck by her pretty little face.

Timid as I always was when truly in love, I did not burn to forge ahead, but yearned and sighed for an occasion where I might introduce myself more intimately into that family. The occasion came up by itself.

On the eighth of May I went to the annual benefit for the late Salpietro without knowing, in fact, that Miss Henry would be there. Among the singers who were assisting that poor old man was the charming Signora Bolla and Viganoni. They asked me to accompany them in a duet of mine from *Rinaldo d'Asti*, "*T'intendo, sí, t'intendo!*"; I agreed with the greatest pleasure to their request, and the duet was encored with enthusiasm.

Having got up from the instrument, I sat on a bench behind my flame and her family, from whom I received many compliments on my music. The recital being over, I offered my arm to Madame Henry to accompany her home, and as we went down the street, her husband asked me if I would favor his daughter with a copy of the above-mentioned duet. What a request, and what a joy for me! I agreed willingly, on the condition that she would sing it with me. This was agreed to.

Having arrived at the door of the house I was invited to come up and dine with the family. Naturally, I did not wait to be asked twice but accepted immediately. However, the dinner was not a repast for me; it was an anguish, a high fever, a delirium. All in all, it was that which Metastasio expresses, with such ingenuity and heat, in a notable passage of his *Galatea,* which I here transcribe.

> To hope with no counsel,
> To fear where there is no danger,
> To strike at shadows and not believe in the truth
> To produce in one's imagination
> A hundred empty phantoms at every moment,
> To dream while awake, and a thousand times a day
> To die without dying,
> To call joy martyrdom,
> To think of others and to forget one's self,
> And to often pass from
> Fear to fear, from desire to desire,

---

[1] Victoire Henry was the daughter of a French dancing master who had moved to London after several years in Paris. She was an accomplished pianist, and studied with Jean Baptiste Cramer, after which she performed and taught piano and singing in London. The marriage with Ferrari was marked by many long absences, as the autobiography outlines, and with Victoire ultimately settled in Brighton, the pair seem to have been quite independent, perhaps even formally separated by the end of Ferrari's life.

This is the frenzy which we call Love.[2]

(Sperar senza consiglio,
Temer senza periglio,
Dar colpo all'ombre e non dare fede al vero
Figurar col pensiero
Cento vani fantasmi in ogni istante,
Sognar vegliando, e mille volte il giorno
Morir senza morire
Chiamar gioia il martire,
Pensar ad altri ed obliar se stesso,
E far passaggio spesso
Da timor in timor, da brama in brama,
É quella frenesia che amor si chiama.)

Introduced so unexpectedly into that family, and received with such grace, I began to frequent the house, and gradually visited morning and evening.

Miss Vittorina did not ignore my attentions, nor did she discourage them. After two or three months, and after having informed her of that which I possessed, of my character, and my intentions, I offered her my hand. She thanked me for my offer but was opposed to the condition that we settle in the Tyrol. I made her aware that in that country I could immediately gain a little independence, and even if my affairs in London were going well, nonetheless I feared a sickness or some other disgrace might render me unhappy; but she was inflexible. I continued, however, to visit her for a number of weeks, hoping to persuade her, but finally she gave me an open refusal.

I then retired from her family with great sorrow and also with some rancor, but not many days passed, and various of her friends, desiring to see the union brought to pass, persuaded her to marry me, with the hope that, as I had spent already twelve years in this country and being there so well known and encouraged, I would soon get tired of the Tyrol, and would reestablish myself once again in England.

On the twenty-eighth of October, then, we went to the altar of St. Martin's in London, and then to the Austrian chapel in the house of His Highness the Prince Starhemberg in Twickenham, after having agreed to leave for the Tyrol the following year. But in the meantime the war between Austria and France broke out, so memorable for the extraordinary defeat of General Mack at Ulm. Various other wars then followed in all of Europe, and such circumstances, united with the habit of living on this island, made me finally resolve to remain here.

---

[2] *La Galatea* is a libretto for a serenata by Metastasio first performed in 1722 in Naples.

Chapter XIV
Sir William and Lady Hamilton - Lord Nelson Etc.

Having finally quenched my longtime thirst to be married, I found myself content and happy, regretting that I had not taken a wife twenty years before, and congratulating myself at the same time for having found a spouse who suited me in every way.

In the year 1805, I was called to Merton by Lady Hamilton, who lived there with her consort in the house of the admiral Lord Nelson. She wanted me to write an Italian cantata in praise of the famous battle of the Nile, fought and won by that hero in Egypt. Happy and proud to have such a request, I promised to put all my effort into succeeding in it. I proposed Serafino Buonajuti as the poet, and he was accepted. She did me the honor of inviting me to dine with the patron of the house and his friends, and during the fruit course she began to sing English ariettas, but while the fair siren was singing, His Lordship was dozing or sleeping, and only woke when the charming singer tapped him on the shoulder.

After the meal I approached Lady Hamilton and told her candidly that I thought that Lord Nelson had no sensibility for music, and moreover, as he did not understand the Italian language, it would be better to have a short poem in English written by my friend Peter Pindar, and so entertain the admiral, who could read of his gallantry while it was being sung. She accepted my suggestion and entrusted me with inviting the celebrated poet to spend a week at Merton, as well as Viganoni and C. Rovedino. We all went, and Peter Pindar wrote the poetry that follows, which I then set to music:

> Pleas'd would I strike the lyre to love,
> In vain the wish, the labour vain!
> For lo! the chords rebellions prove,
> And pour to war alone the strain.
> Change as I will the rebel strings,
> The Harp of martial glory sings.
> Yet who alas! can blame the lyre,
> That pours a sound to Britons dear?
> The song that future heroes fire,
> And bid them kindle as they hear,
> Though dangers seek the wealth of fame
> And bleed to gain a Nelson's name.

I wrote the little cantata for Lady Hamilton to be sung as a solo, the chorus sung by the above-mentioned singers and myself. It was executed in the presence of their families and various of their friends, who received it with favor.

The Victor of the Nile came to compliment me, exclaiming, "Bravo! that was a brilliant action! What do you think of it?" "Superb, my Lord!" I replied, "I would only wish that my music was worth one of your barrage of shells!"

Everyone knows the courage and valor of that great admiral, but Lord Nelson at home was certainly not the most charming of men. He would go down to breakfast wearing a robe full of orders, ribbons, and crosses. If one spoke to him, he would rarely reply. He was sensitive to compliments and to the mention of his naval exploits; the more he was praised, the more he enjoyed it. But woe to him who mentioned the affair of Boulogne or that of Copenhagen! He loved to play vingt-et-un, though for low stakes, and when he won he was cheerful and as happy as a baby. When he lost, however, he cursed like a sailor, not only in English but also in Italian and French as well, although he could say nothing but imprecations in those two tongues. His society was composed of affable and pleasing persons, and he, without making observations, let everyone enjoy himself as he pleased.

After dinner he would take his nap, while the rest of us drank, sang, and laughed merrily.

Sir Hamilton was already at an advanced age, but of good humor and full of courtesy, however, he bored us sometimes with making us hear his instruments, and above all in playing the quartets of his teacher Felice Giardini all by himself with the viola part only. Viganoni, a brave soul, and having known the man for many years, said to him one day:

"But for the love of heaven, most esteemed sir, what in the devil do you find of interest in that viola part that always goes in unison with the bass?"

"A most rich harmony!" replied the cavalier.

"Jesus and Mary!" replied Viganoni.

On that occasion Peter Pindar conducted himself with the amiability he displayed only in society where there was no etiquette. He wrote various pieces of poetry, he improvised several times, and made an elegant apology in verse to Sir William for having criticized him in his burlesque poem The Louisiade. Sir William thanked him as much for his criticism as for his praise, and assured him that he was equally flattered to see his little name remembered by such a great pen.

We were all happy with the hospitality of the company, and so we were just as unhappy to have to leave it.

Upon returning to the city I had the pleasure of seeing the celebrated Naldi's first appearance in the Italian theatre, joined by the no-less-celebrated Horace, in the opera "Le Due Nozze ed un sol Marito." He pleased here, as in so many other works, but he aroused even more devoted followers in the Fanatico per la Musica, accompanied by the astonishing Billington. For this later opera I composed for her a piano solo, in a little scene between her and Naldi, followed by a polacca, and which all together were greatly applauded.

Moreover, during that season I wrote six ariettas dedicated to Lady C. Campbell, and in the summer of 1806, I went to Dartford, invited by my student Mrs. A. Hamilton and her mother the Honorable Mrs. Payne, and with them I went to Portsmouth to join the company of Admiral Hamilton and of Mr. C. Plowden, their relative. I stayed four weeks with them, and I would consider myself an ingrate if I did not say that for thirty years thereafter I was always honored and laden with courtesies by those respectable families.

Towards the month of October, the celebrated Catalani disembarked at Southampton, of whom I will speak in the following chapter.

Chapter XV
Madame Catalani - The Heroine of Raab - English and Italian Poetry.

Angelica Catalani was born at Sinigaglia; she was brought up in a convent in Rome and began her theatrical career as a prima donna seria in Venice at the age of only sixteen.

From there she went to Lisbon, having been engaged there, and as the years passed she visited all the capitals and principal cities of the continent, as well as those of the British Isles. As soon as she arrived in London I had the honor of making her acquaintance, and the pleasure of seeing her and hearing her reveal those rare virtues nature had given her and those delightful talents she acquired on her own.

Although her person and her fame may be known by all, yet they are few who have had the opportunity that I had of frequently meeting her for several years running, of accompanying her at the pianoforte, and of writing for her many pieces of music, so I can speak of her and of that period with more certainty than many others have done.

She possessed a sonorous voice, powerful and at the same time sweet and mellow. I am of the opinion that one could compare her to the splendor of the late Banti, the sensibility of Grassini, the sweet energy of Pasta, the delicious flexibility of Sontag, and the three perfect registers of Malibran.

Fig. 14. Portrait of Angelina Catalani

She owed her style of singing to Pacchierotti, Marchesi, and Crescentini. In the matter of gruppetti, coloratura, trills and mordents, she executed them to the letter; her execution was pure and articulate in every passage or difficulty that might present itself. In the concerted pieces and finales, she animated the singers, the choristers, and the orchestra itself, and her beautiful notes could be heard, clear and not shrieking, over the din. There is neither a Beethoven, a Rossini, nor other musical Lucifer who could have covered up that divine voice. She was not then profoundly trained in music, but yet, guided by what she knew and by her perfect ear, she learned any piece of music in a minute, simple or complicated. In addition to being a superior singer, she was also an excellent actress. Gifted with a nimble and majestic physique, a slender waist, a seductive physiognomy, she was noble in the serious, tender in the pathetic, and funny in the comic. I said that she has been and was, but I am not intending to suggest that she is not still and cannot be still an object of admiration; I am most sure that if Madame Catalani were to return to the stage she would repay the public what she denied them in retiring from her theatrical career.

Madame Catalani has always been religious, modest, and recognized as such by all those who knew her. For every feast she had mass said at her house, for which she herself served. She was an affectionate wife, good mother and loyal friend. She visited and received in her home the leading nobility of London, and was cherished and admired by all. Lady Elizabeth Foster, the last Duchess of Devonshire, said to me one day, "Catalani, in addition to her talents, is the most beautiful ornament of the noblest society, as much for her charm as for her simple and innocent manners." In her own house, and with her friends, she did not stand on ceremony, but always treated them with the most liberal hospitality. She loved to hear stories told, to see billiards played, and to play cards.

In the first years of her dramatic reign in London, I had the opportunity (as I said earlier) to write many pieces of music for her; among which it gives me pleasure to name a few.

> Six Italian arias dedicated to her.
> Six canzonettas, also in Italian, dedicated to H.R.H. Lady E. Leveson Gower
> "Non vi fidate agli uomini," arietta
> "Veh, come è nobile," duet
> "Papa, non dite di no!," canzonetta
> "Vedete, vedete," duet
> "Senti dirò così," aria

I also orchestrated two pieces for her, "Nel cor più non mi sento" by Paisiello, and "Oh dolce contento" by Mozart, with variations which she composed herself and gave to me. That little job required great patience from me, as I had always detested bravura variations on a simple melody and a single strophe, because they betray the sentiment of the words and good sense, and there are few that do not pass so rapidly that they leave no impression or remembrance in the soul, nor consolation in the heart. In spite of this they are most effective for a young singer, full of vivacity and ardor, as the "Erato of Sinigaglia" was at that time; since in such a way one exercises the flexibility of the voice, and at the same time throws dust in the eyes of the public, which is always ready to be made fools of, and to applaud.

Over the course of those two or three years I published a quantity of music for piano, harp, sometimes solo, sometimes in duo, or accompanied by flute, violin, or violoncello, as well as six ariette dedicated to Mrs. Billington, and another six dedicated to Mrs. Jarrett.

In the year 1809, I had the misfortune to be the victim of a most violent ophthalmia, which deprived me of the dear light of the sun for eighteen months in a row, and which prevented me from exercising my profession for another eighteen months. During my blindness I composed three Italian nocturnes for three voices, dedicated to His Royal Highness the Prince Regent; two sonatas for pianoforte and flute; three marches, followed by some bagatelles, which I dictated to my friend Giovanni Mazzinghi, a solid professional, who wrote them down, and who was like a brother to me at that time, if not like a father.

Once I had recovered my sight a little, I began once more to give lessons, to read and write with magnifying glasses, and thus I continued as I am doing now. The first thing that I composed, and which I wrote by myself after my misfortune, was an English arietta by the celebrated Moore, justly saluted with the name of the British Anacreon, which it pleases me to present here, with one of those six which I dedicated to Mrs. Billington.

THE TIMID TEAR
Have you not seen the timid tear,
Steal trembling from mine eye?
Have you not mark'd the flush of fear,
Or caught the murmur'd sigh?

And can you think my love is chill,
Nor fix'd on you alone;
And can you rend, by doubting still,
A heart so much your own?

To you my soul's affections move
Devoutly, warmly true;
My task has been a task of love,
One long long thought of you:
If all your tender faith is o'er,
If still my truth you'll try,
Alas! I know but one proof more,
I'll bless your name and die.[1]

---

[1] Ferrari is of course referring to the Irish poet Thomas Moore, who was extremely popular in the first years of the 19th century as a poet, writer of ballads, singer, and translator. This seems to be an early poem by Moore.

ODE on the CICADA
Happy cicada,
I want to sing of you;
None is so blessed
As to be able to boast like you.
You first drink the frost
And alone atop the trees
Sing your songs.
Yours are the sweet
Fruits of the land where you live,
Yours the friendly
Produce of every season;
You are the delight
Of the rude farmers
Who never vary
Their work.
You are revered as a bard
By one who learns from
You and knows that
With you're the ardent summer returns
Dear to the muses,
And dear you are to Apollo,
Who gave you your rare and strident voice.
 Mistress you are of songs,
Daughter of the green soil
To whom senile age
Does not bring sorrow;
You are not afflicted by woes,
Blood does not circulate in yo,
And you are like the
Immortal gods.[2]

(ODE SOPRA LA CICALA
Cicala felicissima
Cantar vogl'io di te;
Beato altri non v'è
Ch'abbia i tuoi vanti.
Tu bevi pria la brina
E sola in cima agl'alberi
Come regina poi
Spieghi I tuoi canti.
Tuoi del terreno, ov'abiti,
I dolci frutti son
Tuo quanto ogni stagion
Produce amica;

---

[2] Anacreon's Ode XLIII.

Dei rozzi agricoltori
Tu pur sei la delizia
Che non divari mai
La lor fatica.
Qual vate ancora ti venera
Chi da te apprende e sa
Che teco tornerà
L'estate ardente.
Cara alle muse e cara
Sei pure al biondo Apolline
Che a te la rara diè
Voce stridente.
Maestra sei de' cantici,
Figlia del verde suol
Cui non apporta duol
L'età senile;
Te non affligon mali
In te sangue non circula.
E agl'immortali sei
Numi simile.)

Towards the end of the year 1813, I began to write an opera seria, *L'Eroína di Raab*, for Madame Catalani, the late Trammezzani, and for Righi, Di Giovanni, and for his present wife. It was performed in the spring of 1814, and welcomed most warmly; indeed it was given once again in the beginning of 1815, with the latter three performers, and with Signora Marianna Sessi and with the late Signor Gini. The pieces that pleased the most were the duet, "*Ti lascio t'abbandono,*" the two *scenas* for the prima donna, and the canon "*Sento fra i palpiti.*"

After the undoing of Napoleon in the bloody and decisive battle of Waterloo, carried out with such intrepidity and won with such valor by the Duke of Wellington, by Blucher, by Bello, and by their armies, I made another tour of Italy, which I am about to relate.

Chapter XVI

Journey to Roveredo, Venice, and Naples, with Mr. Thomas Broadwood.

Accustomed to the climate, the food, and in general to the customs of England, having become the father of a daughter and of a son, and having a wife fearful and strongly opposed to traveling, I resolved to leave my children in her care, and to go to the Tyrol to dispose of that which I possessed there. I planned to continue my trip in Italy, to buy goods that could be sold at a profit in England and then establish myself in London, starting a small business without abandoning my profession.

I confided my project to Mr. Thomas Broadwood, my good friend, who not only encouraged it, but, as he also desired to make a tour of Italy, he proposed that I should be his traveling companion. Knowing the solidity and judgment of that gentleman, I accepted the offer; but then recalling the risks and imprudences of my dear Mr. Arbert, and of so many other English travelers, I immediately proposed my conditions, and this is what they were: that we should not travel by sea, except in order to cross the Channel; that I would not follow him into any danger or precipice; and that we should not travel by night in Italy, as it was then infested with thousands of assassins who had been let go from the armies of Beauharnais and of Murat. We agreed on these conditions, and so we left on the night of the 30th of September, and with a happy crossing, we arrived in Paris on the 4th of October. Over a few days, I presented my companion to various of my friends, who congratulated me on traveling with such an accomplished young man, and one who seemed to them la raison même. But it was not long after that those sentiments, or principles of curiosity, which so characterize his compatriots, began to develop in him.

We departed from Paris on the tenth, and having left Champagne and Burgundy behind, and having arrived one morning at the top of the Jura, the postillion stopped to let us see Mont Blanc sixty miles away, which appeared, even to my poor vision, as bright as the sun, and so close that one could touch it with one's hands. Here my little Englishman opened the door of the carriage, jumped out impetuously, made his servant come into the carriage, bounced repeatedly on the seat and began to howl like a wolf, "Oh, what a spectacle! How heavenly! Ha, ha!" In truth it seemed like he wanted to fly to the top of the world. As night fell the spectacle became even more interesting; it became dark along the whole horizon, and one could see at the same time the sun shining on the highest part of the mountain in the most glorious way.

We arrived at Geneva about two in the morning, and even though my companion knew that there has never been a man able to go up to the summit of Mont Blanc during that time of the year, yet he made a thousand inquiries to discover whether, with extraordinary means or by force of money, he might be able to do it. He was told that such an attempt would be dangerous, and that the few Englishmen who had attempted it had died and been frozen before making it halfway. He was content then to visit the so-called seas of ice, which are at the northern foot of that phenomenon. In the meantime, I went to the mechanical manufactories that interested me greatly. On the second day after that we left for St. Gingand, a village situated on the right towards the middle of Lake Geneva, and slept there. Just before coming to the entrance of that little place, there was a closed gate in the care of a little boy of twelve years. He popped out of his hut, exclaiming "Messieurs, la visite des vos malles, s'il vous plait."

"Voila les clefs."

"Je ne sais quoi faire de vos clefs: donnez-moi quelque chose pour boire, et je vous ouvre la barrière."

("Gentlemen, I must inspect your bags, if you would." "Here are the keys." "I don't know what to do with your keys: just give me something so I can get a drink, and I will open the barrier.")

The day after we rented a boat to go see the fall of the Rhône, ten miles away on the other part of the lake. The waters of the river fall noisily from the mountains there like the most rapid torrent, and with such vehemence that they do not mingle with those of the lake until they have traveled two miles and been shaken and broken on the opposite shore. Having left the majestic entrance to those mountains, we entertained ourselves by approaching that torrent, now and then putting the left hand in its cloudy and almost frozen waters and the right hand in the tepid and very clear waters of the lake. Having arrived at the place whence we had departed we were joined by my friend's servant, who had followed us on land with the carriage, and from thence passing through Sion, Brigne, through the marvelous Sempione, through Domodossola, Milan, Cremona, Mantua and Verona, we arrived at Roveredo on the first of November. Having agreed to remain three or four days in that little town, I tried as hard as I could to entertain my charming companion, to recompense him for the sacrifice he made in staying there with me. I took him to my castle at Lizzana, to let him see my little estate and the bird-hunting done by almost every individual in that village. We were both afflicted by the sight of a hamlet ruined the year before by a regiment of Austrian soldiers who had been quartered there, and who for lack of wood had cut a great part of my mulberry trees and my vines to provide firewood. As far as hunting went, my companion did not enjoy seeing certain birds caught in the snares or certain others in the arches.

He was already familiar with nets hung horizontally, but he admired greatly the perpendicular nets strung up in the Roccolo. Towards evening I showed him a game of pallone,[1] but as the wintry season was already advanced, the players were cold and lazy, and so they did not want to put on the light and graceful outfits that they usually wore for such an occasion, so that the spectacle was imperfect. Nevertheless, it did not displease him. The day after he went with the coachman Anesi to see the flowery and fragrant Lago Garda, crossing the Adige at the Ravazon gate, passing through Mori, Lopio, Nago and stopping at Torbole, where he embarked for Riba, and from whence he returned in the same way and the same night to Roveredo, happy as a fish, or like an Englishman who has traveled by water.

Mr. Broadwood was greatly entertained by seeing the sheep, goats and little cows in the fields and hills so naturally domestic that they may be approached with the greatest confidence by anyone. If you show them a piece of bread or any sort of vegetable, they take it from your hand and eat it right in front of you. Those dear little beasts are so intelligent that, with the greatest dexterity and no danger, they clamber up on the rocks to seek a bit of grass or some leaves, and also to lick certain salty rocks which please them greatly. But what pleased him the most, and what he marveled at, was to be present at the hunters' target practice, which is done in the way that follows.

They choose a long field, at one end of which they construct a hut, made of wood or of tree branches, like those which you see in England on the downs where they race horses. Towards the other end of the field, five hundred paces from the hut, is placed the target, painted white, which is four feet in diameter. In the middle of this there is a black mark the size of a thaler. Near the side of the target there are stakes planted in the earth, with feathers tied at their tops. The sharpshooter goes into the hut, with his rifle inside, which is called a stutzer. Before looking at the target, he observes whether the breeze is ruffling the feathers, since the slightest breeze will make the bullet move from its course and miss the target, but it is rare that this happens and the bullet does not strike the black sport of the target. Once it is dented, there is a man there ready to fill the hole with a piece of white wood. Five other hunters shoot one after the other, and the one who is closest to the center wins the prize, which is two Bavarian thalers, along with the privilege of taking the feathers from the stakes, which he puts on his hat and with which he triumphantly enters the city, merrily paying for his friends' food and drink with the money that he has earned.

---

[1] This was probably the enormously popular game of *Pallone col bracciale*, where teams hit inflated balls back and forth using a wooden cylinders which fit over the forearm.

While my companion was busying himself with seeing all that was most worth seeing in the vicinity, I was trying to sell my possessions and to balance my accounts with my brother the priest, but I was not successful. The village was then in the greatest misery, nor could you have found anyone who would have wanted to buy even the littlest thing, although the lands had fallen by seventy percent. The negligence, ambition, and extravagance of my brother had put my affairs in such a state that I was obliged to leave them in the greatest confusion.

On the fourth day we left for Trent, as much to hear the organ of Santa Maria Maggiore and to see the painting of the council as to find my old friend Padre Stecher, who had established himself in the city several years before, where he was teaching music for a dozen carantani per lesson (five shillings and three farthings of English money). As soon as we arrived I sent for him, and he came immediately to find me. The pleasure of seeing each other again after thirty-five years was mutual and great. I told him of my surprise to see him there dressed as a priest, and he informed me that the monastery of Mariaberg had been destroyed, the monks sent away, and their possessions disbanded by orders of Napoleon. He let me know, moreover, that our valiant Captain Hofer, who had kept the French busy, had been finally arrested and been most barbarously shot by them. That produced in me such a disgust and an animosity towards Napoleon's cruelty, that I am unable to express it.

Don Mariano Stecher then gave me various of his publications, among them seven superb fugues for organ that I still have: I offered him in exchange some of my bagatelles, which pleased him greatly, and upon examining certain variations that I composed on a Cossack melody, he courteously said to me, "You are giving me gold for my lead." "I wish that my gold weighed half as much as your lead," I replied.

From Trent, we left for Bassano, Treviso, and Venice, where we stayed for two weeks to see the Regatta, the Coccagna, and other festivals that were given in honor of the Emperor of Austria, who was there during our sojourn.

From Venice, we went to Padua, Ferrara, Bologna, Pesaro and Loreto, where one can see benedictions of the crowns, rosaries and other such things in the chapel of the Madonna, as well as the procession of pilgrims on their knees around the church of the said chapel.

We left Loreto on the twenty-sixth, and, passing through Macerata, Terni, Narni, Otricoli, etc. we arrived at Rome on the first of December. We took apartments in the Strada della Croce, at the Piazza di Spagna, in a great house kept and rented out by a famous wig-maker called Luigi, who had a twisted mouth. We were served our meals by a certain Teresa Lotti, a chambermaid, and by a companion of hers, a sort of dwarf nicknamed Twisted, because her waist was like her employer's mouth. Teresa was a charming young woman, full of vivacity, but the twisted one was a little devil, if not a demon. Having become a little more familiar with them, we had them drink a few glasses of wine from Orvieto to make them chatter, so to learn what had happened in Rome after the evacuation of the French. To hear them murmur and blaspheme against the eminences, monsignori, and friars was enough to make you die laughing, and to cause us to ask each other, "Where are we? In Algeria, in Morocco, or in the city of the Holy See?"

As well as the infinite beauties of art and antiquities we saw with our every step through Rome, the extraordinary opportunity presented itself to see a large assembly of distinguished personages who have figured so much in modern history, a group that one would never have expected to find together in one place. Here are a few of them: Pius VII, liberated from Napoleon's persecutions, and restored as pontiff and sovereign; Cardinal Fesch, returned from the prisons of Alexandria della paglia; Cardinal Mauris, who was doing his exercises in a monastery by papal order; Charles VI, King of Spain; his minister and trustworthy prince of peace; the ex-king of Etruria; the ex-queen of Naples; Luciano Bonaparte, ex-prince of the Romans; the last Princess of Wales; and the widow of the English Pretender.

On the sixteenth, my companion proposed to leave that night for Naples, following the Roman courier and accompanied by two dragoons. Although it was against our agreement to not travel by night, I could not refuse

Chapter XVII
Sojourn at Naples - Prince Leopold of Naples - Count Mocenigo - Misfortunes and Death of Paisiello, and his Epicedium.

After an absence of twenty-eight years, what joy and happiness I felt in finding myself once again in Naples, and in seeing my dear Paisiello in good health, and my friends the Coltellinis prosperous and happy! I persuaded my companion to lodge at the Albergo di Venezia, and my feelings were great in finding myself opposite my maestro's house, and in the same apartments where I had begun to climb the ladder of musical composition. Having scarcely changed my clothes, I flew to Paisiello, and although he had been informed of my coming, he was nevertheless a little surprised to see me. I delivered a letter to him, which had been given me by his old benefactor and friend Count Woronzow, from whom he had had no news since his return from Paris, and in which the illustrious and generous lord gave him information about his worthy children, the General Count Woronzow, and Countess Pembroke. He closed the letter with a postscript, which said,

> "Dear Paisiello, I have already passed the age of seventy-two. God knows if we will have the occasion of seeing each other again!"

After having read the letter, which gave him the greatest pleasure, he let me know that he had been made Cavaliere by Murat and confirmed as such by Ferdinando IV, a title which was quite dear to him. He then told me his misadventures, for having been on good terms with Bonaparte, and with his family as well, he lost the favor and pension which he had had from Ferdinando. Through other political circumstances he also lost his pension from the Grand Duchess of Russia, and that from Napoleon, and lived only on the little salary from the Cappella Reale. To see a man of such genius and such merit, advanced to a great age, accustomed for more than a half-century to live like a lord, and now abandoned by the court, the nobility and by his friends in general, deprived of the consoling company of an uncle and a wife who adored him, and reduced, so to speak, almost to misery, was something that caused me pity and at the same time horror. But...

"Tempore felici multi numerantur amici:
Si fortuna perit nullus amicus erit".[1]

There are many friends, if there is fortune,
and when it is finished, there is no friendship.

Supplied with the two recommendations with which his Excellence the Count Woronzow had favored me, one for the Marquis Circello, minister of state, the other for Count Mocenigo, ambassador of Russia, as well as with a letter from the present Duchess d'Orleans for her brother, Prince Leopold of Naples, I took the liberty of introducing Paisiello to these personages, with the hope of being useful to him, and I would probably have been able to succeed in this, or he himself would have succeeded after my departure, if his imminent end had not been written in heaven. Notwithstanding, when I accompanied him to the Marquis Circello, we were welcomed with the greatest courtesy. The marchesa also came to compliment us, and to say a thousand flattering things, but without making any of the invitations to which we had been accustomed from them, Paisiello in Vienna, and I in Paris. We left their palace very cold, and disconsolate.

From there we went to Prince Leopold, and having sent him the little letter from his sister with our visiting cards, we were received with the greatest affability. He offered me his favor in whatever occasion I might have need of it, and then having turned to the maestro, said to him:

"Signor Cavaliere Paisiello, I have heard you and your music spoken of since I was born:

tell me, how many operas have you written in your life?" "Complete operas, a hundred," answered Paisiello. "But if you count the intermezzos, the farces, the ballets, church music, chamber music, etc. I would be able to add another hundred or so."

"And which are those which you consider the best?"

"Royal Highness, I couldn't say, unless they were the *Il Barbiere di Seviglia, Re Teodoro in Venezia*, or *Nina*." And in saying *Nina* tears fell from his eyes. The good Prince, moved by the sensibility of the old man, clasped his hand, saying:

"That one is the best, my dear Cavalier Paisiello, that one must be the best!"

In leaving Leopold's apartments, Paisiello exclaimed:

"Cursed be my luck! If this Prince were King, I would certainly get my pension back!"

---

[1] Ovid.

Happy with our second visit, we tried another to Count Mocenigo, who, after having read the letter that I presented to him, said to me:

"You are recommended to me by Count Woronzow, who I regard as my father, benefactor, and true friend. Everything that I possess in fortune and honors is completely his work, so I am at your service. My house is yours, nor can I say more."

He then asked Paisiello why he had not been to see him before, and he answered that being in disgrace at court he had not desired to present himself to an ambassador, even though he had known his generous sentiments for many years. "My domicile has nothing to do with the court," answered the count. "Come tomorrow then with your student to dine with me, and come back as often as you like, for I will be always happy to see you and to enjoy your company." It was a great pleasure for me to find a man acknowledging his benefactor, and being so liberal, nor did I profit, nor would I profit by his offer, without the most urgent necessity.

Paisiello was reassured that day, and had reason to hope for some subsidy, because in addition to the affability shown him by Prince Leopold and the influence of Counts Mocenigo and Woronzow in Russia, he had also the Prince of Castelcicala, the ambassador in Paris, who was working in his behalf with Louis XVIII. I left Paisiello for some time, and occupied myself with my little commercial enterprise and my traveling companion, who detested Naples during our first days there because it was as cold there as the most severe winters in England, and as there were no chimneys in our apartments, nor apartments with chimneys, we had to be content with a brazier of charcoal, which always gives a headache to those unaccustomed to it.

However, on Christmas Eve (a great festivity there) a usual occurence happened that greatly diverted Mr. Thomas, and which reconciled him to the cold and with the charcoal.

On that evening, until midnight, the common folk and certain well-to-do Neapolitans as well, make a greater racket than the Scottish common folk in Edinburgh from midnight until the morning of the first day of the year. At the end of our supper, we were visited by two couriers from the Cabinet, a certain Ferreri, whom I had known in London, and another, Rizzio, with whom Mr. Broadwood had traveled in Portugal and Spain. After having drunk a few glasses of wine together, they proposed to entertain themselves according to the local custom on that day, that is, by shooting fireworks out the windows, there called bombs. What happiness for an Englishman to make a ruckus outside his tranquil nest! The three bombers went out, and bought three hundred of those cartridges, which they then shot from the window wells. The owner of the house came out complaining that they alone were making more noise than ten neighboring houses, advising them to do charity to the poor, rather than wasting their money on fireworks. They unanimously answered him that he should keep his nose out of other people's business and that they preferred to encourage an industrious shopkeeper, instead of dropping their money in the hands of impertinent and lazy beggars. The owner went away satisfied with the answer.

Having finished the three hundred cartridges, and incited by the owner's observation, they went out once again to buy double bombs, but they could only scare up eighty, which they shot off, one of which fell in the wells of a window opposite our house, and in exploding broke several of its panes. The proprietor of that house immediately sent for a patrol, and very shortly we were assailed by a sergeant and four soldiers in our chamber. The first came up with an imposing air saying:

"Sirs, I am arresting you by order of the government!"

Ferreri jumped up, went over to the sergeant, and said to him angrily:

"To hell with you! You want to arrest an Englishman, an Austrian, and two couriers of the Cabinet! Get out of here immediately, or I'll have you put in jail, you and your pathetic soldiers!"

The poor sergeant was frightened, doffed his hat, and asked our pardon. Mr. Broadwood had everyone drink a glass of wine, paid two silver ducats for the broken windows, and gave the sergeant a ducat; the sergeant thanked him humbly and asked him not to say anything about what had happened.

The two couriers were of the greatest utility to my companion, and to me as well, because while they were diverting him with the beauties and curiosities of the capital and the surrounding area, I was taking care of my acquisitions. One day, however, I went with them to Vesuvius to go into the crater, there then being only that little bit of smoke coming out of its mouth that one sees even when there is no chance of an eruption. We stopped halfway at Portici to observe the statues of San Gennaro and Sant'Antonio, placed facing the mountain of the volcano. The statue of San Gennaro had been exhibited there from time immemorial, but after the invasion of the French, they knocked it down for spite and put up that of Sant'Antonio. After the restoration of Ferdinand, they put up a new statue of San Gennaro, next to the other.

Having gone halfway up the mountain, we found the usual hermit, who advised us to pay attention, because there were little streams of lava here and there which were running under the cinders. I then left their company and went to wait for them at Torre del Greco, where dinner had already been ordered. They continued on, and having joined me two hours later, they told me that as soon as they had entered the crater, they had received a wave of smoke, which had burnt their aces, and soiled their clothes. I congratulated them ironically;

Ferreri and Rizzio were blaspheming against San Gennaro and Sant'Antonio; Mr. Broadwood was exhilarated and as happy as if he had won the lottery.

"Bravo!" I said to him "*Monsier, la raison même!*"

"Go on, coward!" he replied, jokingly, "You don't know the pleasures of life!"

Several days later the plague appeared in the provinces of the kingdom. There was a cordon of fifteen thousand men to impede its progress. I immediately proposed to my friend to leave the city. "What!" he said, "Now is the right time to stay here!"

"And why is that?"

"Don't you see that when we return to London, all your friends will be happier than ever to see us after having escaped from assassins, Vesuvius, and the plague?"

"Dear Mr. Thomas, you are a race of people so extraordinary, that I can't understand you.

You care no more for your life than we care for a fig!"

No more than three weeks passed, and the plague vanished, which in reality was no more than a contagious fever. Then Mr. Broadwood decided to return to Rome.

In the midst of all this, I was visiting now and then with the Coltellinis, and with my maestro and friend. I had him write some pieces of music for Lady Pembroke, but they came out poorly; he had lost his memory, and could no longer produce a measured cantilena, nor link one phrase to another. Having agreed with my companion to leave Naples on January 30, 1816, our preparations for this end were made. Two days before leaving I went to receive Paisiello's directions, and the day after he came to me with a letter which he read me, in response to that which I had brought him from Count Woronzow, in which he gave a summary of his woes, and closed with a postscript which said:

"Your excellence tells me that you have passed seventy-two and that you don't know if we will see each other again. What can I say, as I have passed seventy-four!"

Poor man! He was flattering himself, because life was very dear to him and he had the weakness, as many others do, of concealing his age. He died three months after, and I heard the news in June of the same year in the house of Marquis Bristol, after my return to London. He was reading the gazettes, while I was teaching his charming daughters, Lady Augusta and Lady Georgina Harvey. All at once he exclaimed:

"Ferrari! Paiseillo is dead!"

"*Dio mio*, my lord! I left him only a few months ago in Naples in perfect health, although he was seventy-four."

"You are mistaken - read this paragraph, and you will find that he was eighty-four."

That did not surprise me, and consoled me in some fashion for the loss, because it convinced me of what I had suspected, that Paisiello was rather older than he said. The saying of Mrs. Thrale in her charming poem *The Three Warnings* seems applicable to the circumstance, and here it is in the translation of Stefano Egidio Petronii.

> The tree with deepest root is found,
> Least willing still to quit the ground.[2]

> (*L'arbor che sue radici ha piu sotterra,*
> *Vivo restar vuol piu sopra la terra.*)

Some time thereafter I received from Naples a splendid funeral collection of prose and poetry, preceded by a beautiful portrait of Paisiello, engraved by Guglielmo Morghen. The government, which wanted to make a public display of affection to that true son of the Parthenopean siren, who had shaped for such a long time the delights of the national and foreign stages, invited the most illustrious poets of the country to sing his glories before his marble urn. To give a taste of this collection, we call on the following

STROPHES DRAWN FROM THE EPICEDIUM AT THE TOMB OF PAISIELLO

Hail, O glory and love of the native soil
Whose every part you fill with light.
Nature and Art strove to show us in you
How much they could achieve.
Never will the dust of enemy oblivion
Come to rest on your works;
Because the Farna, ever avenging,
Will blow them away with her beating wings.

The Graces, who uprooted the sacred myrtles
On the cold bed of your eternal dreams
Did not disdain, one day, just to follow you,
To visit the wintery cliffs of Scythia;
Not only to Hyperborean reefs did you more sweetly
Take the breezes of perpetual springs,

---

[2] Hester Lynch Thrale Piozzi (1741-1821), writer, novelist, and patron of the arts. She is an important source for information about Dr. Samuel Johnson. The Three Warnings was published in 1798.

But you taught, midst suspended winds,
To a thousand foreigns echoes Italian accents.[3]

(Strofe Tratte Dall'Epicedio alla tomba Di Paisiello, Di Gabriele Rossetti

Salve, o Gloria ed amor del suol natio,
Ch'empi di luce ogni remota parte;
Tutto in te di mostrarci ebber desio
Quanto potean fra lor Natura ed Arte.
Non mai la polve del nemico obblio
A posarsi verrà sulle tue carte;
Poichè la Fama, vindice immortale,
La sgomberà col ventilar dell'ale.
Le Grazie, che sfondaro I sacri mirti
Sul freddo letto de' tuoi sonni eterni,
Non isdegnaro un dì, sol per seguirti,
Visitar della Scizia I balzi iberni:
Nè sol più dolci all'iperboree sirti
Prendesti l'aure dei perpetui verni,
Ma tu insegnasti, frai sospesi venti,
A mille echi stranieri itali accenti.)

The poet closes with the following apostrophe to Paisiello's shade, asking that he refresh the taste for vocal harmony, which has been so altered by the present school:

Let not the multiform tumultuous foreign
Cacophony no longer dare with haughty pomp
To come and deafen the scene
Upon the Ausionian sands;
But may the gentle primal simplicity
In which Rome and Athens educated the arts
Rediscover, through you, after its long error
The lost ways from the ear to the heart.

(*Fa che non più fastosamente altera*
Osi venir fin sull'ausonie arene
La multiforme bizarria straniera
Tumultuosa ad assordar le scene;
Ma la gentil semplicità primiera
Che nell'arti educò Roma ed Atene
Per te ritrovi, dopo il lungo errore,
Le vie perdute dall'orecchio al cor.)

---

[3] Gabriele Pasquale Giuseppe Rossetti (1783–1854), an Italian poet who emigrated to England in the 1820. He was the father of Dante Gabriel Rossetti and Christina Rossetti. This poem does not seem to have been published elsewhere.

Chapter XVIII.

Departure from Naples. – Brief Stay in Rome. – The Cascade at Tivoli.- Donna Giulia di Dor I Meri. – Florence, and Leghorn. – Return to England.- Arrival in London.

We left Naples on the day that had been set, and without a courier, or any escort, we arrived in Rome on the first of February, after having slept for six hours at Terracina, and the same number at Velletri. We found the apartments we had had before unoccupied, and were happy to take them once more: our host and his serving girls likewise were happy to see us again. The crippled woman, though ugly and getting old, was more amusing than ever and was always speaking badly of the Pope for having reestablished the orders and convents of nuns. But what most upset her was that women were not allowed to walk the streets at night, nor to be seen at the window in the daytime. "Hell!" she would say, "how is it possible for us poor serving women to find a husband if we cannot let our beauties be seen!" Teresa, more moderate than her companion, would say, "God bless the French, who know women's value, and know how to give them gifts!"

Among the eminent persons whom we met in Rome in our journey to Naples, we found the Duchess of Devonshire, with one of her sons, Mr. Foster, returned from a little trip they had made through Italy. She sent us a polite invitation to a salon that she was giving, where the guests would include the widow of the English Pretender, the same woman who had traveled with the highly celebrated Alfieri in England and Scotland under the name of the Duchess of Albania, a name that the illegitimate daughter of Charles Stuart had taken earlier. Unfortunately, we had gone to spend several days at Frascati and Tivoli, and so we were unable to take advantage of such an honor, receiving the invitation only after the party was over.

We had quite a fine time at Tivoli seeing the metal works, and rushing through the villa of Luciano Bonaparte. To offer a description of the latter, I will only say that it originally belonged to a convent of Jesuits, and so the reader will immediately understand that there one finds all the pleasures in life.

Everyone knows the cascade at Tivoli, and yet there are still a few things for me to say about it.

It falls from an immense height, and expands into a sort of lake next to the city, from which it descends precipitously among boulders and caverns, and throwing itself into the plain, finds a bank, and a great hole where it forms a chasm, where the vapor from the waters rises thirty feet in the air, spreading a mist over the earth and stones which makes one slip as if walking on ice. Travelers, in general, stay a certain distance from the chasm, but my little Englishman wanted to walk up to the very edge of the precipice, and he returned a few minutes later sopping wet, as if he had taken a bath. I asked him if, after having been burned by Vesuvius, and refreshed by the waters of Tivoli, he yet desired to take on a new challenge. He answered with the usual English good-nature, "Don't nag me, my dear friend, and let me enjoy myself."

Our stay at Rome was beginning to annoy my companion. "What a difference," he would say, "from the liveliness and merriment of Naples! If here one lives so sadly during Carnival, what will Lent be like? Let's go, let's go!" We left on the 20th for Florence, passing through Viterbo, Montefiascone, Acquapendente, Radicofani, Torimeri, Siena, etc., always stopping before dark in some city or village. One night we slept at Torimeri, and were served dinner by the lady of the inn (Donna Giulia), who was one of the most beautiful creatures one could see, and who spoke the purest Tuscan that I had ever heard. With the fruit she offered my friend a glass of sweet wine, which he accepted, and with which he made a toast. This put her in a good mood, and she told us the little story that follows.

"At fifteen years old I was married, and once the wedding was over, I found myself assailed by a bad fever, which kept me in bed for three months, and even more time convalescing. I had four children whom I lost one after the other, and who are always in my heart. In addition, I have the unhappiness of having a jealous husband, who torments me, persecutes me, and does not let me talk with anyone. If you see me here with you, it is because my servant is sick, but if he were here at home, you would see that he would serve you himself, rather than let me enter your room. Oh, poor me! And my poor lost beauty! If you had known me before I was married you would have marveled; my complexion was white as snow, and my red cheeks like those apples."

My cold Englishman was touched to the soul by this speech, and began to warm, and to seriously fall for Donna Giulia, so that he said:

"What! You complain of the jealousy of your husband! And who, having the felicity of possessing you, would not be jealous? You are as fair as an angel and fresh as a rose, and your voice and speech are so sweet and suave, that they ravish and enchant one at the same time. Ah!"

The ingenuous Tuscan was sensitive to my companion's compliments, but while she smiled happily, while the fool was sighing, and while I was putting out the lights, we could hear in a distance the braying of an ass. "Ah! My husband!" she exclaimed.

"Your husband?"

"Yes, he went with his little ass to the forest nearby to cut wood. Now they have returned, and that beast brays every time he comes near the house. I am thus obliged to leave you, with the greatest displeasure, because if my husband were to find me here with you, I am sure that he would break my bones. And so, good night. Good night."

"Good night, dear Signor Tommaso," I said to him, joking. He feigned indifference, but throughout our journey he could never forget Donna Giulia from Torimeri.

From that little village, we arrived at Florence on the last day of the month.

Although Florence is not a vast metropolis, it is still a considerable city, elegant, and worth seeing. The Arno and its bridges present a grand view, the farms are admirable, and the hills around the city delightful and cultivated in the best way possible.

Cavalier Fontana no longer existed, but his collection of natural history was more complete than when I saw it with Cavalier Campan. I found two friends there from London, the poet Pananti and Mr. Lanzoni. The latter was living either in Florence or a small distance away, in a most beautiful country house near Villa Catalani.

On March 8 we made an excursion to Pisa and Leghorn, and in returning from that port near Empoli, and at a certain bridge of alabaster, Mr. Broadwood discovered a young boy in a little ditch who was pulling boughs off trees and branches from vines. A ruffian arrived and began to beat him with the butt of a pistol in the cruelest manner. Mr. B, moved by compassion, stopped the horses, and jumped down from the carriage, and ran toward the ruffian; the latter jumped over the ditch, and ran away like a madman, so that in a few minutes he could no longer be seen. The former gave a *scudo* to the poor boy, who went home heaping him with blessings.

We stayed another three days in Florence, and left for Turin on the 16th, stopping for a half or a whole day at Bologna, Modena, Reggio, Parma, Piacenza, Tortona, Alessandria, etc.

Outside a gate to the city and fortress of Alessandria, they showed us a man who had been hanged a few hours before our arrival. We asked why, and they told us the horrible story that I present here.

A young cheese maker from Alessandria married a maiden with whom he lived in perfect harmony. In 1812, he had the misfortune to be chosen as one of the conscripts in the immense army that Napoleon sacrificed in Russia. As soon as he had departed, a lawyer friend of his courted his wife, seduced her and took up residence in the husband's house. The latter was spared by the cannons and the ice, and retreating from the defeated army, he wrote to his wife that he was about to return, and then the seducer moved back to his own house. The conscript, a few weeks after his return to Alessandria, disappeared for some time without either the civil or military authorities being able to discover where he was. Finally a poodle, who had been accustomed to go often to the cheese maker, from whom he would get crusts of cheese and learn tricks, was leaving the city one morning with his owner, and when they had gone a certain distance he began to sniff everywhere, went into a field, and began to paw at the earth beneath a large fig tree. His owner followed him, and two peasants who were working in the same field, seeing the animal so engaged, approached and helped to dig up the plot with their hoes. About three feet down they discovered a calf which had been killed and stretched out. They took it out of the hole, and when they wanted to fill the hole once again, the wise poodle jumped in, and began to dig more anxiously, baying, and making terrible cries. The peasants dug once more, and a little further down they found the body of the unfortunate conscript, whom the owner of the dog recognized immediately. The two workers took on the task of carrying the cadaver to their house, and the owner returned immediately to the city to inform the government of what had taken place. They immediately had the gates of the city closed, but while they were carrying out the most extensive investigation, a scoundrel came forward and reported that he and a companion had murdered the poor innocent, enticed by a sum of money that the lawyer, together with the wife of the deceased, had given them. The one who confessed was pardoned, and the accomplice as well. We had seen hanged the infamous seducer, and two days later we were informed at Turin that the infamous meretrix had suffered the same fate.

From entering the Apennines to Turin we traveled almost always on a bed of snow, transported in clouds by the tremendous winds from the Swiss mountains and from the Tyrol, which had fallen, and was resting on those immense plains.

We only spent three days in that area, and that which we enjoyed the most was the Royal Theater, which is certainly the cleanest, most commodious, and most sonorous in Italy.

In the course of our trip through that divine country, music was the thing that interested us the least. The operas of Guglielmi, Sarti, and Paisiello were no longer performed, nor those of Cimarosa. Sometimes one heard those of Meyer and Paerm but never those by Mozart. The music of Rossini was beginning to catch fire, although it was either applauded or booed, depending on the caprices of the public.

Between the 26th and 27th, we crossed over Monte Cenisio, but with great difficulty, because it was covered with snow that was extremely deep. In spite of this we arrived at the summit, and the sun was so strong that we had to take off our cloaks and the wool pants that we were wearing over our boots.

We arrived at Lyons on the 30th, on April 5 in Paris, and on the 8th at Calais, where we had to wait three days for a favorable wind.

On the 12th we embarked in a little English vessel, with about twenty passengers. The weather was terrible; the wind was strong, the sea tempestuous, and an almost icy brine was falling. We left the pier, followed by two French vessels, which, having only traveled a mile to sea turned around and returned to shore. But the intrepid English captain kept going, and although the sea kept rising, and although we had seven octaves of wind against us, he brought us to Dover in only five hours, but the tide was low, and we couldn't enter the harbor until two or three hours later. Various mariners with little boats offered passage to land, but as the waves at the entrance of the pier were as high as those in the Channel, I made Mr. Broadwood swear that he would not expose himself to such a danger, and he was ready to refuse to go. But two or three passengers came (English, of course) and suggested that he go with them. He, from a desire to not appear fearful, and I, wanting to leave the sea, both went down with them into the boat, leaving our baggage with the servant. As soon as we had cast off from the ship, a wave arrived that was so high and frightful that it caused not only my companions to tremble, but the sailors themselves, so that they all began to take off their clothes, in order to jump overboard and swim. I, who can swim no better than a stone, kept quiet, commending my soul to God, and waiting to become fish food at any moment. Luckily in ten minutes we set foot on land, but with our clothes stuck to our skins, and with our coats frozen to our clothes. We went to the York Inn, nor I can I sufficiently praise the hospitality and attention that we received there. We slept there, the next day at Dartford, and on the 14th we arrived at the great metropolis safe and sound.

Chapter XIX
Trip to Brighton - Study of Singing - Residence in Scotland - Return to England.

Three hours after my arrival in London I went to Brighton to see my little family once more, and my consolation was great to find my wife in better health and my children happy and joyous at seeing me again. I stayed with them for five days and then returned to look after my affairs, and to be ready to receive and dispose of my merchandise from Italy. I went immediately to present the homage due to my ambassador, His Highness the Prince Paul Esterhazy, whom

I had already had the honor of meeting earlier, and from that moment to this, both he and his illustrious consort have always filled me to overflowing with courtesy and honors.

A few years later I composed and published a study of singing, in two volumes, one after the other, the first of which, dedicated to Mr. T. Broadwood. It had, and has still, a great following because it is easy and well adapted to England where adequate time is not given to the most difficult aspects of singing.[4]

The second volume, even if superior to the first, nonetheless had less success, nor can I suggest a reason. I had the pleasure of dedicating this volume to the daughter of the celebrated Naldi, one of the most loveable and interesting young ladies. From her infancy she displayed a happy talent for everything. Educated with the greatest care, she became mistress of various languages, of drawing, singing, etc. Having proceeded with the greatest prudence and affability, she conquered the esteem and affection of Count Spard, a Frenchman, who married her many years ago, and with whom she lives very happily, as she deserves.

A few months after the coronation of George IV, I had the honor of dedicating to him six canons in three parts, and among the various little works that I wrote with great success in this genre, these are incomparably the best of all. If it has not become popular, I am to blame, having made the accompaniments more for a capable player than for a common accompanist.

In the year 1823, I was offered a position as a singing master in Edinburgh, for a certain sum of money, with the prospect of making a quick fortune there. Seduced by the offer and by the desire of seeing beautiful Edinburgh again, I went there on the third of May to give it a try, and was so satisfied by the welcomes I received in the city, and from the whole situation I would have there, that I wrote to my wife, proposing to her to join me the following year with my children. She had been advised by the doctors to live by the sea, she could stay just as well in the Scottish capital as in Brighton, and it would be a great advantage to my son to continue the career which he had begun as a surgeon, and to perfect himself in their college and hospitals. The answer was that my letter had greatly agitated her in even thinking of such a trip, and that she was sure that she would never be able to undertake it, neither by sea nor by land. I was disappointed at that point, but later was happier about it, since I could see that my stay in Edinburgh would not be long, having quickly discovered that, outside of the nobility and some travelers or particular individuals, the Scottish

---

[4] This is Ferrari's *Breve tratto di canto italiano*, also published in English translation by William Shield as *Concise Treatise on Italian Singing* (London, 1818).

in general were still not accustomed to Italian music. They much prefer their national melodies and are right to do so, since among the oldest ones, above all, there are some that are very beautiful, and they enjoy together the poetry and the original music of their country. During the two seasons I was there in the years 1824 and 1825, I had my daughter with me for company; she also was received with the greatest courtesy. I believe I must boast of the particular and infinite courtesies that we received from the families of Counts Wemyss, and Elgin, from Mr. H. Hasting Anderson, from the Marquis Riario Sforza and from the French consul, Cavalier Masclet. Mrs. Stark was a good friend of mine, and I am happy to have taken the care to instruct and advance her only daughter so that I have been told she is now the most popular singing teacher in that capital. In addition to Miss Stark I had various others students, who applied themselves more or less to Italian song as one should, and who I name here: Lady Lucy Bruce, Miss Ferrier, Miss Little Gilmore, the niece of Consigliere Hope, and the daughter of General Sir John Hope, the daughter of Colonel Donsmure, the daughters of Doctor Johnstone, the daughter of Professor Russell, and the two Wilkinsons, the younger of which was already, at ten years old, a little prodigy.

A precious acquaintance I made was with the family of a Mr. Robertson, he in Edinburgh, and his wife and two daughters (my students) in Glenesk, between Roslin Castle and Lasswade. Glenesk is a pleasant little place, adorned with the greenest and most luxuriant trees, full of singing birds. Along the fields runs a limpid little river, as useful for the paper mills as for doing the washing. What interested me most was that it quite resembled the area by the San Colombano bridge in Roveredo, so that when I was walking there or spending the night, I did naught else but think or dream of my hometown.

Mr. Robertson was a man on in years, but one of those old men who never get old. He was always joyful, flippant, and extremely liberal, and when he had friends to dinner, he was always the last to get up from the table to go to bed. He took delight, as do many others, in telling and listening to anecdotes and little stories, but he would never forgive those who told improbable tales. He asked me one day, as if something extraordinary, if I had ever been shaved by a woman, because if I should take such a thing into my head he could easily satisfy my whim, as he knew a famous one in the vicinity. I said to him that I had had such a pleasure more than once in France, and that, in fact, I knew that there was an even more extraordinary woman in England who shaved the dead. "Oh," exclaimed the good old man, "you must be making that up." "Well," I added, "my dear Mr. Robinson, if you don't believe my story, I don't know the name nor the address of this woman, but if you would like to write to your correspondent in London, and send him on my account to such a person, he will be informed, and will inform you in more detail of my assertion." My incredulous friend did so and received the following answer.

"From the friends of your Mr. Ferrari I have discovered that although his story seems strange, it is nothing but the truth, and here is what they said to me: Nanny Gunner, wife of a pensioner of the hospital at Chelsea, lives with her husband at Crookham, near Odiham, in the county of Hampshire. She shaves dead men, but not the living; she is extremely active and useful to the whole vicinity...."

My dear Caledonian was surprised and astonished, but not entirely persuaded.

On another occasion, finding myself at his house with various friends, the conversation turned to music, and Mr. Robertson asked me what I thought of the prejudice and absurdity of his Presbyterian brothers in not allowing an organ in their churches because John Knox had declared that he did not want music in churches, asserting that such an instrument was nothing but a wooden box filled with whistles. I answered him that it was not my place to question the opinion of a reformer, but that, as he found the most solemn instrument in music antipathetic, I considered Mr. Knox a man without ears, let alone a soul, and that a church without an organ seemed to me like a garden without flowers, a room without furniture, or a good meal not followed by a cup of coffee. My amiable host understood the jest, and although not used to taking coffee after dinner, he nevertheless ordered that it be made at that instant for his friends. He then told me the two anecdotes that follow.

When he was in Vienna, a celebrated singer of the Italian theatre in that metropolis was contracted for London, and in taking leave of her lover, with whom she had lived for many years, he wept, sighed, and seemed to despair that she had to leave. She said to him:

"Dear Antonietto, I am leaving you, but I am not abandoning you, and my heart will be yours as long as I live, and even after if ever we should meet."

"Adored Bettina, you wound me, you rip out my vitals! Go, my soul, farewell, and be happy."

"Good-bye, Antonietto, my sun, good-bye!"

"Good-bye, Bettina, my star, good-bye!"

As she was about to get into the carriage she took a step back, and said to her love in the coldest tones possible:

"Excuse me, my dear Antonietto, but I had almost forgotten that you owe me a *zecchino* that I loaned you six months ago when we were rushing to the imperial palace."

"Ah, you stingy scoundrel," he answered with disdain, "is this the regret which has you moaning? Here is your *zeccchino*, but I hope that you break your legs before you are halfway through your journey."

A certain Nicola, after having lived for more than fifty years with a certain Lucrezia, fell sick, and one morning he died. His friend was also sick at the same time but survived. Several hours after the funereal event, the executor of the will, an intimate friend of the house, entered Lucretia's bedroom, and she immediately asked news of Nicola, saying that she had been very restless during the night, having known that Nicola had been so unwell the night before. The executor replied that he was much better, since he had gone to the next world. "Is that so!" she replied angrily, "I told him so; it's his fault. He had the bad habit of taking off his clothes and walking around the room for a half an hour before getting in bed; he caught a cold, it went to his chest, and now he's dead, as he deserved. I hope, however, that such a misfortune will not bring any unfortunate consequences. Bring me his will."

In the course of these two seasons, I wrote another singing treatise and six Italian ariettas that cost me a lot of effort, because I wrote both of them with the greatest commitment and *amour propre*. In 1826 I prepared to reestablish myself in London, seeing that affairs in Edinburgh were not going as I had hoped. My daughter was not happy there, because she had lost the company of her friend Miss M. Medley, and what is more, because she was so far from her mother toward whom she had always had such affection. In spite of this I would have stayed yet through that next season, but because of a new regulation at the college of surgery my son was prohibited from entering. I decided to return immediately to my second homeland of England, and I arrived in London on the first day of 1827.

Chapter XX
Italian Opera - Accademia de' Filarmonici - New Voice Study - Benefice at Almacks - Royal Academy - Incidents etc.

No sooner was I arrived than I had the fortune of finding some little things to do. I went to Bromley, and there I found others, enough to satisfy my desire for sleeping outside of London now and then. But what a surprise and what a blow it was for me, entering the college to see all those beautiful trees, which I mentioned earlier, knocked down and cut off at the root, in the season where the poor crows were hatching their eggs! I almost wept and raged at the same moment against such cruel destruction. I thereupon found my old friends in good health, hospitable as usual, but quite saddened by the loss of their trees and the change in their fields.

Having been deprived of Italian musical drama for three years running, I was extremely glad to again obtain free entry to the King's Theatre, and to hear successively the distinguished talents of Signori Curioni, Torri, Velluti, Donzelli, Bordogni, Galli, Galli junior, Zuchelli, Pellegrini, Porto, Benetti, Santini Ambrogi, De Angelis, and the resounding and magnificent voice of Signor Lablache; as well as those of the Signore Pasta, Vestris, Tosi (Puzzi), Carotori (Allen), Schutz, Sontag, Pisaroni, Brambilla, Blasis, Lalande and Malibran Garcia.

As far as the music performed in that theatre is concerned, there is not much novelty. Sometimes during the season they give Meyer's *Medea*, Zingarelli's *Romeo e Giulietta*, Paisiello's *Nina*, Mozart's *Figaro*; all the rest is nothing but Rossini and more Rossini, to keep up with the rest of Europe. In spite of the fact that I have a great regard for the talent and the genius of that composer, I can do no less than observe that hearing always the same style and the same character of music, buffo as well as serious, can only annoy the ears of the listeners, and make them say, as the French do. "*Toujours perdrix! Toujours perdrix!*" (A l w a y s the same! Always the same!)

That spring I published my new volume regarding the theoretical and practical instruction in singing, dedicated to his excellence the Duke of Devonshire. I freely recommend the work to students as well as teachers, being instructive for the former, and not boring for the latter. In it will be found (in addition to theoretical instruction) the way of forming and improving the voice, the intonation and articulation of the student, the way of taking intervals with less difficulty than the usual, as well as the way of giving consistency, flexibility and bravura to the voice.5

Immediately thereafter I published six Italian ariettas dedicated to Miss Jessy Rolls, which will justify what I said in my nineteenth chapter, i.e. that I approve of and admire modern music, up to a certain point, and if someone seeks to criticize me for having modulated too much myself, I would ask him to examine the poetry and music of this little work. There he will find that my modulations and my accompaniments are always intended to express the sentiment of the words.

I went several times to the Royal Philharmonic Society, where I had the satisfaction of hearing the symphonies of Haydn, Mozart and Beethoven, and so many other beautiful vocal and instrumental compositions executed with the greatest exactness and perfection.

Among the singers I have heard and admired at that academy, I am pleased to recall (in addition to those already mentioned above from the opera) Luigi Sapio, whose beautiful voice, well-produced and consistent, and elegant style

---

5 *Studio di musica teorica pratica* (London, 1830)

of singing always give delight to those who hear him. Also, Miss Paton and Madame Caradori, both of whom possess flexible and well-tuned voices, and moreover whose talent and both natural and acquired genius will never fail to delight the public, but even more those of the public who love good music and exactness in singing.

The orchestra of the Philharmonic Society is composed of a great number of eminent professionals, some of whom I have the honor to name alphabetically for the reader.

> First Violin and solo players: F. Cramer, Rieswetler, Loder, Mori,
> Spagnoletti, Weichsell.
> Violas: Lyon Moralt.
> Violoncellos: Lindley.
> Contrabassi, or Violini: Dragonetti, Anfossi.
> Flutes: Nicholson.
> Oboe: Cooke Junior.
> Clarinets: Willman.
> Bassoons: Mackintosh.
> Horn: Platt.
> Trumpets: Harper.
> Trombones: Mariotti.
> Timpani: Chipp.

> Pianists: J.B. Cramer, Mochelles, Neate, C. Potter.

Accompanists: I think it is well to omit the name of these respectable professionals, since every day the duty of accompanist in public academies is nothing but a synonym of V.S. V.S. - *Vostra Signoria, Volti Subito!* (Your Lordship, come back soon!)

Many of the talents praised above have made me desire more than once to have been born thirty years later than I was, and in a city, in order that I might too have profited by today's clear instructions and by the evident progress in instrumental music. Yet, if this had been the case, and if I had had such an advantage, talent, and the means to distinguish myself, I would never agree to compose certain extravagances, nor to attempt difficulties, which though astonishing, are not moving, and which today are executed frequently on every instrument.

I have already said in the first part of this work that in earlier times players sought to sing on their instruments, and that the singers wanted to play with their voices.

Now, the abuse by male singers, and even more so by female singers, has increased to such an extent that they take instrumental cantilenas and passages, put words underneath that have nothing to do with the cantilenas or passages, and sing or (rather don't sing) the whole thing, throwing dust in the eyes and ears of the public that admires them.

The players, jealous of this, are always increasing the difficulties in their music, and here are the consequences.

First of all, the string instruments are supplied with thicker strings, the bow is solid, its hair thick and well-rosined in order to draw more sound, which causes the voices to become faint. The wind instruments want to play higher pitches, in order to be more brilliant, and to make the singers croak, burying them.

And then there is the battle between the players of one instrument and the other. The violoncelli would like to surpass the violins by force of harmonic sounds, the bassoons the oboe, the clarinets the flutes, the piccolos the flageolets, the harps the pianofortes. And here I stop.

As the piano is the instrument most apt for producing a clear execution, a rich harmony, legato, and exquisite, leaping and variable passages, hundreds of players and composers have written volumes of pieces more or less beautiful, easy, difficult, diabolical etc., so that one would say that there is no longer any novelty for that instrument. But no; the field is open as much for present, as well as future, composers, since the use of the pedals, the development of harmony, and the extension of the keyboard will always produce effects novel to the connoisseur, and even newer to he who doesn't know anything.

Thirty-eight years ago, there was no pianoforte in Europe that exceeded five octaves, beginning from the first low F, up to the sixth high F; in that year the addition of a fourth in the treble up to C was made. This succeeded in making a brilliant effect. Some years later a third was added to the bass, down to C, but the lower one goes, the less one can distinguish the vibrations. After many years the addition of another third in the treble up to F was made, whose sounds seem rather to emanate from steel hammers which strike a piece of boxwood, than from hammers of wood, covered with leather, which are striking steel strings.

Now they make them in seven octaves; if I might sleep rather than die, I am persuaded that, after two or three generations, I would find, upon waking up, a pianoforte of ten to twelve octaves, with as many pedals; but then it would be necessary for the player to really stretch his arms and hands, in order to touch the two extremities of the instrument. It would also be necessary, when one plays, to put an ear-trumpet in the left ear to distinguish the vibrations of the bass notes, and an earplug in the right, so as not to hear the rawness of the treble notes.

But to what purpose my observations and my blithering? Music at present is nothing but speculation or business on the one side, a fashion and a madness on the other, and few are the dilettanti who apply themselves to study it as they should, to know its true merit, and to enjoy the most interesting and pleasing ornament of any age.

In the month of February 1828, I gave a benefit at Almacks, under the patronage of my constant protectors her Royal Highness the Princess Esterhazy, the Countesses Tankerville, Carlisle, Cowper, Lady James Hay, the Contessa di St. Antonio (now Duchessa di Canizzaro) etc., which brought me much honor. In the summer of the same year I was attacked by violent gout, which brought with it a contraction of the little finger of my right hand, so inflamed that I was expecting at every moment that it might end in a mortification of the tissue. However by steam baths and frequent rubbings I escaped it, and after a few weeks I began to give lessons again, to accompany, and to compose as I am doing at present.

In the year 1829, walking one morning along Percy Street, I was suddenly assaulted, struck in the chest, and stretched out on the ground, without knowing by whom, or for what reason. A moment after I saw next to me an ox, luckily without horns, but who, with his head and his fore hooves, rolled me into the middle of that street. I was rescued, but I don't know by whom, since for several minutes I was senseless, as much from the fright of seeing that beast over me, as from the contusions which I received in the chest, and from the two cuts on the head that I received rolling. Leeches were applied to me, and in a few hours the pain passed, and in a few days the contusion. To divert myself after such an accident, I composed various little things, among which were three little terzettas in canon for the young ladies Hanrott, now published and dedicated to the same, and which I do not doubt will have a happy result if they are well executed.

At the end of 1829 and the beginning of 1830, I had the pleasure of being present at the opera performances given in the hall of the Teatro del Re, by the alumni of the Royal Academy, and of applauding the happy dispositions and precocious talents of Miss Childe, Miss Bromely, Miss Tucker; of Mr. Brizzi, Mr. E. Seguin, Mr. Smith, Mr. Packer, as well as for the whole orchestra.

Guided by the music director, Maestro C. Potter, they obtained from the public the greatest and well-merited applause. Among the students of this institution, there are young composers, who like some other English and foreign composers in London, deserve to be encouraged not only by the subscribers of the Royal Academy, but also by the directors of the Philharmonic Academy, as much for the good of the art, as for the honor of the two institutions in protecting the living artists who know their trade, who are hard-working, and who only lack experience and the encouragement of the public to make progress and produce beautiful works.

If the last reigning Prince Esterhazy had not spurred Haydn, providing him with an orchestra at his command so that he might have the means of hearing and criticizing frequently his own music, we would certainly not have the sublime and immortal models which he has left us, nor the beauties of Mozart, of Beethoven, etc. which stem from that great genius.

P.S.

As the honor and permission of dedicating the preceding pages to His Majesty has been graciously granted me; and having spoken in these pages of so many illustrious and distinguished personages, as well as of so many princes and sovereigns, it must certainly seem strange that I have hardly mentioned the name of the august monarch to whom I have dedicated the work. Now I will present the reason.

For many years, and in various circumstances, His Majesty has known the sentiments of veneration and gratitude that I nourish for his Royal Person. But I restrict myself to a respectful silence, fearing that, by speaking them, I would offend his modesty. But, if my lips are silent, a sincere voice will always exclaim in my heart:

Domine salvum fac Regem!
(Oh Lord, Save the King!)

The Works of Giacomo Gottifredo Ferrari

*This list combines works contained in library collections and the Works List from the 1920 Sandron edition of Aneddoti.

Works for Stage

-- *Le pescatrici* (not performed)

-- *Les Evénements imprévus*, libretto by T. D'Hèle (Paris, Theatre Montansier, 1791).

-- *Isabelle de Salisburi*, libretto by P.F.N. Fabre d'Eglantine (Paris, Theatre Montansier, 1791).

-- "Se mi tormenti, amor!" - Scena con recitativo (London, Salomon Concerts).

-- additional music for Bianchi's *La Villanella Rapita* (1789)

-- additional music for Sarti's *Fra I due littiganti* (1789)

-- *I due svizzeri* (London, 1799).

-- *Il Rinaldo d'Asti* (London, 1801)

-- *L'eroina di Raab* (London, 1814).

-- *Lo sbaglio fortunate* (1817)

-- *Borea e Zeffiro*, ballet divertisement, (London, 1810).

-- *La Dama di Spirito* (London).

Songs and Vocal Arrangements

-- *La Villanella Rapita* (piano arrangement of the opera buffa above, London, 1797).

-- *Sei Romanze* with piano accompaniment (Paris, 1793).

    -- *Complainte de la reine de France* (1793)

-- *Sei Duettini in Italiano* with piano accompaniment (Paris, 1796).

    -- *Dodici Ariette Italiane di Metastasio*, with piano accompaniment (Paris, 1797, perhaps earlier 1787-1792).

    -- *Sei Canzonette Italiane* (London, 1796).

    -- *Dodici nuove romanze* with piano accompaniment, in 2 vols. (Paris, 1798).

    -- *Le Depart — Grande scène*, with piano and harp accompaniment (Paris, 1798).

-- *Tre Canzonette* with pianoforte and guitar accompaniment, Parts I and II (Leipzig).

-- *Sei Canzoni a tre voci* with piano accompaniment, (Leipzig).

-- *Papa⌐* — song with piano accompaniment (Leipzig).

-- *Sei Ariette* (Vienna: Artaria, 1810).

-- *Six Favorite Italian Canzonets* (London, 1814)

-- *Solo amor:* a favorite new song (Londong, 1815)

Chamber Music, Piano and/or Harp.

-- *Tre Sonate con violino,* op. I. (Paris, 1788).

-- *Tre Sonata con violino,* op. 2. (Paris, 1788).

    -- *Tre Sonata, con violino e contrab.,* op. 3. (Paris, 1788).

-- *Douze Petites Pièces,* op. 4 (Vienna).

-- *Trois Sonates avec violon et basse* op. 5 (Vienna).

-- Concerto in C major, op. 6 (Paris).

-- *Concerto for the pianoforte,* op. 45 (London: Birchall, 1815).

    -- *Trois Sonates avec violon et basse* op. 7 (Vienna).

-- *Caprice pour le clavecin* op. 8 (Vienna).

-- *Trois Sonatines* (Offenbach).

    -- *Trois Sonates avec violon* op. 9 (Vienna).

    -- *Douze Petites Pieces,* op. 10 (Offenbach).

    -- *Trois Solos,* op. 11 (Paris, 1796).

    -- *Trois Sonates avec violon ad lib* (Offenbach, 1797).

-- *Trois Sonates avec violon et violoncelle obl.* op. 12.

-- *Trois Sonates avec flûte* (Paris, 1798).

    -- Trois Sonates dont la deuxième avec violon obl. op. 13 (Offenbach).

    -- *Douze Sonates,* op. 14 (Vienna).

    -- *Trois Sonates avec violon* op. 15 (Vienna).

    -- *Quatre Sonatines pour harpe et violon* op. 16 (London).

-- *Trois Sonates d' une éxècution facile pour harpe et violon* (Paris, 1797)

    -- *Trois Grandes Sonates pour harpe, violon et violoncelle,* op. 19 (Paris: Pleyel, 1798).

-- *Trois Solos* op. 20 (Offenbach and Paris).

-- *Trois Sonates pour le pianoforte,* op. 31 (Paris, 1802)

    -- *Duo pour deux pianos ou harpe et piano* (Offenbach and Paris).

    -- *XXIV Variazioni per il pianoforte* (Naples, 1793).

-- *Douze Variations.* (Naples,1793).
   -- *Ouverture des Les Evénements imprévus pour le piano* (Offenbach, 1797).

-- Sonates faciles pour la harpe, bk. 4

-- *Six Plaisanteries pour pianoforte & flute* (London, 1814)

Writings

- *Breve trattato di canto italiano* (London, 1818; Eng. trans. by W. Shield, 1818)

- *Studio di musica teorica pratica* (London, 1830; Eng. trans., c1830)

- *Aneddotti piacevoli e interessanti occorsi nella vita di Giacomo Gotifredo Ferrari da Rovereto* (London, 1830)

   - ed. *S. di Giacomo* (Palermo, 1920)

Appendix A

Entry in the 1827 edition of Sainsbury's Dictionary. [1] The entry most probably contained information provided by Ferrari himself, and may have spurred Ferrari into collating and publishing his Aneddoti.

FERRARI (GIACOMO GOTIFREDO) is the son of Francesco Ferrari, a respectable merchant and silk-manufacturer at Roveredo, in the Italian Tyrol. G. G. Ferrari, after the usual course of study in the public school at Roveredo, was sent by his father to Verona, to finish his education under the Abbate Pandolfi. There he began sol fa, and to learn thorough-bass, first under Abbate Cubri, and subsequently under Marcola, and at the same time to play on the harpsichord, under Borsaro; these being esteemed the first masters at Verona, at that time. Ferrari showed immediately a great natural genius for music, and, in the course of two years, and, accompanied, and played at sight. He then returned to Roveredo, and was taken into his father's counting-house. But music was already so much his delight, that he determined in his own mind to become a composer, and to learn the theory of every instrument for that purpose. He persuaded his father to let him learn to play on the flute; assigning as a reason, that being on the change of his voice, and therefore unable to sing, the study of the flute would prevent him forgetting his singing. His father, who could refuse him nothing, agreed to his request, and, in a few months afterwards, he played with fluency on that instrument. After this, his family conceiving that he became too much attached to music, he was sent to Mariaberg, near Chur, in the German Tyrol, with the intention of being instructed in the German language. But the good man, his father, did not imagine that the institution of the convent and college of Mariaberg was, that the thirty two monks belonging to it should be all musicians, and could not enter into it without having proved that they could sing or play upon some instrument at sight: that every day, and sometimes two or three times a day, sacred music was performed in the church of the convent: and that the scholars belonging to the college had the right to receive instructions in any branch of music they liked, by paying only ninety Tyrolean florins (eight pounds sterling) a year, including board in a luxurious style, a bedroom to each, washing and instructions, and no extra charge. Here Ferrari perceived that he was in a situation agreeable to his wishes. By constantly hearing both sacred and profane music performed, and by copying a great deal of it, he became a solid musician at an early period of life. He pursued his

1 John S. Sainsbury and Alexandre Choron, A Dictionary of Musicians: From the Earliest Ages to the Present Time 2nd edition (London: Sainsbury's and Co., 1827) 242-243.

206

other studies at school just for the sake of not being punished, but music was his fort. He learned also to play on the violin, hautboy, and double bass, in a slight manner, of course, but well enough to be able to take his first part with other instruments. The celebrated fuguist, Pater Marianus Stecher, who was the school master, gave him also a great many lessons on the pianoforte and in through bass. After spending two years at Mariaberg, Ferrari returned again to his father's counting-house, where he attended for three years, but more from obedience than inclination. His father then died, and being ill-treated by his partners, he determined, without further delay, to try his fortune as a composer.

Prince Wenceslas Lichtenstein, who was then on his way to Rome, took young Ferrari with him. From thence he repaired to Naples, with the intention of taking lessons in counterpoint from Paisiello; but that great dramatic composer having no time to spare, recommended him to Latilla, an able contrapuntist, under whom he studied for two and a half. At the same time, however, Paisiello gave him advice, and, as a friend, instructed him almost daily in theatrical composition. At that period, M. Campan, maître-d'hôtel to the late queen of France, offered to take him on a tour through Italy, and from thence to Paris, which proposition was accepted. M. Campan introduced him to his wife, première femme de chambre to the queen, and Madame Campan introduced him to her majesty, whom he had the honour to accompany on the piano for several hours. Her majesty approved his manner of accompanying, and also admired some Italian notturni of his composition which he sang to her. Some time afterwards, the queen sent Madame Campan to inform Ferrari, that it was her intention to appoint him her singing-master, should the public affairs take a good turn, but the revolution came rapidly on, and every thing was overthrown.

When the Théâtre Feydeau was built in Paris for the Italian opera, Ferrari was appointed conductor, when he composed several pieces of music, which were received with great applause. In the year 1791, having witnessed the horrors of the French revolution, he emigrated to Brussels and Spa, where he gave concerts. He also composed there, and performed a concerto and several sonatas, which were favourably received.

He was, however, never a very great player, but his feelings, taste, and compositions made him appear greater in that respect than he really was.

In the same year, he set the opera "Les Evénemens imprévus," for the Théâtre Montansier, which was very much admired, although it have been composed before by Gretry. The favourite duet of "Serviteur à Monsieur la Fleur," was rapturously encored; this was the first time any piece of music had been encored on the French stage; also after the opera was over, Ferrari was called for, to present himself, when he was greeted with the applause of the whole audience. During the four years he remained in Paris, he composed and published several Italian notturni, duets, modern canons for three voices, some sets of romances, the favourite of which are, "Théonie, pour aimer j'ai reçu la vie," "A l' ombre d'une myrthe fleurie," "Quand l' amour naquit à Cythère," &c. several sets of sonatas for the piano-forte, and for the piano-forte and violin, or flute, &c. &c.

Ferrari was next engaged as a composer to the Théâtre Montansier, with three hundred louis d'or a year; but, fearing that the public affairs would become worse and worse, he emigrated to Brussels, and in the year 1792 to London, highly recommended to some of the first noblemen's and gentlemen's families, as well as to several foreign ambassadors, by whom he was constantly well received and employed for musical tuition, particularly in singing.

His first composition in London, was performed at Salomon's concerts, and was a recitative and rondo, "Se mi tormenti amore" sung with great success by Simoni. In the course of thirty-one years' residence in London, he composed a great many pieces for public concerts, and for the Opera-house, some of which are [list] . . .a great deal of music di camera, such as sets of Italian and English canzonets, duets canone for three voices, sets of sonatas for the piano-forte, sometimes with an accompaniment for the violin, violoncello, and flute, &c. A great many duets and divertimentos for the harp and piano-forte, the first of which (Op.13) has been deemed quite a model for a duet for those instruments. In the year 1804, he married Miss Henry, a celebrated pianist, by whom he had a son and a daughter. In the year 1809, he was afflicted with a complaint in his eyes, and was blind for nearly three years. At this period he used to dictate his compositions to his friends; but at length he recovered well enough to be able to write for himself, with the help of a magnifying glass, and to resume his instructions.

Ferrari's last compositions are without doubt the best; for, without changing either his school or style, he has followed the modem taste with effect. As a part of his latter compositions, we shall mention "L' Addio," dedicated to Miss Ellis and Miss Canning; "Six Italian Canzonets," dedicated to Lady E. Lewison Gower; "Three Italian Canzonets," dedicated to Mrs. Trevor Plowden; "A Greek Notturno," dedicated to the Countess Cowper ; "A Treatise on Singing," and a "First Vol. of Sol fa," dedicated to T. Broadwood, Esq.; a " Second Vol. of Sol fa," dedicated to Miss Naldi; "Six Italian Canons," dedicated to the King; and his last work, just published, "Studio di Musica Teorica practice" dedicated to Lady C.Stuart Worsley.

We do not know why Ferrari has left London for Edinburgh; but we are happy to hear that he is well received there, that his compositions and singing have been admired in many private concerts, and that his instructions are eagerly sought after in the first families and schools of that metropolis.

Appendix B

From The London and Paris Observer: Or The Weekly Chronicle of Literature, Science, and the Fine Arts, Volume 15 (Paris: Galignani, 1839): 283

(Ed. Note: In the following review of Ferrari's Anedotti, the anonymous author takes a very free approach to summarizing the contents of the memoires, getting occasional name spellings and items of chronology wrong, and misrepresenting aspects of Ferrari's life. One wonders if it was written by an acquaintance of Ferrari, who was relying on memory of conversations with Ferrari as well as the Andedotti itself!)

LIFE of FERRARI, the COMPOSER.   London, 1839

(From the Parthenon.)

STRANGE as it may appear, Ferrari was in his day a composer of much celebrity. Such is fame, and so passes away the breath of that short-lived spring called fashion! Yes; the abbe's and the beauties of the old school sang the melodies of Ferrari; at Versailles and at Trianon his talent was never questioned. His reputation grew out of a very trifling circumstance. He contrived to set music to a certain interesting history commencing "Quand l'Amour naquit à Cythère," etc., then in high favour with the ladies of Paris, and which (written by M. l'Abbe' Garron, by the way) sets forth how love, nursed by innocence, but fed with too many sweets by enjoyment, died in the arms of the latter; together with other matters which assuredly the Abbé did not find in his breviary. From that moment commenced the fame and good fortune of Ferrari; all the ladies talked of him, all houses were opened to him, he received his guinea a lesson, and as he was a good-natured easy man, he willingly left to Gluck, and his antagonist, Piccini, all the torments and honours of genius. At length the young Tyrolese visited Naples, and ate his macaroni with the great, the good, the simple-minded Paesiello (sic); and from his sketches of the domestic life of this great musician, we gather that it resembled that of most Neapolitans. Without hopes or fears, present pleasure was his first, his only object. Vesuvius might vomit death, and threaten to bury Naples with its burning cinders, he heeded not, provided the evenings were spent in amusement, the arts poured forth their captivating treasures, and the sun induced that delicious and trance-like langour, which partakes equally of the delights of sleeping and waking, the maestro was contented. Ferrari long enjoyed his tranquil life with Paesiello (sic), his wife, Vesuvius, the pretty singers of Naples, a clear and starry sky, a sea bright as crystal, admirable music, and people ever gay and good-tempered, ever ready to enjoy, and to share their enjoyments with others. Among other things, he was delighted with the Malaga wine, the punch a l'Anglaise, and delicious pastry prepared by Madame Paesiello (sic). The more Vesuvius raged, the greater delicacies covered the table of the musician. The alarum peeling from every belfry, the processions along the sea-shore, the lamps lighted before the images of the Virgin, the stillness of the air, the blackness of the night, the calmness of the sea, the silence on the earth, the disparition of the stars, and the jets of fire that shot from the brow of Vesuvius, all sufficiently astonished and terrified Ferrari, but made no impression on the tranquil mind of Paesiello (sic), who, in his little study facing the volcano, sat calmly composing his Antigone; while the smell of myrrh and incense rose from every street, on every side was heard the drumming and strumming of tambourines, guitars, and mandolines, and groups of dancers were seen under every portico. At Naples Ferrari encountered that modern Venus, the lovely Lady Hamilton, and the celebrated Acton. He traversed the lavas of Vesuvius with the three sisters Cosellini (sic) —Constantine, Annette, and Rosine —" each prettier than the other," he remarks, " and whom he would have married at first sight; more especial! their sister, Celeste Cosellini—all four, in fact, if he had been a Mahometan. Above all, the beautiful Lady Hamilton made a deep impression on his Italian heart, and often did he join his voice to those of the lazzaroni, who, seeing the beautiful Englishwoman riding through their streets, would exclaim—" It is the Holy Virgin herself! Che bella!" Ferrari did not learn much, and Paesiello (sic), who, doubtless perceived that he was not destined to be come a genius, contented himself with bestowing on him a liberal allowance of macaroni and punch a' l'Anglaise, by way of completing his musical education. The Tyrolese, however, wishing to make greater progress, addressed himself to an old lazzarone musician, named Latilla, a sort of personage who would have done anything for a plate of macaroni, and who charged the Neapolitans one carlin, most foreigners two, but the English three carlins per lesson. Ferrari offered him two carlins, but "No," replied the lazzarone, "Tyrolese rhymes with Inglese— and you must pay me three carlins. This Latilla, lazzarone as he was, had good notions on the subject of his art. On one occasion Ferrari showed him a fugue in a quartett by Mozart, and Latilla, striking the table with his fist, exclaimed, " So! Here is something new." " How?" said Ferrari, " Paesiello (sic) has said there was nothing new in music." "That may be," replied the old lazzarone, " but I recognise three kinds of music: that of imitation, which we all compose while young and influenced by admiration for some particular writer; that of expression, by means of which we endeavour to render musically ideas and feelings common to all; and lastly, the rarest kind, veritably original music, the fruit of natural genius and indefatigable industry which create novelty." " But Mozart is still young," "Doubtless he is so, but his pen is old; and l predict that this little man will one day become the Attila of composers." The greatest lazarone of the kingdom was the King himself, who divided his time between the Queen, the Chevalier Acton, and the billiard table ; who never interfered in the affairs of the state, much less in those of his wife, and of whom it was said wittily : --

Hic reglna,

Haec rex,

Hic haec hoc Acton. "

He is Queen, she is King, and Acton is both."

The celebrated trombone-player, Mariotti, came to Naples, after having passed through Rome, where the Pope had given him his blessing. The king wished to hear him. He was a very nervous man, and the image of his Holiness, whose benediction he had just received, was still strongly impressed on his imagination. He played his first piece well, but timidly; the second better; and the third with power and expression, that the King rose from his seat, and, laying his hand on his shoulder, said to him, " you are henceforth first trombone of my Chapel and of my Theatre San Carlos." " Most holy father!" replied the confounded Mariotti, "I thank your holiness!" "My holiness! Come hither," cried the King to his consort in the Neapolitan patois, " come here, and see this mad Bolognese, who has made me a Pope!"

At Naples, Ferrari became acquainted with M. Campan, maitre d'hotel to the King of France, and with him travelled to Rome to hear the music of Pergolesi. They found the Romans busily diverting themselves at the expense of their Pope, Pius V . Pius had just drained the Pontine Marshes, and Pasquin wittily called him, il papa seccatore. " What is his business at Vienna?" inquired Marfosia of him. "E'andato a seccar l'imperatore," replied Pasquin. " You are mistaken," returned the other, " he is gone to say two masses at Vienna, one with out gloria for himself, and the other without credo for the Emperor."

Ferrari, like the good-natured easy musician he was, became acquainted with all the noble dilettanti at Naples, and especially intimate with Count Skavronski, a Russian nobleman, who would take none but musical attendants into his service, and who, by compelling our poor friend to drink with him, brought him to the very verge of the grave. One day a Russian princess sent the count a servant, whom she warmly recommended to his notice. Skavonski was then seated at his piano, modulating, very much to his own satisfaction, from tonic to dominant, and from dominant to tonic, while Ferrari seated near him. assisted him with an occasional bravo! The count, without interrupting his preluding, began his interrogations—' What is your name, friend?" " Barthelemy, at your Excellency's service." "Do you know any thing of music ?" "No, my lord." "But you can play a little on the violin?" "No, my lord." " Nor on the Violoncello?" "Neither, my lord." The count grew impatient, but, without discontinuing his modulations, and without even raising his eyes to the servant, began to sing --" Monsieur Barthelemy is a stupid animal, and I will not have him." The impudent valet, not in the least disconcerted, sang, " Very well, my lord, I care not, some one else will." "Ring the book and inscribe Barthelemy directly in my list of servants," exclaimed the count, delighted at the impudence and ready wit of the man.

In 1787, Ferrari was introduced at Versailles, and was present at the royal mass. Madame Campan undertook to introduce him to the Queen, and, to avoid the formality of a regular presentation, contrived that the introduction should take place as if, accidentally, in her own apartment. Ferrari was discovered at the piano when the Queen entered; he was introduced: and she commanded him to accompany her in some airs from the opera of Le Roi Théodore. "Your protégé," said the Queen to Madame Campan, "is an excellent musician, but he has the fault of most young people,—he times all his movements a little too fast." But Ferrari replied that her Majesty was mistaken; that it was she, on the contrary, who slackened the time, and that he would not, for all the gold in the universe, spoil the music of Paesiello (sic), his master, by humouring the whims of royalty. Bravo Ferrari!

In 1790, Ferrari visited London, and met with the same success he had experienced in Paris. He composed romances and marked appogiaturas, and his pockets were quickly filled with English guineas. At length, glutted with pudding and success, he returned to visit his native country, and brought back from it, not original melodies, but amusing anecdotes, of which the following is a specimen :——One cold December night an inhabitant of a little village in Tyrol threw open his window, and remained standing at it with very little more clothing than nature gave him. "Pierre!" cried a neighbour who was passing up the street, "what are you doing there?" "I am catching a cold." "What for, pray?" "That I may sing bass tonight at mass!" Ferrari's last speculation was the publication of two little volumes of anecdotes, with which his memory was richly stored, and from which the foregoing passages have been selected. The greater number of the amateurs and musicians of the last forty years are there reviewed in a lively, good-humoured, and amusing manner; and the musical world of Rome, Naples, and London, is assuredly better set forth in these unpretending little volumes, than in the musical dissertations and scientific notices of many more professed writers.

Bibliography

Bashford, Christina. "Historiography and Invisible Musics: Domestic Chamber Music
in Nineteenth-Century Britain." Journal of the American Musicological
Society 63,   no. 2 (Summer 2010): 291-361

Bebermeier, Carola. Celeste Coltellini (1760-1828): Lebensbilder einger Sängerin und
Malerin.   Koln: Böhler Verlag, 2015.

Brandenburg, Daniel. "La vita musicale napoletana ai tempi di Giacomo Tritto e
Saverio Mercadante vista dai viaggiatori stranieri." Bolletino Dell'associazione
Civica Saverio Mercadante Altamura no. 2: 7-17.

_____ "'Nirgends ist die Musik zu einem solchen Grade der Volkommenheit
gebracht worden, und nirgends wird sie so fleißig getrieben, als zu Neapel':
Reisende Musiker und ihre Ausbildung in Neapel." Mitteilungen
Der Internationalen Stiftung Mozarteum 49, no. 1-2: 30-39.

Brooks, Jeanice. "Musical monuments for the country house: Music, collection, and
display at Tatton Park." Music & Letters 91, no. 4: 513-535.

Campan, Mme (Jeanne-Louise Henriette). Mémoires sur la vie privée de Marie-
Antoinette,   reine de France et de Navarre. Paris: Boudouin Frères,
1823.

DelDonna, Anthony R. 2012. Opera, theatrical culture and society in late eighteenth-
century   Naples. Farnham: Ashgate, 2012.

Di Profio, Alessandro. La révolution des Bouffons: L'opéra italien au Théâtre de
Monsieur,   1789–1792. Paris: CNRS Editions, 2003.

Durante, Sergio, (Author). n.d. "Die Memoiren des ehemaligen Klosterschülers
iacomo

Gotifredo Ferrari." In Collected Work: Musikgeschichte Tirols II: Von der
Frühen Neuzeit   bis zum Ende des 19. Jahrhunderts. Series:
Schlern-Schriften, No. 322 Published by: Innsbruck, Austria:
Universitätsverlag Wagner, 2004. Pages: 161-172.

Ehrlich, Cyril. The Music Profession in Britain Since the Eighteenth Century: A Social
History.   Oxford: Clarendon Press, 1985.

Fino, Giovanni. Giacomo Gotifredo Ferrari: musicista roveretano. Trent,1928.

Foreman, Amanda. Georgiana, Duchess of Devonshire. London: HarperCollins,` 1998.

Head, Matthew. Sovereign Feminine: Music and Gender in Eighteenth-Century Germany. Berkeley: University of California Press, 2013.

Heartz, Daniel. "Metastasio: 'Maestro dei maestri di cappella drammatici'." In Collected Work: From Garrick to Gluck: Essays on opera in the age of Enlightenment. Series: Opera, No. 1. Hillsdale, NY: Pendragon Press, 2004. Pages: 69-83.

Hunt, Jno Leland. Giovanni Paisiello: his Life as an Opera Composer. New York: National Opera Association, 1975.

Morgon, Elizabeth. "The Accompanied Sonata and the Domestic Novel in Britain at the Turn of the Nineteenth Century." 19th-Century Music 36, no. 2 (Fall 2012): 88-100.

Parker, Roger. "Two Styles in 1830s London: "The form and order of a perspicuous unity"." The Invention of Beethoven and Rossini: Historigraphy, Analysis, Criticism. Ed. Nicholas

Matthew and Benjamin Walton. Cambridge: Cambridge University Press, 2013. 123-138.

Rohr, Deborah. The Careers of British Musicians, 1750-1850: a Profession of Artisans. Cambridge: Cambridge University Press, 2001.

Saint-Foix, George de. "A Musical Traveler: Giacomo Gotifredo Ferrari (1759– 1842)." Musical Quarterly XXV (1939): 455-6.

Sainsbury, John and Alexandre Choron. A Dictionary of Musicians. London: Sainsbury and Co., 1827

Tiella, Marco. "Muzio Clementi e altri 'rinominati pianisti' negli Aneddoti piacevoli e interessanti di Giacomo Gotifredo Ferrari (1763–1842)." In Collected Work: Muzio Clementi: Studies and prospects. Published by: Bologna, Italy: Ut Orpheus, 2002: 413-425.

Troughton, Jane. The Role of Music in the Yorkshire Country House 1770-1850. PhD thesis. University of York, 2014.

Zaniboni, G.G. Ferrari musicista e viaggiatore. (Trent, 1907)

Index of Names